HAMMERSTRIKE

Hammerstrike

Walter Winward

You must either conquer and rule or lose and serve,
suffer or triumph, and be the anvil or the hammer.
Goethe

Heywood Books

© Walter Winward 1978

First published in Great Britain
by Hamish Hamilton Ltd 1978

ISBN 1 85481 016 2

This edition published 1989 by
Heywood Books Limited
55 Clissold Crescent
London N16 9AR

Printed in Great Britain by
Cox & Wyman Ltd, Reading

For Fran again

Rough Plan of Skiddaw Camp, showing main features

Not to scale

OUTER PERIMETER FENCE

INNER PERIMETER FENCE

350 yds

600 yds

30 ft

ADMIN BLOCK

GUARDROOM

INNER GATES

OUTER GATES

WORKSHOP

ARMOURY

CHAPEL

OFFICERS' BATH & HEADS

EXERCISE YARD

SICK BAY

BRITISH OTHER RANKS' QUARTERS

WORKSHOP

STORE

POW KITCHEN

POW ACCOMMODATION

POW CANTEEN

LIBRARY

MT POOL & BICYCLE SHED

GERMAN MESS

BOILER ROOM

BRITISH OFFICERS' QUARTERS

Watchtowers ▪

Author's Note

1. Skiddaw Camp is an invention. Because its fictitious location is near that of an actual camp—Grizedale Hall (POW Camp Number 1)—there may be a temptation to think that they are one and the same. This would be wrong. Neither captors nor captives in Skiddaw are other than imaginary.

2. Although Germans use the metric system of weights and measurement, for ease of reference the English system has been employed more or less throughout. The only exceptions are where I have deemed it dramatically advisable.

3. In writing this book I consulted a number of individuals and organisations. The staff of the Somerset County Library, especially Mr D. Crisp, were most helpful in obtaining books long out of print. Several members of the Embassy of the Federal Republic of Germany, who prefer to remain unnamed, assisted me with wartime ranks and the Luftwaffe chain of command. The Imperial War Museum was, as always, untiring in its efforts to oblige, in particular Mr T. C. Charman, who furnished me with the words of German war songs. And finally the family and friends of the late Oberleutnant Hans-Dieter Mueller were unfailingly courteous in answering my many questions. To all of the above I give my thanks. Any errors of fact are my own, as are the opinions expressed.

Prologue

12 November 1942

Hitler nodded to indicate that the meeting was at an end. Taking his cue, Generalmajor Kurt von Stuerzbecher collected his brief-case from the planning table and backed out of the Operations Room, leaving the Fuehrer, Reichsmarschall Goering, Field Marshals Keitel and Kesselring and their aides to get on with the next business. This was von Stuerzbecher's first visit to the Fuehrer-bunker, but he had been warned that Hitler liked to keep protocol to a minimum. Thus there were no Roman salutes, no affirmations of continued loyalty.

Outside in the corridor he collided with General Jodl, going the other way. As usual, Alfred Jodl was late. Hitler's closest military adviser raised his eyebrows when he saw von Stuerzbecher's uniform.

'Demoted, Kurt?'

'No, an accident.'

He had arrived by plane just as the air-raid sirens began wailing. It turned out to be a false alarm, but in his anxiety to get to hell out of it he had slipped and fallen, covering his uniform with mud and oil. There had been nothing for it but to borrow his pilot's spare, and von Stuerzbecher was now dressed as a Luftwaffe Ober-leutnant. Hitler had thought it a great joke.

'What's his mood?' asked Jodl.

Although there was considerable difference in both age and rank between the two officers, they had known each other since before the war. It would have been an overstatement to call them friends, but neither did each have to watch his back in the other's presence.

'Good enough, considering the news from North Africa.'

'He's got a better nerve than I have, then. Is Himmler in there?'

'No. It seems the SS has been excluded from this little party.'

'But not junior Luftwaffe generals apparently. What's going on?' Is the Reichsmarschall trying to obtain permission to bomb the shit out of Geneva?'

Von Stuerzbecher did not reply. These days it was hard to know who was privy to what. There was little doubt that Reichsmarschall Goering had convinced Hitler that Reichsfuehrer Himmler's attendance would not be required at the discussions which had been going on since mid-afternoon, and possibly the same applied to Jodl. If Jodl was in, he'd be told; if he wasn't, it was better to say nothing.

Jodl laughed at his subordinate's caution.

'Secrets, eh? Well, every state needs its secrets and us more than most. Look after Holland for us, Kurt.'

Jodl thrust back his shoulders and went into the Operations Room. Before the door closed behind him, von Stuerzbecher heard Goering say, with undisguised sarcasm, 'I hope we didn't keep you from anything, Herr General.'

Von Stuerzbecher made his way to street level where, at the entrance to the Fuehrerbunker, he surrendered his pass. The SS NCO who accepted it took in the Knight's Cross with Oak Leaves at von Stuerzbecher's throat and stiffened to attention.

'Heil Hitler.'

'Heil Hitler,' murmured von Stuerzbecher, and went out into the cold Berlin night, glancing skywards, as all old fighter pilots did, to check the weather. It was perfect; a gibbous moon above some low-lying cloud. They'd be over again tonight, the *Tommis*, though whether the target would be Berlin was anybody's guess for the moment.

Von Stuerzbecher's driver peeled himself away from a group of other drivers and stamped out his cigarette as his passenger approached. He opened the staff car door and stood to attention until von Stuerzbecher was inside and seated.

'Back to the airfield.'

Von Stuerzbecher settled himself in a corner and selected a fat cigar from a leather case. No shortage of those yet, thank God.

He fingered the briefcase on his lap but made no attempt to open it. There was a reading light in the back of the Mercedes, but he had no desire to read. He knew the contents by heart. From the moment Goering had given him the problem way back in

2

August, he had spent most of his waking hours planning and re-planning. He had not referred to his notes once throughout the whole meeting.

'If it becomes necessary we shall hammer their hands to a cross,' Goering had said, recognising, by his relative silence, that Hitler approved of the scheme.

It was not difficult to deduce that Keitel and Kesselring did not; they'd heard that sort of vain-glorious comment from Goering before. In 1940, for example, during the *Kanalkampf*, the Battle of Britain as Churchill called it. And it had come to nothing. They'd heard it again when the Reichsmarschall had bragged that not a single bomb would fall on Berlin. He'd been wrong about that, too, and a single glance out of the window of the moving staff car was more than enough to see how wrong.

Generalmajor von Stuerzbecher puffed contentedly at his cigar. Like most fighter pilots, ex- or current, he was on the small side, five feet eight, and stockily built. A native of Hamburg, with his dark hair and somewhat swarthy features he looked anything but the archetypal blond Aryan flier who used to gaze down from the recruiting posters. Most women would have called him handsome. One in particular had thought him special enough to accept his proposal of marriage. But she had died a long time ago and since then there had been no one who meant more than any of the others. In peacetime and at his age, thirty-four, he would have considered himself fortunate to have achieved the rank of Major, let alone his present status. But this was November 1942 and youthful major generals were thick on the ground.

He rapped on the communicating window.

'Step on it.'

Von Stuerzbecher glanced at the phosphorescent dial of his wrist watch. Almost 2200 hours. With luck and good winds the flying time between Berlin and Amsterdam in the Ju 188 he had commandeered for the trip was less than a couple of hours. Nevertheless, he was cutting it a bit fine. The last thing he needed was to run into six or seven hundred Lancasters and Halifaxes heading the other way.

He grinned at the irony of his thoughts. How times changed and how with them changed men. There was a period, about five years, from his early days in the Condor Legion to the latter half of 1941, when he'd gone looking for enemy aircraft. The hours on the ground had been resented and he'd driven more than one maintenance crew to despair by his insistence that the Me 109 be ready for take-off whenever he demanded. They'd been heady days, those, when every young Leutnant wanted his own Staffel and every Staffelkapitän his own Geschwader and the coveted Knight's Cross.

He fingered the sheet-metal tie, as it was irreverently called among air crew. Thirty-one enemy bombers and fighters had earned him that. The Knight's Cross itself bestowed by Reichsmarschall Goering at Karinhall; the Oak Leaves that followed by the Fuehrer in person at Berchtesgaden. Rumour had had it, and he was, if immodestly, enough of a realist to believe it, that the knives and forks, the Swords to the Ritterkreuz, would not have been far behind if he'd been left in command of a fighter station. But Goering had put a stop to that, just over a year ago.

A face to face meeting with the Luftwaffe chief, even for Obersts commanding fighter stations, was an unusual event. If it wasn't for a decoration, it generally meant a thick cigar, a rocket. But on this occasion it was neither.

The Reichsmarschall was looking tired, von Stuerzbecher observed. He hadn't lost any weight; if anything, he'd gained a few kilos. But the flesh hung sadly now.

Goering got straight down to business.

'First of all the pleasant bit,' he said, reading from an official document. 'With effect from October 1st 1941 you are promoted to the rank of Generalmajor.'

Von Stuerzbecher was startled. It wasn't four months since he'd been promoted Oberst.

'Thank you, Herr Reichsmarschall,' he managed.

'Don't thank me yet. You haven't heard the rest of it. As from 0800 hours tomorrow you are relieved of your duties as officer commanding . . .' He threw the document to one side. 'To hell with that formal jargon. From tomorrow morning, von Stuerzbecher, you're grounded.'

'Then I refuse the promotion, Herr Reichsmarschall.'

Goering slammed the desk with a meaty fist.

'You obey orders, Herr Generalmajor. You neither accept nor refuse. You do as you are told. Is that quite clear?'

Biting his lower lip, von Stuerzbecher nodded. Goering's flash of temper vanished as quickly as it had appeared. He pushed

4

across a heavy wooden box containing a dozen Romeo y Julietas. Von Stuerzbecher declined.

'You've been a lucky man so far,' said Goering, peering at what was obviously von Stuerzbecher's dossier. 'You've limped home half a dozen times with your machine shot to ribbons, but you've never suffered more than a scratch yourself. How long do you think that sort of luck can last? I haven't always sat in a chair. I know what it's like on a station. In a crisis—and crises are becoming commonplace these days—you break the rules and take up an aircraft yourself. That is not a criticism; nine out of ten station commanders do the same. But it's a dangerous practice. The air war is a young man's game. I've had it proved to my own satisfaction that after the age of twenty-four or twenty-five a pilot's reflexes slow down. You're an ace, von Stuerzbecher, and aces are far too hard to come by to risk losing them to a lucky burst from a novice Spitfire pilot.

'I could have given you a Group. I could have given you Galland's job or Kammhuber's, but I need you here. I'm putting you on my staff. You may have to cool your heels for a few months, but I'll find a use for you, sooner or later. But no more combat flying. That's an order.'

Cooling his heels had been the understatement of the war, thought von Stuerzbecher, tapping an inch of ash on to the luxurious carpeting of the staff car. Three months doing nothing except sign chits and give speeches; a further five months with a training unit, giving advice to youngsters barely out of school on the best way to stay alive. And then, in August this year, another meeting with Goering.

Again, straight down to business.

'Wehrmacht prisoners of war held by the British,' began the Reichsmarschall. 'Have you any idea what the figures are?'

Von Stuerzbecher hadn't and said so.

'Neither have we,' confessed Goering, presumably referring to the OKW. 'Not an exact count anyway. The problem is, every so often the British send shiploads of them to Canada, which militates against us in two ways. First, until letters from them begin arriving home we've no idea who is where. Second, it makes it difficult for Doenitz's U-boat crews to torpedo indiscriminately. They could well be sending their own comrades to the bottom.

'But at a rough guess we've come up with a figure of eight

thousand. We could be many thousands out in either direction, but that's our working total. The majority are Luftwaffe, with a sprinkling of Army and Navy.' He paused for effect. 'I want you to engineer a scheme for getting them out.'

Von Stuerzbecher thought he was going mad.

'All of them?'

'All of them,' affirmed Goering.

'But you're asking the impossible, Herr Reichsmarschall,' protested von Stuerzbecher. 'No one's ever successfully escaped from the British Isles. In fact, only one man has ever succeeded in escaping from what could be loosely termed British jurisdiction. Leutnant von Werra—and that was from Canada. And it didn't do him much good,' he added.

'Nevertheless, he got home,' said Goering. 'That he was killed on the Russian Front has no bearing on the matter. The one has nothing to do with the other. Good God, man, Allied airmen escape from camps even such as Colditz with monotonous regularity and the manpower involved in tracking down even half a dozen of them is enormous.'

'With due respect, Reichsmarschall, Britain is an island and Germany is not. Furthermore, Allied prisoners on the run receive help from the various underground movements in all Occupied countries. Our own prisoners would have no such assistance.'

'But if it could be done, von Stuerzbecher, if it could be done.' Goering slapped his pudgy hands together in an attitude of prayer. 'Imagine that. If it takes a couple of regiments of German soldiers to recapture half a dozen escaping Allies, imagine eight thousand German POWs on the move. From Devizes Camp in Wiltshire to Comrie Camp in Scotland, eight thousand men on the run. Even if only a fraction of them ever got home, think of the chaos the escape alone would cause on that wretched little island.'

Goering came out of his reverie and was suddenly efficient again.

'I don't have to tell you, my dear von Stuerzbecher, that the war is not going well for us. Certainly, on paper, it looks as though we are holding our own, but a counter-offensive by the Russians or an Allied push in North Africa would be catastrophic. Wars are not always won by numerically superior forces or better strategists. Wars are sometimes won by little things. If necessary, I want to be able to tell the Fuehrer that we can disrupt the whole

6

of Britain's economy, hammer her into the ground. Yes, hammer her into defeat.'

And from that chance remark of Goering's, Operation Hammer was given a name.

At first von Stuerzbecher considered the whole idea to be an advanced case of lunacy, but the more he examined the set-up of the British POW camps, the comparative calibre of prisoners and captors, the more he became convinced of its feasibility. On paper it worked; enough, anyway, for the Fuehrer to have given the go-ahead signal that very afternoon. There were, of course, a thousand minor details still to be worked out and the execution of the plan was a good six months from fruition. But it was possible. And until it became actual, it had been given the highest security classification.

The Mercedes turned off the main highway. Papers were scrutinised and salutes exchanged. The driver coasted to within feet of the waiting Ju 188.

Apart from being granted a top secret label, Operation Hammer was now a matter of some urgency. Hitler wanted the remaining six months' preparation cut by half. Von Stuerzbecher could well understand why. Slowly but surely the tide was turning against the Reich, though God help anyone who dared voice such treason. Just three weeks after the meeting at Karinhall, the Wehrmacht had come to a grinding halt outside Stalingrad, and at this moment Army Group Don was in big trouble. Six weeks later El Alamein had been a bitter blow. And finally, four days ago, the Allies had invaded North Africa.

Urgent indeed.

Von Stuerzbecher left the staff car, buttoning up his leather coat against the icy November wind.

The pilot of the Ju 188, a young Oberleutnant by the name of Moenke, was standing beneath the port wing. Judging by the smell of aviation fuel and oil, the machine was warmed up and ready to go. Moenke smiled to himself when he saw that von Stuerzbecher was still wearing, beneath the leather coat, his own spare uniform. He trusted the Generalmajor would not forget to whom it belonged.

Under his flying leathers, pinned to his left breast, Moenke wore the Iron Cross. But because of his preoccupation with the meeting in the Fuehrerbunker during the flight up, that fact and the youngster's name were the sum total of von Stuerzbecher's knowledge. Once in the air and on course, he decided to dig a little deeper.

'Thanks for the loan of the uniform. I hope the lack of it didn't prevent you from keeping an engagement.'

Both men were wearing flying helmets and throat microphones, but even so the noise generated by the twin 1776 h.p. Jumo 213A engines was enormous. Von Stuerzbecher, in the observer's seat, had to remind himself not to shout.

'Not at all, sir. I always carry a spare in case I'm lucky enough to be invited to a cocktail party at the Adlon.'

Von Stuerzbecher couldn't work out whether or not Moenke was being sarcastic. He decided not. The Adlon Hotel in the Wilhelmstrasse was the scene of many pre-war junkets, but they were a thing of the past. Moenke was bright enough to know this.

'The last I saw of it they were sweeping up the rubble. You'd be lucky to get a cold beer there nowadays.'

'I expect so. Is the Generalmajor's parachute harness quite comfortable?'

The youngster was being ridiculously stiff and von Stuerzbecher thought he knew why.

'Quite comfortable, thank you. You don't much care for acting as chauffeur, do you?'

'May I answer truthfully?'

'Of course.'

'Then with all courtesy, I should prefer to be doing something more constructive towards winning the war.'

'And ferrying generals around the countryside is not your idea of constructive war effort?'

If von Stuerzbecher had expected Moenke to be embarrassed, he was mistaken.

'Tonight, Herr Generalmajor, the terror fliers will be over again. The winter war is not like the summer war. In summer, we can expect them in the early hours so that they can be landing in England by daylight. In winter they come over at any time. Tonight my Staffel will be hunting Lancasters. I should be with them. If, when we get nearer the Dutch coast, you will permit me to switch frequency to one of the radar beacons, you will understand why I should be with my Staffel.'

Damned impudence, thought von Stuerzbecher.

'I have fought the *Tommis*, you know, Oberleutnant.'

'I know, sir. And if you will forgive me you use the correct tense, the past. It is now my turn and others like me.'

Good Christ, thought von Stuerzbecher, he makes me sound like an old man. Which I suppose I am to him. He'd still have been studying geography when I was shooting down my first Spitfire.

In response to a command from a controller south of them at Dortmund, Moenke took the Ju 188 too close to its operational ceiling of 33,000 feet. The thinness of the atmosphere at this altitude made the controls mushy in his hands. There was little he could do with the aeroplane at this height except keep it pointing in the right direction.

The cloud base thickened as they neared the Dutch border, rendering the ground invisible. But six miles above the earth the Junkers was bathed in moonlight. It was, thought Moenke, perfect bombing weather. With the cloud dense up to 17,000 feet, even the Stirlings, with a pitiful ceiling of just over 20,000, would be able to fly where the flak could not get at them until they were well into German territory. It had its disadvantages, of course; the bombing stream would not be able to see its ground markers. But the Pathfinder squadrons had developed aerial marking to such a degree that such a minus factor would have no more than a slight nuisance value.

It was definitely a night when only fighters would be able to prevent further devastation of German cities.

'How old are you?' asked von Stuerzbecher.

'I shall be twenty next month, sir, the week before Christmas.'

'And have you had many successes?'

'In twenty-two sorties I have scored three confirmed victories. All Lancasters. It's not much, but it's a beginning.'

They crossed the Dutch border at Enschede. A few minutes later, passing over Apeldoorn, von Stuerzbecher sensed his pilot becoming fidgety.

'All right,' he said, 'change frequency.'

It took only a few moments' listening to the wireless traffic passing between ground and air to realise that the *Tommis* were on their way and the night fighters had been scrambled. Radar controllers never said and probably didn't know the full strength of a bombing fleet, but to an experienced listener such as von

Stuerzbecher, the number of fighters being given directions could only mean an enemy task force of between seven and eight hundred. And if he were any judge the Ruhr would again be the target. The *Tommis* had been knocking hell out of the heart of industrial Germany in recent weeks and it seemed they would not stop until the last factory was razed to the ground. It was hard to know which was preferable, if preference in such matters could be expressed. Whether it was better that the RAF concentrated on industrial targets or better that they left the factories alone and dropped their death on cities which had no strategic importance, only a demoralising factor.

In the time it took von Stuerzbecher to think these thoughts, the Ju 188, travelling at a speed in excess of 300 m.p.h., had covered five miles. They were now some forty miles east of Amsterdam and about fifty from the Dutch coast. Soon, Oberleutnant Moenke would need to begin his descent. Unless . . .

The Ju 188 had undergone many modifications and performed many roles since it started life as the Ju 88, a *Schnellbomber*. The infinite flexibility of its design had proved so adaptable that it had served as a reconnaissance fighter, heavy day-fighter, torpedo bomber, conversion trainer and anti-tank aircraft. But as a night-fighter, it was unsurpassed. With a top speed of over 320 m.p.h. and equipped with two 20mm cannons, one 13mm machine gun and two 7.99mm machine guns, it could out-gun and outrun any bomber the British put up. What was more, Oberleutnant Moenke was trained as a night-fighter pilot.

Judging by the wireless traffic, the night-fighters had not been scrambled long, which probably meant the long-range Freya radar had only just picked up the bombing leaders crossing the British coast. Von Stuerzbecher had long held the opinion that it was poor strategy to wait until the bombers were on top of continental European soil before attacking. If they could be hit on their side of the North Sea, so much the better. Any Luftwaffe pilot who was forced to bale out would just have to take his chances.

Moenke's Junkers was not equipped with radar; the heavy nose aerials caused a serious drop in speed and manoeuvrability and the Luftwaffe liked to think that major generals got to where they were going without incident. But lack of radar was only a minor drawback. More often than not it didn't function and pilots relied upon a visual for the final attack.

Von Stuerzbecher felt a tremor of excitement. It was over a year since he'd been involved in a scrap.

'How are we off for fuel?' he asked.

'Three-quarters, sir.'

'Then let's get some of that aggression out of your system. Stay on this heading but take her down to twenty-six thousand. I won't be able to do much except act as observer, but in view of what you said earlier maybe that's all I'm fit for at my age. Listen to the radar controllers but don't respond or ask for a fix. We'll bag what we can and go home. Have you got all that?'

Moenke did not need telling twice. 'Thank you, Herr General-major.'

'Don't thank me. If Goering ever finds out what happened, I'll claim you kidnapped me."

Oberleutnant Moenke put the nose down. The twin Jumos roared appreciatively as the atmosphere became less rare and the propellers began to bite.

A Lancaster, the fastest of the RAF's heavy bombers, had a cruising speed of around 260 m.p.h. Crossing the Dutch coast at 26,000 feet, Moenke's Junkers was flat out at 323 m.p.h. Thus the bombing fleet and the Ju 188 were approaching each other at close on 600 m.p.h. With a mean distance of 150 miles between East Anglia and Holland, they should sight the Pathfinders in a little over ten minutes, von Stuerzbecher estimated.

But the sky is a big place, and after a quarter of an hour they had seen nothing.

Von Stuerzbecher was about to instruct Moenke to swing north when the boy anticipated him. Good. The youngster could think for himself. There was a possibility they'd both get home this night.

A minute passed. Two . . . Three . . . Fifteen, twenty miles covered.

A further two minutes, another ten miles.

And then von Stuerzbecher saw them.

Four or five thousand feet below and a mile to starboard, squadron after squadron of them, silhouetted against the clouds. He had no field-glasses and it was hard to tell from the distance, but it seemed that most of them were Lancasters, possibly Halifaxes. They were an awe-inspiring sight.

There was no need to say anything to Moenke. Already he was

making a low sweeping dive to come up below and behind. Height was everything at the beginning of a sortie but useless once a sighting had been made. Underneath, that was the place to strike, at the Lancaster's unprotected belly.

They were not the only German aircraft in the sky. Although still well out over the North Sea, they were now nearer the Dutch coastline and other night-fighters had been despatched on an interceptor course. Even as they watched, one of the leading bombers took a direct hit in the fuel tanks and exploded in mid-air.

As Moenke levelled out at 19,000 feet some of the bombers were already taking evasive action. The pretty airborne pattern which had started in England was now breaking up as the RAF pilots fought to stay alive and keep out of reach of the night-fighters. The apogee of the cloud formation was at 18,000 but many of the *Tommis* were ignoring their natural distrust of cloud and putting their noses down. Von Stuerzbecher spotted one such fugitive half a mile ahead and at roughly the same altitude.

'Lancaster,' shouted von Stuerzbecher, but Moenke was already firing.

Then a succession of events took place so quickly that the brain hardly had time to record one before it was assailed by another.

Oberleutnant Moenke's kill rate of three out of twenty-two sorties was about average, so it was probably excitement or nerves which made him shoot too early. In either case, he was not close enough or low enough to bring his score up to four, and he saw his ammunition wasting itself at eight hundred metres. Simultaneously, the Lancaster's rear-gunner returned the fire.

'Christ,' said Moenke, and side-slipped to port. Which brought him into the sights of a second night-fighter.

The radar controller for this sector had seen Moenke's Junkers edge on to his screen and knew that it was not a German aircraft allocated to him. It should therefore be a *Tommi*, but the screen was now full of *Tommis*. In any case, he was an experienced officer and something about the way the blip was dancing about told him that it was a friendly stray from another sector. The pilot of the second night-fighter saw it differently.

There is not much similarity between a Wellington bomber and a Ju 188. Apart from markings, the Wellington is larger in every respect. But both are two-motor jobs, and to the inexperienced eye, with aircraft weaving and twisting all over the sky at hundreds of miles an hour, they look somewhat alike. It was Moenke's fatal luck that the pilot of the other night-fighter was on only his third mission.

A fraction of a second after the Ju 188 sideslipped to port, the novice pilot opened up with cannons and machine guns. It would be inaccurate to say that Moenke was hit by the novice pilot; it was more of a case of his aircraft running into the 20mm cannon-shells. Eighteen struck home, roughly half and half high-explosive and incendiary, and they were enough to ensure that Oberleutnant Moenke would not be celebrating his twentieth birthday in Christmas week.

Suddenly the cockpit was filled with the smell of oil and death. Momentarily shocked into a state of immobility, von Stuerzbecher forced himself by an effort of will to examine the situation. He was not hit, that was the first thing he decided. The blood on the instrument panel was not his. But Moenke was dead and the Junkers had received a mortal blow. He had to get out. Already the aircraft was dropping into a deadly spiral. A few more seconds and gravity would guarantee that the cockpit became his coffin.

Desperately he reached across Moenke and jerked the lever which released the cockpit canopy. It flew off with a terrifying roar. In spite of his predicament he wasted valuable seconds jettisoning everything that could possibly give away his true rank and status. He was over the sea, and if he didn't die of cold first it was just as likely he would be picked up by a British ship as a German.

The contents of his pockets went fluttering out into the bitterly cold night. Papers, matches, cigars, wallet. He got rid of everything, even money; there was no time to think selectively. The last item to go was his briefcase, which he threw out open.

Between the time he sighted the Lancaster to the time he spilled out of the doomed Junkers, only half a minute had elapsed. Apart from practice jumps he had never baled out of an aircraft before, and his greatest fear as he tumbled through the clouds was colliding with another plane.

The sea looked rough and uncompromising, and hitting it feet first was like jumping off a high wall. He ditched his parachute immediately. Some pilots swore that air in the canopy helped to keep them afloat, others that the canopy could fill with water and drag a man under. He was taking no chances on the latter. His life-jacket would keep him buoyant, at least for a time.

The cold was terrible. Within minutes he could no longer feel his legs. He had no idea how long he was in the water and he reckoned later that he must have passed out. The first thing he remembered was willing hands dragging him from the sea. And a voice saying: 'Looks like we've copped ourselves a Jerry.'

I

15 November 1942

A thin fall of new snow covered Skiddaw Camp. It was going to be cold that winter. Cold enough anyway, as the third week in November finally ushered out autumn, for Oberleutnant Franz Mohr to make a mental note on the subject of fuel for Hut 9's stove.

Crossing the compound from north to south, from the ablutions to the long wooden hut which served as the German Officers' Mess, Mohr threw an anxious glance in the direction of the guard-room and the main gates. There was no sign of activity which probably meant that, so far, Wielen had got away with it. Though God only knew whether he'd survived the night. In the small hours before dawn the temperature had been sub-zero.

When level with that section of the camp which the British called the Exercise Yard and the German prisoners the Pig Pen, Mohr stopped for a moment. It was early yet, not yet 9 a.m., but already a dozen officers had got together a scratch game of volley ball. Playing in an area fifty yards square and mesh-wired, broken in places, in the manner of a park tennis court, the officers had knotted together a dozen scarves to act as a makeshift net. At present it was obviously not serving its purpose, as there was an argument in progress regarding whether the previous shot had gone under or over the scarves.

Willi Schneider called across to him.

'Come and join us, Franz. Perhaps you can teach these buffoons the rules.'

Mohr shook his head.

'You'll get fat.'

'It's the diet.'

15

Willi Schneider could only play with one arm, his right. The muscles in the shoulder of his left had been badly injured when his parachute inexplicably flared thirty feet from the ground after he baled out of his Me 109 over Dover. That was two years ago, in the autumn of 1940. Before that Willi had notched up seven assorted kills. He was, now, just twenty-one.

Franz Mohr continued across the compound, the reason for his earlier anxiety uppermost in his mind.

The previous day, evidently immune to irony, the Camp Commandant, Major Mitchell, had organised a belated Armistice Day ceremony for the dead of the previous war. It was laughable, really; here they were, three and a bit years later into another European war, and he was taking time out to remember the last skirmish. Still, most of the POWs attended and the morning had its bright spot. Taking advantage of the lull in normal camp surveillance, Emil Wielen hopped it.

At first, no one knew how it had been done. When an escape attempt was on the cards, normally the camp was buzzing like a saw both immediately before and afterwards. Which was natural enough as the escaper usually asked his friends to cover for him during the first few hours. But the rules didn't apply to Wielen. He was a loner, a solo artist. In the last six months, he'd been under, over or through the wire three times. Which was pretty good considering each unsuccessful attempt was punished by twenty-eight days in solitary. He hardly gave his captors chance to draw breath before he was on the trot again. Mohr wondered why the *Tommis* didn't put a permanent special watch on him, especially as he generally walked around the compound with a pencil and paper in his hands. Whatever he was measuring, it wasn't the dimensions of a football field.

Wielen had answered his name at the 8.30 a.m. roll-call and was missing at the afternoon head count. Captain Thorogood, the second in command and Adjutant, called an immediate *Sonderappell*, a special roll-call, but the tally still came out one man short. Wielen was *spurlos verschwunden*, vanished without trace. It was evening before news began to circulate of the civilian workman found bound and gagged in the rear of the workshop at the eastern end of the camp. Oberleutnant Wielen had overpowered him, taken his overalls and tool-bag, and calmly walked out through the main gates.

16

Major Mitchell threw an apoplectic fit and gave Otto Breit-haupt, the senior German Officer, the thickest of thick cigars, a real dressing down. Thorogood took it even further and threatened all sorts of vengeance if Wielen wasn't recaptured soon. But that was nothing new. Thorogood hated Germans with a venom that was almost psychopathic. He hated Wielen most of all.

Apart from being a bloody nuisance to the British, Emil Wielen was the one real ace in the camp, though technically many of the POWs were so classified. But Wielen was in a bracket of his own. Not quite twenty-two years old, at the time he crash-landed in the sea off Yarmouth when low on fuel his total confirmed haul was forty-four *Tommi* aircraft. He had Swords to his Knight's Cross, a very rare honour indeed. A law student in 1939, the war had given him, as it had given many others, a chance to find his true vocation.

And bloody good luck to him.

Oberleutnant Franz Mohr paused before the entrance to the Mess to light a cigarette, his second of the day's ration of eight. A tall man for a fighter pilot at five feet ten, he was now in his nineteenth month of captivity. Two of those months he had spent in solitary confinement after the same number of escape bids. As in any other walk of life, there are men who can accept and profit by solitude and there are others who cannot. Franz Mohr fell somewhere between the two categories.

He had viewed the twenty-eight days' punishment following his first attempt with equanimity. It was every POW's clear duty to escape and it was equally the duty of the captors to punish the miscreants. That was one of the rules of the game. A month in the cooler was nothing. In many ways it was a relief not to have to share quarters with eight or nine others. But the fourth week was hard; he began muttering to himself halfway through it.

All of his second term, which had ended on the last day of October, was murder, and hunger was his constant companion. The general diet in the camp had little to be said for it, but the diet in solitary was barely viable. He knew he had lost weight from the way his clothes hung, but he was quite shocked when he caught sight of himself, the day of his release. Where once his hair had been fair and thick and carefully trimmed, now it was greying, thinning and badly in need of attention. Where his eyes had been clear and his face unlined, now the whites were a dull shade of

17

grey and he had the wrinkles of a man of forty. But Franz Mohr was just twenty-four.

Being a prisoner of war Oberleutnant Mohr missed many things: a glass of real malt whisky, concerts, books that were not vetted to see if they were suitable. Most of all he missed women. But in Skiddaw Camp that was one commodity very definitely not on the menu, and the alternatives were practised by very few.

Built in haste in 1941 to take the overspill from Grizedale Hall on Lake Windermere, Skiddaw Camp housed over two hundred POWs, most of them Luftwaffe officers but with a sprinkling of commissioned personnel from the German Army and Navy, together with a number of other ranks who acted, in part, as officers' servants. Disregarding the 'old' men such as Mohr and Major Breithaupt, who was twenty-six, the average age of the internees was twenty-two.

Located at the edge of Skiddaw Forest between the 3000-odd feet of Skiddaw Mountain to the east and Bassenthwaite Lake to the west, the camp was a nightmare for potential escapees. The nearest town was Keswick, five miles to the south, while east there was nothing of size closer than Penrith. The coast was twenty hard miles away, as were the only two ports worth the name, Workington and Whitehaven. But reaching either was only the start of the problem. Beyond Workington and Whitehaven was the Irish Sea.

In choosing Skiddaw as the site for a POW camp, the authorities had used their heads. There was no point in getting out if the coast was the end of the line.

A rough rectangle in shape, the compound measured six hundred yards long by three hundred and fifty wide at its broadest point. In the early days, when the overspill from Grizedale Hall was numbered in tens, a single perimeter fence of rolled barbed-wire, eight feet high, was considered sufficient to deter would-be wanderlusts. It was not until the summer evening that the then Commandant, Lieutenant-Colonel Makepeace, discovered a flock of sheep contentedly grazing near the Sick Bay and his complement of prisoners reduced by four, that both an inner and outer fence was deemed necessary, with a thirty-foot open stretch in between. Taking into consideration that there were eight watch-towers equipped with searchlights along the length and breadth of the compound, in spite of a mere doubling of the fencing, getting out became much more than twice as difficult.

The main gates were a hundred yards off the Keswick road, shielded from the gaze of curious motorists by trees and scrub. The authorities had debated levelling this area but eventually decided against it. Escaping via the main entrance was accepted as impossible and had been until Emil Wielen took his morning stroll. To get out a prisoner had to pass two lots of sentries. The first pair guarded the gate set in the inner perimeter fence and had keys only to that. Once through the inner gate a man had to pass a second pair of sentries on the outer perimeter fence, who, too, had keys only to their own exit. Thus it as impossible for a prisoner or prisoners to overpower the first pair of sentries and force them to open both gates.

Arriving from the outside, once through the gates a new POW was confronted with a baffling number of buildings, all purpose-built with the object of keeping him in and healthy, if not happy. Armoury, Bath-house and heads, Chapel, Dry-goods Store, Exercise Yard, Fuel Store, Guardroom, Hospital, Interrogation Room, Jail, Kitchens, Library, MT Pool, NCO's Mess, Officers' Mess, Prisoners' Accommodation, QM Stores, Recreation Room, Sick Bay, Tailor's Shop, Upper Watch-towers, Vehicle Maintenance Section, Wireless Room. So much for A to W. X, Y and Z were absent. The nearest X-ray facilities were in Penrith, there was no room or need for a YMCA, and not even the Army had found a use for the letter Z.

Apart from time spent in the German Mess, the majority of prisoners spent most of their waking hours in their own huts. During the dark winter months this was unavoidable; curfew was at 4.30, right after the final roll-call, and reveille not until 6 a.m. the following morning. Doors were not locked for sanitary reasons, but any POW found wandering around the compound during the curfew hours had to have a damn good reason or be charged with attempting to escape and spend twenty-eight days in the cooler.

But even in summer months it was always possible to find half a dozen prisoners from each hut lying on their bunks. It was difficult to understand why. Certainly no tunnel escape bids ever emanated from the huts. They were too far from the wire.

The huts were in rows of five and each was not much bigger than a large garage. Each housed ten men in two-tiered bunks, a pair against each longitudinal wall and the remaining one against the wall opposite the door. A wood-burning stove occupied the middle of the floor, its chimney going up and out through the roof. This method of heating was far from efficient. Those close to the stove fried and those six feet away froze. Next to the stove was a trestle-table and two wooden benches. Beside each bunk was a small locker for personal effects. Lighting was by a single naked bulb hanging from the ceiling. This was controlled from the guardroom and remained lit during the hours of darkness. Black-out material covered the windows.

These were the officers' quarters and, paradoxically, the other ranks fared better. Because they numbered fewer and because protocol dictated that they should live apart from their superiors, they had been allocated six huts between thirty of them on the south side of the compound. With only five men per hut, each had a two-tiered bunk to himself, and so far as the majority of them were concerned life here was a damn sight better than fighting on the Eastern Front. With the exception of several of the air crew NCOs, none of them had made an escape attempt. What the hell was the point? Apart from farm work in the summer and snow clearing in the winter, here they had nominal duties and were subject to very little military discipline. Over there, they could be killed. It was better to sit tight until the war was over. In the meantime, they had their cards and dice, occasionally some poisonous alcohol made from potato peelings on an illicit still, and their pin-ups. Even in the Wehrmacht Betty Grable was popular that year, and a glossy magazine picture of the million-dollar legs was about as close as any of them were going to get to a woman this side of war's-end.

Mohr pinched out his cigarette, carefully packed away the stub in his tobacco tin, and pushed open the door of the Mess.

Situated near the southern perimeter wire but overlooked by a watch-tower, the British had provided the structure and no more: four walls, a roof and a stove. But as under a reciprocal agreement with the British captured German officers received two-thirds of their active service pay, certain purchases had been made. What could not be bought had been manufactured, and what could not be manufactured, stolen.

There was a table-tennis table, battered but serviceable, together with half a dozen bats. Balls were harder to come by and anyone who broke one with a fierce hit was fined and banned from the table for a month. In consequence, the game was somewhat lady-like. At the moment, Leutnants Peter Kaehler and Johann Preiss were engaged in a ding-dong battle which looked as though it would last until roll-call.

Across the Mess Skiddaw's snooker champion, Oberleutnant Emke, was engaged in making a marathon break on the moth-eaten baize, while his opponent looked on gloomily.

Aged twenty-three and a big bear of a man, Theodore Emke, when not destroying egos and winning cigarette rations, was the camp comic and story-teller. Shot down over Hull on his tenth mission as pilot of a Dornier 217, Emke swore by everything he held sacred that, before he was able to pull the ripcord of his para-chute after baling out, he'd landed on the tail-plane of a Hurricane and ridden it for several miles before being thrown off. He also swore that he had succeeded in buckling the tail-fin and that he had last seen the Hurricane spiralling to the ground, out of control. It was his considered opinion that he deserved the Ritterkreuz for being the only member of the Luftwaffe to make a 'kill' using biceps alone.

A single-time escaper, Emke was for ever coming to the Escape Committee with weird and wonderful ideas for getting out. Whether he was serious or not no one ever ascertained. August's suggestion was for vaulting the barbed-wire with a vaulting pole, which he planned to make in the workshop. The latest idea was to construct a hot air balloon from rifled inner tubes and float out.

But for all his levity Emke was a great morale booster and a man of indefatigable courage. There were few in Skiddaw who knew it, but at least twice he had brought home a badly mauled aircraft when the intelligent action to have taken would have been to bale out. But this would have entailed leaving injured crew members to their fate, and this Emke had refused to do.

He grinned cheerfully and waved his cue in greeting as Mohr sat down in the armchair he had purchased from the British Mess for six pounds. He'd been cheated, he knew; the armchair was heading for the garbage tip before he stepped in. The stuffing was coming out of the sides and a wayward spring made comfort a hazardous business, but it was the only decent chair in the Mess, and he was proud of it.

On the other side of the table Otto Breithaupt was reading a year-old magazine and Fritz Uhde, Leutnant, writing a letter to his wife.

Dear God, thought Mohr with weary amusement, we look like a bunch of refugees from the soup kitchens.

If that was an exaggeration, certainly the clothing of most of the POWs was a long way from elegance. The emphasis here was on warmth, although in this respect air crew personnel fared less well than their counterparts in the Army and Navy. Naval officers were generally wearing their heavy woollen sweaters when taken prisoner, and from the highest to the lowest among the Army ranks a greatcoat was usually seen. But in order to be captured at all, a Luftwaffe officer either baled out or crashed, and his flying suit suffered as a result. Consequently they wore anything they could beg, borrow or steal. The longer a man had been in captivity, the poorer his apparel became. Mohr's was very old.

'How many does that make this week?' he asked Uhde.

'Six.' Uhde did not look up from his scribbling.

'But you're only allowed to send out four a month.'

'I like to keep ahead. They might change the regulations. Besides, Emke never writes to anyone. I use his quota.'

'Don't the censors think it odd, Emke signing his name to endearments to your wife?'

'I never give it a thought.'

'And what about your little wife?' put in Breithaupt. 'Doesn't she think it strange, receiving protestations of love from a man named Theodore Emke?'

'I never thought of that, either.' Uhde frowned. 'As a matter of fact, she thinks Emke's letters are better than mine. I can't understand it, seeing as how I write them all.'

Mohr chuckled and Breithaupt laughed openly. Uhde had been married a week when shot down over Scotland in 1940. He had celebrated his twenty-first birthday last July and spent most of his waking hours with a pencil in his hand. Nicknamed Horlicks, he had earned the soubriquet during the rail journey from Scotland to London for interrogation. The blinds on the train were unpulled and the first few stations he went through had Horlicks displayed on a hoarding. It wasn't until much later that he realised that the British, fearing invasion, had dismantled many of their station signs and that not every train stop was called Horlicks.

'Shackled for life before his milk teeth are through,' said Mohr, winking at Breithaupt. 'The war has a lot to answer for.'

Breithaupt took his cue. 'He'll get over it. The girl he married in that heady flush of youth and a forty-eight hour pass will turn into a dragon before his eyes. He'll soon find out she doesn't know an egg from a billiard ball or a lamb chop from a flying boot. The nights will be heaven and the days hell.'

'I'll settle for the nights,' said Uhde.

'Assuming you're young enough to enjoy them when you get home. According to the BBC, the British General Staff confidently expect the war to go on until 1952 at least. By that time you'll wish you'd settled for a good cook who can sew.'

'As one or two other people we might know did,' retorted Uhde.

Otto Breithaupt smiled tolerantly, knowing he was the object of the jibe. An incredibly handsome man himself, Breithaupt had chosen to marry a woman who, judging by the photograph he kept of her and their young son on his locker, was five stone overweight and ten years his senior. Only Breithaupt knew that she was unbelievable in bed and could do things with a veal cutlet that made his mouth water even at the memory.

Their game at an end, Peter Kaehler and Johann Preiss relinquished the table to other players and strolled across. Inseparable companions since they completed flying training together, they even looked alike, both being slim and blond and both having had their twentieth birthdays within a month of each other earlier in the year. To complete the coincidence, they had been shot down in separate aircraft within hours of each other and arrived at Skiddaw on different trains but the same day.

An only child, Kaehler had lost his parents in one of the first bombing raids of the war, and subsequently he spent his leaves with the Preiss family in Dresden. To no one's surprise, a firm relationship had formed between the young pilot and Johann's sister, and it was taken for granted that he and Hannah Preiss would marry when the war was over. Hannah's letters to her brother were full of solicitous enquiries concerning Peter's health, and Johann often complained lightheartedly that nowadays his sister hardly knew her brother existed.

'Perhaps you can settle an argument for us, Herr Major,' said Kaehler.

'Oh God.' Breithaupt pulled a long face. 'I'll wager this is about medals again.'

'I don't know why they bother,' said Mohr. 'The High Command does not award Knight's Crosses for table tennis.'

'Perhaps we'll escape one day,' said Preiss. 'Then you'll see Galland and Kammhuber run for cover.'

'Pigs might fly,' muttered Mohr. 'All right, what's the problem?'

'The problem, Herr Oberleutnant,' said Peter Kaehler with mock formality, 'is that my idiotic friend here is suffering from *Stacheldrahtkoller*.' Mohr smiled to himself at the reference to barbed-wire madness. 'In his ignorance, my foolish brother officer suggests that it is necessary to destroy thirteen Lancasters and a Wellington to get the Knight's Cross.'

'And you say?'

'I say ten Lancasters and an escort.'

'Is there a wager on this?'

'Four Players.'

'Then pay the man, Leutnant Kaehler. A minimum of forty points are needed for the Knight's Cross. A Lancaster is three points and the twin-motor jobs two. So if your arithmetic is better than your ability to gamble, you'll find you need thirteen Lancasters and a twin.'

'Yes, but . . .'

'Pay up, Peter.'

'And continue this elsewhere, for God's sake,' interjected Uhde. 'I'm trying to concentrate.'

'But Herr Oberleutnant, Franz, . . .' protested Kaehler.

Mohr heaved himself to his feet. 'Let's leave these two to fight it out among themselves, Otto. I'll play white.'

'Done.'

Breithaupt set up the chess pieces. Mohr moved P-K4. Breithaupt countered with P-K3.

'The French Defence,' muttered Mohr. 'No wonder you always lose.'

'There's nothing wrong with the strategy. It's just unfortunately named, that's all.'

'Yes. I often think the French Defence should comprise knocking over the king and surrendering before a shot's fired.'

Breithaupt laughed. Mohr moved P-Q4.

'Was anything happening outside?' asked Breithaupt.

'Nothing that I could see. Perhaps he's got away with it.'

'I'll be more inclined to believe that in another forty-eight hours. If they haven't got him by then I'll think he's in with a chance. Your move.'

'You think he's a fool to keep going solo, don't you?'

'Not really. I just wish to God he'd let some of us in on what he plans. For all he knows we could have a major break-out pending. If he went the day before we'd all be in the soup.'

'Perhaps so. On the other hand, you can't blame him for keeping himself to himself.'

Major Breithaupt studied the board and shook his head.

'I know your theory, but I just can't believe we have an informer amongst us.'

'More likely you don't want to believe it.'

'No, it's not that.'

Mohr eased forward his king's bishop.

'You've got to face facts, Otto. We all have. In the past six months we've had three attempts scuppered at the last moment.'

'Maybe the British are getting cleverer.'

'That's possible but unlikely. I don't underestimate them, believe me, but the bath-house scheme was too much of a coincidence for me.'

'Not at all. It's one of the obvious places to look. Close to the wire, constant to-ing and fro-ing. They'd be fools not to keep an eye on it.'

'I'd be more inclined to believe you if they hadn't pounced two days before we planned to go.'

'It's logical that they'd leave it so late. Planning escapes keeps us happy and when we're happy we're not a bloody nuisance. They keep us quiet for a couple of months and jump when we're ready.'

'Yes, but what bothers me is precisely how they know when we're ready. You're in check, incidentally.'

'Damn.'

Breithaupt covered the endangered king with his knight. 'Your move.'

Mohr paid no attention. Breithaupt looked up.

'Your move, Franz.'

But Mohr was looking towards the entrance to the Mess. Breithaupt glanced over his shoulder. Captain Thorogood stood in the doorway, his uniform beautifully pressed, his Sam Browne

25

gleaming. He looked like a wealthy patron visiting a workhouse.

'Permission to enter?' he asked in German.

'Permission granted, Herr Hauptmann,' answered Theo Emke, who was closest.

Thorogood walked slowly over to where Breithaupt and Mohr were seated. Neither German got to his feet. The Adjutant studied the chess lay-out for a moment.

'Some news for you, Major Breithaupt,' he said. 'The civilian police have just been on the phone. They've picked up Wielen. He hadn't even got as far as Keswick.' Thorogood tapped the table with his cane. 'I suppose you chaps will realise sooner or later that there's no way home. One of the advantages of being a wretched little island, as I believe Goering put it. Just thought I'd let you know.'

Thorogood turned to leave. He had raised his voice slightly in order that the whole Mess might hear and there were long faces everywhere. Wielen had been caught before, as had others, but each time they hoped for the best.

'Damn,' murmured Breithaupt.

'By the way,' called Thorogood from the door, 'if you're playing black, Major, you're in trouble. Mate in two.'

Breithaupt stared unseeingly at the board.

2

15 November

'Hitler's furious.'

Reichsmarschall Goering drummed his thick fingers nervously on the massive desk top and addressed his three senior commanders: Field Marshals Albert Kesselring, known behind his back as Smiling Albert, Hugo Sperrle and Hans-Jurgen Stumpff. Strictly speaking, Sperrle and Stumpff were not as yet privy to Operation Hammer, but with Hitler ranting and raving over the von Stuerzbecher business, Goering felt he needed all the wise heads he could get.

'I thought he was going to throw one of his fits,' the Reichsmarschall went on. 'Did I have so little control over my junior generals that they went joy-riding whenever they wished? Hadn't I made it quite clear to von Stuerzbecher that combat flying was out? Well, he was guessing there, of course, but as usual it was a damned good guess. Von Stuerzbecher wasn't shot down over occupied territory, therefore he must have been shot down over the North Sea. And what was he doing over the North Sea when his destination was Amsterdam? The Fuehrer added that it would be better for all of us if von Stuerzbecher was dead. Well, gentlemen, we now know that that is not the case.'

The three senior officers looked at one another. Kesselring voiced their thoughts.

'You are quite sure of that, Herr Reichsmarschall?'

Goering eyed him with contempt. Good God, would he have summoned them just three days after von Stuerzbecher's disappearance if he were certain that the man was dead?

'Of course I'm sure. The BBC fliers programme announced

this afternoon that, inter alia, it had captured Oberleutnant Stuerzbecher.'

'*Oberleutnant* Stuerzbecher?' queried Sperrle, the missing general's ex-commanding officer in the Condor Legion. 'How do you know Oberleutnant Stuerzbecher and Generalmajor von Stuerzbecher are one and the same?'

'Because I checked, man, that's how I know. Stuerzbecher, with or without the "von", is not exactly a common or garden name. To be precise we have, or rather had, seven of them on our strength, of which three are Oberleutnants. But I had them all investigated, just in case the British had made a mistake in the rank and their Stuerzbecher is not our Stuerzbecher. Two are dead. Two are on the Eastern Front. One is in Norway and the sixth is right here in Berlin. The seventh is Generalmajor von Stuerzbecher. Make no mistake, gentlemen, the officer the British have taken prisoner is our man. The date of his capture and the other details tally with what we know. We also know that he was wearing the uniform of a Luftwaffe Oberleutnant when he left the Fuehrerbunker on the evening of the 12th.'

'But why did he risk using his own name?' asked Hans-Jurgen Stumpff. 'As you rightly say, there aren't many Stuerzbechers about and the British must have it on record that a senior officer exists with that cognomen.'

'It was probably a chance he had to take,' said Kesselring. 'Otherwise, how would we know he was in enemy hands? He would realise that the names of captured fliers are broadcast by the BBC and he was hoping we would put two and two together.'

'Precisely,' intoned Goering. 'Though I don't have to tell you what will happen if the British also put two and two together and discover that Oberleutnant Stuerzbecher is really Generalmajor von Stuerzbecher. They'll put him through the mincer. They'll roast his balls until he breaks. And when he breaks so does Operation Hammer—and much else besides.'

The silence hung heavily in the room. Outside, it looked as if it might snow. Finally, it was Sperrle who spoke.

'We'll have to get him out.'

'Good God, man, do you realise what you're saying?' Goering's voice rose an octave. 'It'll be three weeks before we even know which camp he's in. And get him out how? With an airborne division? With the Leibstandarte Adolf Hitler Division? Tell him to walk out of the front door, saying he's sorry but he has urgent business in Berlin? You don't know what you're asking.'

'There is an alternative.' Albert Kesselring studied his fingernails for a moment. 'Have him killed. When we know which camp he's in, get a message through to the senior German officer saying that he's a traitor and potential informer and that he's to be executed without delay. I know that Hammer is his brain-child and that his death will set us back a year, but I see no other way out. If we can't rescue him we must ensure that he is not in a position to reveal what he knows.'

'Out of the question,' said Goering. 'Apart from other considerations, no airman is going to believe that von Stuerzbecher is a traitor. He's a hero, a Knight's Cross holder. They would no more believe him to be capable of a treacherous act than they would me.'

'Perhaps,' said Sperrle cunningly, 'they would not believe Generalmajor von Stuerzbecher to be capable of treason, but about *Oberleutnant* Stuerzbecher, who knows?'

'No,' said Goering emphatically. 'Good God, Sperrle, you're asking me to pass the death sentence on one of my best officers for the sake of expediency. I won't have it. What are we, barbarians?'

'It's been done before.'

'Not in my name. And not now, not ever.'

'Then we have to get him out, it's as simple as that.'

Goering toyed nervously with a paper-knife. Nothing but trouble, these days.

'Hitler will have to be told,' he said finally. 'I cannot take the responsibility for something of this magnitude on my own shoulders.'

Kesselring was astonished. 'You mean the Fuehrer doesn't know?'

'Not about von Stuerzbecher being alive, no. The Fuehrer has more to do than listen to the BBC.'

The three Field Marshals exchanged glances, each hoping that Goering was not about to ask one, or all three, of them to accompany him. This was one meeting they felt readily able to miss.

'I don't envy you, Herr Reichsmarschall,' said Sperrle eventually. 'I don't envy you one little bit.'

The meeting between Hitler, Martin Bormann, Hitler's Deputy, and Reichsmarschall Goering took place in the Chancellery on the evening of 15 November 1942. No stenographer was present and no records were kept.

It lasted under ten minutes, and for once Hitler was almost reasonable. He accepted Goering's hypothesis that Generalmajor von Stuerzbecher and Oberleutnant Stuerzbecher were one and the same, and that at least removed the uncertainty from the situation. Von Stuerzbecher was alive, von Stuerzbecher was needed in the Reich; it was just a question of strategy.

He peered over the spectacles he wore only in the presence of his senior commanders and confidantes.

'This is not the happiest of affairs, my dear Reichsmarschall, but wishing matters were different will not alter the facts. Tell me, is von Stuerzbecher reliable?'

'Completely.'

'Then we need have no fear that he will be loose-tongued.'

Goering hesitated too long. Hitler pounced.

'We do have such a fear?'

'Not as long as he is accepted as a mere Oberleutnant. But if it were thought otherwise. . . . There are drugs. . . .'

Hitler dismissed the suggestion with an airy wave of his hand.

'The British do not use such methods. However, it would be inadvisable to leave him in their hands for too long. You have considered the alternative to rescue, I suppose?'

'Yes.'

'And rejected it, I can see that. Well, you know your own business best.

'If I may make a suggestion, Fuehrer,' put in Bormann.

'Please do.'

'The Luftwaffe is not competent to organise a rescue attempt. By definition its sphere of influence is the air. This will undoubtedly require something more subtle than five hundred bombers. It might be advisable for the Reichsmarschall to consult Reichsfuehrer Himmler.'

Goering glared at the Deputy Leader with something akin to hatred. The bastard. As Bormann well knew, there was no love lost between himself and Himmler.

'With due respect, Fuehrer. . . .' But Hitler cut across him.

'No, I think Bormann's idea is an excellent one. Himmler is

undoubtedly the man to see. And I suggest you do it quickly.'

It was both a dismissal and an order. There was no arguing with Hitler when his mind was made up.

'It will be done immediately.'

'I sometimes wonder about the Reichsmarschall,' said Bormann after Goering had left the room.

'Then don't, Martin. Perhaps he is not the man in adversity he once was, but he is still someone I prefer to have with me than against me.'

'Of course.'

Reichsfuehrer-SS Heinrich Himmler was unavailable until much later that same evening, but by 11.30 he knew the whole story. By 11.45 Goering had gone and Himmler was fastidiously rinsing the Reichsmarschall's sherry glass. The niceties were observed even among sworn enemies.

Making himself comfortable in front of an open fire, Himmler's eyes glittered behind his thick glasses. This was a real bonus, Goering coming cap in hand after being instrumental in excluding the SS from the Hammer conference in the Fuehrerbunker. That his exclusion had been the fat Reichsmarschall's work he had no doubt. But now the boot was on the other foot. If the SS could rescue one of Goering's generals, what a pill that would be for the overweight buffoon to swallow.

The only real question was, should he involve the SS? They were not trained for a commando operation, which was what snatching von Stuerzbecher would involve. A small force, probably three or four men. No more.

There was also the question of failure to be considered. No one had ever succeeded in escaping from Britain and getting home. The odds were therefore against it this time. On the other hand, it would be as well to be involved somewhere along the line. If it came off, he would take the credit. If it failed, someone else could shoulder the blame.

The decision taken, he walked quickly to his desk and picked up the telephone.

'Find Standartenfuehrer Weil and send him to me immediately,' he ordered.

3

15 November

It was just after 4.30 p.m. when Oberleutnant Emil Wielen was
returned to Skiddaw Camp under guard. The Military Police had
planned to hustle him quickly through the gates and into the
guardroom before a demonstration could take place, but the
timing of the closed one-tonner's arrival was unfortunate. The last
roll-call of the day took roughly half an hour, beginning at 4, and
the last of the POWs had just answered his name. Roll-calls,
special or otherwise, were held in the Pig Pen, which was at the
western end of the compound, in full view of the guardroom and
Admin offices. There was therefore no chance that Wielen's
return would pass off unnoticed.

Theo Emke was among the first to spot him, and within seconds
a roar went up and ranks were broken. Upwards of two hundred
prisoners surged forward as a man and the MPs found themselves
jostled and pushed as everyone tried to slap Wielen, who looked
fagged out but who was grinning broadly, on the back. The
rumpus was good-natured, without animosity, but even so the MPs
waved their truncheons menacingly and bawled threats.

It did no good. Emil Wielen had poked a pointed stick in the
eye of the British and there were precious few things for the
POWs to cheer about these days.

Finally, the MPs managed to beat a path through the milling
hundreds and shoulder Wielen into the guardroom. But not before
two MPs had lost their caps, two their cigarettes, and one a
brand-new lighter fashioned out of gun-metal. As he disappeared
through the guardroom door, Wielen clasped his hands in the air
in the manner of a victorious prize-fighter.

'Don't try the hills, it's too bloody cold.'

Slowly the mob dispersed. The POWs were ten minutes on the wrong side of curfew and already the guards were yelling that anyone caught out in the open in another sixty seconds would be spending some time in the cooler. They were not joking, either.

Gradually the compound emptied, though not all the prisoners went back to their huts. Keeping well within the shadows to avoid the watch-tower searchlights, Obergefreiter Willi Braune and Unteroffizier Hans Geith made for the boiler-room in the southern sector of the camp. Each had a pilfered packet of cigarettes tucked inside his battledress blouse, but Willi had kept the lighter for himself. They usually worked as a team. Braune would swipe whatever was going and quickly slip the stolen goods to Geith. Later they would split the booty, fifty-fifty.

In the British Army there is no exact equivalent to the Wehrmacht ranks of Unteroffizier and Obergefreiter, but roughly one is a lance-sergeant and the other a corporal first class. Thus Hans Geith marginally outranked Willi Braune and as such had wangled the plum job of orderly to Major Breithaupt, which involved very little more than fetching the Major a cup of coffee every so often and making sure he was awake for early roll-call. Willi Braune was Oberleutnant Mohr's orderly and as such the two NCOs were virtually inseparable. Like most good friends they quarrelled a lot but very rarely did the quarrels become physical. When they did, the cause was inevitably a woman, and the same woman at that.

During a leave taken together early in the war in Willi's home town of Berlin, they both fell for the same girl, Lotti Kreipe. Lotti was blonde, bubbly, eighteen, and a barmaid in a middle-bracket hotel. She was also a first-class prick-teaser and took great delight in playing off one man against the other. Neither of them ever got further than some fairly innocuous kissing and cuddling, but each was convinced that the other had made first base. To make matters worse, Lotti wrote to each of them regularly but never at the same time. Thus when Willi had a letter Hans was stricken with envy until his arrived, usually a fortnight or so later. The previous Christmas, thanks to an administrative balls-up, Willi received two in the same mail-call, and Hans none. Fearing the worst, that Willi was ahead on points in the game, Hans took a swing at Willi, who swung back. The fight didn't last long and

33

they were still good friends afterwards, but it wasn't until March 1942 that the post sorted itself out and each had an equal number of letters.

A *Schusterjunge*, a Berlin street urchin, throughout most of his childhood and adolescence, Willi Braune was what the Germans call *Dreikäsehoch*, three cheeses high. In other words, very short. Early deprivation showed in every line of his workhouse brat's face, but like most poor and underprivileged children he learned the art of survival almost before he could walk. There was nothing Willi could not scrounge or steal if he put his mind to it, which was the one reason Oberleutnant Mohr prized him as an orderly. There could scarcely be another. Willi's coffee tasted like paint stripper and cleaning a pair of boots was beyond him. But if the German Mess was low on, say, eggs, Willi would conjure up eggs. His method of doing so was unconventional, to say the least. Usually he would find out which other commodity was in short supply amongst the POWs, invariably cigarettes, and, working with Hans Geith, proceed to steal cigarettes from a guard. These he would sell to the officers in need and with the money thus obtained bribe the British kitchens to let him have some eggs. It might well be asked why the officer needing the eggs could not do his own bribing, but this would be overlooking Willi's genius. He kept his sources of supply very much to himself. In any case, if the officer did deal with the British kitchens personally, the stolen cigarettes would not be required and so the German lines would be poorer.

Twenty years of age now, Willi Braune was captured in the Australian push on Tobruk in 1941. Although a POW for almost two years, he had no desire to get back into the fray.

By way of contrast, Unteroffizier Hans Geith talked of little else but escape, though talking was as far as his schemes got. In his imagination he saw himself leading a daring break-out and returning triumphantly to Berlin where his heroism and fortitude would be recognised immediately by blonde Lotti and rewarded in bed. In his more rational moments, however, Hans realised that being a prisoner was a bloody sight better than shivering in some freezing fox hole under a barrage of enemy mortars. It was all very well for officers to talk of freedom. On the outside they had more than on the inside. But for the ordinary German soldier (and he supposed it wasn't that much different in the British

34

Army) being on the outside meant obeying damn fool orders, and where the hell was the freedom in that?

A year older than Willi Braune at twenty-one though a POW for a year less, Hans Geith was a strapping five feet eleven with the physique of a light-heavyweight boxer. Add to this his Nordic good looks and an easy manner with women and it might well be asked why Lotti Kreipe had difficulty in making up her mind. But this was not to do justice to Willi's quick mind and indefatigable sense of fun, his inventiveness. Certainly he was no Valentino, but women were never bored in his company.

Glancing quickly over his shoulder to make sure they were not under observation, Willi pushed open the boiler-room door. With Hans at his heels like a faithful retriever, he ducked inside and locked the door by the simple device of jamming a length of iron bar under the handle.

Lance-corporal Harry Cade was already there, sitting on an upturned tea-chest, swigging from the neck of a bottle of beer. In front of him, covered with an army blanket, two more tea-chests served as a makeshift table, a candle flickering at either end. A jug of hot coffee bubbled noisily on top of the furnace. On a cold November evening in the Lake District, there could hardly be a better hideaway.

'You buggers are late,' said Cade.

After two years and one year respectively in POW camps, neither Willi nor Hans had much difficulty in understanding or speaking basic English.

'Sorry, Harry,' said Willi. 'Some trouble at the guardroom.' He looked around at the seating arrangements. As well as the chest Cade was sitting on, three others had been set up. 'Who is the fourth?'

'Harpo Cook. He'll be along later.' Cade fished around at his feet and produced two full bottles of beer. 'Three bob each.'

'They were two shillings last week,' protested Hans.

'There's a war on, mate. Besides, I had to give a couple to the duty corporal so I'm already out of pocket. Three bob or you drink coffee.'

Willi paid for both of them. It didn't matter. Harry Cade was a lousy cards player and he'd have the six shillings and more back before the evening closed.

'We'll play just the three of us until Harpo arrives?'

'Sure. Cut for deal.'

Across the compound in Hut 9 it was freezing. Compared with the luxury currently being enjoyed by Willi Braune and Hans Geith, the officers' conditions in this hut were miserable. The stove had gone on the blink again, spewing out puffs of black, evil-smelling smoke. There was nothing to be done with the offending flue until the following morning and it was a question of either shivering or choking to death. The consensus had opted for the cold.

Oberleutnant Theo Emke had gone to bed, as had most of the others. Fully clothed from head to foot and wearing a balaclava helmet and woollen gloves, Emke was trying to read and keep warm at the same time. The book was *A Farewell to Arms* by Hemingway, one of the volumes permitted by the camp authorities. It was well-thumbed and in French, and Emke was having trouble with some of the sentences. But he was determined to plough on. Tomorrow it had to be returned to Oberleutnant Herburg, the camp librarian, and Emke was not due another volume for ten days.

At one end of the trestle-table, also muffled to the gills, Peter Kaehler and Johann Preiss were arguing the relative merits of the Messerschmitt Bf 109Es and the Spitfire. Kaehler was pro Spitfire, Preiss pro Messerschmitt.

'All right,' Kaehler was saying, 'it did fine in Poland, Norway and France, but look what happened in the *Kanalkampf*.'

'Not the aircraft's fault,' argued Preiss. 'We were in trouble from the beginning because of limited combat time over the target. If we'd been able to carry more fuel we'd have done better.'

'More fuel means less speed. Good God, the Spitfire was already twenty miles an hour faster *and* much more manoeuvrable and you want to reduce the Me's speed even further. That way we not only get more time over the target but we get shot down in greater numbers.'

Preiss conceded defeat. 'Well, we'll have the Gustav next year. The prototype has a 1450 h.p. engine which is larger than the Mark V Spitfire's Merlin.'

Kaehler looked at his friend in amazement.

'*We'll* have the Gustav? Not we, Johann. By the time we get home the Gustav will be a museum piece.'

'Will you two kindly keep it down?' snapped Major Breithaupt from the other end of the table. Huddled in a whispered conversation with Franz Mohr, Breithaupt was not usually so edgy. But Emil Wielen's recapture had depressed him and he was in no mood to listen to the youngsters argue about something over which they had no control. Besides, he was an outsider in Hut 9. By rights, after curfew, he should have been tucked up in his own quarters, Hut 5. It only meant a snap check by a bad-tempered guard for him to be in trouble.

'So, twenty-eight more days in the cooler for Emil,' said Mohr. 'Frankly, I don't know how he stands it.'

'He's tough,' said Breithaupt. 'No criticism intended.'

'And none taken. I freely admit I couldn't take another term of solitary. For me it's either all the way home next time or a bullet in the head.'

'That's foolish talk, Franz.'

'Is it? Look, all of us, all of us in here, are living on borrowed time. If we get out and get home it'll mean the Russian Front and probably a cold grave. If we hadn't been lucky when we were shot down we'd be dead now. One way or another, I don't see much hope for any of us. Once the Americans were in it only became a matter of time. Perhaps not next year or the year after that, but one day the war will be over. And it will take a miracle if we are to emerge the victors.'

Otto Breithaupt's lips tightened. 'You'd better not let Hauptmann Weiss hear you talk like that. For that matter I don't want to hear it myself. Let's put it down to tiredness.'

'As you wish.'

Franz Mohr lit his penultimate cigarette of the day. Quite true, he was tired. Perhaps tomorrow he'd see things differently.

'The trouble with Wielen being in the cooler just now,' said Breithaupt, lowering his voice still further, 'is that he won't be in circulation again until December 14th or 15th, depending upon whether Mitchell sentences him tonight or leaves him to stew until tomorrow morning. And that's assuming Wielen doesn't take a swing at a guard or do anything to get added time. If we're to make our attempt on the 12th as planned, it would be helpful to know what conditions are like on the outside.'

'We're still going, then—regardless of what the weather does?'

'Of course we are. Everything is geared for that day.' Breithaupt frowned worriedly. 'Why, you weren't serious about not taking another shot at it, were you?'

Mohr smiled and shrugged his shoulders. 'I doubt it. Anyway, we're no worse off, Wielen being recaptured. If he'd got clean away we'd still be in the dark.'

'True enough. But I'd like to have spoken to him.'

'Perhaps we'll get lucky, Otto. Perhaps Mitchell will be feeling in a benevolent mood and let young Wielen off with a caution.'

'And perhaps Reichsmarschall Goering will send us all a box of cigars.'

Seated in his office, sucking thoughtfully at an unlit pipe, Major David Mitchell MC was feeling anything but benevolent. Normally a mild-mannered individual, the combination of the pain in his left leg and the business of Wielen had brought on a fit of irritability which he was finding difficult to shake. The pain was the result of a wound suffered at Dunkirk, which had rendered him unfit for active service, a fact which pleased his wife no end. He had done his bit, she was fond of telling him; the ribbon on his breast proved it. If he had to spend the remainder of the war as a policeman, that was fine with her. In his more rational moments he could see her point of view and accept it. She had no wish to become a widow or have to tell their two children that they were now fatherless. She had married an accountant, not a soldier. The sooner he could get back to his civilian profession, the better she would like it.

David Mitchell sighed deeply and audibly. Which was all very well for her. Somewhere along the line she had got the idea that all he did every day was count heads and keep the gates locked. But there was a damned sight more to it than that.

'Well, sir?'

Mitchell became aware that Captain Thorogood was still awaiting an answer to his last question. Perched on the edge of a chair on the opposite side of the desk, the Adjutant tapped the floor impatiently with his cane.

'In a minute, Adrian. Let me think about it.'

A rangy, bespectacled man in his mid-thirties, David Mitchell knew that he was regarded as soft by many of the officers and men, not least among them Adrian Thorogood. Perhaps they were right. No doubt he did see his role more as a keeper of the peace than a winged nemesis, though maybe that would have to alter.

The camp's record for escapes and attempted escapes was a poor one. Not worse than a lot of others but nowhere near the best. Not altogether his fault, however. It seemed to him that when the transfer of the overspill POWs from Grizedale Hall took place, the CO there had seized the opportunity to get rid of most of the bad hats in one fell swoop. After that, it snowballed. Skiddaw became known as the camp where the regular escapers were incarcerated and so anyone with a bad record was sent there.

'Look, sir.' Thorogood decided he'd have to force the pace or the matter would never be resolved. 'What it amounts to is this. If you sentence Wielen tonight, his spell in the cooler begins from today. If you let him sweat it out in the guardroom until tomorrow, we get an extra day out of him. God knows, the way he carries on he'll be on the trot again before Christmas in any case.'

'Not strictly within the rules, Adrian. Habeas corpus and all that.'

'*Rules,* sir.' Adrian Thorogood raised his eyes to the ceiling. . 'Do you think the Nazis obey the rules when one of our chaps goes over the wire? Not likely. He'd be lucky not to face a firing squad.'

'The Germans signed the Geneva Convention just as we did—before we did, as a matter of fact—and the Convention clearly states that twenty-eight days' solitary confinement is the punishment for an escape attempt. Not twenty-nine days, note. And I do wish you wouldn't call them Nazis. It's inaccurate. Not every German belongs to the Party.'

'Every officer in this camp took an oath of loyalty to Hitler and in my book that makes them Nazis.'

'Technically, perhaps. But our men take an oath of loyalty to the King yet I can name you half a dozen individuals right off the cuff who are anti-royalist.'

Thorogood groaned inwardly. What the hell was the matter with the man? At this very moment there were British soldiers, sailors and airmen being blown to smithereens and this old duffer was worried about the bloody rules.

Not yet having attained his twenty-seventh birthday, Adrian Thorogood felt well within his rights to think of his CO as old and a duffer. Although they wore the same uniform and Thorogood too had the purple and white ribbon of the Military Cross sewn to his left breast, there the resemblance between the two officers

39

ended. Mitchell was glad to be out of the firing line and Thorogood could not wait to get back in. He regarded his posting to Skiddaw with distaste, but he was determined to perform his duties efficiently until the brass concluded he was better suited as o/c a rifle company.

Although his dark good looks and fancy name seemed to indicate an upper class background, Adrian Thorogood was far removed from that. The son of a plumber and a chambermaid, he had been christened Adrian after his mother, an incurable romantic, read the name in a magazine story during her confinement. Tougher than she looked, she dug in her heels and argued her husband out of Frank and William. The name caused Thorogood a lot of trouble in his grammar school and was partly the reason he was so handy with his fists. But even the schoolboy scrapping paid dividends. For two years running he had won the regimental boxing championship at middleweight.

Before the war he had worked as a clerk and bottle-washer to a jobbing builder, but he seized the outbreak of hostilities as the perfect opportunity to get out of the rut. No sooner did he complete his basic training than he applied for a commission. To his great delight he was accepted and proved to be a natural. His plan now was to make the Army his career, but he was bright enough to realise that a lot of working-class lads who had stepped a couple of rungs up the ladder would have the same idea. The ones who made it would have a good record behind them. His decoration was a start, as was his fluency in German, but he knew that everything an officer does is taken note of and follows him around for the rest of his days. It was therefore no earthly use lamenting his stint at Skiddaw. It had to be done and done well until a better opportunity arose.

He got to his feet. Mitchell might be an old woman and as soft as shit, but he was the CO.

'Then I'm to take it, sir, that you wish to see Oberleutnant Wielen right away?'

'You are, Adrian.'

'Very good, sir.'

Captain Thorogood donned his cap, saluted and went out.

Alone in his cell in the guardroom but aware that he was being watched carefully in case he suddenly sprouted wings and flew out, Oberleutnant Emil Wielen rubbed his kidneys gingerly. He'd taken a dozen punches and knew he'd be pissing blood for a week. Not from the MPs, whose only concern had been to get him off their hands as quickly as possible, but from Corporal Napley. Napley was a very bribable man and terrified that his blind eye to the escape would be discovered and punished. The beating was to remind Wielen what else could happen if he opened his mouth. Just as if he would. There were few enough corrupt individuals in Skiddaw without losing one to a military prison.

Although normally a good-looking youngster, Emil Wielen's face was showing signs of wear and tear after a night in the open and thirty-six hours without a shave. Even so, his was the sort of character that took adversity in its stride. The *Tommis* might put him down but he wouldn't stay down for long.

On the other side of the bars James Napley, duty corporal, was indeed a worried man, and it was starting to show. A Londoner born and bred, he possessed the sort of greasy handsomeness that made him popular with certain types of women. Too much so, in fact. Five years earlier at the age of seventeen, with three burly brothers threatening all manner of mayhem unless he did the honourable thing, he married the young girl who was expecting his child. The marriage didn't last twelve months, but neither he nor his estranged wife had bothered about a divorce. Which was something he'd omitted to tell the Carlisle girl with whom he had undergone an identical ceremony during the first days of October. And now his new wife was champing at the bit, wanting to go to London with him and 'meet the family' on his next leave.

Jesus Christ, it never rained but it bloody well poured. First the wife and now this bastard German getting caught. Well, he could only hope that those digs in the kidneys had been taken seriously.

Corporal Napley's bribe-taking normally involved small items. Money for keeping his eyes shut while somebody swiped a hammer and some nails; a quid for not reporting a German officer caught red-handed in the wrong hut after curfew; a little black-marketeering on the side—coffee, eggs, whatever the bastards wanted and could pay for. But nothing of the magnitude of, when gate NCO, waving Emil Wielen through when he knew full well Wielen was not the workman he purported to be. Twenty pounds in notes that had earned him, and it had seemed like easy money at the time. A rocket from that bastard Thorogood, sure, but nothing more. And now Wielen had got his bloody stupid self caught again.

41

'Corporal Napley!'

The guardroom rocketed to attention as Captain Thorogood burst in. Napley was the last to get to his feet. Christ, pull yourself together.

'Sir!'

'Get the prisoner over to the CO's office at the double.'

'Very good, sir. You, you and you.' Napley stabbed a forefinger at the nearest three soldiers. 'Get fell in.'

Napley unlocked the door to the cell.

'All right, sunshine, let's go.'

Although it was against regulations for other ranks to address captured officers in such a manner, Wielen had spent enough time in this particular guardroom to realise that protest was useless. It was a fact of life that some British soldiers, like some German soldiers, were ill-bred oafs.

He grinned impudently. Christ, thought Napley, he's going to blow the gaff. Very close to Wielen he whispered: 'One word out of you, mate, and I'm going to see you buried.' To add emphasis, he punctuated the threat with a push in the back.

It was Wielen's fatal error to object to being treated like a pig in a pen. He whipped round on Napley and struck him open-handed across the face.

'You will not touch me,' he snarled. 'You will never lay your hands on me again.'

And then things happened so fast that even at the enquiry later there were arguments over the exact sequence of events. Some witnesses swore that Corporal Napley stood his ground and did nothing. Others were equally convinced that he jabbed Wielen with his rifle and that to get out of the way the German officer ran for the door. In either case, the next thing anyone could recall with any clarity was Wielen outside the guardroom and Napley at the door, swearing he would shoot if Wielen did not stand absolutely still. Yet a third group of witnesses were convinced that Wielen, with nothing to look forward to save twenty-eight days on his tod, was having a last bit of fun at Napley's expense. But the ones who supported the duty corporal's version of the incident vowed that Wielen was making for the gates.

Whatever the facts, no one was in any doubt regarding what happened next. Napley shouted 'Halt or I shoot'—and Wielen didn't halt. In the relative quiet of the post-curfew compound, the shot from the Lee-Enfield was deafening. Wielen fell to the ground, most of his face blown away.

. The shot was heard as far away as Hut 9, where Major Breithaupt was preparing to return to his own quarters. It was followed by a fusillade from the north-east as a nervous watch-tower guard fired at shadows. After a moment's stunned silence, Peter Kaehler made for the door.

'Sit down, you bloody young fool,' rasped Franz Mohr. 'They'll shoot at anything that moves.'

The volley was heard in the boiler-room, where Lance-corporal Cade had just taken a hammering from Willi Braune for the third time running.

'What the bloody hell. . . .' began Cade, knocking over a couple of empty bottles in his haste to get to the door.

But Willi was wiser. 'If you go out there, my friend, you might have to answer a lot of awkward questions.'

It was heard in the CO's office, where Major Mitchell was rehearsing his set speech. Later he was never quite sure how he knew, but he was not surprised when Adrian Thorogood rushed in to tell him Wielen was dead.

They buried the young Oberleutnant the following day. In war there is no time for decent intervals between death and interment. For the German POWs, a sad collection in their old and battered clothes, it was the supreme irony that one of the most decorated officers in the Luftwaffe, veteran of a thousand dogfights, should be shot down while unarmed by a trigger-happy *Tommi*. But they accepted Major Mitchell's explanation, given in person to the senior men, that the whole affair had been a ghastly accident. Mitchell might be their warder-in-chief but they knew him to be an honourable man. It was just another tragedy in a war full of tragedies.

Mitchell himself was not quite sure about his personal honour. In the hastily constituted enquiry the morning after Wielen's death, there was not enough evidence to suggest that the shooting had been deliberate or malicious. Especially as Corporal Napley found a strange ally in Adrian Thorogood, who professed to have seen most of the incident and what else could the Corporal do? Though if Mitchell had overheard the conversation which took place later between his Adjutant and Napley, he might have been more concerned.

43

'I'm not against shooting Jerries, Napley, and I'm certainly not going to have a British soldier court-martialled for doing so. Perhaps if we shot a few more of the buggers the war would be over a damn sight quicker. But I find it odd that it was not only you who pulled the trigger, it was also you who allowed Wielen to escape. So just bear it in mind that I'm not a fool.'

The final act was for the CO to send the papers to Division with the recommendation that no further action be taken. Forty-eight hours later, the matter was history.

4

Christian Eicke awoke slowly, every muscle in his body aching.
His mouth tasted like the innards of an old boot. Cautiously he
opened his eyes. He was in a cell, no doubt about it. Even if, in
the half-light, he could barely see the heavy iron door with the
grille in it, there was no mistaking the fetid smell of prison. But
why? And much more to the point, where?

He tried sitting up and made it at the second attempt. But the
effort proved too much for his stomach and he only just made the
latrine bucket before puking.

He felt a little better after that. Perching himself on the edge
of the planks which served as a bed, he fished in his tunic pockets
for a packet of crumpled cigarettes. Once alight, he made his
mind a blank, knowing from past experience that it was useless to
make a conscious effort at recall, that the events of the previous
night would percolate through in their own good time.

Unless he'd done something completely idiotic, he was still in
Cologne, a bloody bad place to be, what with the *Tommis* bombing
the shit out of it at regular intervals. Early on in the evening he
had gone out and started hitting the bars. By nine, with no food
inside him, he was three parts drunk. It was around then he'd got
into the argument about the camps.

'We Germans are a civilised race. The camps are Allied propaganda.'

'My arse. I've seen them.'

'You're drunk, Oberleutnant.'

'Probably.'

Later on he'd picked up a little blonde fraulein, a fraulein who

45

turned out to be a frau. Though maybe she'd told him she was married and he'd been too drunk to care. Either way, to the best of his recollection her husband had chosen to arrive home at an inopportune moment, while the blonde's heels were drumming a tattoo on Christian's back. The fight hadn't lasted more than a couple of punches. The husband opted for discretion when he realised that Christian, drunk as he was, was much younger, much stronger. But he'd returned half an hour later with three bully boys in tow. And that was that. Christian thought he remembered hitting the street in an untidy heap, but the rest was a blank.

He touched his ribs gingerly. The bully boys hadn't settled for just tossing him out. They'd made sure he stayed out by putting the boot in.

He got to his feet, doused the cigarette, and hammered on the cell door. His wrist watch had stopped at twenty minutes after midnight, but he judged, from the muted sounds he could hear, that it was early morning and the prison was coming alive.

Finally, after five minutes' banging, the grille was pulled open and the face and shoulders of a young Gefreiter appeared.

'Yes, Herr Oberleutnant?'

'Never mind yes. Let me out of here.'

'I regret that is not possible.'

'Not possible my aching arse. If this door isn't open in ten seconds you'll be spending the rest of the war in Russia.'

'I have my orders. If the Oberleutnant will be good enough to wait.' The Gefreiter started to close the grille.

'Hold it.' The youngster studied Christian patiently. 'Look, I'm sorry. Forget about the threats. Put them down to a hangover. But I have to get out of here.'

'I understand that, Oberleutnant. But until my orders are changed I can't release you.'

'Okay, go and get them changed. Where am I incidentally, civilian or military lock-up?'

In spite of the Gefreiter's uniform, it was not impossible for Christian to be in a civilian prison. But he was relieved when he was given the name of the barracks.

'Bring some coffee back with you.'

Christian returned to the plank bed. Being in a military prison wasn't too bad. He could easily have been picked up by the

Gestapo or the Kripo, and that wouldn't have been funny at all. Mind you, he told himself, don't go hoisting the flags too soon. The OKW doesn't go much on its officers being picked up in a bloodied, drunken heap.

It was ten minutes before he heard the sound of feet in the corridor and the rattle of keys. The door swung open and the Gefreiter came in, carrying a wooden platter containing some black bread and cheese and a large mug of coffee. Behind him stood an Hauptmann wearing the white *Waffenfarbe* and letter 'L' which designated an Infantry Training Regiment. His uniform was so immaculate that it must never, surely, have been anywhere near a battle. Crumpled, unwashed and unshaven as he was, Christian felt a moment of shame.

The Gefreiter placed the coffee and cheese on the bed and retreated. Christian seized the mug and drank half the contents in one swallow. It all but took the lining off his throat but it made him feel a lot better. The Hauptmann took one step inside the cell and sniffed distastefully. Christian eyed him over the rim of the mug.

'Oberleutnant Eicke?' Christian nodded at the inane question. 'Hauptmann Westerhoff. It's customary to get to one's feet when a senior officer enters the room.'

'Add it to the charges.'

'We'll see about that later. In the meantime, kindly finish your coffee quickly and get cleaned up. Gefreiter Wecke will show you where. He'll bring you to me when you're respectable. You are, of course, to consider yourself under open arrest.'

'Of course.'

Hauptmann Westerhoff clicked his heels and went out.

'Is he always that efficient this early in the morning?' Christian asked Gefreiter Wecke. 'What in God's name is the time, anyway?'

'It's twenty-five minutes to seven, sir. And if you'll forgive me I think it would be wise to make a move. Hauptmann Westerhoff does not like to be kept waiting.'

'Too bloody bad for Hauptmann Westerhoff,' said Christian, but finished his coffee in a single mouthful and followed the NCO to the washroom.

Shaving tackle, soap and a towel, together with toothpaste and a toothbrush, had been laid out for him. A shower and a change of uniform would have made him feel as good as new. Even so, after fifteen minutes' scrubbing, scraping and brushing, he was ready to face whatever lay ahead.

'Okay,' he said, 'lead on.'

Gefreiter Wecke preceded him along a series of passages before stopping in front of an unmarked door. He knocked timidly. 'Good luck, sir.'

Christian went inside, closing the door behind him. Hauptmann Westerhoff was behind the desk, smoking a foul-smelling French cigarette in a holder. Feeling less bloody-minded now, Christian stood loosely to attention until summoned closer and instructed to sit down. Hauptmann Westerhoff studied him closely.

He didn't look much, this Oberleutnant Eicke. He didn't even look German. More like Irish with that dark curly hair and almost black eyes. His papers gave his age as twenty-five, but that was either a mistake or he'd had a lot of nights like last night. Closer to thirty would have been Hauptmann Westerhoff's guess, though the external evidence of the fight, the bruised cheekbone and cut upper lip, could have had something to do with that.

Christian waited as long as he thought necessary before asking: 'What are the charges?'

'Insubordination will be another one unless I start hearing Herr Hauptmann at the end of such questions.'

Casually, Christian fumbled in his breast pocket for the Knight's Cross. He rarely wore it where it should be worn, around his neck, but he frequently found its display useful in getting him off the hook.

Hauptmann Westerhoff goggled at it. The Ritterkreuz, this oaf? Good God.

But there was no further mention of insubordination and his tone contained a little more respect as he read from a document in front of him.

'Let's see. The lady's husband is an Oberst, so we can begin with assaulting a senior, very senior, officer. Of the three men who . . . helped . . . you into the street, one has a fractured jaw, another a couple of cracked ribs, and the third cannot see this morning out of either eye. Then there's the drunkenness in a public place, the obscene language, and the stealing of a military vehicle.'

'The *what*?'

'While the Military Police who picked you up dusted themselves off—you gave them trouble as well, by the way—you snatched the keys of their vehicle and drove away. You were singing *Stille Nacht, Heilige Nacht*. A little early for Christmas carols, I would have thought. You'd probably still be going if you hadn't rammed a street lamp.'

'Jesus Christ.'

'When they caught up with you, you . . .'

'No more,' groaned Christian. 'They'll throw the book at me.'

'I'm afraid the book isn't big enough, Eicke,' said Westerhoff. 'You're a one-man Panzer Division. There are things you've done that aren't even in the wretched book.' He returned the document to the desk. 'But no one's going to throw anything at you.'

'I don't understand.'

'No more do I.' Westerhoff smacked his lips in disapproval. 'But those are my instructions. I got in touch with your unit when you were brought in and was ordered to put you on the first plane for Berlin. You have friends in high places evidently.'

'Not that I know of,' said Christian, unable to believe his luck.

'Nevertheless, no one is pressing charges. Your bags have been packed and are waiting for you, together with your orders, at the aircraft. If I were you, I'd get on my way before someone changes his mind.'

Utterly bewildered, Christian stood up and made for the door. From behind him, despairing of ever receiving a salute or any other form of recognised courtesy from this officer, Westerhoff called out: 'Also if I were you, Oberleutnant, I'd take time out to get myself a bath. Really, you smell quite appalling.'

The orders were unequivocal. Oberleutnant Eicke was to present himself to Standartenfuehrer Weil in Berlin on 18 November, 1942, at 4.30 in the afternoon. Which puzzled Christian even more. What the hell did the SS want with him? Unless in shooting off his big fat drunken mouth last evening on the subject of the camps he had been overheard. Those bloody camps; would he never be rid of them?

He remembered vividly that day on the Eastern Front. A bright, sunny afternoon, full of hope. The vanguard of the Division had outstripped its supply lines and dug in, consolidating the position.

49

There wasn't much activity from the Ivans and Obersturmbann-fuehrer Hoess had said: 'Come on, Christian. Let's go and wangle some tea.'

They drove seventy or eighty kilometres before reaching the camp. It seemed much like the others he had seen except that it was more heavily guarded and the inmates, mainly Slavs and Polish and Russian Jews, more undernourished. There was also a peculiar, not entirely unpleasant, smell he couldn't put a name to.

The Commandant was an old friend of Hoess's and they took wine and cake in his pretty little house far away from the main compound. The Commandant's wife was the perfect hostess, keeping the conversation general and flowing. With the wine beautifully cool and cake delicious, the war seemed a long way off.

'Goebbels appears to think the Russians will be crushed before winter,' remarked the Commandant, when the talk finally got around to the fighting.

'Don't believe everything you read in the *Voelkischer Beobachter*,' said Hoess. 'I sometimes think Goebbels isn't talking about the same war the rest of us are in. We take a beating up front and Old Clubfoot turns it into a magnificent victory.'

'I should have you shot for treason,' grinned the Commandant.

'Save your bullets. Let the Ivans use theirs.'

'You sound fatalistic, Erich,' said the Commandant's wife.

'Realistic. Neither Christian nor I expect to survive the year. No matter what you read, casualties are reaching an unacceptable level.'

'Is that true, Herr Sturmbannfuehrer?' Christian was asked.

'It's an opinion, anyway,' he answered, 'and one a lot of us subscribe to. The Ivan is far tougher than we were led to believe and Russia is a massive country. Even if we beat them on the ground, an occupying army would find it enormously difficult to administer such a vast territory. I think it was Nicholas the First who said he had two generals in whom he could confide—Generals January and February. We're going flat out but unless we make even better progress the weather will beat us if the Ivans don't.'

'Dear me,' tutted the Commandant, 'more treasonable speeches. I'm getting very worried about the SS.'

The talk drifted to other topics and then it was time to go.

'I'd show you around,' said the Commandant, 'but I'm afraid I have work to do. However, if I can grab hold of a junior officer . . .'

'No, no,' said Hoess hastily. 'I've seen it all before and I don't think I need a repeat performance.'

They thanked their host and hostess and took their leave. Travelling back towards the main gates in the staff car, Christian suddenly pointed.

'Good God, look at that.'

Two guards were systematically beating a young girl, obviously Jewish. She couldn't have been much more than fifteen and they were belabouring her with fists and boots, unmindful of her screams, trying to get her to join a long queue of other inmates who were evidently awaiting their turn in the showers. A wizened old man, possibly a relative, looked on helplessly.

'Stop the car,' ordered Christian, and was out before Hoess could stop him.

Angrily he strode over to the guards, pushing them to one side. He held out a hand to the girl. She cowered before him, her eyes filled with terror.

'Come on,' he said, 'no one's going to harm you.' But the girl remained transfixed. Christian turned on the guards. 'I ought to have you shot. You're a disgrace to the uniform you wear.'

Neither guard was much impressed by Christian's rank or his anger.

'We are merely doing our duty, Herr Sturmbannfuehrer. The girl cannot work. She has sickness in her lungs. She must go with the others.'

'Go where?'

For the first time Christian saw that the shower queue consisted mostly of the very old and the very young. The few in-betweens looked ill.

'Go where?'

The guards exchanged glances. Was it possible that this SS Major was as ignorant as he appeared?

'For the love of God, Christian,' called Hoess, 'get back in the bloody car.'

Hoess's shouting triggered some response in the girl. She began to cry and sobbed something in a dialect Christian did not understand.

'What is it, girl? Do you speak German?'

'She says that she is going to be killed and that she does not wish to die,' murmured the old man.

'Killed? What d'you mean, killed? From the disease in her lungs? Is it tuberculosis? They have doctors here.'

'Ah, yes, doctors,' said the old man.

'For Christ's sake, Herr Sturmbannfuehrer,' screamed Hoess, 'get back in this damned car! That's an order!'

Confused, realising he had walked into a situation that was beyond him, Christian returned to the car. It moved off immediately. Looking over his shoulder he saw the girl being pushed into line. She had stopped struggling.

'You'll have us both up against a wall,' barked Hoess, red-faced with anger. 'This is a *Vernichtungslager*.'

Christian sat stunned. *Vernichtungslager*. Extermination camp. He had heard rumours of such places but had put it down to propaganda. But it was true, all true. The Commandant and his pretty wife, with their cold Rhine wine and home-baked cakes, were overseers of death. The meaning of the sickly sweet smell he had been unable to identify became clear.

That same afternoon, after drinking a bottle of brandy, he was placed under close arrest for attempting to strike a superior officer.

And so on, thought Christian, as the aircraft crossed the river north of Magdeburg. One bottle of brandy had led to another and another. But it would be dishonest to say that his heavy drinking was still the fault of what he had seen in the east. That may have started it, but now he enjoyed the habit for its own sake. He was sliding down the slippery path to alcoholism and he couldn't get off. He needed something to force him off, but he didn't know what.

At precisely 4.30 p.m. Christian was ushered into the Standartenfuehrer's office, though really, pulling rank, Weil had turned it into more of a sitting-room. It contained a desk and filing cabinets, but they were almost out of place. Drawn up on either side of an open fire were two high-backed leather armchairs. Between the armchairs a small table held a silver coffee service and china cups and saucers. Beside the tray was a bottle of French brandy and two goblets. It was hard to believe that this was Berlin and that outside they were still clearing up the dead and dousing the fires from last night's raid.

Seated in the chair facing the door Weil barely glanced up from the papers on his knee when Christian came in. In looks he was not unlike his chief, Reichsfuehrer Himmler: the same close-cropped head, the same thick spectacles through which he peered myopically. On the wall above the fireplace hung photographs of Himmler and Hitler, while near the window, on either side of the desk, stood the furled standards of the premier Waffen-SS Divisions: the Leibstandarte Adolf Hitler and the Das Reich. On the wall opposite the fireplace, beautifully worked in gold thread on a piece of damask cloth, was the SS motto—*Meine Ehre Heisst Treue*. Loyalty is My Honour.

Two paces inside the door Christian, now bathed and in a clean uniform, stood rigidly to attention. It was one thing to be impolite to lowly Hauptmanns, quite another not to show courtesy to a Standartenfuehrer.

Weil glanced up. 'Come in, Eicke, come in. Come in and sit down.'

Christian walked the length of the room and took the second armchair, sitting erect, his cap on his lap.

'And for God's sake relax, Oberleutnant. No one can see you here. If we're to gain anything from this meeting I don't want you to feel you're on the parade square. I was about to have some coffee and brandy. Would you care to join me?'

Christian stammered his acceptance. The Standartenfuehrer poured for both.

'Help yourself to cream and sugar. And brandy. Don't be bashful. I know from your dossier that you're a drinking man.'

To hell with it, thought Christian. If he wants to treat me like Martin Bormann, I'm not going to say no.

He poured himself a massive slug. By comparison Weil's glass looked empty.

'Your very good health, Oberleutnant.' Weil smacked his lips. 'Even if the French cannot do anything else, they know the secret of manufacturing brandy. I often think that all ethnic groups, perhaps I mean nationalities, have things they do well and things they do not so well, and that they should concentrate on their strengths. The French, for example, are peerless in making wine, the Americans are magnificent businessmen. The English should stick to managing colonies, under proper supervision of course. The Italians . . .' He paused and smiled, not unpleasantly. 'Well, perhaps not every nation has a gift.'

'The Germans, sir?' Emboldened by the brandy and the congenial atmosphere, Christian didn't give the question a second's thought.

'The Germans? We are the world's conquerors. Or don't you listen to the Fuehrer's speeches?'

Standartenfuehrer Weil was still smiling. My God, thought Christian, that's a bit near the mark.

'I can speak to you in that somewhat disrespectful manner,' went on Weil, reading Christian's mind, 'because I understand that you too are frequently guilty of disparaging comment and outrageous action. That is so, is it not?'

It's a trap, Christian decided. The coffee, the brandy, the avuncular attitude. One word out of place and I'll be dangling by my balls from a meat-hook.

'I'm not sure what the Standartenfuehrer is referring to,' he said carefully.

'Come, come, Eicke.' Weil drummed his fingers irritably. 'It's all here, in the dossier. Would you like me to read some of it to you?' He flicked open the cardboard cover. 'Oberleutnant Christian Eicke, formerly Sturmbannfuehrer Eicke of the SS Panzer Division Totenkopf. Quite a drop in rank and status there, Eicke. From a Sturmbannfuehrer in the crack Death's Head Division to an Oberleutnant on garrison duties. Iron Cross First Class— Poland 1939. Knight's Cross—Russian Front 1941. I hear you think a lot of the Ivans as soldiers. Well, no matter, no matter. So do we all. Now.'

Weil skipped a couple of paragraphs.

'Ah, here's an interesting snippet. Drunk and striking a superior officer April 1942. Severely reprimanded. You were lucky to have Obersturmbannfuehrer Hoess speak up for you there. May 1942— drunk and disorderly, contravening Section so-and-so. May again, drunk. Then there's a gap. I imagine the clerk got sick of the repetition. July 1942, court-martialled for striking an NCO. Again only a severe reprimand. You were damned lucky, Eicke. They could have shot you. I would have done. Drunk, drunk, drunk and disorderly. Fighting, abusive to senior officers. And the last entry: Demoted to the ranks and dishonourably discharged from the SS on the orders of Reichsfuehrer Himmler personally. Re-enlisted in the ranks of the 131st Infantry Regiment almost immediately. Promoted Oberleutnant October 1942. Currently based in Cologne.'

Weil tossed the file to one side.

'A pretty sorry record, eh, Eicke? Sturmbannfuehrer at the age of twenty-three and Oberleutnant putting out fires and arresting black-marketeers two years later. A pretty miserable decline for a man of your previous record. What the hell happened? I've looked and looked, but nowhere does it say directly, only hints.'

Christian gripped the brandy goblet until his knuckles whitened. 'If the Standartenfuehrer will forgive me I choose not to answer.'

Weil brought his fist down with a crash on the arm of the chair. In spite of being several feet away, the coffee table jumped a couple of inches.

'No!' he roared. 'The Standartenfuehrer will not forgive you! Where the hell do you think you are, Oberleutnant? There's a bloody war on and it's no place for prima donnas. So pour yourself another brandy and listen to me. Because you'll answer civilly when I ask you a question. And unless you watch your manners very carefully, your next stop will be the firing squad you've luckily escaped for so long.'

Christian did as he was told and poured himself a second brandy. He sipped it gingerly. Weil's anger disappeared as quickly as it had begun. Many high-ranking officers had learned that trick from Hitler, whose rages were invariably stage-managed.

'I'll rephrase my question,' said Weil. 'Your service record tells me of a sudden change of character. One day you're a bemedalled officer with a crack SS Division, travelling rapidly up the promotion ladder. The next you're on your way to becoming an alcoholic with psychopathic tendencies. I want to know why.'

'Psychopathic tendencies?' Christian felt light-headed and wondered if Weil had put something in the drink. 'A phrase from a Jewish science. Perhaps you should consult Freud, Herr Standartenfuehrer.'

'If that remark is meant to annoy me, Eicke, you haven't succeeded. The Theory of Relativity is a Jewish phrase, but I can't ignore it because of that. Very well, if you won't give me a straight answer, I'll do it for you. It was the camps, wasn't it? You saw the camps?'

It seemed a long time ago and strangely irrelevant now. 'Yes.'

55

'Good,' said Weil, 'we progress. You saw something you neither liked nor approved of and took the adolescent escape route of hiding your head under a blanket of alcohol. Very well, I'm not going to defend the camps. It might surprise you to learn that many people in a much higher position than you feel the same. If the war goes badly for us, every German, whatever the colour of his uniform, is going to pay a terrible price for the work of a handful of madmen. But I want to know more about you, Eicke, so I'll ask you another question. Was it the systematic slaughter of civilians that disgusted you? If so, what d'you think the R.A.F. does when it bombs our cities? Does every bomb only hit a target of strategic importance, a factory, a steel mill? Is that even the intention? Are German civilians immune from being blown to pieces? Perhaps you'd care to explain your theory to some soldiers who are both widowers and childless. It is a regrettable fact of war, Oberleutnant, that innocent people suffer, the weak suffer.

'Have you ever attacked an entrenched position of fifty men with fifty of your own? Of course you haven't. Such an act would deserve you a place in an asylum. You either wait until you out-number them five to one or soften them up first with artillery. That's rather like five bullies in a school playground ganging up on one boy. But it is war. Perhaps you've read Macaulay on the subject. "He knew that the essence of war is violence and that moderation in war is imbecility." '

'Quotations,' sneered Christian. He was no longer intimidated by Weil. 'I'll give you one. "There is such a thing as legitimate warfare; war has its laws. There are things which may be fairly done and things which may not be done." Cardinal Newman. Bombing cities or opposing an inferior force with a superior one are legitimate tactics. The camps are another thing. I understand war, Herr Standartenfuehrer.'

'Good. I'm glad of it. I may yet find a use for you.'

Christian wished to God he'd get on with it and not treat him as an enemy of the Reich, which he wasn't. He was a German soldier and he wanted a German victory. Things would be different then. The criminals would be hanged and honest men put in their places. But either Weil could give him something to do which was worth doing or let him get back to Cologne and a fresh bottle.

The Standartenfuehrer reached for Christian's dossier and flicked through it until he found the entry he was looking for.

'It says here that you were educated in England and that you speak English fluently.'

'I was there for six years, sir—from 1930 to 1936. My father's business made it necessary for him to spend almost as much time in England as he did at home and it was decided that I should go to school there.'

'Why was that? We have excellent schools and universities right here in Germany.'

'I believe it was because he wanted me to understand the British way of thinking. He's in shipping and it's his opinion . . .' Christian paused, embarrassed. 'It's his opinion that the British build the finest ships in the world.'

'I think Admiral Raeder would probably agree with you,' said Weil wryly. He studied Christian for a moment before going on. 'And your sister, how did she take all this? You gallivanting around England while she was stuck at home?'

'My sister, sir?' Christian hadn't thought of Heidi in years. 'My sister was a semi-invalid from adolescence on. She died in 1936, which was one of the reasons I returned home.'

'Ah yes, here it is. Cause of death, leukaemia.'

Christ, thought Christian, there wasn't much missing from the SS files.

'And how is it now, the English?' asked Weil.

Christian shrugged. 'I'm probably a bit rusty, but a language is not something one forgets easily.'

'Good, excellent.' Weil placed the dossier on the floor beside his chair. 'You're a lucky man, Oberleutnant, as I've said before. Not many of us are granted second chances but you're about to get one. How would you like to do some real soldiering, the kind you're obviously well suited for, instead of rotting in Cologne?'

Christian did not hesitate, though later he thought that the charges Hauptmann Westerhoff had itemised had something to do with his decision. 'I'd like that very much, sir.'

Ten minutes later he was not so sure. He listened in astonished silence as Weil explained, leaving out only the name of the officer, that a Luftwaffe general had been captured by the *Tommis* and Germany needed him back desperately. At this moment they did not know where the officer was being held, in which camp, if indeed he had reached a camp, but that information would be available via normal POW channels in the near future. When it arrived, with a tiny handful of men, probably not more than two or three, Oberleutnant Eicke was to go in and snatch the general.

Christian thought he was going out of his mind. Take two or three men and invade a British POW camp, rescue some bloody fool who'd got himself caught, and get that same bloody fool home to Germany. Impossible.

'If the Standartenfuehrer will forgive me,' he said, 'the Standartenfuehrer is off his head. It can't be done.'

'Good. I'll tell Generalmajor von Stuerzbecher's mother.'

'Von Stuerzbecher? *Kurt* von Stuerzbecher?'

'The same.' Weil looked up innocently. 'You know the general?'

The bastard, thought Christian. Now he understood the reference to Heidi. For five years, from the summer of '31 until Heidi's death, Kurt von Stuerzbecher had courted Christian's sister. He tried everything in his power to persuade Heidi to marry him, but Heidi said no, not until she was better, which they all knew would never be the case. But Kurt refused to give up. He was a guest in the Eicke house in Hamburg whenever an opportunity arose. During the long summer vacations from school in England, while Heidi was resting, Kurt and Christian would spend their afternoons together. It was Kurt who had taught Christian how to catch the fattest trout and how to bring down the highest-flying pheasant. In spite of the difference in their ages, nothing was too much trouble. If Kurt could not spend as much time as he wished with the sister, he was determined to spend it with the brother.

They saw little of each other after Heidi's death. Kurt joined the Luftwaffe and became an ace with the Condor Legion; Christian had his studies to complete. They tried keeping in touch, but the bond that had held them together was broken. They bumped into one another from time to time, drank together, talked about the old days; and it was enough. To Christian Kurt was like a brother; it wasn't necessary to constantly reaffirm old loyalties.

'Would the Standartenfuehrer mind answering a question of mine?' asked Christian slowly.

'Go ahead.'

'Why was all this necessary?' He indicated the brandy, the

coffee in the china cups. 'You could have given me a direct order. As a soldier, I would have had to obey it.'

'It's one thing to give an order, Oberleutnant. It's quite another to know that the order will be carried out in the best possible way. A simple reading of your dossier was not encouraging. I wanted to see if you were the same man the file says you are now or the one you used to be.'

'And?'

'You're one of the few available men with the qualifications to pull this off. You speak English and you know England. Your record shows that this is the sort of operation that used to appeal to you. You need to lose about ten pounds in weight and throw away the bottle, but if anyone can do it, you can. If you succeed, you'll have rendered the Reich an inestimable service.'

'And if I fail? It's still impossible, whether the officer is Kurt von Stuerzbecher or not.'

'Perhaps it is. But you'll at least try and find a way now, won't you? There's a lot at stake. Success will ensure that your former rank is restored and that your file reads less like that of a convicted felon. You might even get the cauliflower to that Knight's Cross of yours.'

'I'll need time,' said Christian.

'That you have. It'll be two weeks, perhaps three, before we know in which camp von Stuerzbecher is being held.'

'And I'll want a free hand in picking my own team. I won't have any interference in that, no SS bully boys palmed off on me just because they have a good killing record.'

'Granted. You'll almost certainly be in civilian clothes, of course, so don't choose anyone who looks too German. But apart from that you can recruit anyone you wish. Let me have their names and I'll see to it that they're released from their present duties. The same applies to you, naturally. Cologne will be told that you have been seconded to my office. I suggest you make your HQ here in Berlin. If you have any trouble finding suitable accommodation, let me know. We have special arrangements for important personnel.'

Alone, Standartenfuehrer Weil walked to the window and watched Christian cross the street below. Soon he was lost in the crowds.

He hoped he had made the right decision, selecting Eicke. It

59

was a gamble, but he had the best qualifications. More to the point, he fitted the specification the Reichsfuehrer had stipulated. An SS man who was no longer SS. Himmler could claim success for a victory and shrug off a defeat. On balance, it was an hour well spent.

5

Throughout the war the London Cage was housed at 8, Kensington Palace Gardens. Officially known as the Prisoner of War Interrogation Section (PWIS), it was, as the title implies, a preliminary interrogation centre for captured Germans.

In the early days of the war, when no German flier expected the conflict to last longer than a few more weeks, the downed pilots unwittingly gave their interrogators more intelligence than the latter could have dared hope for. Apart from name, rank and serial number on the questionnaire which all new arrivals were obliged to fill in, all kinds of other questions were posed: home address, unit, nature of mission, and so on. Although it may seem incredible, these were frequently answered in detail. The apparent ingenuousness of the approach was partly responsible; a simple form to complete instead of rubber truncheons in a cellar. But more than that the fliers had received very little instruction in security. In its arrogance the Luftwaffe did not expect many of its pilots to be shot down. It was not until Franz von Werra's escape and debriefing that lectures on the method of dealing with interrogation were made mandatory. In consequence, by 1942 the interrogator's job had become much more difficult. Of necessity, therefore, he became more subtle.

Normally a POW could expect to spend no more than a day or so at the Cage before being despatched to a regular POW camp such as Grizedale Hall, Skiddaw, Devizes, Lodge Moor, Sheffield, or Comrie, Scotland. Some were held longer and some sent elsewhere for further grilling. It all depended upon what value the limited resources of British Intelligence placed on the captured individual. In Kurt von Stuerzbecher's case he had been there for six days.

After being put ashore at Harwich in the early hours of the 13th, he was taken under escort to London, arriving at Liverpool Street Station as dawn was breaking. In the usual manner he was given a questionnaire to complete. After scanning it briefly he filled in the barest details. His name, dropping the 'von' and changing his first name to Karl; his rank, demoting himself six grades to Oberleutnant; and a fictitious serial number.

'You haven't finished,' the Staff Sergeant said when he collected the document.

Many afternoons spent with Christian Eicke had given von Stuerzbecher a good command of the English language. But he affected only partial understanding and made his accent more guttural than it actually was. It was possible at a later date that a hidden knowledge of English would be of value.

'It is all that is permitted.'

The Staff Sergeant shrugged. It was the stock answer. In any case, it was none of his business. He was merely the office boy.

Alone, von Stuerzbecher examined his surroundings. The room was small, fifteen feet by twelve, and the window barred and shuttered. The only furniture was a wooden table, a couple of chairs, and a camp bed.

He made his mind go blank. By this time the Luftwaffe High Command would know that he was missing and the telephone lines would be buzzing. But there was nothing he could do about it. More than likely he would spend the remainder of the war as a prisoner, but as long as that was the worst that happened he would put up with it. He had committed a criminally negligent act by flying into the *Tommi* bomber stream and now he would have to pay for it. While the British believed him to be a mere Oberleutnant, however, incarceration would be tolerable. If they ever found out his true rank—well, it didn't bear thinking about. In one respect the Geneva Convention worked in his favour, more so than normally. Giving only his name, rank and serial number precluded any awkward and unanswerable questions regarding his unit.

The door opened and a youthful British Captain entered, carrying von Stuerzbecher's questionnaire and a notebook and pen.

'Good morning, Oberleutnant,' he said breezily and in German, and introduced himself as Captain Harrison.

'Good morning,' answered von Stuerzbecher, getting to his feet. Christ, those were the sort of details he'd have to remember. With his assumed rank of Oberleutnant, the British Captain was senior to him.

'Sit down, please.'

Captain Harrison took the chair on the other side of the table. He looked at von Stuerzbecher thoughtfully before tapping the questionnaire.

'This won't do, you know,' he said. 'If we're to let your people know you're safe, I'll need more information than this.'

'I'm not allowed to divulge any more than I have, as you well know.'

'Oh, I agree that those are the rules, but like most rules they're unrealistic. I'm not asking you to reveal the strength of your squadron or its position. But if you'll simply give me your home address I'll see that your wife and family are informed.'

'I'm sorry, that can't be done.' Von Stuerzbecher shook his head firmly.

Harrison frowned. 'Surely your home address can't be of strategic importance.' He tried a joke. 'Not unless it's in the Wilhelmstrasse.'

'I'm sorry, Herr Hauptmann, but you know as well as I do that my home address *does* have strategic importance. Alone, perhaps not. But pieced together with information obtained from other prisoners from the same town it might tell you whether or not your bombing sorties are having any success.'

'Rubbish, Stuerzbecher. I'm merely trying to be helpful. I'd have thought a man of your age would have realised that.' He scribbled something in the notebook. 'How old are you, anyway? Thirty-five, thirty-six? A bit old to be an Oberleutnant, I would have thought.'

Von Stuerzbecher remained silent.

'A bit old, anyway,' continued Harrison, 'to be an Oberleutnant on operational duties. I could understand it if you were behind a desk, but flying over the North Sea? That I find puzzling.'

'Nothing puzzling about it at all. I am an experienced flier. Germany needs experienced fliers. Q.E.D.'

'Well, that's something, anyway.' Captain Harrison made a note. 'You're a pilot, not an observer or radar man.'

Von Stuerzbecher cursed inwardly. God, he'd have to watch his tongue. The slightest slip and he was done for.

'My name is Karl Stuerzbecher, my rank is Oberleutnant . . .'

'Yes, yes,' said Harrison testily. 'I have all that. But it's still puzzling. Most of your pilots we shoot down are in their late teens or early twenties. You're in your middle thirties. So either Germany is running short of youngsters more quickly than we thought or you're not what you purport to be.'

Von Stuerzbecher said nothing.

'And another thing that intrigues me,' went on Harrison. 'According to the fellows who brought you in, when you were picked up you were carrying almost nothing that could be termed personal effects. I find that very strange, particularly the absence of cigarettes, lighter or matches. I can see from your fingers that you're a smoker.'

'When one is baling out of a damaged aircraft, one does not bother with such trivia as cigarettes and matches.'

'True enough. On the other hand, one normally keeps cigarettes and matches in a side pocket.'

'Not in my case. In any event, you were the one who suggested cigarettes, not I. I'm a cigar smoker. One cigar would last me a whole sortie. I don't need to carry spares.'

'Cigars, eh. I would have thought cigars were difficult to come by in Germany, especially for the lower ranks. If your Armed Forces are anything like ours, brigadiers and above grab the best of whatever's going.'

Abruptly Captain Harrison stood up.

'Would you like some coffee, Stuerzbecher? Sorry I can't manage breakfast but that won't be for several hours yet.'

'Coffee would be most welcome.'

'I'll arrange it.'

After telling the Staff Sergeant to rustle up a mug of coffee for the prisoner, Captain Harrison descended a floor, walked a short distance along the corridor and rapped lightly on an unmarked door. Half a minute later he was explaining his misgivings about the new POW to a full Colonel.

'Something very fishy, sir. He's far too old to be an Oberleutnant on active service and he tells me he smokes cigars. We might have caught a mackerel here.'

The Colonel was unconvinced. It wasn't the first time he'd been told there was a mackerel on the hook, even a whale, but most turned out to be sprats. Still, he could afford to overlook nothing, at least for a day or so.

'Put a few political questions to him then leave him on ice for twenty-four hours.'

Von Stuerzbecher was in the process of draining the mug when Harrison returned.

'Coffee all right?'

'Excellent, thank you. May I ask when I shall be assigned to a camp?'

'Oh, soon, soon. Just a few more questions. I need the answers to these to make sure you're put in the correct camp. We try not to mix the ordinary German with the hard-core Nazi. We find there's more blood spilt by doing that than anywhere on the front.'

Harrison spread open his notebook, as though preparing for a lengthy session.

'You're not a Nazi, I suppose, are you?'

Von Stuerzbecher was puzzled but saw no reason to answer untruthfully.

'But of course I am. We all are.'*

'I see.' Harrison made a note. 'Then you agree that the Anschluss of Austria and the invasion of Czechoslovakia and Poland were legitimate acts.'

'Of course,' answered von Stuerzbecher without hesitation. 'As you would no doubt agree that the colonisation of India, Africa and much of the rest of the world were legitimate acts. It may come as an unpalatable shock to you, Herr Hauptmann, but empires, British or German, are not founded on the principle of charity.'

Whether Captain Harrison took the bait as a ploy or whether he was genuinely annoyed that von Stuerzbecher had the temerity to compare Germany with Mother England, the Luftwaffe officer was never later quite certain.

'You're not seriously trying to compare our methods with yours?'

''Cause no, effect yes. The ethnic African didn't greet you with open arms. He fought you. You were stronger and therefore won. It matters little to a conquered people that they are subjugated by the sword or the tank. The end product remains the same.'

'Philosophy, Herr Oberleutnant?'

'Geopolitics, Herr Hauptmann. Britain became a maritime

*Author's note: It was not until late in the war or indeed after it that the word Nazi took on the sinister meaning it has today. Most officers, if not actually members of the Party, were pro-Hitler.

power and acquired a far-flung Empire because she is a tiny, isolated island with a genius for administration. Germany's Empire will be contiguous with her present borders. Germany has no interest in overseas British possessions. It was a mistake to try to colonise parts of Africa. Germany's destiny lies to the east, the rest of Europe and Asia.'

'*Lebensraum?*'

'If you wish. And it is pointless to turn up your nose at it, Herr Hauptmann. *Lebensraum* is no longer an idea; it is a reality.'

'You obviously haven't been reading the latest reports from Stalingrad.'

'A temporary set-back. We've had them before; we shall no doubt have them again. But be clear about one thing: the German people are far too dynamic to be limited to territory assigned by the Treaty of Versailles.'

'That old chestnut.'

'Chestnut perhaps. But if you attempt to emasculate a nation, you'd better make sure you get both balls.'

Captain Harrison smiled. 'You don't talk like a mere Oberleutnant, Stuerzbecher.'

'Perhaps mere Oberleutnants in the Wehrmacht have a better perspective of history than their equivalent in the British Armed Forces,' retorted von Stuerzbecher.

Nevertheless, he said no more. This apparently harmless debate was not taking place because Captain Harrison wanted an early morning argument. The British officer was a skilled interrogator. God knows how many times he had had similar conversations. One slip of the tongue would reveal that von Stuerzbecher had been in the Fuehrer's presence less than twelve hours previously, and an audience like that did not happen to mere Oberleutnants.

It was time to shut up.

'I think we are getting beyond the bounds of our respective roles,' he said lightly. 'Our personal beliefs and philosophies are irrelevant to my present status.'

Captain Harrison did not attempt to argue. Unhurriedly he closed the notebook and pocketed his pen.

'I agree. I think I've heard enough.'

'Which means I'll be sent to a camp?'

'You seem very anxious to leave us.'

Von Stuerzbecher said what any Oberleutnant would have said.

'Herr Hauptmann, you know as well as I do that even lowly Oberleutnants possess information which you would be glad to have. My base, the strength of my unit, new aircraft, conditions in Germany, morale. Of course I am anxious to leave you. What German officer wouldn't be?'

'Well, we'll have to wait and see.'

Harrison paused with his hand on the door-knob.

'The Medical Officer will visit you shortly, to ensure that you've suffered no ill-effects from your ducking. Your meals will be brought to you here. I know what the Geneva Convention says about exercise and fresh air for POWs, but you'll forgive me if, for the moment, we do not obey the letter of the law. We'll have another chat tomorrow.'

In the event, tomorrow took place at 3 a.m. the following morning, 14 November.

Von Stuerzbecher was sleeping fitfully on the camp bed. Apart from the orderly who brought his meals, he had seen no one but the Medical Officer for almost twenty-four hours.

The MO had given him a thorough examination. This was less due to concern for a fellow human being than to discover the general state of his health. Medical Officers were a vital cog in an Intelligence unit, as their reports could frequently indicate the sort of diet a prisoner had been getting prior to his capture. Any form of malnutrition could indicate food shortages in the Reich, and that kind of information was of incalculable value to the British.

Von Stuerzbecher was fully awake the minute the door was flung open. This time it wasn't Captain Harrison but an RAF Squadron Leader in full uniform. He sat himself on the far side of the wooden table and produced the ubiquitous notebook and pen as if by magic.

'Good morning, Herr Oberleutnant,' he said cheerfully in good and accentless German. 'My name is Squadron Leader Manson. Sorry about the miserable hour, but I'm sure you people of the *Nachtjagdgeschwader* are used to getting up at uncivilised hours.'

Von Stuerzbecher rubbed his eyes to clear them. The Luftwaffe equivalent of Squadron Leader was Major, and this was how he addressed his new interrogator.

'Please don't apologise, Herr Major. I could do with a bit of company.'

'Good, good. Well, just a few more questions and you'll be

67

seeing the last of us.' Abruptly he switched to English. 'It was a Ju 88 night-fighter you baled out of, wasn't it?'

Von Stuerzbecher understood the question perfectly but faked bewilderment.

'I'm sorry, Herr Major, but I didn't catch that.'

Manson repeated the question in German.

'I'm afraid I can't answer that. If you've found any of the pieces you'll know and if you haven't I'm not at liberty to tell you.'

Manson smiled his understanding and produced his cigarettes. Hesitating only briefly, von Stuerzbecher accepted one with thanks.

They puffed away in silence for a couple of minutes before Manson said: 'You know, when I was first told that we'd captured an Oberleutnant who is my age, I was most anxious to meet you. Promotion's slow in our bloody mob, but it must be murder in the Luftwaffe. Unless you've been a bad boy, of course. We've got a couple of those in the RAF; Wing Commander one day, cleaning the latrines the next. Was that it?'

Von Stuerzbecher held his peace. Manson changed tack.

'Look, old man, you've got to answer some of my questions or you'll be in this room for the duration. I'm not asking you to betray any military secrets. Good God, I'd have no respect for you if you did. But my CO has given me a job to do and he won't take no for an answer.'

'I'm permitted only to give my name, rank and number. Anything more is forbidden.'

'As you wish.' Manson put down his pen and closed the notebook. 'I can see I'm not going to get much out of you. Still, I admire you for it. Not many of your chaps see it that way. They're only too happy to sing like canaries and get the hell out of here.'

'I don't believe that, Herr Major.'

'Don't you, by God. You've obviously got a great deal more faith in your fellow flier than I have. I tell you frankly, Stuerzbecher, sometimes there's so much baring of souls going on in this room that I feel like a bloody priest. Most of it's guilt, I suppose. When your pilots see the devastation they've inflicted on London they're filled with remorse. Inevitable, don't you think?'

'The RAF are not exactly dropping feathers on our cities.'

'Come, come, there's no comparison. We aim for strategic targets; you chaps aim for civilians.'

68

'That's not true, Herr Major.'

'Not true my foot. Apart from anything else, those radar-equipped Ju 188s give our heavy bombers a hell of a problem. The aerials might cut down their air speed, but they're still very fast for a night-fighter. Far faster than a Lanc, anyway. How do you find landing them? Surely the aerials give the plane a very dangerous stalling speed.'

'I wouldn't know, Herr Major. Aerials? Radar-equipped Auntie Jus? This is all a mystery to me.'

Manson nodded, as though coming to a conclusion. Then without a word he got up and left the room.

Von Stuerzbecher sighed with relief. Round One to him.

Apart from meals, they left him alone throughout the 15th and 16th November, and on the 17th tried a plant, a German-speaking British officer in the uniform of a Luftwaffe Leutnant. Ushered into the room just after lunch as a newly captured flier, it took von Stuerzbecher under a quarter of an hour to judge the man to be a fake. He was too garrulous. Suspecting hidden microphones, no German officer would be that talkative.

They removed him in the late afternoon, on the pretext of a separate interrogation, and that was the last von Stuerzbecher saw of him.

In the small hours of the 18th Captain Harrison returned, accompanied this time by a full Colonel. Although weary through irregular hours and lack of proper exercise and ventilation, von Stuerzbecher was immediately on the alert. Under normal circumstances the interrogator's rank was just one grade higher than the prisoner being questioned. A Luftwaffe Oberleutnant, therefore, rated a British Captain. (The Squadron Leader was an exception, belonging to RAF Intelligence, whose questions were, or would have been with encouragement, on technical subjects beyond the ken of Army officers.) But this—a full Colonel; there couldn't be many of those around.

Von Stuerzbecher got to his feet in a hurry and stood rigidly to attention. The Colonel introduced himself as Wilkin.

'All right, Jamie,' he said to Captain Harrison, 'you can leave us. I don't think Oberleutnant Stuerzbecher is likely to attack me.'

Alone with Colonel Wilkin, whose German had a Bavarian lilt, von Stuerzbecher was given permission to sit, which he did with an air of resignation. He had not yet been permitted to shave or to bath and he felt filthy. By way of contrast, Wilkin looked as if he had just stepped from the fitting room of a military outfitters. His uniform was clean and beautifully pressed, his Sam Browne dazzling. He was not much older than von Stuerzbecher, but already his hair was greying.

'I must ask your forgiveness for what must appear to be gross discourtesy,' he began. 'Normally, we are not so inhospitable to our guests. In fact, the majority of them don't stay with us this long. But you puzzle us, Oberleutnant. You puzzled Squadron Leader Manson, you puzzled Captain Harrison, and their reports have puzzled me. What, we are all asking ourselves, is a German officer in his middle thirties doing with the rank of Oberleutnant? By rights you should be my equivalent, an Oberst, perhaps higher. We're very curious, to say the least. We've talked about it and we've come up with several alternatives.' He enumerated them on his fingers. 'One, you're not a pilot at all but a desk wallah who for some reason found himself in an aircraft; two, your rank is not what you state it to be; or three, and much more important, you are not military personnel. You are, in effect, a spy.'

'Ridiculous. I was in uniform.'

'True, but why were you in uniform, why were you not wearing a regulation flying suit? It's Captain Harrison's theory that you had civilian clothes in a suitcase, which you were forced to abandon when you were shot down.'

'Absurd. A fairy tale.'

'Oh, I agree it's an uncomfortable thought,' said Wilkin smoothly, 'and the consequences are even more unpleasant still. But you were found not only in walking-out dress but without any documents whatsoever, not even identity discs. We only have your word that you are Oberleutnant Karl Stuerzbecher of the Luftwaffe. You see our problem, don't you? If you are the officer you claim to be we need proof. If you're not an officer at all, I'm afraid your next interview will be with a firing squad.'

Von Stuerzbecher thought as quickly as his tired brain would allow. Whether or not the firing squad was a bluff, he would have to treat it as being serious. The alternative was to reveal his true rank and name, and that was out of the question. But thirdly, he had to get out of this wretched London Cage as soon as possible. The longer they kept him here, the more likely they were to discover his true identity. He decided to try a bluff of his own.

'Perhaps you've heard of Leutnant Franz von Werra, Herr Oberst,' he said.

'I have indeed,' answered Wilkin. 'In fact, I had the pleasure of interrogating him myself. A rather pompous young man, I thought, full of his own self-importance. And some of his claims for aircraft destroyed were pure fiction.'

'Nevertheless, Herr Oberst, von Werra escaped and got home to Germany. Before being posted to a new Staffel he was debriefed at length by our own Intelligence people, and from him we learned much of your methods. For example,' von Stuerzbecher lied, 'he told us that it was not unusual for British Intelligence to judge a pilot to be a civilian and therefore a spy, and threaten the firing squad. You know as well as I do that it is every officer's duty to rid himself of documents which may be of value to the enemy. I had more time than most and threw away everything. We do not underestimate you, Herr Oberst. A cigarette lighter made in a certain city might tell you more than any imprudent statement; a packet of cigarettes with a girl's telephone number scribbled hastily on the back; a newspaper cutting. These items could tell you more than we wish you to know.

'My fellow officers have frequently accused me of being a cautious individual, and perhaps they are right. But in an emergency there's no time to select what one will keep and what one will dispose of. It's better to get rid of it all.'

Von Stuerzbecher drew a deep breath and hurried on.

'I am who I say I am, Herr Oberst—Oberleutnant Karl Stuerzbecher of the Luftwaffe.' He allowed a trace of bitterness to creep into his words. 'If I have been passed over for promotion, if I am not the flier Adolf Galland is or von Werra, that is not for me to judge. To call me a spy is ridiculous and to send me before a firing squad with no more than an unsubstantiated assumption is an act unworthy of the uniform you wear and the rank you hold.'

Colonel Wilkins twiddled this thumbs for several minutes after von Stuerzbecher finished speaking. 'Very well,' he said finally, 'very well.'

He stood up, rapped on the door for the guard to open it, and went out. Von Stuerzbecher heaved a long sigh and shut his eyes.

Captain Harrison was waiting for Wilkin in the Colonel's own office.

'Well, sir?'

'I don't know, Jamie, I just don't know. He's either a brilliant liar or he's telling the truth.'

'I think he's lying, sir.'

'They're all lying, Jamie, they've all got something to hide. Anyway, we can't keep him here any longer. This is a busy hotel and we've already wasted enough time on him. I think you'd better make arrangements to send him on.'

'We could move him out to Cockfosters, sir, let them have a crack.'

'No, they're up to their eyes too. Send him to a camp. If we've made a mistake, that's our bad luck. There are still plenty of other fish to fry.'

And so early in the morning of 19 November, Generalmajor Kurt von Stuerzbecher was at last given shaving tackle and a sliver of soap and told to prepare to move out in half an hour.

With two other prisoners he had never seen before he was driven through bomb-torn London in a closed one-tonner and handed over to his travelling escort at Euston Station. Twenty minutes later he was on his way north.

6

19 November

For the third time that week it had snowed overnight in the Lake District and Skiddaw Camp was covered with a fluffy new inch or two of the white stuff. There was more on the way, too, judging by the temperature in the compound and the fat-bellied clouds louring over the Cumbrian Mountains. Not that the weather affected the volley ball players. In the Pig Pen they were already at it, although it was barely 9 a.m.

Crazy, thought Private George Cook, who was on early turn as compound picket and who was shivering uncontrollably as he made his rounds. He watched one-armed Willi Schneider miss a strike, fall in a heap, and jump up laughing. Mad as bloody hatters. Like a bunch of schoolkids.

Which was rich comment coming from George Cook, who, at nineteen, was hardly more than a schoolkid himself. The owner of a round, cherubic face which saw a razor less than twice a week, if there was any justice in the world George Cook wouldn't have been in uniform at all. His temperament matched his choirboy features, and the results of his induction education tests had labelled him below average. He wasn't clinically stupid, but he was very slow. Slow to understand an order, slow to carry it out, slow to do the thousand and one things the Army required of him.

There are some men, it is said, who grow into uniform, grow to be part of it and it part of them; there are others who never make it, who should never be asked to try. George Cook was one of the latter. Nicknamed Harpo by the Germans because of his blond curls, he was permanently bewildered by the apparently endless discipline and rules. Things which it seemed obvious to do were forbidden and things which seemed ridiculous mandatory.

73

His one prayer was that his number would remain that of a camp guard, that he would never be sent overseas or asked to point a rifle in earnest, and that one day soon they would let him return to the West Country girl he was engaged to.

A wild hit by Leutnant Peter Kaehler sent the ball through a gap in the wire netting. It landed at George Cook's feet.

'Throw it back, Harpo,' shouted Kaehler, in English. It was a standard phrase, known to most of the POWs. The ball frequently landed outside the Pig Pen.

Private Cook hesitated; he wasn't sure whether to do so would be an infraction of the rules. Besides, he didn't like being called Harpo, the dumb Marx brother.

'Come on, Harpo.'

Other voices joined the chorus. It wasn't the morning for hanging around.

Shyly, George Cook grounded his rifle and picked up the ball.

'You can put that down right away, Private Cook!'

George Cook froze in mid-movement. If it was part of his misfortune to be slow, it was equally unfortunate to be assigned to the same unit as Corporal Napley. Cook wasn't sure why, but Napley seemed to delight in making his life a misery. Worse, whenever he was doing something wrong, Napley was always around, like an avenging angel.

Corporal Napley had got out of bed the wrong side. The previous evening his Carlisle wife had again suggested, insisted, that on his next leave he take her to London to meet the folks. With Christmas only a few weeks off and leave pending, he had been unable to think of a way out. So he had agreed. Later, regretting his rashness, he had proceeded to drown the memory of his promise in beer. He was now feeling the after-effects and the sight of George Cook with a ball in his hand and his rifle in the snow only improved his temper marginally. But it was better than nothing.

He marched up to Harpo, who still hadn't the sense to drop the ball and snatch up the Lee-Enfield.

'What the hell d'you think you're doing? D'you think the Army pays you to act as ball-boy to a bunch of bloody krauts?'

'No, Corporal.'

'No, Corporal. Then drop the bloody thing, for Christ's sake, and pick up that rifle.'

Harpo did as he was told with as much alacrity as he would ever manage, coming roughly to attention. Corporal Napley walked slowly around him, like a terrier stalking a cornered rat. The POWs crowded the wire netting to see what would happen next. Since Emil Wielen's death a few days earlier they were wary of Napley. No matter what Major Breithaupt said, none of them believed the official verdict of accidental death, and more than several of them had made a private vow to send Napley to his Maker if the opportunity arose. But in the meantime they were treading carefully.

'You're a bloody disgrace, Cook, d'you know that? You look like a hundredweight of flour in a pound bag. What do you look like?'

'A hundredweight of flour in a pound bag, Corporal.'

'Correct. I could have you court-martialled for what you just did. Haven't you got any more bloody sense, putting your rifle down where anyone could swipe it? What are you trying to do, start an armed revolt?'

'It was right next to me, Corporal.'

'It was right next to me, Corporal. Next time, keep it in your hot little hand. You got that?'

'Yes, Corporal.'

'If they want their ball back, let the buggers get it themselves.'

It occurred to Napley to burst the POWs' ball, now lying at his feet, with Cook's bayonet. He voted against it. It would only cause trouble and he wanted none of that until the Wielen business died down. Instead he gave it a vicious kick. It flew a few yards and stuck in the snow.

Inside the Pig Pen Peter Kaehler looked at Willi Schneider who nodded at Johann Preiss. Without a word the volley ball players left the Pen, ostensibly to retrieve the ball. Corporal Napley was less than twenty yards away when the first of the hard-packed snowballs hit him on the back of the head. As he turned, livid with rage, another couple caught him flush in the face.

'You bastards!' he screamed.

But there were a dozen POWs and only one of him. He took to his heels, the prisoners' jeering laughter echoing in his stinging ears as they continued to pelt him until he was out of sight.

Harpo Cook took advantage of the disturbance to make himself

75

scarce. Rounding the back of Hut 16 he collided with Lance-corporal Harry Cade, who had witnessed the whole incident. Without knowing why, Harry Cade felt protective towards George Cook. Probably, he thought, because Cook was always being picked on by Napley.

'I'll fix that bastard one day,' swore Cade. 'I'll bury him.'

'He doesn't bother me really, Harry,' said Harpo.

'Then he should. Christ, George, I sometimes wonder what you've got in your balls apart from porridge.'

Harpo laughed. Harry Cade was his friend. He couldn't get into much trouble when he was with Harry.

'Are we playing cards later?' he asked.

'I am, but I don't know why I bother to let you play. Christ, I spend half the night taking money from Braune and Geith and you spend the other half giving it back.'

Harpo knew this wasn't true. Harry invariably came out the loser against the Germans.

'I'll see you later, then.'

'Okay,' said Cade, 'later.'

On the verandah outside his office in the Admin Section, CSM Bernard Purser had also witnessed Corporal Napley's flight. He approved; he didn't like Napley. There was a time when a man had to earn his stripes and work to keep them. Nowadays, any fool with a loud voice had two up before he was dry behind the ears. Still, the Adjutant swore by Napley so there was little he could do about it.

CSM Purser returned to his office and carried on checking the sick list.

With the CO away at a meeting and Captain Thorogood taking the opportunity to do some shopping in Carlisle, Bernard Purser was effectively in charge of the camp. There were junior officers on Skiddaw's strength, of course, but like most old soldiers the CSM's opinion of junior officers was nil. They were good for nothing except scrounging cigarettes and tea.

CSM Purser scratched his initials on the sick list and tossed it into the out-tray for Captain Thorogood to endorse on his return.

Now aged forty-three, Bernard Purser was the archetypal professional soldier from the top of his closely cropped head to the tip of his highly polished boots. He had been in the Army most of his adult life and had won the Military Medal in France in 1918.

Now that *had* been a war, he was fond of saying to anyone who had never witnessed it personally. Men stuck in trenches and told to stay there, regardless, until it was time to be relieved or to advance. And there was precious little relief. Knee-deep in mud for weeks on end and covered with lice so familiar they had names, that was the role of Tommy Atkins. He was a fighting man through and through, as hard as nails. He'd have eaten most of the present-day Armies of either side for breakfast and still have found room for a snack.

Not an unkind man by any means, CSM Purser was nevertheless known as a terror on the parade ground, capable of throwing the most violent rages if so much as a speck of dust were to be discovered on a soldier's rifle. Only he knew the rages to be simulated. The way he saw it, the senior NCO in a camp was father, mother and wet-nurse to the other ranks. A soldier might be put on a charge for rust on his bayonet, but afterwards it would become second nature to respect his weapon, and one day he would be glad of it.

To the Germans he was known as Sergeant-Major Tomorrow, after his habit of answering any question with that word. ('When are the Red Cross parcels due?' 'Tomorrow.' 'When are we going to get more blankets?' 'Tomorrow.' 'When will the war be over?' 'Tomorrow.' With a grin.) The Germans, as far as was possible, liked and respected him because they knew he was too wise to hate them simply for being Germans. Before she was killed in the Blitz, his wife had also respected him. Neither of them were people of great emotion, so love was out of the question. But respect, yes, even though she never fully understood why his job was his whole life. He still missed her.

CSM Purser had suffered two major disappointments in his life. The first was that he had never made RSM. He did an RSM's job in all but name, but he had never been granted the status. In the field or even with a training battalion, he felt he would have made it. As it was, he knew he had reached the end of the promotion road.

The second disappointment was that his only son, only child, for that matter, had elected to join the Royal Navy. With the boy now on convoy duty somewhere in the North Atlantic, it somehow gave them less in common.

He checked the desk alarm and compared it with his wrist

77

watch. It was almost 9.30, time to put on the kettle and get out the board. In a couple of minutes Oberfeldwebel Ernst Reitlinger would be knocking at the door, carrying a sheaf of papers. The documents were a blind. Whenever the CO and the Adjutant were away, Oberfeldwebel Reitlinger and CSM Purser got stuck into a game of draughts. The set-up had bothered Purser at first; it could have been called fraternising with the enemy. But when young Tom Hastings, the only officer on the British side to know of the meetings, told him that 'fraternisation' came from the Latin word for brother, the CSM had felt better about it.

Although not much given to self-examination, Purser sometimes wondered about his relationship with Reitlinger. Here they were, literally on different sides of the fence, yet it would be true to say that the Oberfeldwebel was the best friend he had. Admittedly they were roughly the same age, held similar rank, and had both fought with distinction in the 1914-18 conflict; but it was nevertheless an odd situation made odder by the fact that neither spoke much of the other's language. Enough to get by; enough to say good-morning and how-are-you and what-lousy-weather. But no more. Their only real means of communication was through the universal medium of the draughts-board; that, and a cup of hot, sweet tea. But that was how it should be with old soldiers.

Across the compound in Hut 5, Major Breithaupt's hut, the Escape Committee was in session. Or rather, for the moment, it was not. The four members had reached an impasse, divided as to whether the snow would affect, even postpone, the break-out planned for 12 December. Major Breithaupt and Oberleutnant Franz Mohr were of the opinion that if the snow continued to fall between now and then, the whole business would have to be rethought. The other two were all for going whatever the conditions.

'Good God, if we let the weather put us off we don't deserve to get out.' Those were the sentiments of Kapitänleutnant Heydt of the German Navy. 'If we miss this opportunity we won't get another crack until the spring. It was the same last year; once the snow sets in this early it'll be with us until March. By the time we get home the whole bloody country will be run by Jews and gypsies.'

'Defeatist talk, Wilhelm?' smiled Mohr.

'You know bloody well it's nothing of the sort.' Heydt flushed

78

angrily. 'But we're German officers and we're doing no damned good penned up over here. If the Luftwaffe hasn't got the balls for it, the Navy has.'

'It'll be a Committee decision,' said Breithaupt firmly. 'There'll be no more unauthorised attempts.'

'Then for God's sake take the decision, man, or we'll be here for ever.'

Otto Breithaupt eyed Kapitänleutnant Heydt with distaste. Heydt was what the propagandists meant when they talked of 'real' Nazis; blond, blue-eyed and fanatical in the extreme. As the commander of a U-boat operating out of the French submarine base at Lorient, Heydt had sunk 80,000 tons of Allied shipping before he was twenty-three, two years ago. He would have still been at it if his ship had not developed engine trouble and been caught on the surface by a Coastal Command Mosquito. He had surrendered without firing a shot and remained bitter about it. In any other commander, not scuttling the U-boat and leaving his crew to their fate would have earned the tag of coward. But Heydt's courage was a matter of record, as was his intense dislike of the Luftwaffe, whom he considered to be overfed and under-employed.

'Let's go over the pros and cons once more,' said Breithaupt patiently. 'The 12th is three weeks away and all our arrangements are geared to being completed by that date. If we don't go then, we don't go at all, and we're likely to have a dozen very disgruntled officers on our hands. If we do go, we're up against the weather. Let's assume it's actually snowing on the 12th. Admittedly that will hamper our pursuers, but it's not going to help us much either. We won't be able to stick to the roads. Normal people do not wander around in such conditions. We shall therefore have to go across country, and I don't have to tell any of you what the terrain is like between here and the coast. It's rugged, even for fully fit men who have trained on a proper diet. The snow will make the going twice as difficult, and that's not to mention the tracks we'll leave. Those are indisputable facts.'

Mohr nodded his agreement; Heydt shook his head furiously; Hauptmann Heinrich Weiss merely looked bored.

The question of escape was academic to Weiss, whose face was hideously scarred. The pilot of a Ju 88 shot down over London in 1940, Weiss was the only member of the crew to have survived.

An anti-aircraft battery had made the kill, a lucky shot hitting the bomber amidships and setting it on fire. Weiss had baled out with his flying overalls ablaze. The initial free fall, far from putting the fire out, had only fanned the flames upwards, into his face. Civilian surgeons had done their best, but plastic surgery was in its infancy and there was none to spare for the enemy. Apart from the scars on his cheeks and jaw, he had virtually lost the sight of one eye, over which he now wore a patch. There was no way he was going to be able to walk through twenty miles of enemy territory without being spotted.

Not yet twenty-four, Hauptmann Weiss was as fanatical a Nazi as Heydt, though it was hard to tell whether the hatred which burned inside him was due to political conviction or bitterness because of his disfigurement. Somewhere in Germany he had a wife, who wrote to him regularly. He never replied to the letters. For him, that part of his life was over.

'What's your opinion on the subject?' Breithaupt asked him.

Weiss took his time answering.

'I think we're putting the cart before the horse, Herr Major,' he said eventually.

'How so?'

'We're talking about whether the escape should go ahead as planned. Like Heydt, I'm all for it. Even if we don't succeed or only partly succeed, we'll cause the British a hell of a lot of trouble, and in no small respect that's a contribution to the war effort. But I'm assuming, of course, that the *Tommis* don't already know of our plans for the 12th.'

Breithaupt groaned out loud. 'Not that again.'

'Yes, Herr Major, that again. I'm not alone in thinking we have an informer amongst us—though I exclude those at this table, naturally. I believe Oberleutnant Mohr subscribes to the same theory.'

Mohr nodded. It was something of a fixation with him and he was glad Weiss had raised it.

'As I told you the other day, Otto, the three attempts we've had scuppered at the last minute must be more than coincidence.'

'And as I said,' intoned Breithaupt, 'we mustn't underestimate the British. They're not fools, they know we're going to try and get out. All they've got to do is keep their eyes open.'

'Using that as a working hypothesis,' said Weiss, 'we're being absurdly optimistic to attempt an escape at all. We might just as well sit back and wait for the war to end. I agree with Mohr; coincidence must be ruled out. As head of security I know just how careful we are. Unacceptable though it may be to you, Herr Major, I have come to the conclusion that we're being sold out.'

Breithaupt gnawed at the end of his pencil stub. Weiss was correct in one respect; he, Otto Breithaupt, didn't want to believe that there was a traitor in the camp.

'I assume that theorising is not the end of it, Hauptmann Weiss,' he said finally. 'You have something practical in mind to root out this so-called informer.'

'I have.'

'For God's sake,' broke in Heydt, who was tired of this talk of treachery. 'Do we go ahead on the 12th or not?'

'I suggest we shelve that decision until we hear what Hauptmann Weiss has to say,' said Mohr. 'It's no use us giving the green signal if we get no further than the wire.'

Breithaupt concurred. 'Let's hear your scheme, Heinrich.'

'It's really quite simple,' said Weiss. 'I'm sure we all have our own ideas about who the alleged traitor is, but whether we are justified in our suspicions we don't know. I have therefore devised a method which will give us the answer once and for all.

'To begin with I suggest we each write down three or four names here and now. Any name that appears more than once will mean we're all thinking along the same lines. Once that is established we can proceed.'

It was a positive suggestion and even Breithaupt agreed that it could do no real harm. 'Do we include NCOs?'

'Only the more senior ones, those who have actively participated in escapes or have shown their willingness to do so. We can forget about the very junior ranks; they're more interested in comfort than betrayal.'

Each man thought carefully before condemning a fellow officer or senior NCO. When the lists were completed they were handed to Weiss, who spread them out on the table in front of him.

'It seems we have two common denominators, gentlemen,' he announced, 'Two names that are common to several lists. One appears three times, the other four. Although Kapitän-leutnant Heydt evidently trusts his own officers and ratings implicitly.'

'There are only a dozen of us,' snapped Heydt, 'and I know them all as well as I know myself. You asked my opinion, you've got it.'

'Get on with it, man,' Mohr urged.

'Very well. The name that appears three times is Oberfeldwebel Reitlinger.'

'Nonsense,' said Breithaupt, who'd considered Reitlinger before dismissing the notion as absurd.

'Nevertheless,' said Heydt, 'he and CSM Tomorrow are as thick as thieves. If I didn't know Reitlinger to be a family man I'd suspect they were lovers.'

'They play checkers, that's all. If you're going to use that as a basis for treachery, this whole exercise is a waste of time.'

'He has opportunity, Herr Major,' put in Weiss. 'Three of us think he's a possibility. We can't afford to overlook him.'

'And Martin Bormann's Joe Stalin's cousin,' muttered Breithaupt.

'And the other name?' asked Mohr.

'The other name is much more interesting. Oberleutnant Kapp.'

Each of them had an immediate mental image of Oberleutnant Kapp, late of the 186th Artillery Regiment, and Franz Mohr at least wondered if he'd put the name on the list because he, personally, didn't like the man. There was very little to like. Kapp was *Dreikäsehoch*, bespectacled and skinny, and one of the very few German officers to be captured during the British rout at Dunkirk. No one could prove it but it was thought that Kapp had surrendered at the first available opportunity. How he had ever got his commission was a mystery to most of them; Party influence, it was suspected. But apart from being physically unattractive, Kapp was the camp moaner, the Jeremiah. As far as he was concerned food parcels were always late, mail misdirected, and the standard of cooking and hygiene abysmal. Even the handful of fellow Army officers shunned his company and sometimes he would disappear for hours on end. This latter was far from being proof of his guilt; a clever informer would make it his business to be seen. But it was something to be considered.

'So, Kapp,' said Heydt.

'We haven't proved anything yet,' Breithaupt interrupted quickly. 'I for one doubt that it is Kapp even though I put his name on my list.'

'Well, that's my business from now on.' Weiss threw the lists into the stove. 'We'll soon know, one way or another.'

'How do you propose to go about it?' Mohr asked.

'I intend to set a trap. I shall leak information, gradually, over the next few days, that an escape is being planned for, shall we say, two weeks from now. Naturally neither Kapp nor Reitlinger will be given the same information. On the due date we shall keep a careful watch. If the *Tommis* turn up in force at either of the fictitious exits, we'll know which is our *Spitzel*.'

'And then?' asked Heydt.

Weiss drew a hand across his throat, but Breithaupt was having none of that.

'There'll be no drumhead courts-martial while I'm senior officer,' he warned. People like Weiss tended to forget that courts-martial were forbidden; only the *Tommis* could mete out disciplinary action. In theory, that is. In practice it was somewhat different.

'Well, we haven't caught our rabbit yet, have we?' Weiss smiled his twisted smile. 'The scheme might not work. If it doesn't, we'll have to try again.'

Breithaupt shook his head. 'Sometimes, Heinrich, I swear to Christ you enjoy this sort of thing.'

'It's a contribution, Herr Major. What else can a man in my position offer?'

Breithaupt got to his feet.

'As far as I'm concerned that's all for today. We'll see how Heinrich's plan works out then discuss the 12th again. Let's get to hell out of here. My chaps must be freezing outside. Walk with me, Franz?'

It was snowing again and they huddled deep inside their threadbare clothes.

'What about the new batch of POWs?' asked Mohr. 'Would you like to meet them?'

'If you wouldn't mind. I've got a hundred other things to do.' He chuckled. 'Besides, the train's bound to be late.'

'Don't grumble about the trains, Otto. It means our bombers are still doing the job.'

7

19 November

During the Second World War most escapes from POW camps, on either side, were made via tunnels, and the one planned from Skiddaw for 12 December was no exception. In one respect, the porosity of the soil in that part of northern England, while hindering progress, helped the POWs. Few tunnel escapes had been tried from Skiddaw and none had succeeded, which led the British to believe that it could not be done. Mostly escapees got out by using sheer bluff, as Emil Wielen had done, or by stowing away in the back of civilian refuse carts or delivery vans. In the early days, before the doubling of the perimeter fence, two officers won temporary freedom by throwing a makeshift rope ladder over the barbed-wire, which was not electrified, and scrambling out in that manner. When such schemes worked they were a great morale booster, but they had one obvious drawback: only one POW, at the most a couple, could get out at any one time. Breithaupt's plan for the 12th involved a dozen.

Although he had no way of knowing whether or not Major Mitchell and his staff, via an informer or by keeping their eyes open, were aware of the tunnel, Breithaupt was pretty sure that, either way, the Commandant wouldn't pounce until the last moment. As he had pointed out to Oberleutnant Mohr, this had the dual effect of keeping the POWs happy and untroublesome while they were digging and demoralising them when their efforts proved valueless at the eleventh hour. That had been Mitchell's *modus operandi* in the past and there was no reason to think he would change a winning pattern.

Getting under the wire was only a fraction of the problem for would-be escapees. On the outside they needed clothes that would pass casual scrutiny, money for emergencies, provisions; they needed maps, compasses, a knowledge of the terrain. It was not the slightest use building a tunnel to rival the Simplon if they were discovered sitting at the side of the road, wondering which way was west. For this reason Skiddaw was invariably a hot-bed of clandestine cottage industries.

Clothes were the most important item. The majority of POWs looked like POWs, either because they still wore some of their flying gear or because of the regulation overalls issued by their captors. So the first thing was to change the colour and shape of their clothing, which was the responsibility of an Oberleutnant who was a tailor in civilian life. Dyes were obtained from berries, collected during the autumn and squirrelled away, and ordinary ink. The bark from some trees, too, when soaked in hot water, produced a reliable brown pigment. Thus a pair of grey-blue Luftwaffe trousers, which against regulations many of the air crew wore in combat, would be transformed. Admittedly not every attempt proved successful and what should have been dark blue or brown turned out to resemble something like camouflage netting. But this was wartime Britain and many of the indigenous population wore what looked like cast-offs.

Once dyed, trousers were restyled, reassembled and pressed. But not too well. Several fugitives had been spotted for what they were because of a knife-edge crease in their trousers.

Tunics proved more difficult. There was no way, without proper equipment, that the military cut could be disguised and the tunic turned into a civilian jacket. But at least the colour could be altered and under a dyed overcoat (a doctored greatcoat) would not be too noticeable.

After clothing the second most important item was money; money for fares if the going got rough, for purchases if the provisions ran out; and for bribes if an escapee was fortunate enough to reach a port and find a corruptible skipper. It was a curious paradox of camp life that money for bribes had first of all to be obtained by bribery. POWs were paid in scrip, not currency, and scrip was useless outside the camp. The amount varied according to rank, but an Oberleutnant in 1942 would obtain roughly the equivalent of six pounds sterling per month. The black-market exchange rate was four for one.

Apart from Corporal Napley there were other guards in the exchange market. Although it was an indictable offence and the

85

punishment severe if discovered, it went on all the time. Many of the captured fliers possessed expensive wrist watches, pocket watches, fountain pens, and other items capable of being converted to hard cash. The going rate varied according to the natural laws of supply and demand, but any POW who could hang on to his possessions for long enough was assured of a respectable price. And legitimate currency was of course smuggled in by new arrivals, sometimes in a very odd manner. Mostly it was concealed in book-bindings and suchlike, but the Hauptmann who swallowed ten one-pound notes after baling out and waited for nature to take its course was very disappointed when he found no takers for the end-product.

After money came provisions, usually chocolate. An alert observer should always have been able to tell when an escape was on the cards as few of the POWs were ever seen eating their rations.

Penultimately it was a matter of knowing which direction to go in and what to avoid. Recaptured POWs were an invaluable source of information in this. A route which was passable in June was sometimes out of the question in December; a house where someone had obtained a glass of water in August could well be a temporary billet for troops in November. These were things to know.

In view of the camp's proximity to the coast, maps and rough compasses were not considered essential equipment for potential runaways from Skiddaw. Nevertheless, they were provided if required; if, for example, a prisoner decided not to head for Workington or Whitehaven but inland. Each recaptured flier, after his twenty-eight days in the cooler, was thoroughly debriefed by the Escape Committee and a reservoir of intelligence assembled from which maps were drawn. Most of the POWs got no further than a few miles, so there was an embarrassing plethora of knowledge concerning the hills and roads within the immediate vicinity of the camp. Further on was more of an unknown quantity but even so the disposition of the major roads was known.

Lastly there was the question of attitude once out of Skiddaw, and on this lectures were given by officers who knew something of England and the English, standing-room only.

Many POWs were recaptured because they looked and behaved like POWs. An ignorance of the language was not in itself a draw-back; the English, it was pointed out, are a secretive race not much given to social intercourse. They are reserved in attitude and demeanour. Not for nothing did the proverb originate of an Englishman's home being his castle. Once inside, with the portcullis down and the drawbridge up, he is not interested in callers and neighbours. He's not much interested in them outside the castle, either. Therefore, the POWs were told, even if you have a working knowledge of English, don't be too chatty; don't try to curry favour by tossing out 'good mornings' at random, if by some misfortune your route takes you through a town or village. More important still, don't skulk. The Englishman is a proud individual who makes way for no man. And here, usually, the story was told of the English spy in Cairo during the First World War. His disguise as an Arab was perfect, his accent faultless. Yet he walked through the bazaar as if he owned it, something no Arab would ever do. So keep your head up and never run, unless it's for a bus.

But all of the aforegoing presupposed that a POW was on his way, and as yet none of them were.

As senior German officer, in consultation with the remainder of the Escape Committee Major Breithaupt had given long and careful thought to the positioning of the tunnel. From the inner perimeter wire to the outer was a standard thirty feet, nine and a bit metres the way the Germans calculated it, so at first glance it mattered little where the tunnellers started, all other things being equal. But the western boundary housed, as well as the guardroom, the Admin offices and the armoury, which was always heavily guarded. The opposite end of the compound was also out, which was a pity as quite close to the inner perimeter wire stood the POW's kitchen, canteen and a room which served as a library. The snag here was that the nearest cover beyond the outer wire, a clump of trees leading into a copse, was seventy yards away, over sixty-four metres. Unless a prisoner wanted to run that far in full view of the watch-tower guards, tunnelling anywhere close to the trees would take the rest of this war and most of the next.

The best idea had been to begin in the officers' bath-house and heads, on the north side. With all the comings and goings from that building, an escape burrow there was considered foolproof. But two days before the selected POWs were due to leave, Captain Thorogood descended with half a company of armed men, and that was that. A second tunnel anywhere in that region would have to wait a while.

Which left the south side, though really there was nothing there save the MT Pool (again heavily guarded), the British officers' quarters (definitely not), the long wooden hut which served as the German officers' Mess (too obvious), and the all-denominational chapel. Breithaupt had not even considered this as a possibility until the afternoon in August young Peter Kaehler rushed into Hut 5.

'Sir, I've just come from the Chapel . . .

'Congratulations. I've been saying for a long time that what we need around here is more religion and less griping. What are you trying to do, Kaehler, pray your way out?'

'Of course not, sir. But it's one of the coolest places in the camp on a day like this and the Chaplain's hardly ever there except on Sundays so he doesn't mind . . .'

'Will you kindly slow down, Kaehler, and get to the point. I have work to do even if junior officers do not.'

'I'm trying to, sir.' Kaehler took a couple of deep breaths. 'There's a way out from there, Herr Major, I swear to God there is. It's just a wooden structure, the chapel, like the Mess, but through lack of space or something they've pushed one end of the altar right up against the south wall. And it *moves*, sir.'

'Moves? Have you and Preiss been making that potato wine again?'

'No, sir. But it does. I tried it.'

'Tried what? What moves, you dunderhead?'

'The altar, sir, the bloody altar. I leaned against it and the bloody thing damn near toppled over, God knows why.'

'God indeed, Leutnant Kaehler. Show me.'

In purpose-built Skiddaw the chapel appeared to have been erected as an afterthought. It wasn't difficult to imagine the military planners, in their anxiety to cater for the overspill from Grizedale Hall, omitting it from their original drawings and then, as the camp took shape, thinking, Oh Lord, isn't there something in the Geneva Convention about a place of worship for POWs? Can't find the precise reference, old man, but we've got a few hundred square feet doing nothing down there on the south-west perimeter; that'll have to do. Nothing too fancy, though; we're not competing with Sir Christopher Wren. Didn't know the Jerries prayed, anyway.

And nothing too fancy was what the POWs got; a wooden

structure with a wooden floor seventy or eighty feet long by thirty wide, with benches as pews and an altar like an oversized desk.

Kaehler was right, Breithaupt saw immediately; no one had bothered to nail the altar down, perhaps thinking that its own weight would keep it in place, and what was the point in going to more trouble than was necessary for POWs? What was more, the altar was hollow, just a big box really, large enough to take a man. Underneath its base were only the floorboards.

'Grab a couple of reliable men and keep watch,' he ordered Kaehler. 'I'm going to take a look.'

It took Otto Breithaupt the rest of the afternoon to prise loose a couple of boards, but what he saw when he had finished, via the dim light of a pencil torch, gave him immense satisfaction. There were no solid foundations. The corner posts had each been sunk into a bed of concrete, but that was all; the rest was just earth. And the gap between the beams which supported the floorboards and the earth itself was a good five feet, almost high enough to stand up in. In their anxiety to get the camp completed on schedule, the *Tommis* had made a mistake which was going to cost them dearly.

Back in his hut Breithaupt did some rapid calculations. The tunnel could be started just inside the south wall of the chapel, which was some twenty feet or six metres from the inner perimeter wire. The distance between the inner and outer wires was thirty feet, about nine metres, and from the outer wire to the cover of the trees, much closer on this side of the compound than at the eastern boundary, about fifty feet or a little over fifteen metres. Allowing for the fact that the tunnel would have to be approximately a metre wide by a metre high, the quantity of earth they would need to shift was around thirty cubic metres. The space beneath the floorboards of the chapel was six or seven times as big so there would be no problem about getting rid of the excavated soil. Just dump it, it was as simple as that.

A relay of good tunnellers, allowing for shoring up and labouring under arduous and exhausting conditions, could shift half a cubic metre a day. In theory, therefore, in sixty working days they should be in a position to attempt the break. Not every day could be a working day, of course; too great an interest in the chapel by too many POWs would raise suspicions. Three or four days a week should be about average, say fifteen weeks from the time they started. The second or third week in December would see them ready to go.

A major problem to be overcome before digging could get under way was finding a good reason for having a lot of men regularly beating a path between the main compound and the chapel, and here Breithaupt had a brainwave. He formed a choir and asked permission to hold choir practices in the chapel. The Commandant was all for the idea; anything that kept the prisoners out of his hair without interfering with the running of the camp could only be a bonus. Captain Thorogood wasn't so sure.

'They're up to some bloody thing, sir. Good grief, why do they want to stay indoors when the sun's cracking the flags?'

'Nonsense, Adrian. But if it'll make you any happier, keep an eye on them.'

The Adjutant did just that, but Breithaupt outfoxed him. For the first two weeks of choir practice not a cubic centimetre of earth was moved, not a spade lifted; the choir did precisely what all choirs do: rehearsed. And if the rendering of the various hymns was less than holy, well, that only meant more homework.

Captain Thorogood eventually gave up. If the bloody Jerries were up to something, he'd find out about it sooner or later.

Gradually the tunnel progressed. While the choir thumped out its unmelodious offerings above them, the duty diggers burrowed away, not the least of their problems being ventilation. But there was little to be done about that. It simply meant stopping once every five or ten minutes and sometimes crawling backwards to breathe the (comparatively) fresh air beneath the chapel.

The pattern of digging never varied. By feeble torchlight, the POWs worked in teams of two. While the lead man of the pair chipped away at the earth in front of him with implements fashioned from old cans, pilfered chisels, even sharpened mess-tins, the second man filled a cut-off trouser leg, tied with string at one end. When the 'sack' was full he retraced his steps until he was underneath the chapel and dumped the contents. The exercise was then repeated.

Shoring up was the most difficult and unpopular task, as on those days no forward movement was made. The POWs were always on the prowl for planks, bits of iron, or anything else that could be used. The end products would have given a mining engineer heart failure, but it worked, for the most part.

The days it didn't work were towards the end of the summer, when the rains came and soaked the desiccated soil, causing minor falls and snail-like progress. The roof of the tunnel was a good two metres below the surface of the compound and the chances of a gaping hole suddenly appearing remote. Still, they had to be careful. No one knew what the effects of a heavy downpour would be. Breithaupt's estimate of half a cubic metre a day proved to be about average, though it was sometimes less, never more.

Nevertheless, by the end of September they were under the inner perimeter wire, and by the last day of the following month outside the compound itself. Now, as November ran towards its wintry close, they were reaching the end of the trail. The Escape Committee had calculated that the last sackful of earth would be removed on 11 December, and the break-out was planned for the following night.

With luck, every man jack of the POWs who had worked on the tunnel was thinking. Providing nothing went wrong at the last minute; providing the roof didn't cave in or Captain Thorogood develop second sight or somebody rat on them; providing all of that.

Each of them knew that what they were attempting had never succeeded before and that every tunnel took on a personality of its own, sometimes friendly, sometimes hostile. This one, nick-named *Kaninchenbau*—Rabbit Warren or Rabbit Run—had been lucky for them. Only one minor upset had occurred, though that could have easily become a disaster.

It took place one morning when the Chaplain walked into his domain just as the tunnelling crew were emerging from beneath the altar. Leutnant Uhde, who was supposed to be door guard, had let his mind wander to his young wife and had not seen the Chaplain until it was too late. Franz Mohr saved the situation by rallying the POWs around the altar and getting them to sing an impromptu rendering of *Stille Nacht, Heilige Nacht*—Silent Night. When the Chaplain remarked that wasn't it a bit early to be practising carols, Mohr responded that the choir needed all the rehearsal it could get. The Chaplain, somewhat short-sighted, was compelled to agree and left them to it.

So the tunnel was a lucky one, but with only three weeks or so to go now before K-day (for *Kaninchenbau*), the men occasionally showed signs of strain. Friends snapped at one another for no apparent reason and those who had been selected to make the attempt found themselves drawing further and further apart from those who were to stay behind. No one argued with the decision regarding who should go; that was up to the Escape Committee and final. But it was hard for those not on the list, to watch those who were check and recheck their iron rations, clothing, maps. It was also hard to understand why Breithaupt had limited the number to a round dozen, though most of them accepted that twelve missing in a snap head-count would create only confusion, while fifty or sixty would send the balloon up.

Leutnants Kaehler and Preiss were going. Kaehler was a must because it was his alertness which had set the whole scheme in motion. And where Peter Kaehler went, Johann Preiss went. Franz Mohr was going, though Otto Breithaupt debated the wisdom of this at first. If this escape did not succeed, Franz could well go to pieces with a further twenty-eight days in the cooler. But he'd worked hard on the digging and deserved his chance.

Kapitänleutnant Wilhelm Heydt was going and taking with him four of his naval officers. Heydt had put forward his own name and those of his subordinates, and there was no arguing with him. It would have been difficult to negate his claims, in any case. Whether Breithaupt liked the man or not, the fact remained that he had served on the Escape Committee for a year without asking for a place on previous runs. It was his due and Otto Breithaupt could not deny it.

Leutnant Fritz Uhde was going. He was one of the lucky ones. At the beginning of any escape bid, the officer who originated the idea plus any one other POW he nominated were first on the list. After that, depending upon what the method of egress was, the Escape Committee chose a further eighty per cent. With a tunnel attempt it would be the strongest, those who could dig without showing strain, as naturally enough only the individuals who worked on the tunnel could expect to use it. The remaining two or three places were chosen by lot, screws of paper in a cap, the successful ones marked with a cross. Fritz Uhde had drawn a cross and was already smelling his young wife's scent.

Oberleutnant Werner Herburg was going—by accident. Nominally the camp librarian, with no more arduous a duty than ensuring that books, a great prize, were fairly distributed, it was Herburg who owned the chess set Franz Mohr and Otto Breithaupt usually played with. It had been received the previous Christmas, 1941, sent by Herburg's mother via the Red Cross. The British examined it with a fine tooth comb for contraband and, finding nothing, passed it on to the officer concerned. It was used regularly without incident until July 1942, when it was accidentally dropped by Peter Kaehler at the end of a session. It broke into four layers. Between each layer, carefully folded, were ten English five-pound notes, a total of one hundred and fifty pounds, a fortune. Further examination failed to reveal any more treasure, but it was obvious that Frau Herburg was a clever lady. She had overlooked the obvious hiding places and opted for the obscure, hoping that somehow the money would be discovered. As it rightfully belonged to her son, who without hesitation put it into the common fund, there was no way the Committee could exclude him from the next serious break-out.

The penultimate place went to Oberleutnant Theo Emke. It was impossible to leave Emke out. In spite of his hugeness, which gave him great difficulty in the tunnel, he had twice the work-rate of any other officer. Those huge biceps and hands could damn near dig a tunnel by themselves, and he never grumbled. He would be sadly missed by all save the would-be snooker champions, but his place was on the outside.

For the final spot to make up the round dozen, Major Breithaupt first of all suggested Hauptmann Weiss. Weiss declined. 'In the Reich I will be given a desk job; here I am useful.' No one argued.

Breithaupt then considered himself—but quickly rejected the idea. He wanted to get home and into the fight again as much as anybody, but his place was in Skiddaw, co-ordinating. It might be presumptuous and arrogant of him, but here he had a value greater than his value to Germany in the air. Many of the POWs were only kids; they needed guidance; he had a duty to see they did nothing foolish. His self-imposed task (he refused to think of it as self-sacrifice) could keep him in Skiddaw for the rest of the war, but that was the luck of the draw.

So the twelfth and final place was left open. There was no obvious candidate, but one never knew when one might appear.

At three o'clock that same afternoon Oberleutnant Mohr was summoned from his hut by his orderly, Obergefreiter Willi Braune. The expected batch of new POWs had arrived. Normally this was treated as a gala event by the old-timers, all anxious to see if they knew anyone amongst the new arrivals. But today the weather kept them huddling around their stoves. Blobs of snow the size of small fists, driven by a rising wind, had been falling since noon and it was impossible to see further than a few feet.

'The perfect day for an escape, Herr Oberleutnant,' said Willi. 'The *Tommis* will never find us.'

Mohr smiled to himself. 'Us, Willi? When was the last time you went under the wire?'

'I've never been given the opportunity. It's always the officers who make the breaks.'

'Then I'll see to it that you're included in the next. It's a bit tricky though. We're charging the main gates in broad daylight.'

'Herr Oberleutnant . . . ?'

'We need someone to fling himself at the guard's bayonet while the others get out.'

'Perhaps I'll wait for something better.'

'Perhaps you will. All right, Willi, you can go back to whatever you were doing. There's no point in us both catching pneumonia.'

Willi made his way across the compound to the boiler-room. With any luck Harry Cade would already be there, coffee bubbling. Charging the main gates, for Christ's sake. What did the Oberleutnant take him for, a lunatic? It was all very well for the officers; if they got back it was a full page spread in the *Voelkischer Beobachter* and tea with the Fuehrer. For other ranks it was heigh-ho for the front line. No bloody thank you. There was a lot to be said for being a prisoner.

Franz Mohr wrapped his threadbare coat more tightly about him and put his head down. God, but it was a wicked day. Kapitänleutnant Heydt or no, if the weather was like this on the 12th no one was going anywhere.

At the door to the guardroom CSM Purser was waiting for him. Mohr stamped his feet and shook himself like a terrier.

'Good afternoon, Sergeant Major,' he said in English. 'I trust if this weather continues you will not be taking roll-call in the open.'

'I really couldn't say, sir, though I think it's unlikely. We'll probably just do a head-count in the huts.'

'I should hope so. Well, by how many bodies have you depleted the Wehrmacht this time?'

94

'Just three, sir, all Luftwaffe Oberleutnants. They've seen Major Mitchell, but the MO is busy. Their examination will have to wait.'

'Very well. Lead me to them.'

Mohr followed the CSM into the guardroom. The three captured officers were standing in a line, facing the door. Mohr looked them up and down. His eyes widened in astonishment and it was all he could do not to click his heels.

On the far left of the trio, von Stuerzbecher saw instant recognition pictured on the face of the newcomer, and to defuse a potentially catastrophic situation he stepped quickly forward.

'Oberleutnant Karl Stuerzbecher, Luftwaffe,' he barked. 'Good to see you again, Hans.'

It took a moment or two, but Mohr got the message.

'Good to see you, Karl, though your memory fails you. It's Franz, not Hans.'

'Of course. Forgive me. It was such a brief meeting.'

This conversation, for the apparent benefit of the other two POWs, was conducted in German and the CSM did not understand a word of it.

'All right,' he said, 'that's enough of that. You can chat as much as you like outside. Get going.'

'Of course, Herr Feldwebel.' Mohr beckoned the others. 'Follow me, gentlemen.'

Outside, Franz Mohr thought quickly. For obvious reasons von Stuerzbecher did not want the British to know who he was, but less obviously he didn't want his two companions to know either. Mohr had to get rid of them.

'Look,' he said, 'I'd like to have a word with my old friend Karl before the others commandeer him for news of home. So I'll leave you to find your own way to the Mess.' He pointed. 'Go diagonally across the compound and it's the first wooden structure you see after you pass the Motor Pool. Welcome to Skiddaw, by the way. I hope you won't be here long.'

The other two were only too glad to get out of the cold and within a few strides had disappeared behind a curtain of snow. In spite of himself Franz Mohr now came to attention.

'Herr Generalmajor,' he said respectfully.

'None of that,' warned von Stuerzbecher. 'I'm Oberleutnant Stuerzbecher without the von from now on and don't you forget it. Let's keep walking. Who are you and where did we meet, incidentally? I seem to know you.'

Mohr introduced himself. 'We met at a party in Paris in the summer of 1940. You were only an Oberstleutnant then, but needless to say we heard of your subsequent promotions. Is it true that the *Tommis* don't know who you are?'

'As far as I know. And it's essential, Franz, that they don't find out. I can't tell you how essential, but believe me, a great many German lives depend on it.'

'You're safe as far as I'm concerned, sir.'

'I expect so, but what about the others? Is there anyone else here likely to recognise me?'

'Hard to say, Herr . . . I mean, Karl. There are a couple of hundred of us here and it's possible you've met some of them before. Then again, I wouldn't have recognised you myself except for the fact that you were good enough to talk tactics to me for half an hour. If you'll forgive me, you've changed.'

'We all have, Franz. Who's the senior officer?'

'Major Breithaupt.'

'Breithaupt, Breithaupt. No, I don't think I know him, but we'd better remedy that as soon as possible. Also, I've got to get a message home right away, letting them know where I am. Not the normal POW's letter, though that will have to do if there's no alternative.'

'The Navy has a code, sir . . . I'm sorry . . . Karl. They're a bit jealous about letting anyone use it, but I'm sure they'll make an exception in your case. It'll mean letting Kapitänleutnant Heydt in on it, though.'

'Can't be helped. All right, Major Breithaupt first and then Kapitänleutnant Heydt. And I know you must have a thousand questions you want to ask me, Franz, but much later if you don't mind.'

'Of course.'

8

3 December

The same weather conditions which were creating havoc in northern England were also being felt in Germany. Not that the Berliners were worried; it could snow from now till Armageddon for all they cared. It might be nasty, squelchy stuff in peacetime, but in wartime it was a gift from the gods. It made the young girls' faces bright and hid the bomb-torn buildings. More important, it kept the *Tommis* grounded. Even the terror fliers couldn't take off in weather such as this. The current joke was that Goebbels would shortly announce in the *Voelkischer Beobachter* that the snow was the result of some new secret weapon. It was cold, bloody cold, but cold was better than dead.

Inside Oberleutnant Christian Eicke's rented apartment it was far from cold, not all of the heat being generated by the roaring fire.

'You're off your bloody head, Christian.' Feldwebel Josef Schelling looked from the map of England spread out across the table to his superior officer and friend. 'When the SS came and grabbed me from the Front I thought my time was up. Now I know I was right. A Division couldn't do it. You've got one Ritterkreuz, for the love of God; what the hell do you want with another? We wouldn't stand a chance.'

Christian ran a hand through his dark hair. 'It's precisely because fourteen thousand men couldn't do it that the three of us can.' He grinned disarmingly. 'Anyway, you're forgetting something. I'm not asking you, I'm telling you.'

'That's below the belt, Christian.' The third member of the trio, Obergefreiter Wolfgang Schultz, pulled a long face. 'When we arrived you said this was a volunteer operation.'

97

'So it is. But I'm the volunteer. You two are conscripted.'

'Bloody hell.'

'You mean there's no way I can get back to somewhere nice and safe like Stalingrad?'

'None.'

Josef Schelling shrugged. 'In that case I volunteer. But you might have chosen someone other than Schultz here. If the British don't kill us, he will.'

'Balls.'

As a matter of fact, since he had come to the conclusion that three was the optimum number for the operation, Christian had given both other members of the team considerable thought. To begin with he had listed everyone he could think of, officers and other ranks, who were in any way suitable for the task at hand. He had examined their qualifications carefully and only with the greatest reluctance rejected them. The list finally narrowed down to the two men opposite him. NCOs or not, Feldwebel Schelling and Obergefreiter Schultz had, in effect, chosen themselves. There was no one with whom Christian would rather work, no one he would trust more with his neck. Though to look at them they were a most unlikely couple.

Born in 1904 in Düsseldorf (though now he was approaching forty he sometimes gave his year of birth as 1908), Josef Schelling was a giant of a man, three full inches over six feet with shoulders to match and a chest that threatened to burst out of his regulation tunic. A mechanic by trade, he had supplemented his income between the wars by prize-fighting in fairgrounds. His face still bore the marks of those days, though he swore that his broken nose was due to a fall after too much beer. Drinking beer was his favourite pastime and he had been known to put away three crates in an evening.

On loan from an Infantry unit and attached to the Engineer Battalion of the Totenkopf SS Division, his fondness for the bottle was the source of much trouble in the early days. Promoted Oberfeldwebel three times, three times Schelling had been busted to the ranks before Christian took him in hand. As his immediate superior officer Christian was responsible for two of the demotions and he was at a loss regarding what to do with the big fellow. He could have him shot, that was one solution. Getting drunk anywhere near the Front was not treated as a joke in the SS, even for NCOs on attachment. He could toss him into a military prison for the duration. But that didn't appeal either. There seemed too much good in the man to take the easy way out.

The second time Schelling appeared before him, Christian had the answer.

'It seems to me,' he said, 'that you're always in trouble because you have too much time on your hands. I've therefore arranged with the Battalion Hauptscharfuehrer for you to be drilled every moment you're not actually eating, sleeping or on patrol. What's more, whatever the ground conditions you will be required to parade in full walking-out dress, which must of course be cleaned and pressed. Let's see if a little fresh air and exercise can't cure you of your addiction to beer.'

It took ten days but eventually Schelling realised he couldn't beat the system, and Christian was not surprised when the ex-Feldwebel requested an interview. He was only amazed it had taken so long. Drilling under the beady eye of the Hauptscharfuehrer for five hours a day on normal days and all day on rest days wasn't funny; neither was scraping inches of mud off a uniform and boots in preparation for the next inspection.

'Permission to speak, Herr Sturmbannfuehrer?'

'Permission granted.'

'I respectfully request to be taken off punishment. As the Sturmbannfuehrer rightly predicted, fresh air and exercise takes away a man's appetite for beer.'

'Good.' Christian reached in his desk drawer and produced a bottle and two glasses. 'But not schnapps, I trust. Sit down.'

They finished the bottle together, and Schelling gave no more trouble after that. And being a natural leader of men he gradually worked his way up the promotion ladder again.

When Christian was transferred to the Recce Battalion of the Totenkopf Division, he took Feldwebel Schelling with him. Reconnaissance was a dangerous business, with the Battalion sometimes operating half a dozen miles ahead of the rest of the Division. On such occasions it was comforting to know that he had at least one NCO who was both reliable and courageous. Or in this case two, for included in the transfer was Wolf Schultz.

Obergefreiter Wolfgang Schultz had been a long-standing friend of Josef Schelling before Christian met either of them. A fully accredited hero, Schultz wore with pride one of the Army's most coveted awards, the *Panzervernichtungsabzeichen,* the badge for the single-handed destruction of a tank. Or rather he wore two, for on two separate occasions he had taken out a Russian tank without using an anti-tank weapon.

There were some who sniggered at the sight of the huge Schelling and the diminutive Schultz going out on the town together, and who nicknamed them Lennie and George after the two characters in John Steinbeck's *Of Mice and Men.* But sarcastic comments were always made in private, for in spite of his size Wolf Schultz was a fighter of renown. What he lacked in weight and height he made up for in speed and guts, going at an opponent with arms flailing like miniature windmills. In order to put him down and make him stay down, you had to knock him out; anything less, regardless of the state he was in, simply enraged him and put him back into the fight with twice as much energy and venom as before. Many a man who fought Wolf Schultz was beaten because his arms grew too heavy to deliver the coup de grâce.

Schultz openly confessed to wishing he was six feet four with the looks of Clark Gable. Instead he was five feet eight, weighed 140lbs, and resembled a recalcitrant cherub with a bad case of rabbit teeth. But this drawback in no way prevented him from pursuing one of the most active sex lives anyone in the Totenkopf Division, not renowned for its celibacy, had even known. If the Division was miles from anywhere and the nearest female company a nanny-goat, Schultz would somehow find a willing woman. He put it down to an acute sense of smell, which he said was the equal of a stallion's at breeding time. Others put it down to luck and indefatigable energy.

On transfer to the Reconnaissance Battalion, Christian took him on at Schelling's request. At first Christian had his doubts, only slightly mollified by sight of the tank badges. What on earth could this skinny individual do? Schultz answered the unposed question with a vengeance on their first sortie by taking out, alone, a Russian machine gun nest that was holding up the advance. Christian's misgivings disappeared in a flash at the sight of the Obergefreiter racing up a heavily defended slope with the speed and agility of an Olympic sprinter.

Subsequently, prior to Christian's ignominious dismissal from the SS, the three of them did everything together, in battle and out of it. If it was dangerous, it was for them. And it was a measure of the deep friendship that existed between them that neither two commented on Christian's new rank of Oberleutnant. They knew some of the story; the rest would be told if and when Christian elected to tell it. In the meantime, they thought it completely natural that, faced with his present problem, Christian had sent for them. They would have felt insulted had he done otherwise. They would respect and calculate the hazards, of course, and they would grumble; but that was just part of being an old soldier.

'It's still impossible, Christian, whether I volunteer or whether I'm dragooned.' Feldwebel Schelling frowned at the map of England. 'The British aren't going to let us walk calmly in, free the General, and walk out again.'

'First of all,' said Christian, 'forget von Stuerzbecher's rank. If the British knew that they'd stick him in a special camp and we'd never get at him. But as far as we can gather he's got away with posing as an Oberleutnant.'

'Don't the *Tommis* have lists of names of senior officers?' asked Schultz. 'I thought we did.'

'We do. So do they. But they can't update them with any degree of regularity or accuracy. As the war goes on, promotions are made weekly. It's impossible to keep track of every junior general in the Luftwaffe. Aces like Galland and Kammhuber, yes. They'd be as well known in England as they are here. But Kurt von Stuerzbecher is not exactly of the front rank. If he were, he'd have Kammhuber's job or Adolf Galland's.'

'It's still impossible,' said Schelling.

'I wish to God you'd stop using that word,' said Christian irritably. 'Although I must admit I said exactly the same thing to Standartenfuehrer Weil. But that was before I knew where the camp was.'

He could see they were not convinced.

'Look,' he said, 'the *Tommis* expect POWs to make escape attempts. That's why they guard the camps. I've no exact figures, of course, but I was allowed to see von Werra's account of his bids and it seems to me that more POWs get out than we ever knew. What they don't do is get home. They're normally caught within hours of going under the wire, and that's because they have only the vaguest idea of where they're going and what they're going to do when they get there. The *Tommis* rely heavily on the fact that England is an island. There's virtually no way off for an escape bid organised from the inside. But one organised from the outside, that's different. Because it's never happened before the *Tommis* won't be ready for it. That's our advantage.'

'Christ,' muttered Schultz, 'you mean we've actually got to get him out of the camp as well as bring him home?'

'How the hell else d'you think we're going to snatch him?' demanded Christian. 'I can't go up to the Commandant and ask him if it's okay for von Stuerzbecher to take a walk, see you Christmas.'

'But it's im . . .' began Schelling. 'Sorry, Christian, but it's ludicrous. There are just three of us. We know approximately where the camp is but we don't know what its defences are, what the surrounding countryside is like. We know von Stuerzbecher's inside but we don't know where. There must be hundreds of POWs in there. We don't know what his routine is. We don't know what time he gets up and what time he goes to bed. We've no way of getting a message to him, telling him to be ready at a certain hour. Wear a blue carnation so we'll recognise him. With all due respect, Christian, this is the most arrant piece of nonsense I've ever heard.'

Christian nodded. 'Except for the last sentence I'm inclined to agree with everything you say. We don't know what the camp's defences are, we don't know where von Stuerzbecher is, we don't know what routine he follows. I also accept that there's probably very little chance of getting a message to him, but I can't solve any of these problems over here. I won't have a clue what's going on in Skiddaw until I've taken a look inside.'

'Now I know I'm going mad or deaf,' groaned Schelling. 'Correct me if I'm wrong, Wolf, but I thought I heard our so-called superior officer say he was going to take a look *inside* a British POW camp. Like a tourist.'

'That's what comes of being stationed in Cologne. All that bombing has sent him crazy.'

Christian grinned. 'All right, all right, but examine it logically. I can't make any concrete plans for getting von Stuerzbecher out until I know where he is and what security is like. And I can only find that out by paying them a visit. I speak fluent English don't forget, which was partly the reason Standartenfuehrer Weil pulled my name from the hat.'

'And we speak none.'

'Let's hope you won't have to.'

'And let's hope Generalmajor von Stuerzbecher starts broadcasting for the *Tommis* so that we can call this whole thing off,' said Schelling. 'What's so special about him anyway, or aren't we supposed to ask that?'

'I'm not sure myself,' admitted Christian. 'All I know is that somebody wants him back.'

'Beautiful.' Schelling shook his head at the prospect. 'Three German soldiers marching along the country roads in northern England. Hasn't it occurred to anyone that we might be a bit conspicuous?' Christian said nothing. Schelling's eyes narrowed. 'We will be in uniform, I suppose?'

'Er, not exactly.'

'What does not exactly mean?'

'It means we'll be in plain clothes.'

Schultz held his head in mock despair. 'Oh Christ, let me off. Do you know what the British do to the German soldiers caught wandering around in plain clothes, Christian? They put them up against a wall and shoot them. No messing, no formalities, just a firing squad.'

'I've thought of all that,' said Christian, 'but there's no way round it. It's twenty miles from coast to camp and twenty miles back again. Uniforms are out.'

'We could drop in at night, on a regular bombing run, and be on our way before sun up,' suggested Schelling.

'That's out. There'll be no dropping in and dropping out. We can't take a chance on somebody seeing a parachute and sounding the alarm before we've even started. We'll go in by U-boat.' He jabbed a finger at the map. 'Somewhere around here, Maryport, or maybe a little further south. It'll depend what the Navy thinks. With any luck we'll come out the same way.'

'Christ, submarines,' said Schelling. 'I hate the bloody things.'

Christian was surprised. 'You've travelled in one?'

'Of course I haven't. Why should I travel in something I hate?'

Christian didn't attempt to argue the logic of that.

'When are we due to leave?' asked Wolf Schultz.

'The sooner the better. The availability of a U-boat is a major factor, but there's no point in hanging around. Say a week or so, December 8th or 9th. In the meantime, you can bunk in the spare room.'

'Where you can keep an eye on us.'

'Where I can keep an eye on you,' agreed Christian.

He checked the time and reached for his cap. He had an appointment with Weil at 8 p.m. and he did not want to be late.

'You'll notice the liquor cabinet is well stocked,' he said, 'courtesy of the management. Help yourselves, but take it easy. We may have a lot of cross-country hiking to do and I want you two to be up to it.'

'If the Oberleutnant will excuse the impertinence,' said Schultz cheekily, 'the Oberleutnant is looking a bit podgy himself.'

'The Oberleutnant,' said Christian, 'has lost two kilos in the last week and he intends to lose two more before we sail. I'm serious, Wolf,' he added sombrely. 'The difference between spending Christmas in Berlin and not spending it at all could depend upon how fast you can run.'

'Reminds me of old times,' said Schultz, when the two NCOs were alone.

Schelling shook his head mournfully.

'I wish you hadn't said that. The only thing I remember about the old times is that whenever the three of us were billeted together, you could bet your life someone was going to start shooting at us.'

Standartenfuehrer Weil was delighted to see that Christian looked much fitter than at their last meeting. He'd lost some weight and his eyes were much clearer, the surrounds less puffy. Weil was far from happy, however, with Christian's choice of personnel for the venture.

'A Feldwebel and an Obergefreiter? Couldn't you have done better than that, Eicke?'

'I've worked with them before, sir. They're the best there is.'

'I hope you're right. From a brief reading of your plan, if you can call half a page of outline a plan at all, you're going to need a couple of supermen.'

'As I explained in my covering letter, sir, there's nothing more I can tell you until I've seen Skiddaw for myself. From what I can gather from Leutnant von Werra's account, Grizedale Hall, where he was interned, was no more than an English country house converted into a POW camp. Skiddaw seems to be somewhat different.'

'Yes, I understand your difficulties.' Weil picked up a document from his desk. 'I have a signal here from Admiral Doenitz. He has a U-boat undergoing minor repairs at Lorient in Brittany. It will be ready to sail at 0800 hours on the 7th. You and your party are to report on board at 2300 the previous day. The captain is Korvettenkapitän Stieff.

'The U-boat will stand off your suggested landfall of Maryport and you will be ferried ashore by dinghy. The exact spot will depend upon weather conditions, enemy activity, the propensity of mines, and so forth, but you will be landed during the hours of darkness on December 9th/10th. So much for getting in.'

The Standartenfuehrer studied Christian carefully before going on.

'On the direct orders of Admiral Doenitz Korvettenkapitän Stieff has been told that he is not to risk his ship in any way whatsoever. Do you understand that?' Christian said that he did. 'In any way whatsoever,' repeated Weil. 'If there is any manner of danger prior to the landing he is to abandon the operation entirely, and he is to be the final arbiter as to what constitutes danger. The same applies once you are ashore. You will not be picked up if in doing so the safety of the U-boat is threatened.'

Christian nodded his understanding. On the scales of relative values, one Luftwaffe Generalmajor did not equal one U-boat.

'It's been left to you,' continued Weil, 'to work out a system of signals with Korvettenkapitän Stieff, but under no circumstances will he stand off Maryport later than the evening of the 14th. If vous with the U-boat by the 14th you will not get home. I'm sorry you are not there by then, he is to assume you've failed and make for the Atlantic. Bear that in mind, Eicke. If you do not rendez-it has to be like that, but the U-boat is needed elsewhere.'

'I understand, Herr Standartenfuehrer.'

'Good. You will not, incidentally, be the senior non-naval officer aboard. I have arranged for Obersturmbannfuehrer Kirdorff of the Prinz Eugen SS Division to act as liaison officer between Stieff and yourself. He is there as a precaution, to look after your interests—in case Stieff takes Admiral Doenitz's orders too literally. You do not know Kirdorff, I believe?'

'No, Herr Standartenfuehrer.'

'Fine. That's how it should be.'

Weil consulted his notes.

'Now looking down your list of requirements, most of this is easily arranged. Civilian clothes with appropriate labels, British identity papers, currency, English cigarettes, ticket stubs, etc. But I'm not sure that all you should be taking as a weapon is one 9mm Luger. It's not much of a defence.'

'Our best defence will be to remain unseen,' said Christian. 'But if we are unfortunate enough to be asked to identify ourselves it's no use having perfect documents backed up by three machine guns. We'll have to bluff it out. The pistol is for emergencies only.'

'Very well.' Weil shut his notebook. 'That seems to be it, Oberleutnant. I shall want to see you once more, on the morning of the 6th. You will then be given sealed orders, not to be opened until von Stuerzbecher is safely out.'

'Sealed orders, sir?'

'A contingency plan, Oberleutnant, for use if things do not work out as you anticipate.'

9

At 0630 on a bitterly cold but snowless morning, CSM Purser received a telegram from the Admiralty. The signalman who delivered it left quickly without waiting for a signature of receipt. *We regret to inform you that your son, Able Seaman David Ramsey Purser, was killed in action* . . . Et cetera. It gave the date but not the time and, curiously, Bernard Purser felt he would have liked to know the precise hour of the boy's death. What was he doing then? Drinking beer in the Sergeant's Mess? Reprimanding a soldier for sloppy dress? Sleeping? There was a lot missing from these official telegrams, though no doubt David's CO would write him a personal letter sooner or later. He would probably never be told, however, whether his son had died well or badly, quickly or slowly; whether a shell had put an end to his life instantly or whether he had drowned, his lungs full of oil, calling out for someone.

Bernard Purser stared at the yellow message form for a long time. Somehow a mug of sweet tea appeared miraculously by his bunk, but he did not recall drinking it. Even so, when he next looked; it was empty.

He wondered what they did with the bodies of youngsters killed at sea. He should know that. Good God, he was a senior NCO after all. A pretty pickle he'd be in if he were ever asked the question and didn't know the answer. Though it was different on dry land. There, a soldier killed in action was buried in firm soil as soon as there was a lull in the fighting, his identity discs placed with the others. He'd seen plenty of that in the first little lot. Sometimes the Orderly Room table would be piled high with discs, all awaiting a telegram. He supposed the Navy did it differently. Full honours and a canvas shroud and Union Jack if there was enough time. And if there was enough left of the body to put in a shroud.

Bernard Purser was not the sort of man to feel self-pity or to get instantly and incapably drunk and go hunting for the nearest German to beat senseless. Perhaps it didn't make him much of a soldier, but he knew full well that, on this very day, some father in Hamburg or Berlin or Dresden had received an identical telegram and that he, too, was bewildered at the insanity of it all. It was probably a capital charge to even think it, but he wondered if either the Imperial General Staff or the German High Command saw boys like Able Seaman Purser as anything more than units.

In the manner of these things the news of Sergeant-Major Tomorrow's son's death spread quickly throughout the camp, and that morning, at early roll-call, there was none of the usual skylarking. No one faked absence by refusing to answer his name. The POWs were soldiers also and many of them had lost friends or relatives in three years of war.

At 0900, in spite of the fact that Major Mitchell and Captain Thorogood were in camp, Oberfeldwebel Ernst Reitlinger knocked timidly on CSM Purser's door, half expecting him not to be there. But the CSM was having none of that. 'Take the day off, S'arnt-Major. Take a week's compassionate.' 'No thank you, sir. I've got nowhere to go.'

The Oberfeldwebel stood in the open doorway, clutching a piece of old newspaper tied with string. Inside were twenty-four new draughtsmen, twelve black, twelve white, hand-made since midsummer from cast-off bits of wood. He had intended them as a Christmas gift for his friend, but this seemed as good a time as any to present them.

'Come in, Ernst. Sorry there's no tea on the boil this morning. Damn-fool orderly forgot to bring the milk.'

Oberfeldwebel Reitlinger stammered that it was okay, that he couldn't stay in any case, that he just wanted to leave the parcel. For the first time since becoming a POW he felt bitterly his ignorance of English. What was adequate for playing draughts was quite useless for saying what was in his mind. So he said nothing. Instead he put his gift on the desk and left.

CSM Purser fingered the string binding it for a long time, but he did not open the parcel.

Shortly after 9 a.m., near the entrance to the MT Pool on the south side of the compound, Obergefreiter Willi Braune assisted by Unteroffizier Hans Geith was about to attempt his personal coup of the war.

Willi's keen nose had told him for several weeks that an escape was brewing, and he pondered how to make a profit from it. Not knowing about a potential break-out was not an unusual state of affairs, even in a camp as small as Skiddaw. The Escape Committee took the decision in secret and only those who were to go under the wire were told the precise date and the manner of egress. The Oberleutnant tailor who dyed and restyled uniforms was fully employed all the year round, as were the forgers of counterfeit documents. There was nothing to be gained, therefore, by watching them for sudden bursts of activity. POWs who were not privy to the plot might suspect something, but it was an unwritten rule, for security reasons, that no questions were asked.

Willi had considered the problem at length. What would an escapee need more than anything else, apart from a private airfield and the start-trolley to a fully fuelled aeroplane? Well, there was money, for openers. Prisoner or not, a man could never get enough of that. Trouble was, there was no way of laying his hands on any quantity of the stuff, and even if he did that was a profit in itself and he would keep it.

There were weapons, of course, but here he knew he was drifting into the realms of fantasy. The armoury was watched closer than a Berlin brothel-keeper watched his best girls for signs of lovesickness, and it was common knowledge that any unauthorised approach meant being shot on sight. Apart from that, no escaping POW would risk being caught with a weapon, which also meant a dawn meeting with a firing squad. So guns were out.

A vehicle, naturally, would be the stroke of the century, never mind the war. Get Major Breithaupt a one-tonner and Major Breithaupt would undoubtedly see that Obergefreiter Braune was promoted to Brigadefuehrer Braune with the Knight's Cross and a five-bedroomed house in the Wilhelmstrasse thrown in as ballast. But again that was indulging in fantasy. The guard at the entrance to the MT Pool had the same instructions as the guard on the armoury: shoot to kill anyone who even looks like a car thief. Still, Willi considered himself a salesman and the best salesmen ascertain what their customers require before calling. You couldn't sell a Mercedes to a man who had three and you couldn't expect a housewife with a dozen brushes to buy a thirteenth. But the Mercedes-owner might like a motorcycle and the housewife could well be interested in a cleaning cloth. So if a vehicle was needed but a vehicle was unobtainable, the customer would have to settle for a substitute. Such as a bicycle.

On the occasional escorted walks the POWs were allowed outside the camp when the weather was fine, Willi had seen many a British civilian riding a bicycle. Apart from the fact that it was a cheap and convenient method of transportation, needing neither complicated servicing nor rationed petrol to get from A to B, a man on a bicycle was somehow never suspect; he was going somewhere or coming from somewhere for all the world to see, right there in the middle of the road. A bicycle gave an aura of honesty and industry. If Willi could get a bicycle his reputation would be legend, not to mention his pockets bulging.

He did not even need a whole bicycle; he already had a frame. He had found it one day the previous spring, rotting and rusting after a winter spent in the open. But the brake cables appeared to be intact and the rear reflector was still attached to the rear forks. It even had a chain. The only problem was no wheels. But Willi had taken it and hidden it under a mound of coke in the boiler-room.

The bicycle shed was next to the MT Pool, but unguarded and outside the barbed-wire fencing which protected the vehicles. When a bicycle was not being used, its owner immobilised it by padlocking the spokes of the rear wheel to the rear fork, using a small chain.

Over the weeks Willi had noticed a pattern emerge. Because the British Army was like the German Army, each soldier had his own allotted space, numbered; woe betide him if he parked his machine in another's space or another parked in his. Secondly, most bicycles were used at least once a day, regardless of the weather. Because there was a constant movement of traffic in and out of the camp, the main roads had been ploughed clear of snow. If a bicycle was not used for a couple of days, chances were that the *Tommi* who owned it had gone on leave. If it were stolen, it would not be noticed until the *Tommi* returned. But Willi did not need a whole bicycle; he needed just the wheels.

In some respects stealing just the wheels was more difficult than stealing an entire machine. A frame by itself would, under normal circumstances, be noticed immediately and questions asked. It would therefore be necessary to choose a machine parked in the furthest, darkest corner of the shed, if possible one of a group of three or four whose owners had all gone on leave at the same time.

It was Willi's custom to check the shed after the 8.30 roll-call, keeping a note on a scrap of paper of those machines that were in regular use and those which had not been moved for forty-eight hours. Twice he thought he was in luck, but on both occasions the target bicycles were out again on the third day. But a POW learns nothing if not patience, and on the morning of the fifth Willi's was rewarded.

Three bicycles had remained untouched for four days. He had considered striking the previous afternoon, but a 72-hour pass was not uncommon so he left it until the fifth. They were still there. Obviously the *Tommi* owners were on a long leave.

There was still a snag, however; the corner of the shed where the bicycles stood was the corner nearest the MT Pool—and the guard, who never kept his eyes in one place for more than a few seconds. It would be necessary to distract him.

Willi discussed the matter with Hans Geith.

'You could always slip him a bribe,' suggested Hans. 'Give him some money or cigarettes to look the other way.'

Willi turned that down. 'We've never dealt with this one. He might be honest. He might even accept the bribe, and still raise the alarm.'

Besides, suborning the *Tommi* didn't appeal to Willi's sense of occasion. This was a problem in tactics and should be resolved by the superior use of intelligence.

'Then a diversion,' said Hans. 'I could rope in a couple of others and we could start a fight.'

A fight was the most common way the POWs got what they wanted. While the guard's attention was elsewhere, the required article was plundered.

'No fear.' Willi shook his head emphatically. 'That would mean more shares. We're only splitting the profit two ways.'

'The rate you're going there won't be any profit to split. By the time you've worked out how to get the wheels, the *Tommis* will be back.'

'You could talk to him,' said Willi craftily. 'Hold him in conversation while I get them off.'

'Oh no.' Hans was having none of that. 'I'll do the wheels; you can handle the rest of it.'

'But stealing the wheels is the most difficult and dangerous part. I'm giving you the easiest bit.'

'Which I decline with thanks. I'll work in that dangerous, dark corner of the shed while you talk to the guard. It has to be me, in any case. We haven't got a spanner and my fingers are stronger than yours.'

'Bloody ingratitude. I suppose you'd like me to pinch his rifle while I'm about it.'

'You could always blame it on *Stacheldrahtkoller.*'

Willi's eyes lit up. 'Hey, that's it.'

'Run off with the guard's rifle? Are you off your head?'

'No, but I could pretend to be. Barbed-wire madness. I wouldn't really snatch it or anything bloody stupid like that, but I could fake being a bit crazy. You know, roll in the snow, things like that.'

'You sure you're *not* going nuts?' asked Hans suspiciously.

'Of course I'm not, you dumb-head. But have you got any better ideas?'

Hans hadn't, and so at a few minutes after 9 a.m. Willi prepared to put on the acting performance of his young life.

While Hans loitered near the east corner of the bicycle shed, Willi sauntered across to the MT Pool, hands in pockets. The *Tommi*, he noticed when he got closer, was about his own age, twenty or so, and a little jumpy at this unheralded approach of a POW. Better not make him too jumpy, Willi cautioned himself, or Hans'll get the wheels and I'll get a wooden suit.

When he was about thirty or so feet away he began to chuckle to himself. Watched by the curious guard, he crouched on all fours and started digging in the snow.

'Morning, Colonel,' he said in English. 'You won't tell anyone, will you?'

The guard decided the best policy was one of non-participation. Willi didn't mind. The *Tommi* would be forced to pay attention shortly. It was human nature.

'There is gold in the ground here,' said Willi. Months of conversation practice with Harry Cade and Harpo were paying dividends now. 'I discovered it yesterday.'

The guard muttered something that sounded like 'daft', but he was fascinated in spite of himself. Out of the corner or his eye Willi saw Hans Geith slip into the shed and crouch by the rear wheel of the bicycle nearest the wall.

Willi scrabbled about until his fingers touched a pebble. He waved it triumphantly.

'You see, gold. I told you. There is a fortune here, just for the two of us.'

The guard changed the position of his rifle. 'You stay where you are. Don't come an inch closer.'

Willi feigned bewilderment. 'You do not wish to share the gold?'

'That's a little bloody rock, you silly bugger.'

'A rock?' Willi scratched his head. 'No, my friend. To you it looks like a rock, but it is really gold.'

'Oh Jesus.'

Hans was fiddling with the padlock on the rear wheel. Willi sent out a silent plea. Don't mess with the bloody lock. Tear a few of the spokes out.

He got down on his hunkers and plunged his hands into the snow, coming up with a dozen pebbles.

'I'll be rich. And you too will be rich, my friend, my very good friend,' he told the guard. 'Join me and be rich. You shall have cars, houses, beautiful women. Join me and become wealthy.'

He threw a handful of pebbles into the air and turned a cartwheel. Then another. He fell on his face in the snow and sat up giggling. Hans had the rear wheel off and was grappling with the butterfly nuts on the front forks.

Willi spread his arms in a gesture of universal brotherhood. 'Don't be afraid, Colonel. No one will ever learn our secret. Fill your pockets and be free.'

'I'll fill you full of bloody holes in a minute.' The guard punctuated the threat by lifting his Lee-Enfield waist high. 'Now clear off before you get into trouble.'

'Trouble?' Willi tried a handstand that didn't come off. 'What trouble? Rich men do not have trouble, they make trouble. Let us both make trouble by starting another war. I'm fed up with this one.'

'Right.' Thoroughly sick and tired of this lunatic German, the *Tommi* brought his rifle to the on-guard position. Willi eyed the bayonet nervously. 'One more word out of you and I'm going to stick you. Get the hell out of here. *Verstehen?*'

Hurry up, you stupid bastard, urged Willi. Hans was levering at the last nut with all his strength. Hurry up before my share of the profits goes on bandages.

He backed off a couple of paces. 'You do not wish the gold? You do not want my gold?'

'All I want is that you clear off from these bloody gates. If you come any closer I swear to Christ I'll blow a hole in you.'

Willi continued to retreat as the guard advanced. His position was such now that Hans could not be seen unless the guard swivelled through one hundred and eighty degrees, going left. Willi was determined not to allow this by moving to his own left.

'Very well,' he said with dignity, 'you are not a comrade. I refuse to share my gold with you.'

'There's no gold, you mad bastard. You're holding a handful of pebbles, rocks, bits of stone.'

'Stones?' Willi opened his hands and looked at the contents. Thirty yards away, Hans loosened the last nut, slipped off the front wheel, tucked both wheels under his arm and made off in the opposite direction.

Willi let the pebbles fall one by one to the ground. 'Yes, you are right. Someone has stolen my gold.'

Head down and shoulders slumped, he walked off.

Hans was in the boiler-room ahead of him, tears streaming down his face.

'Oh Christ,' he spluttered, 'I could hear every word. I couldn't get the bloody nuts off for laughing.'

'You shouldn't have been listening,' said Willi petulantly. 'Another couple of minutes and that idiot would have shot me. Come on, let's see if they fit.'

Willi took hold of the boiler-room shovel and began shifting coke. A minute later he said, 'I could have sworn I put the frame here.'

'A bit to your left,' advised Hans, hunting through his pockets for the nuts and washers he had stolen along with the wheels.

But the frame wasn't a bit to the left; neither was it a bit to the right. And after fifteen minutes frantic shovelling they knew it wasn't there at all.

'Somebody's stolen it,' said Willi, aghast at the thought. 'Some bugger's been in and taken it. Of all the bloody thieves . . .'

Hans Geith was more philosophical.

'Well, we've got the wheels now. All we need is a frame. Hey, don't throw lumps of coke at me . . .'

Much later in the day in the German Mess, Theo Emke read aloud to Oberleutnant Hans Baum the letter Baum's mother had sent her son. After three years of war most German civilians had got the message about censorship and careless talk and Frau Baum's two closely written pages were a model of generalisation; so much so that the blue pencil had hardly been used. She expressed the hope that her only son was well and that he was taking good care of his health, the most precious of God's gifts. His sister Helga asked after him all the time and was growing up to be a proper little lady, keen on her studies and with no interest in boys. She was making something for his birthday and was hoping she would be allowed to send it. ('I won't tell you what it is, it'll spoil the surprise.') Father had had a bad cold but was getting over it. It had, however, blocked his nose something awful and Frau Baum was quite sure his snores could be heard ten kilometres away.

There was more in the same vein, quite a lot of it to do with the health (or lack of it) of Hans Baum's relatives. An aunt had sprained her ankle, an uncle had developed some kind of rash. Another aunt thought she'd lost her cat and was *very* surprised when it returned, trailing half a dozen hungry kittens.

The letter was quite creased now, having been received a month earlier and read almost daily to Oberleutnant Baum. Theo Emke in no way objected to this self-imposed chore and was quite sure, if and when he escaped, someone else would take it over. For Hans Baum could not read himself. In the autumn of 1941, while on a bombing mission over southern England, his aircraft had received a direct hit from flak and he had witnessed the rest of his crew fry in their own fat before some instinct for self-preservation forced him to bale out. He had not spoken during his interrogation and he had not spoken since. He passed his days in the Mess or in his hut, carving crude figures of men from pieces of wood. He could not answer his name at roll-call, but the camp authorities were tolerant. Strictly speaking he should have been repatriated or, at the very least, transferred to a special hospital for the mentally ill, but thanks to some administrative balls-up he was still in Skiddaw.

Understanding that the reading was at an end, Oberleutnant Baum held out his hand. Emke folded the letter carefully and passed it over. Baum put it in a side pocket. From the other side of the table Leutnant Fritz Uhde looked at the pair of them with an expression of sadness and pity.

'I still say you're making a mistake, Emke. You're not doing Baum or Frau Baum any favours by kidding her on.'

'Shut up, Fritz,' said Emke, not unkindly, and glanced anxiously across at Hans. None of them were ever quite sure how much he understood. Certainly he recognised the names of his sister and the others his mother wrote of, but that seemed to be the limit of his comprehension. However, Emke was taking no chances.

'She'll find out sooner or later,' persisted Uhde. He was at a low point in one of his interminable letters to his young wife and wanted something to occupy his mind. 'Even if the war goes on for another ten years she'll have to know in the end.'

'So let her find out in ten years' time, then,' retorted Emke, though he was far from convinced that the action he was taking was the correct one.

Frau Baum knew it was Theo Emke who penned her son's letters, but she was under the impression he dictated them himself. Without ever saying so directly, Emke had allowed her to believe that Hans had lost the use of his right hand when shot down and that he was too idle to learn to write with the other one. Whether Hans was renowned for idleness at home or not, Emke didn't know, but Frau Baum appeared to have swallowed the story. ('And thank that kind Oberleutnant Emke from the bottom of my heart. I don't know what we would have done if we hadn't heard from you via him.')

Uhde was probably right on balance, Emke conjectured, but it was too late to do anything about it now. Having kept up the subterfuge for over a year, he could hardly turn round and tell Frau Baum that her son was a mindless imbecile and there must be doubts whether he would ever again live a normal life.

In any case, after the 12th, with any luck, it would no longer be his problem. He had already spoken to Otto Breithaupt and Breithaupt had promised to do what he could to find a replacement scribe. Frau Baum would wonder (because there was no way any censor would allow her to be told that Oberleutnant Emke had successfully escaped), but there was no helping that. Perhaps he could go and see her when he got home, break it to her gently. But he doubted he had the courage. Rather face a hundred Spitfires in a crippled Ju 88 than tell a mother that her son would never be the same again.

Hans Baum shuffled his chair backwards and got to his feet. For a moment he looked steadily at Emke, and Emke thought he was trying to convey his thanks. Then the moment passed and Hans walked slowly from the Mess.

Over in Hut 5, as dusk began to close in and the shouts of the guards, summoning the POWs to the last official roll-call of the day, were heard in the distance, huddled around the stove Major Breithaupt, Oberleutnant Mohr and Kurt von Stuerzbecher were engaged in the argument they had been having, off and on, for the last ten days; that of wishing on von Stuerzbecher the twelfth and final place in the Rabbit Run. Otto Breithaupt and Franz Mohr were all for it; von Stuerzbecher was not so sure.

To his way of thinking, he should sit tight until someone in Germany got a message to him, possibly via Kapitänleutnant Heydt using the naval code. Then, and only then, would he be free to act. If act was indeed his instruction. It could well be that the High Command would wish him to stay put; that was not inconceivable. As Oberleutnant Stuerzbecher he was just one more anonymous POW; as an escaper, if he were recaptured, he could well be marked down as a troublesome individual and subjected to further and more intensive interrogation. He had survived the London Cage by the skin of his teeth; he might not survive, as an Oberleutnant, a more lengthy examination.

Breithaupt and Mohr knew nothing of Operation Hammer, of course. Together with Hauptmann Weiss and Kapitänleutnant Heydt they knew him only as a senior officer successfully masquerading as an Oberleutnant. It was perfectly natural, therefore, that they were puzzled at his reluctance to escape.

'I don't understand you, Karl,' said Breithaupt. Along with the three others who were privy to von Stuerzbecher's real identity, Breithaupt now called him Karl without second thoughts or deference. 'If you don't get out now you may not get out for months, perhaps not ever. Whether we pull it off or not, just making an attempt on such a grand scale will force the *Tommis* to tighten up security all round. It will never again be possible to escape in more than ones and twos, and as an Oberleutnant and a newcomer, your name will be well down the list. Good God, the 12th's only a week away and already hints are being dropped about the spare place. I can't hold it open much longer.'

'I understand your difficulties, Otto,' said von Stuerzbecher, 'but appreciate mine. I must wait until I've heard from Germany.'

'But that could take weeks,' protested Breithaupt. 'Heydt's letter will have only just arrived. There's not a snowball in hell's chance you'll get a reply before the 12th.'

'Then you must let the last place go to someone more deserving.'

'You know I can't do that, either.' Breithaupt shook his head. 'If by some miracle a few succeed in getting home and it becomes known, as it will, that a General was left behind while mere Leutnants were given places, I'd be pilloried in my absence.'

'You can get Franz here to tell the OKW that I gave you a direct order.'

'That's exactly what he can't do,' put in Mohr. 'Otto's senior officer, in practice if not in fact. It matters not that you outrank him considerably. As head of the Escape Committee what he says goes. He can order you out or order you to stay behind, just as he pleases.'

'Then he must order me to remain.'

Abruptly, von Stuerzbecher took a decision. Through no fault of his own, Otto Breithaupt was in an intolerable position. He would tell him, both of them, so much and no more, though even going that far might lay him wide open to a charge of indiscretion.

'Look, it must have occurred to the pair of you, as it must have occurred to Heydt and Weiss, that an officer of my rank possesses more war secrets than the rest of the camp put together. I was damn lucky that in all Skiddaw only Franz had met me before. But if I escape and get recaptured, there's a possibility I'll be transferred to another camp where I may be recognised. If that happened I'd put my chances of remaining an anonymous Oberleutnant for more than a few days no greater than evens.

'The Colonel at the London Cage, as I told you, was very curious why someone of my age held such a lowly rank. No offence intended, Franz. If he learned he'd been duped, he'd put me through the mincer. As the war progresses interrogation techniques improve, and I've no way of knowing how long I could hold out before I said something I shouldn't.' Von Steurzbecher tapped the table to emphasise his next words. 'And believe me, gentlemen, I am not exaggerating when I say that some of the intelligence I possess could mean the difference between victory and defeat. I must stay here until I am told what I have to do.'

Breithaupt and Mohr exchanged glances. This put a different complexion on the matter.

'If that's your decision,' said Breithaupt.

'It is. And I assure you . . .'

Von Stuerzbecher did not get a chance to finish. The door was flung open and Corporal Napley poked his head in.

'Come on, you three, are you deaf? *Appell*, roll-bloody-call. If you're not on parade in two minutes it's the cooler for you . . .'

Towards midnight, in the peace and quiet of his quarters, CSM Purser poured the last of the whisky and fingered a couple of the draughtsmen Oberfeldwebel Reitlinger had made. He had been drinking heavily since 9 p.m. but he felt in no way drunk, though a doctor would have diagnosed otherwise.

It was bloody nice of Ernst to have spent his leisure hours carving those; he must have been at it for months. He had months to spare of course, but it was still a handsome gesture. Usually when the POWs made something they tried to sell it; it was one of their few ways of earning extra money.

The telegram from the Admiralty lay on the table and he read it for the hundredth time, the words dancing as he tried to focus. Christ, he'd drunk more than he thought.

Poor David, never really had a chance. Like so many of the youngsters the war was claiming, never had a chance to meet the proper girl, get married, have a few kids, build a home. If the Chaplain was to be believed, David was okay now. But it was hard to accept that the same God who was now embracing David was apparently unconcerned about the living. That was the trouble with Christianity, something he'd never considered before; everything was geared to death.

Leaving a quarter of an inch of whisky in his glass, Bernard Purser staggered to his bunk and, fully clothed, fell headlong on to it. By the time he was snoring, 5 December had passed into history.

IO

6 December

Immediately after morning roll-call Hauptmann Weiss collared the rest of the Escape Committee for an *ad hoc* meeting at the south-east corner of the Pig Pen. The trap to catch the informer was to be sprung the following night.

'You've left it late enough,' said Kapitänleutnant Heydt sourly.

'These things take time,' retorted Weiss. 'I could hardly go up to Oberleutnant Kapp and tell him directly that an escape was being planned. He'd have smelt a rat instantly. Still less could I approach Oberfeldwebel Reitlinger. The information had to be filtered through to them.'

'How are you working it?' asked Franz Mohr.

'Very simply. Kapp has been told that an attempt is to be made from the Sick Bay at nine o'clock tomorrow evening. If Thorogood operates according to the established pattern, he'll make his swoop then, trying to catch us in the act. If he moves before he'll find nothing because there is nothing. He'll have to be there at 2100 to see how we plan to get out.'

'And Reitlinger?'

'He's been told the same time and date, but a different place; from behind the library. You'll notice that I've devised routes well away from each other, one on the north side and one on the east. That's a precaution in case there's a lot of running around tomorrow. We don't want any mistakes regarding the identity of our traitor.'

'You're still assuming there is one,' said Breithaupt.

'I'm convinced of it. In any event, we'll know one way or another tomorrow.'

'What about look-outs?' asked Heydt.

'That'll have to be us, I'm afraid. I know there's a risk involved, wandering around the compound with Thorogood on the rampage, but you'll appreciate I couldn't let anyone else in on the deception. I suggest Heydt and myself watch the Sick Bay, and you, Herr Major, with Oberleutnant Mohr the library.'

'On the assumption that Kapp is the better bet and you want to be in at the kill.'

'On that assumption precisely, Herr Major.' Weiss smiled his twisted smile.

Breithaupt nodded. 'Very well, we'll do as you suggest. 2100 it is, though I for one will not be disappointed if we have a wasted night.'

'The Major has a touching belief in the goodness of his fellow man.'

'It's what we're fighting for, isn't it? Now if you'll excuse us, Heinrich, the rest of us have a choir practice and we're late already.'

'By all means, Herr Major.'

From his office window Captain Thorogood saw the meeting break up. Although he had no concrete intelligence on the subject, he was fairly certain that what he had just witnessed was a gathering of the Skiddaw Escape Committee. As senior German officer Breithaupt was bound to be on it. Breithaupt and Mohr were as thick as thieves so the Oberleutnant would be a member too. Kapitänleutnant Heydt was the ranking naval officer and there was little doubt, if Thorogood were any judge of men, that he'd insist on the Kriegsmarine being represented. One-eyed Hauptmann Weiss was an enigma, but a clever and fanatical enigma. They'd need his brains and capacity for cold, unemotional assessment.

But what the hell were they plotting? They were undoubtedly up to something. With the exception of Wielen's solo run, the camp had been too quiet for months. It was unnatural.

Abruptly he left his own office and rapped on the door of Major Mitchell's. The Commandant was studying the outgoing mail and wondering whether he should let a reference to 'the good food and excellent working conditions' slip by before passing the letter on to the official censor. On balance he thought not; his German wasn't fluent enough to detect a hidden meaning in the sentence, but as it was patently untrue it must be regarded as suspect.

'Yes, Adrian?'

'Permission to hold a *Sonderappell*, sir.'

'A special roll-call?' Mitchell frowned and checked the time. 'The normal one was only completed half an hour ago.'

'Which is the time to nab them, sir. They won't be expecting it.'

'Nab them? Nab who? What's going on?'

'Nothing, sir, which is what's bothering me. We've been too quiet for too long. They must be up to something.'

'I thought you were always informed when trouble was brewing.'

Mitchell smiled to himself at his Adjutant's discomfort. He knew Thorogood liked to pretend that the forestalling of an escape bid was due to his own alertness.

'Not always, sir. Do I have your permission?'

'Is it snowing?'

'Sir?'

'If you're going to call a *Sonderappell* it will undoubtedly mean that you'll want to parade the prisoners in the Exercise Yard and keep them there until you've finished. If it's snowing I'll get all manner of flak from Major Breithaupt about maltreatment.'

Adrian Thorogood held his temper. Bloody effeminate old fool. God knows how the Allies were expected to win the war if Mitchell's attitude were reflected in other camps.

'With due respect, sir, Major Breithaupt is a prisoner of war. I don't think we should pay too much attention to whether or not he thinks it's a good idea. In any case, it isn't snowing.'

'Very well, you have my permission. Do you want me on it?'

'Not unless you want to be. It'll take me ten minutes or so to get my men organised. I'll pop my head in when we're ready to move.'

'As you like, Adrian.'

Thorogood saluted and made for the door. Mitchell called after him.

'And Adrian . . . Try not to look so disgruntled when I make a suggestion or comment on one of yours. One day you might find yourself sitting in this chair or one like it.'

God forbid, thought Thorogood, and went to find the CSM.

Gathered around the altar in the chapel and belting out a carol with gusto, Major Breithaupt's choir were enjoying themselves when Thorogood struck. Theo Emke, whose stint it was as door guard, was the first to suspect that all was not well.

'There's something going on outside,' he called out urgently. The choir fell silent.

'Be a little more specific, Emke,' said Breithaupt calmly.

'Sorry, sir, but there are *Tommis* running in all directions. Look out—one of them's heading this way.'

'Get back over here,' ordered Breithaupt. 'And keep singing—all of you.'

It was something he had always feared would happen and prayed never would: some kind of disturbance while two of his moles were underground. In this case, the moles were Peter Kaehler and Johann Preiss, and there was no chance of getting them out. They were two metres under and up to thirty metres away from the altar. Even so, he kicked its base in the hope that they would hear.

The chapel door was flung open and Lance-corporal Harry Cade shouldered his way in, bayonet fixed.

'All right, you lot, *Sonderappell* right away. Get over to the Pig Pen and get fell in. Right now. *Verstehen?*'

The choir looked fearfully at Breithaupt, awaiting his lead.

'What's the matter, Corporal? Somebody escaped?'

'Don't ask me, mate, I only work here. Come on now, let's move it.'

Breithaupt stalled for time, hoping that Cade would leave them to make their own way across.

'All right, Corporal, we'll follow you.'

But Harry Cade remained in the doorway.

'No chance, old son. I'll follow *you*. Now get going.'

There was nothing they could do but obey. Harry Cade made sure everyone was out and shut the door behind him.

Throughout the remainder of the camp a minor panic set in among the POWs as they tried to secrete forbidden goods.

The Oberleutnant tailor lifted a floorboard in his hut and shoved in the tunic he was refashioning. Fortunately the tailoring system was geared to special roll-calls and whenever an article was finished it was passed on immediately to the POW concerned. Even so, if the tunic were discovered it would mean several wasted weeks as well as the loss of a cache.

In Hut 21 two of the camp forgers, working independently at the trestle-table, each got rid of a set of identity documents by the simple expedient of placing them in a waterproof bag kept to one side for such occasions. Their pens and inks were placed in a separate bag. Once outside, both bags would be tossed into the nearest rain barrel, to be collected later.

Elsewhere, men were hiding currency they should not have, compasses, maps, hand-fashioned tools. It was most unlikely that a body search would be carried out, but it was better to be safe.

On Major Breithaupt's standing orders, certain minor items were left to be discovered. Captain Thorogood would consider it most odd if a hut search revealed nothing and he would continue looking until something turned up. It was as well to let him find a few unimportant bits and pieces.

In the boiler-room Willi Braune and Hans Geith finished their morning coffee slowly. On learning of the *Sonderappell*, the boiler-room had been Harry Cade's first port of call, and ten minutes after he cleared the chapel the POWs were assembled in the Exercise Yard, in hut order.

A *Sonderappell* usually took one of two forms. First there was the head-count made by the junior NCOs under the supervision of CSM Purser. If that tallied with the total on the CSM's clipboard, the prisoners were kept standing in the Exercise Yard for another hour or so while squads of soldiers searched the huts and the German Mess for contraband. If it did not tally, every POW's name was called individually and a close watch kept to make sure prisoner A did not answer for prisoner B as well as for himself. When it was finally established who was missing, the fun really began.

Rarely did the head-count tally, mainly due to the POWs' natural desire to cause as much trouble as possible for their captors. A hut that should have a complement of eight would be found to contain seven, the eighth having bent down to tie a bootlace. In the recount, a prisoner from an adjacent hut would move smartly to his right or left and make the total nine. But CSM Purser's NCOs were up to these dodges and the tocsin wasn't sounded until it was established beyond all doubt that someone had bolted.

Apart from the sick and bed-ridden, who were not expected to parade, there were 219 officers and other ranks in Skiddaw, and the first count put the number at 212. That didn't matter. As well as the prisoners fooling around, CSM Purser was accustomed to innumerate junior NCOs. In any case, the total was increased to

214 when two Luftwaffe officers appeared from the direction of the heads, having been caught literally with their trousers down.

CSM Purser tried again. This time he made it 217 and there were no late arrivals. Either his NCOs were dafter than they looked or Skiddaw was minus two birds. There was nothing for it but to call the roll.

Each junior NCO supervised three or four huts, and it was Hut 9's misfortune to be in Corporal Napley's domain. That Napley had not missed Kaehler or Preiss in any of the three head-counts was excusable. Certainly he could see that where there should be eight bodies there were only six, but the CSM alone kept a full list of who was indisposed. It was not until the absentees were checked against that that their names would be known.

Against a background of shouting Corporal Napley called the roll, starting with the senior officer.

'Oberleutnant Mohr.'

Franz Mohr clicked his heels and announced himself present.

'Leutnant Uhde.'

'Ja.'

'Oberleutnant Emke.'

'Ja, Herr Brigadefuehrer.'

Napley scowled. 'That'll be enough out of you. Leutnant Kaehler.' No reply. Napley looked up. 'Leutnant Kaehler?'

'I think he's sick,' said Mohr.

Napley made a mark on his pad and another against the absent Preiss. Two of the bastards. Just two missing and both his.

He marched across to the CSM.

'Leutnants Kaehler and Preiss absent, S'arnt-Major.'

'Any explanation?'

'Oberleutnant Mohr thinks they're both sick.'

'Not on my list they're not. All right, Corporal.'

It took five more minutes to establish that only Leutnants Kaehler and Preiss were unofficially absent and, ordering his NCOs to keep the POWs where they were, the CSM went to report to the Adjutant.

From his window in the Admin. Block Adrian Thorogood had witnessed the various counts and the roll-call and knew from experience that all was not as it should be. In some perverse manner he felt pleased. It was a black mark, of course, not to have a full complement, but his judgement in springing the *Sonderappell* had been vindicated.

He returned to his desk as Bernard Purser knocked and entered the office.

'Two prisoners missing, sir. Leutnants Kaehler and Preiss, Hut 9.'

'I see. No explanation, I suppose.'

'None, sir, but . . .'

'Yes?'

'I was going to say, sir, that if they've hopped it they've been damned quick about it.'

'They *are* quick, S'arnt-Major. Every German in Skiddaw is quick and prepared to take any opportunity to escape. It might sometimes be overlooked by other members of this establishment but we have over two hundred dedicated Nazis out there whose only desire is to get back to the Fatherland and begin bombing our cities again. All right, fetch Major Breithaupt and the senior officer from Hut 9 to me. The rest of them can stay out there and freeze.'

'Very good, sir.'

Alone, Adrian Thorogood debated the advisability of telling Major Mitchell he was short a couple of Germans. He decided against it. The Commandant would doubtless invite Breithaupt into his office for a cosy chat and a cup of tea, and that was not the way Thorogood planned to handle the matter at all. If two of them had got under the wire Thorogood wanted to know how. To that end he'd keep the POWs standing outside in the cold all night if necessary.

There was a tap at the door and CSM Purser ushered Breithaupt and Mohr into the office. The two Luftwaffe officers stood to attention, eyes to the front. Purser took up a position near the window.

'At ease, gentlemen,' said Thorogood. Mohr and Breithaupt relaxed. 'It seems two of our birds have fled the nest and I'd like to hear your views on the subject. You first, Oberleutnant; they're in your hut.'

'I have nothing to say, Herr Hauptmann.'

'You mean you don't know anything or you won't say anything?'

'I mean I know nothing.'

'I see. You're trying to tell me that two officers under your supervision can disappear into thin air and you know nothing about it. If you ran your Staffel the way you run your hut, I'm surprised you shot down any aircraft at all. What about you, Herr Major? As senior German officer and head of the Escape Committee, surely you have something to contribute?'

Breithaupt acted dumb. 'Escape Committee? I'm sure I don't know what the Adjutant is talking about.'

'Your acting ability does you credit, Major. The theatre lost a valuable recruit when you joined the Luftwaffe.'

Thorogood lit a cigarette and studied the burning match thoughtfully for a moment or two before blowing it out.

'I'm going to make a couple of guesses, gentlemen. My first guess is that Leutnants Kaehler and Preiss are not outside the camp at all.' He watched them for a reaction. There was none. 'My second guess is that you, or some of you, are digging a tunnel or planning some other method of escape and that Kaehler and Preiss were trapped inside when the *Sonderappell* was called. If those two assumptions are anywhere near the truth, I'm going to turn this camp upside down until I find the prisoners and their place of concealment. When that happens, all of you will be allowed to return to your quarters. Until then you will remain in the Exercise Yard, in ranks. You will not be permitted to smoke and neither will you be released to eat. You will make that announcement to your men, Herr Major.'

Breithaupt's jaw muscles tightened angrily at this flagrant violation of the regulations.

'I will make the announcement, Herr Hauptmann, but prior to doing so I formally request an interview with the Commandant.'

'Your request is noted and denied. You can make your own arrangements for seeing the Commandant at a later date. In the meantime, let me remind you that I have German-speaking officers outside. You will tell your men exactly what I told you to say, and nothing more. Take them back, S'arnt-Major.'

In the meantime, Peter Kaehler and Johann Preiss were only just beginning to realise that they were trapped.

Working at the extremity of the Rabbit Run when the *Sonderappell* was called, neither had heard Major Breithaupt kick the altar. Even if he had made ten times the racket it was doubtful if the two young Leutnants would have paid much attention. Another metre, a metre and a half, three or four more days, and they'd be ready to break out. The excitement was more than they could bear, and they concentrated totally on the job at hand.

If it had been possible to see the diggings from an aerial viewpoint, the POWs who had worked on the Rabbit Run would have marvelled at their efforts. Operating purely by instinct and common sense they had tunnelled almost in a straight line and were, in fact, several metres beyond their estimated position. Had they broken the surface now, their exit would have been hidden from the camp by the nearest of the trees. But Leutnants Kaehler and Preiss had no way of knowing this and continued excavating as though their lives depended upon it, fearful that the 12th would arrive and they would not have dug far enough.

It was a filthy, debilitating business and most of the POWs were exhausted after an hour. Theo Emke could manage twice that, but Emke was an exception.

Neither the front man nor the rear man of each team had the easier task, though they changed positions as often as was necessary. The front man had only to dig and shovel the earth behind him, but he was working with primitive tools in almost total darkness with virtually no oxygen. Torn finger-nails and bleeding hands were the least of his worries. Even after the war, POWs who had been involved in tunnel projects were subject to sudden, seemingly irrational fits of claustrophobia. The rear man had the advantage of breathing the comparatively fresh air beneath the chapel every so often, when he took a filled sack back to empty it, but he had to crawl, at an agonisingly slow pace, a total of sixty metres every trip. Sixty metres might not sound much, and isn't much, on the surface. But on bended knees in the cold December ground, with sudden falls of soil causing panic and always a mouthful of dirt, it was far from a rest cure.

At the end of an hour, which most prisoners learned to gauge with uncanny accuracy, both members of the team would retrace their steps and wait until Breithaupt judged the coast to be clear and let them out. While waiting, they used a canvas bucket full of cold water to clean off most of the dirt. As they worked naked, leaving their camp clothes in a heap to be donned when they were finished, this chore took more than a few minutes. But it was essential they didn't rush it. The surest way for the *Tommis* to smell a rat was for a dozen POWs to go into the chapel looking like the choirboys they purported to be and emerging like coal miners. Once in the chapel, any grime that had been missed was removed for them until they looked as good as new. The only thing they could do little or nothing about was their hands and nails. No matter how hard they scrubbed, the dirt remained ingrained, the callouses immovable. It continues to be surprising that, throughout the war, POW camp authorities on neither side instituted a hand check as a matter of daily or weekly routine. One glance would have been sufficient to reveal which of the prisoners was working on a tunnel.

But it's the most obvious things which are frequently overlooked, as Kaehler and Preiss were beginning to realise. Without help from above there was no way of moving the altar and getting out.

'What the hell d'you think has happened?' Peter Kaehler kept his voice down to a whisper. They had both tried, without response, tapping the inside of the altar. Shouting was out of the question for fear a *Tommi* guard was on the prowl.

'Buggered if I know.' Preiss was shivering. 'But I hope to God they get us out of here before I freeze to death.'

'There must be some sort of a panic on. Major Breithaupt wouldn't just walk off and leave us.'

'Be just our bloody luck, wouldn't it, if someone else has gone under the wire and we're included in the missing. They'll stick us in the cooler whatever happens and bang goes our chance for the 12th.'

'Christ, I hadn't thought of that.'

Preiss shone the torch up through the floorboards beneath the altar.

'Maybe if we got a plank or something and gave it a shove . . .'

'And it topples over just as Sergeant-Major Tomorrow walks in through the front door. The Major would have our guts for guitar strings. Forget it, Johann. We're stuck here until someone lets us out.'

'Which might mean the rest of the day.'

'Which might mean the rest of the bloody week.'

Thoroughly depressed, they lapsed into silence.

Including the time spent on the head-count and the roll-call, the POWs had been standing in the Pig Pen for over an hour. To a man they were frozen stiff, but Major Breithaupt had ordered them not to break ranks. Most of them had now guessed why they were being punished en masse. Although the precise location of the tunnel and the exact date of departure was a secret known only to a handful, none of the prisoners were fools.

'Bloody bad security,' Breithaupt heard a naval officer in an adjacent rank mutter. He was not one of Heydt's men selected to make the escape, and he was feeling bitter. 'I don't mind the bastards making a run for it, but they might at least make sure the rest of us don't suffer if they're caught in the act.'

It was obvious that Breithaupt was meant to overhear the complaint, but he chose not to comment. It was an unjust accusation but an understandable one. POWs were subject to the most intolerable stresses and deprivations, one of the least being loss of liberty. Not out of malice by their captors but because there was a war on, they were fed inadequate food; the vitamins and minerals needed to keep the nervous system vital were largely absent. The majority of them knew that their homes and families were being bombed almost daily by the RAF and the Americans; if a wife or child were killed they might not know about it for weeks. The absence of women was a further demoralising factor. None of them had even been near, let alone made love to, a woman in two years. Given these circumstances it was perfectly natural that nerves became frayed and tempers were held in check only by an effort of will.

Three ranks away Fritz Uhde had also overheard the naval officer's criticism. 'He's right, you know. We should have been prepared for something like this.'

'Shut up, Fritz,' said Franz Mohr pleasantly. 'If you want to stay behind and take over as head of the Escape Committee, I'll see Otto Breithaupt gets your place in the tunnel.'

Fritz Uhde shut up. He wasn't really being ungrateful, he told himself, but he was fearful that as a result of today's happenings something would go wrong with the escape.

'Sorry, Franz.'

'That's all right.'

But it was far from all right, thought Mohr. If Thorogood was as good as his word, he would keep them standing here until hell froze over.

He was wondering what to do about it when Theo Emke solved the problem for him. Only God and the Luftwaffe knew why

Emke was still an Oberleutnant; he had all the qualities for much higher rank.

'What we need is a sing-song,' he grunted, and immediately suited the action to the word. *'Unsre Flagge und die wehet auf dem Maste . . .'* His deep bass voice rang out across the compound. 'Come on, you miserable buggers, let's hear it.'

Within seconds a dozen voices joined in, and a moment later the whole compound was singing.

> *Unsre Flagge und die wehet auf dem Maste*
> *Sie verkündet unsres Reiches Macht;*
> *Denn wir wollen es nicht länger leiden*
> *Dass der Englischmann darüber lacht . . .*

The *Tommis* knew. this one well by now. It was a favourite German taunt. *Denn wir fahren gegen Engeland*. We're sailing against England. Translated it went:

> Our flag waves as we march along
> It is the emblem of the power of our Reich;
> And we can no longer endure
> That the Englishman should mock it.

The NCO i/c the Pig Pen detail tried a feeble 'Silence in the ranks,'—but no one could hear him and he soon gave up.

Another hour went by. And then two. Taking Captain Thorogood's orders literally, the squads of soldiers under the overall command of the CSM turned the German lines upside down. Some of them, like Lance-Corporal Harry Cade and Harpo, acted within the spirit of the law and simply searched the obvious places; others like Corporal James Napley, obeyed the law to the letter.

It was Napley's squad who turned over the German Mess. Franz Mohr's precious armchair was poked and prodded by Napley's bayonet until the stuffing was bulging from a dozen new slashes. The net on the table-tennis table was torn in two, and a ball, left lying around by mistake, stamped on. The snooker table was pushed on to its side and kicked until it fractured. Priceless books, priceless to the POWs, were defaced. The prisoners had little, and that little Corporal Napley took a delight in destroying.

The bath-house and heads, being the site of a previous break-out attempt, were given special attention. The prisoners' library was next on the list, followed by their canteen. Even the coke in the boiler-room was moved and Willi Braune's two bicycle wheels impounded.

It was fortunate for the Germans and unfortunate for the British that the huts, being roughly in the middle of the compound and therefore far away from the perimeter wire, were considered unlikely bolt-holes and searched last. Bedding was pulled apart and the floors examined cursorily for loose boards. But by this time the troops were tired and fed up, and little of value was found.

The chapel was virtually ignored. Admittedly it was used as a place of worship by both captors and captive and lately the choir had got more use out of it than anyone else; but unconsciously the troops did not see it as part of German territory, in much the same way as British front-line soldiers didn't believe that the God they prayed to would have much truck with Nazis. A couple of *Tommis* poked their heads in, but that was as far as it went. Some atavistic superstition warned them of sacrilege.

At the end of two and a half hours CSM Purser had to report almost total failure. The squads had missed the Oberleutnant tailor's cache and no one had even considered looking in the rain barrel. The haul was a few small coins, two torches, a sharpened nail-file, the beginnings of a pencil-written journal, and a small-scale map of Greater London. It was enough to send Adrian Thorogood purple with rage.

'The men can't have searched thoroughly, S'arnt-Major. If they had they'd have found Kaehler and Preiss.'

'Perhaps they're already out, sir. It might be an idea to alert the civilian police and the Home Guard.'

That was Major Mitchell's theory too, and Thorogood had already made the necessary telephone calls. He could still hear the police Inspector's sarcastic voice.

'It's been done, S'arnt-Major, though I'll stake ten years' promotion they're still in the camp. Even if they're not, how in God's name did they get out? They didn't do a Wielen and walk through the damned gates. You've already told me there are no gaps in the wire. So they must have gone under the bloody thing. Which means a tunnel. Which also means that if you can't find Kaehler and Preiss you should at least be able to find the bloody tunnel.'

'If you'll forgive me, sir, it's not logical that a tunnel would be constructed and only two POWs escape. If there were a tunnel we'd be missing a lot more than two.'

'Not if it's still being dug and those two bastards were trapped in it at *Sonderappell*. Not then.'

The CSM had an idea. 'Then why not call off the search, sir. If Kaehler and Preiss turn up later today or tomorrow, you'll know you were right and we can begin looking for the tunnel. If they don't, we'll know they've got out somehow.'

Thorogood thought about it. It was a reasonable suggestion. Two men could not survive underground for more than a few hours. If there was a tunnel, they'd have to emerge.

'All right, S'arnt-Major Purser, that's not a bad idea. But before we put it into practice I want you to repeat the whole exercise and this time include our lines. I wouldn't put it past the bastards to be trying something there. If that doesn't work, we'll try it your way.'

They were sitting in the dark now; torch batteries were at a premium and not to be wasted. Somewhere to their right they could hear water dripping and on several occasions some small animal or other had made scuffling noises. Johann Preiss hoped it wasn't a rat.

'What time do you think it is?' he asked.

'Don't know. One o'clock, maybe two.'

Preiss shivered in the blackness and massaged his legs to keep the circulation going. His stomach told him that Peter's guess was a couple of hours out. Even a thin bowl of Skiddaw's soup would go down a treat right now.

'I wish to Christ I knew what was going on up top.'

'I'd be a lot happier if I knew what the hell we were going to do when we get out. Whatever the reason, there must be a *Sonderappell* on; there's no other explanation for Major Breithaupt leaving us down here. And when we turn up the *Tommis* are going to want to know where the hell we've been.'

'Maybe we can tell them we escaped, didn't like the food rationing, and came back.'

'I'm serious, Johann. We can't just appear from nowhere like bloody pixies.'

Preiss caught the drift. 'Don't even think of it,' he said. 'Don't even suggest that we stay down here another six days.'

'I don't see what else we can do. The best that can happen when we show ourselves is a couple of weeks in the cooler, which means we'll miss the 12th anyway. The worst that can happen is that they'll comb the camp from end to end, looking for the tunnel. They're bound to find it sooner or later, which means no one else gets a chance either. It's better they think we're already over the hills and far away.'

'But six days! What kind of a state do you think we'll be in to make a run for it then?'

'We'll manage. Breithaupt will get food to us and there's just enough room here to do exercises. We'll make it into a kind of competition, see who can do the most push-ups and knees-bends.'

'You'll cheat,' said Preiss, and laughed quietly at the absurdity of the statement. 'You must want to get back to Hannah very much,' he added.

'If she were not your sister I'd tell you just how much.' Kaehler allowed himself a moment of fantasy. 'Imagine it, Johann, a couple of weeks from now and we could be seeing her, your whole family. Think of those veal cutlets your mother cooks.'

'Don't, for Christ's sake.'

'And new potatoes running with butter.'

'Peter, I'll cave your head in. I think I'd commit murder for a plate of new potatoes right now.'

'Just keep thinking about them. The time'll pass quickly, you'll see.'

When it started snowing at 3 p.m., Captain Thorogood opted to forestall Major Mitchell and call off the hounds. The men had been through the whole dreary business a second time and had come up empty-handed; searching the British lines had proved to be a complete waste of energy. Besides, the POWs in the Pig Pen were getting restless. The singing was sporadic and unenthusiastic now, but a rowdier element was starting to toss snowballs at the Pen guard. They'd been out in the cold for close on six hours and they were hungry and tired. If he kept them any longer he'd have a riot on his hands. Tomorrow was another day. If Kaehler and Preiss turned up, he'd begin again. But part of him was already agreeing with the general consensus that, somehow, they'd got away.

'All right, S'arnt-Major, dismiss the prisoners. We might as well abandon the afternoon roll-call as well.'

When CSM Purser made this announcement and it was relayed in German by Breithaupt for the benefit of those who did not speak English, the POWs managed an ironic cheer and began to break ranks. They were stopped in their tracks by Breithaupt's next words.

'I know you're tired and hungry and that uppermost in your minds is the thought of hot drinks and food. You've been kept here all day by the British, but I want you to show them that if necessary you would have stayed here all night. German servicemen are not ragtag and bob-tail troops even when they're prisoners of war. So I want you to march out of here as though you were recruits on the drill square. Dismiss.'

The CSM had not understood a word of it, but to his amazement he saw 217 Germans come to attention as a man and file smartly out of the Pig Pen.

The three other members of the Escape Committee waited at the exit for Breithaupt. Men like Theo Emke and Werner Herburg were also hanging around, but Breithaupt waved them off. Decisions first, inquest later.

'Bastards,' said Franz Mohr, when he saw the wreckage in the Mess. 'Pointless bloody vandalism.'

Breithaupt seemed to have expected something of the sort. 'Don't blame them all, Franz. We've got people like that on our side too.'

They gathered round a table at the far end, leaving others to clean up.

'All right,' said Breithaupt, 'before I say what I think I'm open to suggestions.'

'We can't do anything about them tonight.' Heydt made his voice hard. This was no time for romantic rescue gestures. 'It's a bad business, but if we go anywhere near that chapel the *Tommis* will descend like locusts.'

Weiss concurred. 'But it's worse than that,' he added. 'I've been thinking about it for the last three hours. We can't really let them out at all.'

'Franz?'

'I'm afraid I agree with Hauptmann Weiss. If they suddenly reappear tomorrow the *Tommis* will know for certain we've a tunnel somewhere. If they don't, they'll think Kaehler and Preiss have escaped. There's no alternative; they've got to stay down there until the 12th.'

'I hope to God they've come to the same conclusion.' Breithaupt hated the thought of subjecting the youngsters to a week's incarceration. 'The question is, is it possible to survive that long?'

'They're young,' said Mohr. 'They're as healthy as any of us are. In any event, we've no choice. Either they take their chances or we lose the tunnel. Those are our options.'

Breithaupt mulled it over. 'All right, we'll put it to them. But pass it around that tomorrow morning I want every man on the escape to forfeit a quarter of his rations. They're going to be starving and they deserve every assistance we can give them. They'll also need blankets. Franz, I'll leave that to you. Every other man to give up one of his blankets. You might dig up some reading matter and give them one of the emergency torches as well. Christ, they've got to have something to do down there.'

Peter Kaehler and Johann Preiss were in surprisingly good condition when Major Breithaupt reached them immediately after roll-call the following day, though they fell upon the food wolfishly and didn't speak until their bellies were full.

They'd slept fitfully, they both admitted, and they'd completely lost track of time. It was also a bit creepy, being buried alive beneath a place of worship. But yes, they could stick it out until the 12th, as long as the food kept coming. They had no bloody option really, did they? Anyway, down here there were no parades. A few mice and worms and maybe a rat or two, but nothing they couldn't cope with. Major Breithaupt felt quite choked up when he left them.

II

7/8 December

Fortunately it was still snowing, the flakes leaping and dancing in the cold north wind, half veiling the watch-tower searchlights. In less inclement conditions it would have been possible for the guards to pick out four furtive shapes moving quietly across the compound.

At fifteen minutes before nine o'clock Franz Mohr and Otto Breithaupt slipped from their respective huts and met, as arranged, behind Hut 20, from where they had a more or less clear view of the library, a tiny wooden structure at the eastern end of the camp. Half a mile in front of them, though they could sense it rather than see it, the mountain which had given the camp its name lunged darkly into the night sky. A few minutes later, Kapitänleutnant Heydt and Hauptmann Weiss took up a position opposite the Sick Bay.

Mohr rubbed his hands and blew on them to keep warm.

'I hope this isn't a waste of time. It's no night to be chasing wild geese.'

'And I hope it *is* a waste of time.' Breithaupt's voice was muffled by the black balaclava covering his head. 'In any case, don't grumble at the weather. If it's like this all over Europe there'll be many a family in Germany thanking God that the Lancasters are grounded.'

'I don't know about that. Von Stuerzbecher hinted only this morning that the *Tommis*' new radar enables them to pinpoint a target with unerring accuracy regardless of conditions.'

Breithaupt grunted with annoyance. 'He shouldn't talk about such things.'

'Maybe I misunderstood,' said Mohr hastily.

'No, you didn't.' Breithaupt sighed the long sigh of the very weary. 'I know it's difficult for him, playing the dual role. He has to think twice, three times before he ever opens his mouth. Anyway, it's no secret the war's going badly.'

'You called it treason when I suggested the same thing a couple of weeks ago.'

'Whistling in the dark, Franz. You can't fight this sort of war on two fronts, and post-war historians will prove it. It either had to be the Russians or the Americans and the *Tommis*. It could never be both.'

Franz Mohr was mildly shocked. 'It sounds as if you've already accepted defeat. If so, why are we still fighting? Why are we even considering an escape?'

'We're still fighting and you and the others are going to escape because no one's told us otherwise. We're soldiers, Franz; we do as we're told.'

Breithaupt was silent for a moment.

'It's strange, isn't it, how victory or defeat can hang on such a slender thread as the whims or forgetfulness of a few individuals? There was a lot of talk—very private of course—that the Fuehrer never invaded England because he felt an instinctive empathy, as I suppose many of us do, with the British. If he had, it might all be over by now.'

Mohr snorted quietly. 'A better reason might be that we didn't command the air over the Channel and we hadn't enough landing craft. I'm afraid I don't subscribe to unconscious motivations.'

'They exist, nevertheless. Do you recall the story, I don't know how apocryphal it is, about Marshal Blucher's forces at Waterloo?' Mohr said he didn't. 'It seems that a squadron of French cavalry fought its way through Blucher's lines and got as far as the cannon. When the officer in command asked who had the nails with which to spike the touch-holes, no one had bothered to bring them. They'd all been so anxious to get on with the charge that they'd forgotten the reason they were going.'

'For want of a nail the horseshoe was lost, etc,' said Mohr.

'Something like that. It seems to me that we Germans are like that squadron of French cavalry. We keep pressing forward but we're not quite sure where we're going or what we're going to do when we get there.'

'Christ, that's a bit deep.'

Breithaupt shook his head and grinned wryly.

'Sorry, Franz. I'm not long-suited in philosophy. But it's this sort of thing'—he gestured in the general direction of the library—'that gets me down. If we have to fight an enemy within as well as the *Tommis* . . .'

'You'll soon know,' said Mohr, and placed a cautionary hand on Breithaupt's arm.

But it was only Obergefreiter Willi Braune heading for his card game in the boiler-room. The door opened, revealing a momentary glow, then closed again.

'That was your bloody orderly, wasn't it?'

'It was. Yours is probably already inside. Didn't you know? Braune and Geith play cards most nights with a couple of *Tommis*.'

'I did not know. I'll put a stop to that first thing in the morning.'

'Not a good idea, Otto. It does no harm and the other ranks don't have much to look forward to. Besides, let's not upset Braune and Geith; they're the best thieves in the camp.'

'Perhaps you're right. Christ, I'm cold. If nothing happens in the next few minutes it looks as though Weiss was wrong.'

But on the north side of the compound Hauptmann Weiss was feeling far from wrong. It was, he estimated later, approximately three or four minutes after nine o'clock when the watch-tower searchlights at the north-east and north-west corners swung suddenly inwards, as though at a prearranged signal, and illuminated the area around the Sick Bay. In an instant, that whole section was full of *Tommis*, making no attempt at stealth. Directing operations was Captain Thorogood in person, and Weiss picked out CSM Purser and several others he knew by name. In all, there were some fifteen or twenty armed soldiers in the vicinity.

But neither he nor Heydt stuck around to count them. Thorogood would soon discover there was nothing to be found and he might widen his area of search. It would go badly for any POW caught out in the open.

'We've seen enough,' he whispered, making no effort to hide his exultation.

Mohr and Breithaupt had also heard the rumpus and drew the only conclusion possible.

'So Weiss was right after all.'

Breithaupt's voice was full of bitterness. 'Yes. Tomorrow we shall have to have a word with Oberleutnant Kapp.'

In March 1941 Kapitänleutnant Otto Kretschmer's submarine, the U.99, was sunk by a British destroyer, HMS *Walker*, and Kretschmer himself taken prisoner and incarcerated at Grizedale Hall. Apart from keeping in touch with Admiral Doenitz using a code devised prior to the war, before being transferred to a Canadian POW camp in May 1942 Kapitänleutnant Kretschmer found a way to circumvent the regulations governing courts-martial.

Under the Geneva Convention prisoners were not allowed to sit as a court-martial board on other prisoners; punishment, whatever the nature of the offence, could only be meted out by the captors. Kretschmer got round this by setting up what he called a Secret Council of Honour to try those whose courage or loyalty were in doubt. In all but name it was a drumhead trial, but Major Breithaupt, in spite of earlier misgivings, was determined to use the artifice in the case of Oberleutnant Kapp.

At 0930 on the morning of the 8th, after a roll-call which revealed Leutnants Kaehler and Preiss still to be missing, Oberleutnant Kapp was summoned to Major Breithaupt's hut, Hut 5. The regular occupants were told to make themselves scarce and a guard placed on the door, both inside and out. Because of the secret nature of the proceedings Breithaupt selected Emke to watch the inside and Werner Herburg the out.

It had occurred to the Escape Committee that if their suspicions regarding Kapp were correct, Captain Thorogood would be looking for an explanation from him before long. Breithaupt wanted the Council of Honour out of the way before that event took place, if he allowed it to take place at all. However, in spite of the seemingly damning evidence against the bespectacled Artillery officer, Breithaupt had no intention of countenancing a kangaroo court or assuming him guilty until that fact had been proven beyond all doubt. To begin with, therefore, he invited Kapp to sit at one end of the trestle-table. Breithaupt sat at the other, flanked by Mohr on his right and Heydt and Weiss on his left. It had been decided to call evidence only in written form, and each man had in front of him a signed deposition from the officers who had fed Kapp the false information.

Breithaupt called the meeting to order and addressed Kapp directly.

'Last night,' he began, 'an escape attempt from the Sick Bay was thwarted at the last moment by the appearance of Captain Thorogood. We are making enquiries into how Thorogood could possibly have known of the time and place of the attempt, and we believe you can help us in this.'

'I, Herr Major?' Kapp's face was a picture of innocence. 'How should I be able to help you?'

'You were one of the few people to know the full facts. This enquiry is to establish whether through careless talk or . . . or other reasons you passed the information on.'

'I assure you I did not, Herr Major. Not only did I not pass any information on, I had none to pass. This is the first I've heard of such an attempt.'

Like most born liars Oberleutnant Kapp was totally convincing in his denial. If the trap had not been baited with such care Breithaupt would have been inclined to believe him.

'I see,' he said. 'Hauptmann Weiss?'

'This Council does not believe the Oberleutnant's last statement,' said Weiss. His one good eye stared at Kapp coldly, like that of a hangman measuring his victim for the rope. 'For the last two weeks I have personally been responsible for the rumour of the Sick Bay attempt reaching you. I have used only those officers whose loyalty I trust implicitly and they told no one other than you of the rumour. Note the word rumour, Oberleutnant. It is used advisedly. There was no attempt from the Sick Bay last night, nor is one planned. The place was chosen deliberately to see if the *Tommis* would appear. As you well know, they did, and they could not have been there unless they had information. That information could only have come from you.'

Heinrich Weiss rubbed his eye in an effort to stop it twitching. Since the crash it always did that when he was excited, and he was excited now. So far as he was concerned Kapp was as guilty as sin, and the quicker he was put where he could do no more harm, the better. In his opinion the Council was a complete waste of time, but he was wise enough to know that Breithaupt would not sanction lynch law. To get the verdict he wanted he would have to play within the rules.

'We're waiting, Oberleutnant,' said Major Breithaupt.

'Waiting for what, Herr Major?' Kapp took off his spectacles and polished them vigorously. 'Hauptmann Weiss is saying in effect

142

that I am guilty of a treasonable relationship with the British. I resent that imputation, and I repeat that I knew nothing of the Sick Bay escape plan until a few minutes ago. I would furthermore remind the Major that this Council is illegal. You have no right to try me.'

'You suggest we hand you over to the British?' asked Heydt.

'I suggest we terminate this farce here and now and that you allow me to go about my business.'

'No doubt with Captain Thorogood,' sneered Weiss.

'That's a damned lie!'

Breithaupt rapped on the table with his pencil.

'That will be more than enough, gentlemen,' he said sharply. 'You will remember that in spite of the location you are German officers and that this, whatever Oberleutnant Kapp says to the contrary, is a properly constituted Court.'

He picked up a document from the table in front of him. Kapp was almost convincing, full of plausible indignation, but the words written down were incontrovertible evidence that he was not telling the truth.

'You say, Oberleutnant, that you had no knowledge of the escape until just now. Yet I have here a signed statement from two officers whose honour cannot be impugned that you were told the day before yesterday that an attempt was to be made at 2100 last night.'

'Name them,' demanded Kapp.

Breithaupt gave him the names of two Oberleutnants who assisted Weiss with camp security.

'They too are lying,' snapped the Artillery officer.

'Both of them?' queried Mohr.

'Both of them. I recall no such conversation and I would again remind the senior officer that this Council is illegal.'

'I can have the two officers brought in,' said Weiss generally.

Kapp hesitated. 'That will hardly be necessary. For some reason unknown to me they will only repeat in person the same lies they have already put their signatures to.'

'Why should they do that?' asked Heydt.

'I don't know. Perhaps I've done something to offend them. It is not unheard of for some individuals to use a public court for private vengeance.'

Weiss pounced. 'Then you accept the legality of this body?'

143

'I do no such thing,' blustered Kapp. 'But since I appear to have little choice in the matter I insist upon being allowed a defence.'

'Another officer?' asked Mohr.

'Another officer, one chosen by myself with the power to examine witnesses. It would only take a day or so to arrange . . .'

'No,' said Breithaupt. 'If we permit you to leave here you will go straight to the British for protection.'

'You're assuming me guilty,' cried Kapp. He was sweating badly now. As fast as he cleaned and polished his spectacles they misted up again.

'We're simply examining the evidence.'

Which they continued to do for a further ten minutes, though really it was a monologue. With hardly a pause for breath Kapp kept on denying that he was a traitor and protested that he was being treated unjustly.

Weiss could see that Breithaupt wanted a confession. Although the evidence, apart from the man's attitude, pointed overwhelmingly to Kapp's guilt, Weiss knew that the Major was the sort of individual who wanted every 'i' dotted, every 't' crossed. He therefore offered Kapp an escape route that was not really an escape route at all.

'Perhaps the Oberleutnant made a mistake earlier when he professed not to have heard of the Sick Bay attempt,' he said cunningly. 'Perhaps, unwittingly, he was guilty of no more than careless talk and is now frightened to tell us.'

Kapp committed the fatal error of seizing this straw. Had he stuck to his original denial he might have got away with it because the evidence against him was at best circumstantial.

'Hauptmann Weiss is right,' he said after a moment. 'I didn't want to say anything before because I was afraid matters would go badly for me. But yes, I do remember the conversation with the two officers concerned and I also remember talking about it.'

'To whom?' demanded Heydt.

'I don't recall.' Kapp wiped his palms on his tunic. 'Another officer, I think, outside the Pig Pen yesterday morning. I was excited at the prospect of another escape being made and I wanted to see what others thought. There were several NCOs nearby and I think the guard known as Harpo was also in the vicinity. He could have overheard me, or the NCOs . . .'

'You disgust me!' Breithaupt hammered the table with a closed fist in sudden anger. 'To save your own neck you're willing to malign some nameless NCO or fellow officer. Why did you do it, Oberleutnant? Money, better rations, some promise or other?'

'Herr Major, I swear to God . . .'

'You'd swear your own mother's life away if you thought it would save your treacherous hide.' Breithaupt was white and shaking. Mohr had never seen his friend so angry. 'There are men out there, Kapp, brave men, officer and NCO, who suffer deprivation gladly rather than rat on their comrades. Treason is far too kind a word for what you've done, because I've no doubt that if we looked hard enough and dug long enough we'd find that the other failed escapes were the result of your collaboration. God knows, if I had a gun I'd shoot you myself here and now. Oberleutnant Emke!'

Theo Emke came to attention and clicked his heels. 'Herr Major?'

'Get this man out of my sight and see that he talks to no one. If he tries to run for it or call for help you are to break his neck instantly. I'm sorry to burden you with such a responsibility with the inevitable consequences, but I want you to tell us here and now, so that Oberleutnant Kapp can hear, that you accept it.'

'I accept it, Herr Major. If Oberleutnant Kapp so much as sneezes without my permission, it will give me great pleasure to kill him.'

'Thank you, Emke. Let Oberleutnant Herburg know where you'll be so that we can recall you when we have finished our deliberations. Now get him out of here.'

Kapp opened his mouth to protest, but Emke's hand on his collar soon silenced him. He went through the door as meek as a lamb.

Breithaupt heaved a long sigh. 'I'm sorry about that outburst, gentlemen.'

'You were too easy on him,' said Weiss. 'You should have ordered Emke to kill him right away.'

'This is still a properly constituted Court, Herr Hauptmann. There'll be no sentence until we've had the verdict, though I take it there's no disagreement on that.'

'None,' said Heydt. 'Guilty.'

'Guilty,' said Mohr.

'Of course guilty.' This from Weiss.

'And my vote makes it unanimous,' said Breithaupt. 'The question is, what do we do with him?'

'Do with him?' Weiss was quite frankly astounded. 'What do we do with him, Herr Major? We dispose of him as quickly as possible, as a warning to others who might be inclined similarly.'

'And what do you suggest we do with the corpse?' asked Breithaupt. 'Don't misunderstand me; I've no intention of going soft on Oberleutnant Kapp. But now we've found our traitor I'm more interested in the living than the dead. If we execute him it will almost certainly be impossible to hide the body. When the British find it they will institute an enquiry and they will know that such an execution could not have taken place without at least my consent. In their eyes the Council of Honour is illegal and therefore not competent to pass the sentence of death. We will in effect have committed murder and we'll be tried accordingly under British law. And let none of us doubt what the verdict of that Court will be. We will not even be given the choice of a firing squad. The sentence will be death by hanging.'

'Otto . . . Major Breithaupt is right,' Mohr broke in before Weiss could protest. 'And don't think for a moment it's only his own skin he's worried about. As senior officer he's automatically involved, but let's not fool ourselves for a second; Captain Thorogood may not have proof that the four of us in this room constitute the Escape Committee, but he could hazard a pretty good guess. It would mean the rope for all of us.'

'Ridiculous,' said Weiss angrily. 'Are you trying to tell me that four German officers cannot find a way to make the death of one criminal look like an accident? Like you, gentlemen, I have no wish to give the British hangman employment, but I would rather have it that way than let Kapp go free. Good God, what was the point in trapping him if all we do is to pat him on the head and tell him not to do it again?' He turned to Kapitänleutnant Heydt for support.

'I don't believe I heard Major Breithaupt suggest any such thing,' said Heydt. Breithaupt looked at the naval officer with new respect. 'Under normal circumstances we would of course march Kapp directly outside and put a bullet through his head. But these are far from normal circumstances. With the 12th so close we can't afford to take unnecessary risks . . .'

'You can't maybe.'

'. . . and neither can Kapp simply disappear. If he is not seen around Captain Thorogood will add two and two together and assume the worst. Neither can we execute him, hide him in the Rabbit Run, and make it look like an escape. With Kaehler and Preiss already missing Thorogood would tear the camp apart to find Kapp. We were lucky once; we can't expect the cards to fall for us again.'

'They had a similar problem at Grizedale Hall a year or two back,' said Mohr. 'A naval officer accused of cowardice. They gave him the choice of running for it and not coming back, or being killed.'

'I remember it.' Heydt had begun his POW career at Grizedale Hall. 'The *Tommis* caught up with him but he kept on running. They shot him in the back.'

'Unfortunately that wouldn't work here,' said Breithaupt. 'If what we suspect about Kapp is true, he just about threw his weapon down at Dunkirk and volunteered to be taken prisoner. He's not the sort to take that option. If we give him a choice between running and being executed he'll run all right—but to Thorogood.'

'Which leaves his immediate dispatch the only solution,' argued Weiss.

'Not necessarily,' said Breithaupt. 'I've been thinking about this carefully. I can see one or two obvious objections, but what about using Kapp ourselves? What about giving him the choice between having his neck broken or taking orders from us? Thorogood thinks he has an informer in our midst; very well, let's see he gets all the information he can use—but tailored to our own needs.'

'Absurd!' snorted Weiss. 'Insanity. If we let Kapp go the first thing he'll do is ask the Adjutant for a transfer, telling him why.'

Breithaupt did not agree. 'Perhaps not. I think I can persuade Oberleutnant Kapp that we can track him down no matter where he goes, which is not so far from the truth. Using the Doenitz code we can let High Command know that Kapp is a collaborator and see that they pass on the message to the other camps. It would take time but it's more than possible.'

'Nonsense.' Weiss could see his victim slipping away. 'Kapp would know that all he's doing is buying time. When the war's over he'll be tried by a properly constituted court-martial, which will undoubtedly sentence him to death. He might live this year, but next year he's a dead man.'

Breithaupt and Mohr glanced at one another but neither bothered to point out that such a court-martial would depend very much upon who won.

'Perhaps you're right,' acknowledged Breithaupt, 'but an eleventh-hour reprieve is always welcome. In any case, I don't see we have much choice. No matter what you say, Heinrich, killing the wretched man is out of the question. We agreed earlier that a majority verdict on the sentence is one we should all accept, but I'd prefer it to be unanimous. I'm therefore willing to spend a little more time trying to persuade you that getting Kapp to work for us is the most sensible decision to take.

'We had a stroke of bad luck the day before yesterday with Kaehler and Preiss getting caught in the Rabbit Run. To the best of our knowledge Thorogood thinks they've gone under the wire. But the one thing we can do without is him suddenly becoming inquisitive again. The *Tommis* overlooked the chapel last time; maybe next time they won't. So let's say we brief Kapp to tell Thorogood that, although he made a mistake last night, he's heard that a mass break-out is being planned for the middle of January and that Kaehler and Preiss have already gone to test the route. He doesn't know yet how they escaped, but he expects to find out over Christmas. Knowing the way Thorogood's mind works he'll be quite happy to leave us alone until the second week in January. He won't even bother to look again for Kaehler and Preiss. And by the second week in January, gentlemen, a dozen German officers should be sending us picture postcards of Berlin.'

'Beautiful,' said Franz Mohr delightedly, and even Heydt managed a rare grin.

But Weiss was still far from happy.

'And after the middle of January? Or rather, after 12 December—because on 13 December Captain Thorogood will know for certain he's been made a fool of.'

'After 13 December, Hauptmann Weiss, I don't think Kapp will have much credibility left as an informer. We all know that Thorogood hates Germans and I doubt if the good Captain will worry one way or another what happens to Kapp once his usefulness is at an end. An accident as you suggested, perhaps? It shouldn't be difficult to arrange.'

As far as Heydt and Mohr were concerned, the matter was decided. But Breithaupt wanted his unanimity and he waited anxiously to hear from Hauptmann Weiss.

'Very well,' said Weiss finally. 'I agree. But I want it made quite clear that what happens to Kapp after the 12th is my business alone.'

'Of course,' said Breithaupt.

They had Kapp brought back. Hang-dog and sweating profusely in spite of the temperature, the bespectacled Oberleutnant listened with growing astonishment as he learned that he was not to be executed on the spot. With an alacrity that was shameful, he agreed to everything Breithaupt suggested, though the Major was careful to omit the actual date and place of the fictitious escape. As far as Kapp was aware something was being planned for the middle of January and he was part of a diversionary tactic.

'And make no mistake,' Breithaupt concluded. 'You are being offered your life only because you can be useful to us. If we suspect that you are still collaborating with the British, that you are passing on information which does not emanate directly from this Committee, you will surely die. Wherever you try to hide, we shall find you. Take him out, Emke.'

Hauptmann Weiss's one good eye followed Kapp to the door. Major Breithaupt could say what he liked, but Weiss had already made up his mind that Kapp would not survive the night of the 12th.

12

9 December

Korvettenkapitän Dieter Stieff was as cheerful a character as any
of them had ever come across. A native of Kiel he looked about
nineteen, though Christian knew this could hardly be the case.
Even in a war where the promotion system had gone berserk, the
German Navy did not give that sort of rank and command of an
expensive U-boat to nineteen-year-olds.

Obersturmbannfuehrer Kirdorff was also something of a surprise.
Christian had been expecting a much older man, but Kirdorff
turned out to be a couple of years this side of thirty. He greeted
Christian's party on coming aboard, and that was more or less the
last anyone saw of him. He took his meals alone and slept in a tiny
cabin next to the radio shack.

After sailing from Lorient dead on time on the morning of the
7th, there was nothing to do for the two days it would take to
reach the north-west coast of England. Stieff took the long way
round, skirting the Ile d'Ouessant well to the west and heading
out into the Atlantic. Sailing through St. George's Channel and
up into the Irish Sea was asking for trouble, he explained. At
longitude 12 degrees he swung the U-boat north and followed the
Irish Coast.

On the morning of the second day, while cruising at periscope
depth, they spotted a large convoy heading east. The urge to take a
pot-shot at the merchantmen ferrying foodstuffs from Canada and
the United States to England was almost irresistible, but Stieff
overcame his natural inclinations. 'There'll be plenty of time to
play hide and seek with the *Tommis*.'

The most hazardous part of the journey took place on the 9th,
going through that stretch of water between the north-east coast of
Ireland and the south-west coast of Scotland, the North Channel,

from the Mull of Kintyre down to the Mull of Galloway. Stieff openly confessed that these were unfamiliar waters and that he proposed to make part of the run in daylight and on the surface.

Christian was not in the least happy at the prospect of being picked up on coastal radar and meeting up with the Royal Navy or a Mosquito of Coastal Command. 'I thought the whole idea of a U-boat was to travel underwater.'

'That's the theory,' said Stieff nonchalantly, 'but I'm one of those people who likes to see where he's going. You can stay top-sides and watch if you wish. If there's any danger we've always got a minute or two.'

Christian took one look at the choppy seas and the heavy clouds hanging over the Scottish mainland and felt threatened enough.

'No thanks,' he said.

Although the German Navy was not usually so democratic as to quarter the officers with the men, Stieff was no slavish disciple of protocol. 'As you'll be working together you might as well eat and sleep together,' he said in Lorient, and promptly turned over his 2 i/c's cabin to Feldwebel Schelling and Obergefreiter Schultz. Christian himself bunked with Stieff, and all four men took their meals together, apart from the other officers and crew.

In spite of the cramped conditions it proved to be an admirable arrangement. Stieff was an excellent host and raconteur and a fine mimic. His impersonations of Germany's leaders had the other three in fits of helpless laughter, though Schelling and Schultz were a little embarrassed at first and kept looking over their shoulder for Kirdorff.

Leaving Stieff to the business of getting them safely through the North Channel, Christian sought out his men. He found them in their cabin, making a final equipment check.

Apart from the clothes they stood up in and a spare set of civvies in a rucksack for von Stuerzbecher, they were taking a three-man tent, cooking utensils and food (with British labels), and iron rations. Christian was to carry the Luger, a compass and, after much private debate, a large-scale map of the area. He had pondered the question of a map at great length and eventually decided it was indispensable. Although after much study he was fairly certain he knew the topography of the area, its hazards and pit-falls, like the back of his hand, there was always the unexpected to be catered for. They might not be able to come out the way they went in, and it would be the height of irony if they succeeded in all other aspects of the venture but could not find their way back to the rendezvous before Stieff was compelled to abandon them. Christian hoped they would not be seen, but if they were he intended passing the group off as hikers, a not unlikely pastime for the British even in the depths of winter. Hikers carried maps, so a map became part of their kit.

In a side pocket of Christian's waterproof jacket were the sealed orders Standartenfuehrer Weil had given him in Berlin. As they were so close to landfall he was tempted to break the seal now, memorise the contents and destroy them. But Weil had decreed otherwise, and Christian decided to play it by the book.

He'd examined himself for nerves and found none. He was feeling better than he had done for months. Weil might have selected him because he knew England and the English and was a close friend of von Stuerzbecher's, but the Standartenfuehrer was not to know he had more or less saved Christian's life. The drunken days in Cologne and elsewhere seemed no more than a distant nightmare, and he hadn't touched more than a couple of glasses of beer in over two weeks. He had lost the excess weight too, and was now not far short of perfect fitness, mental as well as physical. He had something positive, worthwhile, to do, and it made him feel good.

'Everything all right?' he asked.

'It will be when I get out of this can,' growled Schelling. 'Christ, how these people put up with it for weeks on end is beyond me.'

'Look at it from their point of view. Imagine us crawling around England in the depths of winter when we could be as snug as bugs under fifty fathoms of ocean.'

'Are we on schedule, Christian?' asked Wolf Schultz. Neither he nor Schelling had been on deck since Lorient, and the U-boat could be in the Pacific for all they knew.

'As far as I know. Stieff expects to be somewhere off the lower end of the Solway Firth, between Maryport and Workington, by nightfall, but it'll be 2100 or thereabouts before we're ashore. Do you want to go over the whole thing once more?'

Neither Schelling nor Schultz were the jittery types, but it was still good military practice to keep a man's mind occupied until it was time to go.

'Might as well,' answered Schelling. 'If Wolf gets lost it'll be useful if he knows where to surrender.'

'Balls. The only way I'll get lost is looking for you.'

Christian grinned and spread open the map.

'As near as possible Stieff wants to stand offshore just south of Maryport, but that will depend very much on enemy activity. However, there's not much of strategic importance in this part of the world so it shouldn't be a problem. He'll heave to as close as he dares, and we'll be rowed ashore by dinghy.

'From Maryport or wherever it is, we strike due east. I'd like to go cross-country, avoiding roads, villages and towns, but that will depend upon conditions underfoot. If we're forced to use roads we'll go via Broughton Moor, Dovenby, Bridekirk, Blindcrake and Bewaldeth, skirting Bassenthwaite Lake to the north and going down its east side to the camp. It's about twenty miles or thirty-one kilometres door to door, so I don't expect to be at the objective much before dawn. In fact, I'd like to work it that way, get somewhere within the vicinity of the camp by daybreak. It'll probably take the rest of the day to reconnoitre and figure out a way to let von Stuerzbecher know we're here, but I've got a couple of thoughts on that subject. I'll tell you about them later.

'The next bit's the easy bit,' Christian smiled. 'We liberate von Stuerzbecher and take him home.'

'With half the British Army chasing us,' grunted Schelling.

'And with only a couple of days to do it in,' added Schultz.

'Nobody said it was going to be easy, but I think we're agreed that if we can't find a way to free von Stuerzbecher in a couple of days, we'll never find it.'

'Doesn't matter anyway,' said Schelling. 'If we're not back by the evening of the 14th we've got a long swim home.'

'Precisely.' Christian folded up the map and put it away. 'Tomorrow's the 10th and by tomorrow night we should know if the job's possible. Strictly speaking that only leaves us two whole days to get it done, because if we're to rendezvous with Stieff on the night of the 14th at the latest we'll need to travel back during the dark hours of the 13th and hole up during the day. If we can't get von Stuerzbecher out on the 11th or 12th, we can't get him out at all.'

Wolf Schultz grinned mischievously. 'Maybe that's how we should play it. Take a stroll through the English countryside for a few days then come back and report failure. No one's going to blame us for trying.'

'We're not going to fail,' said Christian seriously. 'That's the last thing we're going to do.'

Later on in the day Stieff came below to report that they had just rounded the Mull of Galloway without incident and that darkness had fallen ten minutes ago; that the weather was atrocious upstairs and that it didn't look much better over the mainland; that they were making a steady eight knots on the surface and that he expected to be in position between 2000 and 2100.

'I must say I don't envy you,' he commented. 'If it's not snowing it'll be sleeting, and if not sleeting raining.'

'We've seen worse,' said Christian. 'If this were Russia we'd think it was spring.'

'You look the part anyway.' Not wishing to leave anything until the last moment, all three were dressed to go. 'If I didn't know differently, I swear I'd shoot you on sight as British spies. I particularly like the hair.'

Christian smiled self-consciously. It was one of the details he was pleased to have remembered, instructing Schelling and Schultz to give the barber a miss. Fortunately neither of them wore their hair closely cropped, as British cartoonists liked to depict German soldiers, and Christian had always favoured a style just above his collar. In the short time he'd had it wasn't really long enough to satisfy him absolutely, but all three were wearing it longer than would have been permitted in Germany.

'Thanks. I expect we'll be court-martialled for slovenly appearance when we get home.'

'When you get home,' said Stieff, 'I doubt if anyone will mind if it's halfway down your back.' Abruptly he was serious. 'You're quite clear about the signals?' he asked Christian.

'Quite clear. We return to where you drop us wherever that happens to be. On the night of the 13th or 14th, at exactly 2000, we flash two long two short, wait sixty seconds, then repeat the signal. Fifteen minutes later we do the same thing again. On neither occasion will you reply.'

'It's safer. It's unlikely your signal will be seen, but a patrol could pick up our acknowledgement. But we'll be there, never fear. Your first signal will tell me you're ready to be taken off and your second will guide the dinghy in. I could also be there on the 12th if you wish.'

Christian shook his head. 'No point. Even if everything goes like clockwork, to be at the rendezvous on the 12th would mean travelling overnight on the 11th, and there's no chance we'll be able to do that.'

No one bothered to mention what would happen if the U-boat did not receive a signal on the 14th; that would have been tempting fate.

'All right, then.' Stieff stood in the companionway. 'I'll get back upstairs and start driving this crate. I've instructed the galley to prepare the biggest and best meal they can muster. It shouldn't be long.'

'I wish he hadn't said that,' muttered Josef Schelling, when Stieff had gone. 'I remember what happens after the men eat a hearty supper.'

Now observing full silent routine, Christian and his party scrambled over the bows of the U-boat and into the waiting dinghy at 2050 hours. To prevent their civilian clothes getting too wet too quickly, Stieff had thoughtfully equipped the trio with oilskins and sou'westers. These would be brought back on landing by the crew of the dinghy.

His eyes not yet accustomed to the darkness, Christian wondered how the hell Stieff knew where they were, for looking east not a light showed anywhere. Even screwing up his eyes and adopting the ridiculous but usual landlubber's pose of leaning physically forward, Christian could see nothing. The night was moonless, the sky black and angry. It was still raining, though that could well be snow inland.

As the dinghy pulled away from the U-boat's side, glancing over his shoulder Christian thought he could make out Stieff in the conning-tower. There was no sign of Kirdorff. Neither were there any whispered 'good-lucks'; farewells and silent prayers had already been said below. All that could be heard now was the wail of the wind and the sound of oars.

Stieff had chosen the three biggest members of his crew to man the inflatable dinghy, but even so Christian could sense that the prevailing wind and the run of the tide were pushing them further south than they wished to be. By gesture he managed to convey that his party would take a couple of spare oars, but the Obersteuermann in command shook his head and thumbed out into the darkness. Christian understood; the passengers would be better employed keeping an eye open for stray mines.

It seemed an hour but it was probably no more than twenty minutes before a darker patch of sky turned out to be coastline, and a change in the sound of the waves indicated they were nearing shore. Minutes later, the dinghy scraped the bottom.

Christian, Schelling and Schultz slipped quietly out of their oilskins. With Schultz carrying the rucksack and Schelling the harness which held the tent, Christian led them over the side. Again, from the sailors, there were no vocal incantations to the spirits of good fortune; either they would reunite with their passengers in a few days or they would not. That was all there was to it.

Under the lee of the cliff which towered ahead of them, Christian tried to calculate his bearings. Neither he nor the others watched the dinghy disappear into the night. They were ashore all right, but none of them wanted to hang around.

'We've got to find a way up this lot,' he shouted. It shouldn't be much of a problem; even if he was further south than he reckoned, nowhere did the map show the cliffs rising above a couple of hundred feet. 'Wolf, scout left, Josef right.'

They found a path in no time.

'Take it easy going up,' warned Christian. 'The last thing we need now is a broken ankle.'

13

It was no longer snowing but all the signs pointed to another fall before morning. In the meantime they had the cold to contend with.

They had been trekking for two hours and Maryport and the coast were a long way behind them. Christian estimated they had covered five miles or so and he was quite happy with their rate of progress. Although they were using the roads, as a precaution he had set the phosphorescent dial of his British Army compass to ten degrees south of east. In an emergency that heading would put them on a collision course with the River Derwent.

The night had so far been uneventful—with one exception. On the outskirts of the hamlet of Dovenby they had come across a detached house standing in several acres of ground. As they were about to pass it the stillness was suddenly shattered by the sound of a car engine and the driveway illuminated by headlights. In a panic they flattened themselves against the hedgerow. The car shot down the driveway and skidded to a halt before entering the main road. Christian could see the occupants quite clearly, a man and a woman. And a window must have been open because he heard the man say: 'For the love of God we'll only be away five days, don't worry about it.'

When his heart stopped thumping Christian filed the information. An empty house could well be useful on the way back.

Attempting to travel cross-country had proved to be impossible. In places the snow was two or three feet deep and they had all sunk into it up to their knees before the idea was abandoned. The return trip might be a different proposition, but for the moment they hugged the sides of roads, ready to leap into a ditch at the slightest danger. Apart from the incident with the car, so far they had seen only one truck, full of singing troops, and a solitary motorcyclist; travelling at night had its advantages. It took time, of course, but even so they were beyond Blindcrake by 1.30. Half an hour later Christian called a halt.

'If all England's like this,' said Josef Schelling, gulping down a can of self-heating soup, 'can anyone tell me why we want to conquer it?'

Christian massaged his calves while eating a bar of chocolate. 'It's not all like this and not even this is always the same. You should see it in the summer, or in summers before the war, at any rate. The place is crawling with hikers and climbers—at least half of them girls,' he added pointedly for Schultz's benefit.

'I don't think I'd know what to do with a girl if I was presented with one on a plate,' said Schultz. 'My privates have shrivelled up and disappeared.'

'I thought I saw something small drop on the road a while back.' Schelling grinned in the darkness. 'But it was such a pathetic little thing I didn't think you'd miss it.'

Schultz made an obscene gesture with his fist. 'Speak for yourself, Feldwebel. If anything drops off me the British'll think it's an air raid.'

'Bury the cans,' warned Christian. He squinted at his wrist watch, bought in Bond Street in happier times. It was 2.30. With luck they should be through Bewaldeth by 3.30 and on top of the objective an hour or so after that. Sunrise in this part of the world for the time of year was a few minutes before 8 a.m. He wanted to be several hundred feet up Skiddaw with a good view of the camp before then.

They were level with the northern tip of Bassenthwaite Lake ten minutes the wrong side of Christian's e.t.a. Although in theory it was a straight run down the Keswick road now, Christian nevertheless reset his compass to read 150 degrees. They would only be able to follow the road so far and he wanted no guessing games when they left it.

Three-quarters of an hour later, ahead of them in the distance, they were puzzled by a pattern of lights which got no closer. Static convoy? Air raid defences? It took a couple of minutes to work it out.

'Stupid of me,' said Christian. 'They're the searchlights from the camp.' He experienced a surge of elation; the first part of their mission was almost over.

As they left the road to make for the lower slopes of Skiddaw, it started to snow. But it was only a short-lived squall.

They were all desperately tired now, having covered the best part of twenty miles in something under seven hours. But they found reserves of energy from somewhere and by 5.15 a.m. they were a thousand feet up the mountain, looking down on the camp.

The searchlights made it as bright as day, and it was all pretty much as Christian had expected; row after row of wooden huts in the middle of the compound and administrative and other buildings dotted around the inner perimeter wire. The searchlights appeared to function automatically, judging by the way they traversed in a regular pattern, though doubtless there were armed guards in each watch-tower to operate them manually if there was a breakdown in the power plant. Anyway, there wasn't much more he could do until daylight, when the first item on the agenda would be to establish the POW's routine. In the meantime, rest, food and sleep.

'Put the tent up somewhere where it can't be seen from the camp,' he told Wolf Schultz. 'Over there by that rock face looks a good place.'

'Camouflage?'

'Yes, but not too much. We don't know yet whether this area is used by shepherds and I'll lay odds the *Tommis* come up from time to time. I don't want to make it too obvious that we're trying to hide.'

'I'll take the first watch until dawn,' offered Schelling.

'All right. But if you see anything or anyone, for God's sake wake me up. And keep a note of anything important that happens down there. Parades, roll-calls, anything of that nature.'

All three were really far too exhausted to eat, but they forced themselves to munch some hard tack and chocolate. Five minutes later, Christian and Wolf Schultz were asleep.

When Schelling shook them awake with the news that the camp was coming alive, it seemed as if they had only just closed their eyes. In fact, it was a few minutes after sun-up. For a change the sky was relatively clear and it looked as if they might get away without a snowfall for at least part of the day.

After a cold breakfast Christian insisted they should all shave; if they were unfortunate enough to be spotted nothing stood out more than a man with a day-old beard. Afterwards, while Schelling got some rest, Schultz kept watch and Christian settled down to the dreary business of establishing the camp routine.

He decided against using binoculars. It was always possible some sharp-eyed sentry would see the lens reflection up on the mountain and wonder what the hell was going on. In any case, the POWs were almost close enough to touch, though he was still too far away to make out individual faces.

Morning roll-call took place at precisely 8.30 in a fenced-off section of the compound. He made a careful note of the time, the disposition of the prisoners, and how long the operation took, though that was the only note he made for three hours. It seemed hardly worth recording that after roll-call the POWs split up and went their separate ways. Some strolled around the compound, others brought out a ball and batted it around the fenced-off section. But the majority disappeared back into their huts and into several buildings on the south side, to his far left. There was nothing to be gained by watching a ball game or men wandering aimlessly, so he switched his attention to the main gates. Short of a miracle, that was going to be his way in and out.

Like many others before him, Christian looked at the main gates and despaired when he realised that, with two notable exceptions, the inner perimeter gate was never open at the same time as the other. Unless a man's business in the big wide world beyond Skiddaw was accepted as legitimate by both lots of sentries, he was trapped in that stretch of no-man's-land which separated the fences.

The first exception was for men coming the other way, returning from leave or a trip to town or a night on the tiles or the thousand and one other reasons that mean constant activity at the entrance to any establishment containing the military. Less stringent precautions were taken here, the theory being, as Christian had worked out for himself, that while there were a couple of hundred Germans anxious to say goodbye to Skiddaw, only a lunatic would want to say hello.

The second exception was for vehicles, of all shapes and sizes, going in either direction. Heading out, anything larger or more suspicious than an open-topped jeep was searched thoroughly by the sentries on the inner gates. Once that was done, however, the vehicle was waved through both gates. Coming into camp, providing the driver's papers were in order, there was even less formality. It therefore seemed that the only way in was on wheels. Christian had neither the papers nor the uniform to pretend to be a *Tommi* and he could hardly hijack a military vehicle plus driver on the open highway. It followed that his method of entry would have to be via a civilian car or van.

For the remainder of the day he concentrated exclusively on civilian vehicles, paying particular attention to anything that might belong to a local tradesman. He was well prepared to spend the following day repeating the exercise, for if the same vehicle appeared twice at approximately the same hour it could mean a regular delivery service and be worthy of further investigation.

But by the time the second roll-call of the day was taken at 1600 hours, his list was far from impressive: four civilian private cars (three of them almost certainly belonging to camp personnel, as they came in from some overnight business but did not go out) and two vans. He had risked binoculars on the vans. One was an ancient contraption of nondescript colour, seemingly held together by bits of wire and will power. And judging by the way the driver stood and talked and smoked a cigarette with a couple of *Tommis*, he was well known. The second was bright yellow in colour and bore the legend Foster's Bakery. The driver of this took it straight up to what Christian assumed to be the guardroom, leapt out with a wooden tray of loaves, spent under thirty seconds inside, and drove off along the Keswick road, in the direction of that town, like a bat out of hell. Either he was in a hurry to get home or he had a lot more deliveries to make.

The time of entry of the first van was recorded as 3.20 p.m., that of the second was 3.55, just as the watch-tower lights were being switched on and the POWs assembling for roll-call.

By 4.30 the roll-call was over, the POWs dispersed, and Christian had learned nothing more. And with the Germans now presumably locked up for the night, he doubted if there was anything more to learn, not that day.

He was also very tired. With only a couple of short breaks for food and a slightly longer one for a session of violent exercise to prevent himself freezing to death, he had kept the camp under surveillance for nine hours. Three hours' sleep after a twenty-mile route march was hardly adequate preparation for that sort of vigil. Still, it was not something he could have delegated to his NCOs. They were good men, brave as lions and thoroughly reliable, but the ultimate responsibility for freeing von Stuerzbecher was his alone. They had been extremely patient all day, however, and it was high time he let them know his thoughts.

Over a heated can of soup followed by a surreptitious cigarette, he told them his idea of using a civilian vehicle. Neither was impressed by his apparently suicidal urge to get into the camp.

'It's too risky, Christian,' said Schelling. 'First of all you've got to steal a van, then pass yourself off as a relief driver. Even if you succeed in doing both without the alarm being raised, you won't get further than the guardroom, at any rate not much further. I was also watching the procedure. Deliveries are made just inside the inner gates. The *Tommis* are not going to risk letting a civilian driver have the run of the camp. God knows what might happen to him or his vehicle.'

'Neither do we see the necessity,' said Wolf Schultz. 'We're here to get von Stuerzbecher out, not join him behind barbed-wire or worse. I don't see why we don't steal a pair of cutters and go in through the fence.'

But Christian negated that. 'It wouldn't work. There are twenty-five or thirty huts in the compound and von Stuerzbecher could be in any one of them. It might take us a week to ascertain which, and in a week the U-boat won't be waiting for us. On the other hand, if I could get in near roll-call I could possibly do something to let von Stuerzbecher see me. You saw where they held the *Appell*, in the fenced-off section where the men were playing ball?' The other two nodded. 'It's only thirty or forty metres from the guardroom. If I was there around 8.30 or 1600 and created a disturbance von Stuerzbecher would at least know help was at hand. Don't forget we're old friends. He'd recognise me at once.'

'Then what?' asked Schultz. 'He's not going to run up and embrace you, jump in the van, and drive off with you into the setting sun.'

'No, but he'll realise I wouldn't be showing myself unless I wanted something from him, some information. I wouldn't be such a fool as to drive into Skiddaw in broad daylight if I already had a viable scheme for freeing him. He's only been a POW himself a few weeks, remember. He'll be fully aware that our knowledge of Skiddaw is sparse.'

'Go on,' said Schelling.

'If he's as bright as I know him to be,' Christian continued, 'he'll work out some sort of signal for us. It could take any form so we'll have to keep our eyes open, but if it tells us no more than which hut he's in or where he'll be at any particular time and day—well, that's at least more than we know at present. It may then mean taking up Wolf's idea about the cutters.'

There was a long silence.

'It's a bit bloody bare, Christian,' said Schelling finally. 'We're working on practically nothing. Christ, for all we know there might be a camp inspection by Churchill tomorrow.'

Christian shrugged his shoulders. 'I agree, but we're up against a deadline. If I had a month to plan it I'd not only get von Stuerzbecher out but the rest as well. But . . .' He stopped and frowned as a sudden thought occurred.

'What is it?' asked Schelling.

'He's planning to use the pair of us as battering rams,' suggested Schultz, who could already see the eye-whites of the firing squad.

Christian didn't hear him. He thumped his palm excitedly. 'We're short of knowledge, right? We need more information than we've got, right? Now who in the world, in Germany, England or anywhere else you care to name, knows more about the inner workings of a military base than even the troops themselves?'

'Civvy workers,' said Schelling.

'Tradesmen?' offered Schultz.

'Right,' said Christian, 'right both times. And where do civilian workers and tradesmen go when they're not working and they're not at home?'

'A concert?'

'A cinema?'

'A beer house?'

'Precisely,' said Christian. 'A beer house, a pub, there to discuss politics, lament the day's events, and gossip. Gentlemen, I regret you cannot accompany me, but I'm going for a drink.'

When Christian saw the yellow Foster's Bakery van parked outside the tiny pub a mile down the Keswick road, his pulse rate shot up thirty points. Careful now, he cautioned, don't get so bloody excited. And for God's sake don't walk in and order a glass of schnapps.

The pub was no more than two ground-floor rooms of a private house, converted into a single bar when the owner got a licence, an occurrence not uncommon in the north of England and something Christian had seen scores of times during the pre-war years. Before the advent of Skiddaw Camp it had catered to no greater trade than the occupants of the dozen houses which made up the tiny hamlet, but now it was used by off-duty soldiers as well.

There were three of these at the dartboard when Christian walked in, but they gave him no more than a perfunctory glance. That was how it should be. As far as he was concerned he passed muster. His boots, clothes and rucksack were the accoutrements of a hiker, and in physical appearance he looked more Irish than German. If there was any discrepancy in his accent, which he doubted, a casual listener would put it down to Hibernian origins. In any event, he thought it beyond the compass of most men's imaginations to envisage an ex-SS officer turning up in a rural pub.

Apart from the soldiers, the only other customers were two old men playing dominoes and a youth in his late teens or early twenties propping up the counter. It took no great genius to deduce that this was the driver of the van, but if Christian needed further confirmation the youth quickly provided it.

'And if old Foster thinks I'm getting up at the crack of dawn to do early turn tomorrow, he's got another think coming.'

The barmaid nodded uninterestedly and turned her attention to Christian, who flashed her one of his best smiles.

'What can I get you?' she enquired. Usually it was 'What'll you have?' or 'There's no spirits, don't you know there's a war on?'— but for a thirty-eight-year-old unmarried lady with a weight problem smiles were a rare event, unless they came from one of the lads at the camp, anxious to see if she'd share a bed with him. It was easy to tell a gentleman, was her private thought.

'What I'd like is a whisky, but I suppose I'll have to settle for a pint,' smiled Christian.

The barmaid gave the matter some thought. The whisky stock was very low and the guvnor would have her life if she sold any to non-regulars. But he'd struck lucky recently with a case of black-market brandy and she'd been told she could sell that to all-comers.

'Fine,' said Christian, when she suggested it. He added soda and paid with a pound note. 'Have one yourself.'

With the rucksack now on the floor beside him, he pocketed his change and swallowed half the drink in a single gulp. 'That's better. I was beginning to think my blood had deserted me.'

'Bit cold for hiking,' commented the barmaid.

'Too true. But I had a couple of weeks' leave due and I decided to spend it up here. Anything to get out of London.'

'Still, the weather might have been kinder.'

Christian permitted the smile an encore. 'You're right there. I did think of sleeping under canvas, but I soon got rid of that idea. Somebody might have to dig me out in the morning.'

Christian could sense that the van driver was annoyed at losing his audience, and he was grateful when the barmaid was called away to serve the soldiers.

'Come far today, then?' He was the kind of young man who couldn't keep his mouth shut for long.

'From Cockermouth,' answered Christian, sticking close to the truth. 'I had hoped to get as far as Keswick before it got dark, but I couldn't get a lift and the roads were worse than I thought.'

'Alan's going to Keswick,' chipped in the barmaid, working the beer pumps.

'Yeah, but I'm not in the market for lifts. No offence,' he said to Christian, 'but old man Foster would have my tripes if he found out I was giving lifts. Christ, and my dad says I'm lucky, not being in the army. He doesn't have to work for Foster.' He lowered his voice confidentially. 'I've got a perforated ear drum. If it wasn't for that I'd be with your mob.'

Christian smiled to himself.

'He sounds a miserable bugger, this boss of yours,' he said sympathetically, 'I wasn't eavesdropping, but I couldn't help over-hearing what you were saying when I walked in, something about an early turn.'

'Bloody right.' Alan launched into a tirade about employers in general and Foster in particular. The barmaid glanced over pityingly when she saw Christian had been collared and Christian tried to convey that he was only listening out of politeness.

It transpired that Foster ran a one-man bakery in Keswick and that usually he had two drivers. But for the past four days the second driver had been laid up with flu and it was left to Alan to do all the deliveries, which entailed getting up at 5 a.m. and working through until 6 p.m. or thereabouts. After finishing he had to have a couple of beers, didn't he, and he wasn't getting to bed before midnight, sometimes not at all if he missed going home and went to see his girl friend instead. Because Penrith, where she lived, was a hell of a long way from Keswick, where he lived.

'I've tried getting one of my mates to split the shifts with me, but they're not interested, not just for the week or so it'll take the other driver to get on his feet again. Though if Foster thinks I'm going in at the crack of dawn tomorrow, he's got another think coming. I don't care if his customers don't see another loaf from now till Christmas.'

Christian's mind was working overtime. He didn't much believe in luck, but here was a situation which could readily be exploited.

The young man Alan sometimes slept at home and sometimes with his girl friend, so in all likelihood neither his parents nor his girl would miss him if he didn't turn up for a couple of nights, especially as one lived in Penrith and the others in Keswick. Each would assume he was with the other. That was point number one. Point number two was that Alan had been seeking a relief driver but had found no takers. He was a garrulous, argumentative sort of person so it stood to reason that he'd told Foster he was sick and tired of the whole business. The baker would not be surprised, therefore, if he didn't turn up one morning—or if someone else turned up in his place. With one driver already out Foster would simply thank his lucky stars that he had someone to make the deliveries.

Now it was just within the realms of possibility that Alan would jump at an offer to share his workload for a couple of days, but regretfully Christian knew he couldn't make such a suggestion. A man on leave from the Armed Forces wouldn't take time out to help a total stranger, not when he didn't know the area. Which left only one alternative, because refusing such a gift as the yellow van was a sure way to make the gods angry: Alan would have to be put out of the way, at least for a few days.

But first Christian needed to know a great deal more.

'Have a drink,' he offered. The barmaid nodded sagely. It was perfectly obvious to her that the good-looking stranger was buttering up young Alan to get a lift as far as Keswick. And why not? Alan was a miserable so-and-so at the best of times and it would do him good to be used for a change. Besides, Keswick was too far to walk this late in the day and there wouldn't be many other vehicles heading in that direction, not with the weather being what it was. It was a pity, though; the stranger was one of the few who wouldn't have to ask twice to hop into her bed, if she could sneak him up the stairs past the guvnor at shutting-up time. A lovely man. An officer without a doubt, you could tell by the posh way he talked and his manners.

Having successfully pigeon-holed Christian, she went about her business.

Christian and his new-found friend drank steadily together for a couple of hours, though after the initial brandy Christian switched to beer. One or two customers came and went, but Christian was only interested in the soldiers. Sooner or later they would be heading away from Keswick, back to Skiddaw, the way Christian intended taking Alan, and needless to say he didn't wish to pass the *Tommis* en route.

They looked set for the night and Christian was beginning to despair, but around half-past nine the money ran out and they left.

'Another?' asked Christian. Alan had already sunk seven pints, apart from whatever he'd drunk before Christian arrived on the scene, and it was beginning to show in the ruddiness of his cheeks and slurred consonants.

He debated the suggestion but opted in favour of discretion. 'No, that's plenty for me. Too pissed to drive if I drink any more. Never get us to Keswick.'

'Us?'

Alan blinked at him. 'You don't think I'm going to let you walk all the bloody way, do you?'

'But I thought you said Foster didn't let you give lifts.'

'Bugger Foster. Anyway, that's just something I say. You've always got these army blokes from the camp trying to cadge a lift, so I tell them I'm not allowed to. But that doesn't apply to you, Charlie.'

Christian had introduced himself as Charles Kay, the name on his forged papers.

'That's very good of you, Alan.'

'Not at all, not at all. Pleased to help. Lez go, shall us?'

They said good night to the barmaid, who threw Christian a wan smile.

Outside, the cold night air hit Alan like a heavy door as he lurched over to the van. 'Christamighty, an' I thought they were waterin' the beer.'

The address of Foster's bakery was emblazoned under the proprietor's name, but that was ancient information to Christian. He had the whole story now, chapter and verse. He not only knew the address, he knew the time Alan was supposed to be there the following morning and even something of the geography of his rounds. But most important of all he had learned that there was no set time for the delivery to the camp. Usually, Alan tried to make it early in the day, but his whole route had been at sixes and sevens since his co-driver became ill. They expected him when they saw him.

'You like me to drive?' asked Christian.

'Chris', no.' Alan fumbled for his keys and found them at the third attempt. 'I'm okay.'

Which didn't suit Christian at all. Once the youngster was behind the wheel it would be difficult to shift him. He took a quick look round; there was no one in sight.

'Alan,' he whispered softly.

Alan half turned. 'Yeah?'

Christian's punch was perfectly timed. It caught Alan on the point of the jaw. He went down without a murmur.

Quickly, Christian unlocked the van and bundled the inert body into the passenger seat. Thirty seconds later he was behind the wheel. It was years since he had sat in a vehicle with a right-hand drive, but once he had identified the headlight switch and the trafficator control, there was nothing to it. As long as he remembered to stay on the left-hand side of the road (Schelling was right; why on earth did they want to conquer such a crazy island?), it would be plain sailing.

He passed the slip-road leading to the camp at a steady 30 m.p.h. and half a mile further on pulled off the main highway. He half-concealed the van's bodywork with a few branches, but didn't bother to make too thorough a job of it. He'd be up before the birds tomorrow.

Alan was still unconscious, but he was a lightweight and Christian had no difficulty, in spite of the cumbersome rucksack, slinging him across his shoulders in a fireman's lift.

The lights from the camp were some distant aid to direction-finding, but even so it was a further three-quarters of an hour before Christian stumbled noisily upon Schelling and Schultz.

'Jesus Christ,' swore Schelling, 'you scared the hell out of us. I thought it was a brigade of commandos or at least a bear. What the hell have you got there?'

Christian lowered Alan carefully to the snow-covered earth.

'The key to Skiddaw, gentlemen. And if someone will be good enough to find me something to eat, I'll tell you all about it.'

14

Wolf Schultz shook him at 5 a.m. and announced that it was bloody freezing and there was some ground fog about. Apart from that it was clear. With the exception of a light fall around midnight, it hadn't snowed all night.

Christian sat up and rubbed the sleep from his eyes. A couple of feet away in the tiny tent, his hands bound but otherwise unfettered, the van driver looked at him in silent terror.

Not even his best friend would have called Alan Miles an intelligent youth, but he was bright enough to realise that it was either a question of doing as he was told, keeping his mouth shut, or having it shut for him. For good. That these people were Germans and that their business here had something to do with the camp, he had no doubts. But it was nothing to do with him.

While shaving, Christian repeated the warning he had given the previous evening.

'You're going to be quite safe as long as you don't give us any trouble. In a day or two we'll be gone and you'll be free to leave. But if you make any attempt to attract attention, you'll be shot. Is that quite clear?'

Alan nodded dumbly.

Outside Christian flapped his arms to get the circulation going. It was still three hours to sun-up, but the searchlights from Skiddaw gave him some light by which to see.

'We'll have to play it today by ear,' he told Josef Schelling, 'but keep an eye on the camp. You won't be able to miss that little yellow van. If anything goes wrong, use your own judgement. But my advice would be to get the hell out and make an early rendezvous with Stieff.'

Schelling grunted. 'What about the Englishman?'

'He'll be quiet. He's scared stiff.'

'I didn't mean that. We won't be able to leave him behind when we go. The second they find out von Stuerzbecher's missing, the *Tommis* will be all over these hills. If he's left alive to tell them he was held prisoner by three Germans, they'll know the break-out was organised from the outside.'

Christian had already considered this, but for the present he shelved the decision. 'Maybe we'll take him with us, release him on the coast.'

There was a moment's silence. 'I'll do it,' offered Schelling, leaving Christian in no doubt what 'it' was.

'If anyone's going to do it it'll be me. But it may not be necessary. Wish me luck.'

Schelling watched Christian pick his way carefully down the slope. Soon he was lost amongst the trees.

Bodywork covered with a light mantle of snow and frost, the yellow van was where Christian had left it. He examined the area for footprints; there were none. The engine turned over at the third attempt. Choke half out, he pulled on to the road and headed for Keswick.

Old man Foster was far from pleased that his only available driver had sent an unknown replacement without so much as a by-your-leave. That was typical of the younger generation, no sense of responsibility.

'What's your name, son?'

Christian told him, remembering to call himself Charlie and not Charles. The latter was a bit too upper class, as the English term went.

'You're not from around here, not with that accent.'

Christian said that he was originally from London, but (recalling where Alan's girl lived) had spent the last few years in Penrith. He added that he'd been over the delivery round with Alan and to prove it rattled off a list of names and addresses. Foster seemed satisfied.

'But don't think I'm paying you both.'

'No need,' Christian reassured him. 'You pay Alan, he'll pay me.'

'You're a trusting sort of sod, aren't you?'

It took an hour to load up the various trays of freshly baked loaves and buns, but by 7 a.m. Christian was ready to leave.

'And make sure you're back here by two o'clock for the afternoon deliveries,' was Foster's parting shot.

A couple of miles outside Keswick Christian parked on a grass verge. It was getting lighter now, the road busier, but no one paid any attention.

His first task was to push to the extreme back of the van the three dozen loaves destined for Skiddaw. Secondly, he opened the bonnet and disconnected the battery leads. It was doubtful if anyone would stop and ask him his business, but if they did he wanted a good reason for being there.

He sat and smoked for an hour, and at 8.15 reconnected the leads. If he drove steadily he should be outside Skiddaw at 8.25.

At 8.20, in Hut 9, Franz Mohr said: 'Come on, let's not give the *Tommis* any excuse to put us all in the cooler.'

'You've got a bloody alarm clock in that head of yours,' called Theo Emke. To Hans Baum, with a slight gesture, he indicated that it was time for roll-call.

On the bunk once occupied by Emil Wielen, Kurt von Stuerzbecher, fully dressed, decided he would indulge himself for two more minutes in the comparative warmth of the hut. Though probably, he told himself, it's not the warmth that interests you at all; it's the unwillingness to face another boring day, compounded by the fact that tomorrow's the 12th. But he would go, he concluded. He would tell Otto Breithaupt immediately after roll-call that he would accept the last place in the Rabbit Run. It was probably an error of judgement, but he had spent far too much of his life being active to tolerate another second of captivity.

In twos and threes and occasionally alone, the POWs made their way over to the Pig Pen. Probably not more than half a dozen saw the yellow van come to a halt outside the main gates.

The *Tommi* guard walked round to the driver's side, his expression one of cautious puzzlement. 'Foster's?'

It was an idiotic question, but Christian knew what he meant. He also knew that the military had little time for the civilian population, and vice versa.

'If that's what it says on the side of the van, that's where I'm from.'

'All right, mate, keep your shirt on. Where's the other driver?'

'If you mean Alan, he's either sick or hung-over or getting stuck into that girl of his over in Penrith. Now open the gates, will you? Old Foster told me to make you first on the list because you buggers have been complaining. But I can't hang around all day. Either get the gates open or I'll leave you till this afternoon.'

'All right, all right. Christ, anyone would think you owned the business.'

The guard waved an arm and both sets of gates swung open. Christian drove on slowly. Ahead of him, no more than forty or fifty yards away, he could see the POWs assembling for morning *Appell*.

From his previous day's observations Christian remembered that Alan, once through the inner gates, had turned sharp left and pulled up tight against what was evidently the guardroom. But he was a new driver, wasn't he? Any fool could see that. He would be forgiven if he didn't park in the right place.

Instead of parking with his nearside adjacent to the guardroom, he drove in a wide arc so that the nose was now facing the gates; the rear doors, out of which he would remove the bread trays, were directly opposite the Exercise Yard. It brought the van and the POWs ten yards closer to one another. Given more time that ten could have been twenty, but he wanted to start his performance before the *Tommi* NCOs, already consulting their lists, began calling the roll.

A corporal and two privates descended the guardroom steps. Christian opened the rear doors.

'You're early today,' said the corporal to Christian's back.

'That's right. I'm early because I get up early. While you were still dreaming of Betty Grable I was on the road. Now where the hell are those bloody trays?' He made a pretence of searching.

'Shake it up, can't you? It's bloody freezing out here.'

Christian brought his head out of the depths of the van. 'I'm damned if I can find them. There are supposed to be three dozen loaves here for you lot.'

As Christian looked up there was an immediate flicker of recognition in the corporal's eyes.

'I know you, don't I? You're not the regular driver, but I know you from somewhere.'

Christian knew precisely where, but it was better that it came from the *Tommi*.

'I've got it. You were in the pub last night, you and the other driver. He was knocking it back like he'd won a sweepstake.'

'Which explains why I'm doing the round today while he's still tucked up in bed.' Christian scratched his head. 'Anyway, someone's forgotten to load your stuff so you'd better take somebody else's. I'll sort it out later.' He beckoned the nearest of the privates. 'Here, grab one end of this.'

The *Tommi* took one end of the tray while Christian took the other. Suddenly the contents were on the ground, in the snow and the slush.

'You bloody fool!' yelled Christian. His words echoed throughout the compound. 'Now look what you've done!'

The *Tommi* protested that it wasn't his fault, that Christian had let his own end slip. But Christian would have none of that and continued to rant.

In Hut 9's rank Theo Emke and Fritz Uhde grinned at each other when they saw what was going on. Serve the *Tommis* right. All that fresh bread and not a morsel of it for the POWs. They would get the stale stuff, yesterday's leftovers, last bloody week's leftovers. The way the van was parked they could not only see the loaves, they could smell them. A couple of hundred mouths watered.

Von Stuerzbecher stood on tiptoe and peered over Franz Mohr's head to get a better look. The loaves on the ground between them, the driver seemed about ready to take a swing at one of the *Tommis*. To make matters worse, some of the nearer prisoners were now jeering raucously, and the driver, in his anger, turned round to give them a vicious V-sign.

The blood drained from von Stuerzbecher's face. Unless his eyes were going, the man now glaring at them all from less than forty metres away was his old friend Christian Eicke.

'Are you all right?' asked Emke anxiously. 'You look as though you've seen a ghost.'

'I'm fine.' Von Stuerzbecher's mind was racing. 'Theo, I don't think I've ever felt better.'

The corporal from the pub had hold of one of Christian's arms. He wasn't at all happy with the situation. This driver had biceps like iron.

'For Chrissake take it easy! What's a few lousy loaves of bread?'

'They may be a few lousy loaves to you'—Christian was still shouting—'but it means I've got to make another trip back here this afternoon. If I give you what's left there'll be nothing for anyone else.'

'So you make another trip. It's not the end of the world.'

'And who's going to pay for the stuff on the ground?' Christian gave one of the loaves a kick.

'The Army will. Just tell your guvnor to book it out to the camp. And for Christ's sake get a hold of yourself.'

Christian decided it was high time he did exactly that. Judging from the jeers, just about every German on parade had witnessed his histrionics.

'All right. But don't expect me back before midday. If you're short of bread until then, blame him.' He gestured towards the unfortunate private, who was still protesting that it wasn't his fault.

Leaving the loaves where they lay, Christian got behind the wheel. The guards at both gates had also seen the incident and they waved him straight through without a search.

'Bloody madman,' swore the corporal. 'I wish I had him in my platoon for a couple of weeks. You two berks, pick up those bloody loaves and get rid of them.'

'You're sure?' asked Major Breithaupt.

'Of course I'm sure.' Von Stuerzbecher thumped the table with his fist. 'Good God, I spent most of the Thirties with the Eicke family. I was going to marry Christian's sister. I know him as well as I know myself.'

Immediately after roll-call von Stuerzbecher had sought out Otto Breithaupt, who in turn called an emergency meeting of the Escape Committee. They were now in Hut 5, trying to figure out the significance of Christian's presence, assuming it was Christian Eicke.

'A man's memory can play peculiar tricks,' murmured Kapitän-leutnant Heydt, 'especially in a place like this. You were some distance away, the light was poor. You'll forgive me, I know, but it seems almost unbelievable that a German officer appears on our doorstep just weeks after you were shot down.'

In spite of their inevitable doubts all four members of the Escape Committee were looking at von Stuerzbecher with renewed interest. He was a very senior officer, they knew, but it wasn't unknown for even senior officers to exaggerate their own importance. If he hadn't made a mistake, however, he was as valuable to the Reich as he had hinted, for the presence of a German officer disguised as a British civilian could only mean one thing.

'I tell you it was Eicke,' insisted von Stuerzbecher. 'Look at that ridiculous business of the bread and the trouble he caused. And look how he made certain that everyone within earshot would know he was coming back at midday. It was play-acting, pure and simple. He arrived at roll-call and created a disturbance because he wanted me to see him. He knew damn well I'd recognise him, which is no doubt why he was selected for the mission. And he's coming back at noon in the hope that I can get a message to him.'

Franz Mohr admitted it made sense. 'If he'd found a way to get you out—I assume that is his intention—he'd have had no need to take the risk he did. I just hope to God it isn't his intention to smuggle you out in the back of that wretched van.'

'That won't be necessary.' Otto Breithaupt was now convinced that von Stuerzbecher's eyes had not deceived him. 'By one of those absurd coincidences that happen in war, Herr Eicke has arrived at precisely the right time. He won't have to find a way to free you. Tomorrow night you'll be free in any case. I take it you'll now accept the last place in the Rabbit Run?'

Von Stuerzbecher wasted no time on false humility. 'I will.'

'Then that's settled. But it leads us to the problem of letting Eicke know our intentions. This is not just for your sake,' he told von Stuerzbecher, 'but for everyone's. If Eicke isn't told of our plans he might try something on his own, and that could ruin Rabbit Run for everyone. Any ideas?'

Heinrich Weiss had one and he massaged his one good eye while he mulled it over. Eventually he said: 'With Eicke expecting some kind of signal a dozen methods could be used. But I think his choice of vehicle has provided the answer for us.'

The other four listened as Weiss outlined a tentative scheme. When he had finished Heydt remarked. 'I hope for all our sakes this is not a question of mistaken identity. If it is, we are going to have on our hands one very surprised British driver.'

It was five minutes before noon when Christian neared the camp for the second time. He was pushing his luck in more than one respect, and he knew it. By this time, dozens of Foster's customers would have telephoned the bakery, complaining that their deliveries were overdue. Foster would doubtless put down the first few calls to his temporary driver's inexperience and lack of familiarity with the route. But soon he would get worried. He might even call the police.

The outer perimeter sentry recognised the van and gave the signal for both lots of gates to be opened.

Bloody fool, thought Christian, hitting the horn in acknowledgement; I could have a dozen Storm troopers with Schmeissers in the back.

Obergefreiter Willi Braune and Unteroffizier Hans Geith were lounging near the Pig Pen when Christian pulled up by the guardroom. And if the camp staff had been paying attention they would have noticed that many more spectators than usual, officers and other ranks, were watching the volley ball game. Even more significant the whole group, some twenty or twenty-five strong, sauntered forward as Christian opened the van's rear doors.

'Your guvnor's been on the blower playing merry bloody hell.' The corporal Christian had rowed with earlier, the same two privates in tow, delivered the message with malicious glee as he descended the guardroom steps. 'Wants to know where the hell you've been.'

'Is it my fault if the van breaks down?' complained Christian. 'Christ, if he spent some of his profits keeping his vehicles in a proper state of repair we'd all get along a lot better.'

'You should join our lot, mate, then you'd know all about cockups.'

'I'm not that stupid.'

'Here, watch it.'

Christian never did find out what he was supposed to watch. Led by Braune and Geith, a score of POWs made a sudden dart for the van, calling rapidly to each other in German. Although he had been expecting something to happen, Christian was unprepared for this, and he found himself thrust to one side as dozens of hands

177

reached past him and into the van for the freshly baked bread.

The *Tommis* were transfixed with bewildered horror. They didn't even make a move for their rifles. Neither did the watch-tower guards or the other British personnel in the vicinity have an opportunity to raise more than a feeble bleat of protest before what became known as the Great Bread Raid was over, with POWs dashing in all directions, clutching their spoils.

Christian thought he caught a glimpse of von Stuerzbecher's face in the melee, grinning fiendishly, but everything happened so fast he could easily have been mistaken. Nevertheless, he felt something thrust into his pocket.

'Jesus Christ.' The guard corporal stared bug-eyed at a score of disappearing backs. 'Jesus Christ on a bicycle.'

Christian knew he'd be expected to throw a fit. 'What the bloody blue blazes was all that about?' he raged. 'Look at the mess!' The area around the van resembled a battleground, and what had not been filched was unrecognisable as food. 'What am I going to say to old man Foster? Don't you feed these bloody people, for the love of God?'

The corporal could see his stripes disappearing like straw in a gale and he was happy to hand over the whole matter to the CSM, who had come out of his office to see what all the noise was about. It was one of those days when the Commandant and the Adjutant were away simultaneously, and CSM Purser took it upon himself to defuse the situation. After reassuring Christian that full restitution would be made for the damaged and stolen foodstuffs, he asked that the matter be kept private. 'It won't do the war effort any good, lad, for half the population of Keswick to know what went on.'

Christian promised to say nothing. It wasn't often a British senior NCO apologised to an Oberleutnant and that in itself was reward enough.

When Major Mitchell returned and was told of the incident, he summoned Otto Breithaupt. Breithaupt professed not to know the names of the perpetrators; it had all happened so quickly. Though doubting the truth of this, Mitchell accepted it. There was little else he could do. He was, in any event, more concerned about the apparent inefficiency of his staff than a few loaves of bread. It could have been the armoury under siege and not just a delivery van. But Breithaupt was told that although no individual would be punished, the POW community would pay a collective fine amounting to the cost of the damage.

Breithaupt agreed that this was probably the best solution, and left the Commandant's office feeling mightily pleased with himself.

As night fell, a thousand feet up Skiddaw Christian, too, was feeling highly satisfied with the day's events.

After leaving the camp he had driven the van five miles towards Penrith before dumping it up to its axles in mud in a clump of trees, and hiking back. With any luck, it would be weeks before it was found.

It had crossed his mind to use it for the trip back to the coast, but he had quickly abandoned the idea as too risky. Come morning it would be on someone's missing vehicles list, and it was far too distinctive a colour to be driven with impunity.

While Wolf Schultz prepared a cold supper (fresh bread tonight), Christian reread von Stuerzbecher's note. In block capitals it said simply:

TUNNEL BREAK-OUT TIMED FOR 2200 DECEMBER 12th. STRUCTURE EXTREME WEST SOUTHERN PERIMETER.

Christian identified the building without difficulty, in the far left-hand corner of the compound from where they were camped. Christ, they must have been working on it for months, long before Kurt was shot down. But while it solved one problem, it created another.

'He won't be coming alone, that's a hundred per cent certain,' Schelling had pointed out. 'But what do we do with the others?'

'That's not our affair. Our job is to get von Stuerzbecher home.'

'You can't just abandon them, Christian.' This from Wolf Schultz. 'They won't stand a chance.'

'Neither will we if we start hiking across England with half the Luftwaffe in tow. If it's no more than a couple, perhaps I'll think about it. But more than likely there'll be a dozen of them. You don't construct a tunnel for a handful.'

It pained him to say it but it had to be said. Coming in had been relatively easy; no one was expecting them. Getting out would be a thousand times more difficult. It might be morning before the escape was discovered, but when it was all hell would be let loose, with the coast a favourite target for the pursuers. Even four men were going to have trouble; more than four was asking a miracle.

They fed themselves and their prisoner and settled back to the dull if dangerous business of waiting for a whole day and night. Although physically tired after his early start, Christian was still very much mentally alert, and he volunteered to take the first outside watch.

They had decided earlier that with so much illumination emanating from the camp, it was quite safe to smoke, and Christian lit up. It was still desperately cold, too cold to snow, and there was a vicious wind blowing from the north-east. For no reason at all he thought of the survival manual, where he remembered reading that for every knot of wind on wet clothes the body temperature dropped one degree.

Replacing the cigarettes in his breast pocket, his fingers touched the sealed orders given to him by Weil. Abruptly he decided to disobey the Standartenfuehrer's instructions by opening them immediately. Christ knows what would be happening thirty hours hence.

The single sheet of paper was couched in official language and signed by Reichsfuehrer-SS Himmler himself. But paraphrased it read that if there was any danger of Generalmajor von Stuerzbecher being retaken alive by the British, Oberleutnant Christian Eicke was to shoot him personally.

15

12 December

Throughout the war, with one or two notable exceptions, troops
selected for prison camp duties were of a far inferior calibre to
those with fighting units. Like Major David Mitchell, many of the
officers had suffered wounds rendering them unfit for active service though not totally incapacitated; others were too old; still
others, such as Adrian Thorogood, had their papers temporarily
slotted into the wrong pigeon-hole.

If it can be said that repetition dulls the senses, the Skiddaw
guards were totally blunt, for anyone with half an ear attuned to
atmosphere would have sensed, during the 12th, an air of sup-
pressed excitement among the POWs. Even those who were
not in on the break knew that something was imminent. Willi
Braune summed it up. 'If we have a full complement of prisoners by the end of the week, I'll apply for a commission in the
RAF.'

All over, last-minute preparations were being made. Civilian
clothes were checked, money counted, counterfeit papers stashed
away, prayers said. The prayers would be needed most of all. Of
those due to make the break only Franz Mohr and one of the naval
officers spoke a little English. Apart from von Stuerzbecher, of
course.

There was to be no choir practice this day and no work on the
tunnel. As far as anyone could estimate they were through now,
under the trees on the south side. An hour's digging upwards, less
than a cubic metre of earth, and gravity would do the rest. They
would be out. Not least of those to heave a sigh of relief at the
prospect were Leutnants Kaehler and Preiss.

Apart from being unutterably filthy, the two junior officers were not much the worse for wear, in much better condition than anyone could have expected a week ago, although they were completely disorientated. Time had become meaningless. They slept when they were tired and stayed awake when they were not. Bone-chilling cold was a major problem, but that was partly alleviated by the extra blankets Breithaupt had smuggled to them and increased rations. By far and away the worst part of their stay underground was the unavoidable smell of their own bodily functions. Johann Preiss, at least, knew he would never forget that.

They passed part of their waking hours in physical exercise, paying particular attention to the legs. There wasn't enough room, or oxygen, for running on the spot, but they each managed five hundred knee-bends a day and one hundred push-ups. When they wearied of that they tried elementary isometrics. It says much for the feeling of friendship they had for one another that at no time did either lose his temper.

During their non-active hours, which were in the majority, they played guessing games or described in detail a seven-course meal, right down to the last cup of coffee and the positioning of the silver. To begin with they invented a different meal each day, but Kaehler's descriptions were so spectacularly graphic, so mouth-wateringly accurate, that Preiss decided he didn't want to hear any more.

Sometimes they read, but torch batteries were at a premium and this activity was limited. In any case, their favourite pastime, one that did not require light after the initial stages, was going over their escape route.

On the second day of their incarceration Major Breithaupt produced a torn-out page of a school atlas map of northern England. 'I'm sorry I can only let you have this overnight, but you'll appreciate it's in great demand.'

The scale was too small to be of much practical use on the outside, but nevertheless they memorised the major roads and towns thoroughly.

It was a convention of escapes from Skiddaw, as it was from most other camps, that routes were never discussed except by those who were travelling together. Neither Kaehler or Preiss, therefore, knew if anyone else would be going their way. On balance they doubted it. The obvious places to make for were the ports of

Workington and Whitehaven. From there, with luck, an escapee could stow away on a coastal vessel sailing for Liverpool, and from Liverpool it was a simple matter, in theory, to find a ship going to neutral Eire. The trouble was, what was apparent to the POWs was equally apparent to the British, and both ports were always closely watched, particularly after a break-out. It was certainly quicker to get to the west coast than to anywhere else in the British Isles, but it was pointless arriving if the coast was crawling with *Tommis*.

'We'll fix the bastards,' enthused Peter Kaehler. 'We'll take the main road to Carlisle and then head for Newcastle.'

Preiss traced the route with his forefinger. 'There are ports galore on the east coast. If we can't steal some kind of boat we don't deserve to get out.'

Neither considered the difficulties, the almost insurmountable obstacles to be overcome before they reached German-occupied territory. Like their counterparts in German camps, if they had sat down to calculate the odds against them they would never have made a move.

'While the *Tommis* are running around in circles on the west coast, we'll be hundreds of kilometres away.'

'And we'll be home for Christmas.'

Oberleutnant Theo Emke felt more or less the same way, but with the advantage of four or five years in age over the two young Leutnants, he was more realistic about his chances. Still, the important thing was getting out, as Major Breithaupt had impressed upon all the Luftwaffe officers. 'Look upon it as a bombing mission. You don't expect to hit the target every time and there are always some losses. But you have a nuisance value far out of proportion to your chances of success. While the *Tommis* are looking for you, they can't be doing the thousand and one other things they should be doing.'

Theo Emke was travelling alone. Earlier in the month Werner Herburg had made a tentative suggestion that they make the run together, but Emke had brushed him off as politely as he could. It was not that he disliked Herburg, far from it, but he felt his chances would be enhanced going solo. About the only person he would have taken was Hans Baum, but that of course was out of the question. It was hard to know if Baum was even aware of what was going on, though as morning became afternoon Emke was conscious that Baum's eyes were always on him, like a dog who is being left behind on a summer walk. It became too much for Emke finally, and he went out into the compound, casting an anxious glance skywards as he did so.

He wasn't the only one worried about the weather. It hadn't snowed for the last couple of days, not more than the occasional flurry, and Fritz Uhde knew that the difference between success and failure depended upon whether it snowed heavily their first night out.

For Uhde there was no question of not getting back to Germany. Although he had told no one in the camp, the reason he wrote so often to his young wife was because he was uncertain of her fidelity. At the end of the week in which they first met, she had made it quite clear by word and gesture that she wanted to go to bed with him, and the night that followed gave him more pleasure than he thought humanly possible There was nothing she wouldn't do, no experiment she wouldn't try. And while he was with her and she was his, he was the happiest man alive.

But he was wise enough to realise that while he was the immediate object of her sexuality, if he were absent for any length of time she would find it difficult to sleep alone. She wasn't a whore, but she had basic needs that had to be satisfied. If he wasn't there to provide an outlet, sooner or later someone else would. He had to get home, that was all there was to it.

The naval officers under Kapitänleutnant Heydt were to travel as a pack. They knew there were risks in this—if one was recaptured they all were—but they considered the risks worth taking. For them there would be no nonsense about stowing away on a boat to Eire or anywhere else. There were five of them and they were fully experienced in all matters of the sea. If they couldn't steal a ship, any sort of ship, and sail it to Brazil if necessary, they didn't deserve their badges of rank.

'The trouble with pilots,' Heydt was fond of saying, 'is that they have no stamina for long missions. Take away their aeroplanes and breakfast in the Mess and they're lost.'

To a man the naval personnel agreed with him. (It's no secret that in the armed forces of any nation the air branch is thoroughly disliked by the army and the navy, who see air crew the way a marathon runner sees sprinters. They take risks, surely, but only for an hour or two each time. Then it's heigh-ho for home and a medal. An hour in the air does not compare with weeks at sea or months knee-deep in mud.)

On his stroll around the compound Theo Emke came across Werner Herburg, who looked up hopefully. But Emke merely smiled and walked on.

Herburg shrugged philosophically to himself, he couldn't blame Emke for wanting to go it alone, but it would have calmed some of the butterflies now racing around his stomach to know that he would have a companion on the break.

Werner Herburg was a realist and knew he had only been included in the dozen for Rabbit Run because of the money found in the chess set. He had put it all into the escape fund because that was his nature; he had certainly not expected Major Breithaupt to reward him with a place on the break. What was more, if he were honest with himself he knew he should have told Breithaupt at the beginning that he'd far rather the place went to someone else, someone more deserving; for he didn't really want to go, as he had never really wanted to be a flier. That the High Command thought him ideally suited to the job of piloting a bomber didn't alter the fact that he was of the opposite opinion. Every mission, and they'd been few enough before the Spitfire got him, had been preceded by bouts of physical sickness. But somehow he'd got the aircraft off the tarmac and brought it back all but once. If the truth were known, however, he was not unhappy in the camp. He didn't even really want to go home. Home meant a domineering mother (who ideally should have taken his place in the Luftwaffe) and the horrific thought of further missions.

Still, he was stuck with it now and, as he had done throughout his life, he would try his best.

For different reasons Franz Mohr, now playing chess in the German Mess with Otto Breithaupt, was also determined to try his best. He couldn't afford to do anything else. Another twenty-eight days in the cooler would finish him.

Major Breithaupt moved a knight and successfully forked Mohr's remaining rook and bishop.

'You'll notice that with my customary chivalry I'm taking advantage of your preoccupation to beat the hell out of you.'

Mohr smiled thinly. 'It'll be the last time.'

'Let's hope so.'

185

Mohr opted to save his rook and moved it out of reach. Breithaupt studied the board keenly.

'You're all set, of course. I mean, I'm not keeping you from anything?'

Mohr's outside clothes were already bundled up, papers and money in the trousers pocket. Emergency rations, mostly chocolate, were in a waterproof wrapping. It would take him under five minutes to prepare. 'Nothing.'

'Good. Don't forget to send me a postcard.'

'I just hope it's from Berlin and not the London Cage.'

'It will be—from Berlin, I mean. I have a good feeling about this one.'

After much deliberation, Breithaupt took the bishop.

'It'll be your turn one day, Otto.'

'Not me,' Breithaupt grinned cheerfully. 'I'm indispensable here, haven't you heard? Besides, with you and Heydt both going that means two spare seats on the Escape Committee. If I went too Hauptmann Weiss would fill them with his cronies and run the camp like a reform school.'

'It still seems bloody unfair.' Mohr decided that attack was the best form of defence and swooped down on Breithaupt's back rank with his queen. 'Unless the *Tommis* are fortunate enough to capture an Oberst, you'll remain senior officer until the end of the war.'

'The penalties of organisational brilliance, dear boy. In any case, I'm only senior officer technically. Karl outranks me so much that a day's pay of his is equal to a month's of mine.'

'Only for another few hours.'

'With luck.' Breithaupt moved a pawn to give his king an escape hatch. 'You know, I still can't get over it—yesterday, I mean. It's just as well I hadn't offered the last place to someone else.'

'He could always have tagged on the end.'

'And make thirteen? No chance. There'd have been a riot.'

'Another would have made fourteen.'

Breithaupt shook his head. 'We discussed that at the beginning if you remember. In theory there's nothing to prevent the whole wretched camp going out, but those watch-tower lights, in spite of the automatic traverse, don't make it easy. Even with the trees as partial cover, if a guard turns round at the wrong moment you're all in the soup.'

'It's the first man out who'll have the greatest burden,' said Mohr. 'He'll be going up blind, unable to see which way the guards are facing.'

'There's nothing we can do about that; it's one of the hazards of the business. It'll be you, incidentally, the first man.'

'Me?' This was the first Mohr had heard about the escape order.

'I can't send Emke, he's too much of a bloody giant, and Heydt insists that the navy go out together. Kaehler and Preiss I'm leaving until last. There won't be much light coming down that hole, but it'll get them used to the outside again. They'll be as blind as bats otherwise. Uhde's too young to trust in the vanguard, and I'm a bit worried about Oberleutnant Herburg. Oh, he'll be all right, I'm not suggesting anything different, but he's rather timid. That leaves you or Karl. I can't send him first because I don't know what orders the people on the outside have been given. It may well be that they're to get him the hell out of it above all else, and it'll be necessary for the first man to make sure the coast's clear for the second man, and so forth. Which leaves you. Karl will go second. If they whisk him away immediately it'll be up to you to wait around for the third man. Sorry and all that, but noblesse oblige.'

'It's all right. A minute more, a minute less, it makes no difference. Unless we get a whole night's start they'll catch up with us anyway. You're in check, incidentally.'

Breithaupt moved a bishop between Mohr's queen and his own king. 'I'm calling a final briefing immediately after this afternoon's roll-call,' he said, 'but there's no harm in telling you now that you'll all move across to the chapel in escape order, which means you first, beginning at 2000 hours. Five minute intervals between each man. Even allowing for delays, you should all be inside the tunnel by 2100.'

'The door will be open, of course?'

'I've arranged that. I was going to do it myself, but I want to be last across. I'm using Braune and Geith. As they seem to spend most of the dark hours flitting between their huts and the boiler-room, they might as well make themselves useful. They think we're having some sort of meeting there.'

'He's a good man, Willi Braune.'

'They both are. I was most impressed with the way they handled that bread business yesterday.'

Mohr moved his rook horizontally. It was now in the column adjacent to his queen with a free run down the board.

'You said you'll be last across. Does that mean Hauptmann Weiss won't be coming to wave goodbye?'

'Correct. He says his one eye isn't really good enough for moving around unseen in the dark, but frankly I suspect a trace of envy. It's all very well him saying he doesn't want to go home because of his injuries, but it must be hard, watching others take advantage of your own planning.'

'It's the same for you.'

'No, it isn't.' Breithaupt eased forward a pawn to threaten Mohr's rook. 'We stay for different reasons. I admit that when I slide the altar back into place I'll feel a twinge of something, but it won't be envy. Uncertainty probably. Perhaps even a touch of despair. I won't know anything, won't even know whether you're alive or dead or on the high seas until I get a postcard or message or they frog-march you back through those bloody gates. That will be the hardest part, not knowing.'

'You'll also have to arrange for a new chess partner,' said Mohr slyly, his finger on the rook.

'True enough.'

'Though perhaps you'll choose someone nearer your own weight next time. Checkmate.'

Franz Mohr pushed forward the rook. Otto Breithaupt stared at the board in disbelief before bursting into gales of laughter.

Christian gave the order to strike camp and pack up a few minutes before 8 p.m. Although it was still two hours to break-out, they had to get down the mountain and skirt the camp far to the south before coming in through the trees opposite the tunnel exit. Now all that remained was the vexatious question of Alan Miles.

'You can't leave him, Christian,' said Schelling urgently. Normally a kind and generous man away from battle, Schelling was also the archetypal realist. 'If you leave him in the open overnight he'll die of exposure, if he doesn't summon help first. If he's still alive tomorrow the *Tommis* will certainly find him.'

'We're taking him with us. We'll release him at the coast.'

'You're a fool, Christian.'

Christian remembered the *Vernichtungslager,* the extermination camp, and his argument with Standartenfuehrer Weil. Either he had meant what he said then or they were the self-excuses of a drunk.

'I'll thank you to remember who you're talking to, Feldwebel,' he said coldly.

Schelling stiffened to attention. 'As you wish, Herr Oberleutnant.'

Christian shook his head sorrowfully. Perhaps Schelling would have understood a little more if he'd known of Himmler's orders concerning von Stuerzbecher. But if it ever became necessary to shoot a senior officer, and an old friend at that, the responsibility was his alone.

He walked across to where Alan Miles, his hands still bound, was cowering against a tree. Alan understood no German, but he sensed that the two men had just been arguing about him and that a decision had been reached.

'In a minute or two we'll be leaving here and taking up a position opposite the camp,' Christian told him. 'You'll be coming with us. At ten o'clock some German POWs will be making an escape bid and from you I want to hear not a sound. We'll be very close to the wire, but if you make the slightest attempt to attract attention, by word or gesture, you'll be shot. Is that perfectly clear?'

'Yes. Are you going to let me go then? I won't say anything.'

'You'll be released some time tomorrow, possibly the next day. You will be unharmed. I might add that the decision to keep you alive is mine. At least one of the others and probably both would have you killed here and now.' The youngster shuddered uncontrollably at the thought. 'So don't upset them. More important, don't do anything to upset me. I may have lost their trust by allowing you to live, but I won't hesitate to win it back if you so much as breathe out of turn.'

'Ready to move,' called Schultz.

'Okay,' said Christian, 'let's go.'

At approximately the same time as Christian and his team began making their way down the mountain, Willi Braune broke into the chapel while Hans Geith kept watch for patrolling guards. It was an ordinary padlock and presented no difficulties, though Willi was careful to rearrange the broken mechanism in such a way that a perfunctory examination would reveal no trace of damage.

This done, they hid in the shadows until the searchlight beams swung past them before heading back to their hut. There was no card game this night; Lance-corporal Cade was on duty. But there was one scheduled for tomorrow and they were both looking forward to it.

At 2000 hours on the dot Oberleutnant Franz Mohr took a last look around Hut 9 and slipped out into the compound. Over his shoulder in a sack he carried the clothes and accessories Peter Kaehler and Johann Preiss would wear for the break.

Situated in the second row of POW accommodation, Hut 9 was two hundred yards from the chapel and almost diametrically opposite it. But this was a help rather than a hindrance as Mohr could glide from row to row, north to south, before making a final dash for the shadows of the German Mess on the southern perimeter wire. From there it was simply a matter of following the wire along, behind the Mess and behind the MT Pool, until he reached the chapel. The watch-tower between the Mess and the MT Pool presented no problems, thanks to the automatic traverses the *Tommis* insisted upon using. In theory no section of the compound should be unilluminated for more than ten seconds, but in practice it didn't work out that way. The machinery was old and malfunctioned from time to time; rather like a domestic clock, it went faster or slower as the mood took it. The idiosyncrasies of each searchlight were well known to the POWs, though in any case ten seconds was more than enough time to move from building to building.

One . . . two . . . three . . . four . . . Mohr made the shelter of the central watch-tower without difficulty. He experienced a moment's panic when he heard voices, but he realised that they were coming from above his head, inside the tower itself, and that he was out of the guards' range of vision.

One . . . two . . . three . . . four . . . The whole length of the MT Pool during the seconds of darkness, a quick breather, then on to the chapel.

They had all realised weeks ago that getting from the rear of the chapel to the front and in through the door was going to be the most risky part of the manoeuvre. In sequence, the chapel door was illuminated by two of the searchlights on the north side of the compound. The one in the north-east corner swung anti-clockwise from north to south and back again. Ten seconds after it began its return trip the central light, whose main function was to illuminate the southern wire, lit up the same door. But because of a faulty cog somewhere in the mechanism, one time in four the central light was only six seconds behind. After that, things got back to normal. But as even ten seconds was cutting it a bit fine to get to the front of the chapel, open the door, go inside and close the door again, it would obviously be fatal to make the attempt when the interval between the lights was only six.

Mohr hugged the wall and counted. One to ten. Wait. One to ten again. Wait. One . . . two . . . three . . . four . . . five . . . six . . . Wait. North-east light coming back . . . and vanishing. Go.

Clutching his bundle Mohr raced for the door. Three . . . four . . . He saw the lock and froze. Five . . . six . . . Christ, hadn't Willi Braune . . . Seven . . . eight . . . He wrenched at the padlock. It came away in his hands. No time to do anything about that now. Nine . . . He threw himself inside and pushed the door shut behind him, leaning against it breathlessly, his heart pounding.

Ten . . .

But no shouts in the distance, nothing to show that the watchtower guards had spotted anything out of the ordinary.

Although the uncovered windows let in a certain amount of light, he waited a minute to allow his eyes to become accustomed to his surroundings before moving quickly towards the altar and putting his back against it. It moved an inch or two, then a couple of feet. Below, Preiss and Kaehler stiffened at this new and threatening noise.

'Peter? Johann? Are you there? Shine your torch, will you? I can't see a damned thing.'

The dim beam lit up Mohr's anxious face.

'Franz? Is it really you? Is it time?'

Mohr tossed down the bundle. 'It's me and it is. Your clothes are in there. Get into them as quickly as you can. This place is going to start filling up.'

One by one at the predetermined interval of five minutes the remaining POWs followed Mohr into the chapel and down into the Rabbit Run.

Next came von Stuerzbecher with Fritz Uhde hot on his heels. Uhde had miscalculated and allowed only a three-minute gap. After Uhde Werner Herburg arrived, panting like a man with a heart condition. The naval officers came next, with Kapitänleutnant Heydt bringing up the rear. At a quarter to nine Theo Emke's big feet and broad shoulders appeared.

'Christ, there's a smell down here. Haven't you been washing your socks, young Kaehler?'

'Shut up, Theo, and make yourself useful,' said Mohr. 'Take something to dig with and start making a hole. The rest of you, you all know the order of escape so let's keep it organised.'

Major Breithaupt was last to arrive, at three minutes to nine. Franz Mohr was waiting for him when he dropped through the floorboards beneath the altar.

'Is everyone here?'

'All except Emke. I've sent him up ahead to begin the hole.'

'Good.'

Breithaupt peered into a darkness only partly relieved by Kaehler's torchbeam. He didn't want to make a speech, but the Rabbit Run, the mere existence of it, was a major achievement and he couldn't let the occasion pass without saying something.

'I can't stay to see you off,' he began, 'because that altar has to be replaced before someone discovers the chapel door's been forced and decides to investigate. But it goes without saying that I wish each and every one of you all the luck in the world. Have a drink for me when you get home, but *get* home.'

There were murmurs of thanks and vows that they would.

'One other thing. Most of you will have guessed by now that Karl is not who he purports to be. I mention this only because he has some people waiting for him on the outside, though as he's number two they'll probably be on their way before the rest of you are out. But if you see them, ignore them, keep your distance. Don't try to join forces. That's it. Good luck.'

And then he was gone. A slight touch on Franz Mohr's shoulder, and he was up through the floorboards. The heavy altar was pushed back into place.

'Kaehler, shine the torch that way,' said Mohr. 'Let's see how Emke's getting on.'

Once within the area of the huts, Otto Breithaupt made no show of furtiveness. If anyone asked, he was on his way to the heads. Near Hut 7 he thought he caught a glimpse of Hauptmann Weiss, but he could have been mistaken. In any case, there was no reason why Weiss shouldn't be on the prowl.

Christian's team were in position opposite the chapel at 9.40. Sixty or seventy yards into the copse, they nevertheless had a more or less clear view of the south-west section of the compound.

Nothing moved save the trees. The wind was picking up, blowing roughly nor'nor'east. There was undoubtedly more snow on the way, but Christian refused to think about it. If it came, it came. He would worry about it when it happened.

He held up five fingers three times. Schelling, over to his right, and Wolf Schultz, standing guard over Alan Miles, signalled their understanding. Fifteen minutes to go.

At 9.48 Theo Emke came back down the tunnel in a state of great excitement. 'I'm through. I just felt a bloody great chunk of snow on my head.'

Mohr took the sharpened mess tin they were using as a shovel. In spite of the fact that he was trembling with anticipation, he issued the final orders coolly and concisely.

'Right, you all know the exit procedure so stick to it. We'll be a bit low on oxygen in there so no more than three people in the tunnel itself at any one time. The man in front will have the torch. Two flashes means he's under the hole. The next man can then come up. A single flash means wait. Good luck, everyone.'

On his hands and knees, the torch in his right hand, Mohr crawled the length of the tunnel, only stopping when he could go no further. He looked up and almost wept with exultation. Emke and gravity had done a magnificent job, and for the first time it was possible to stand up in the Rabbit Run. A foot or two above his head was a hole six inches in diameter, ready for widening. Through it and beyond he could see the lights from the camp. They were out.

'Look.'

Schelling pointed. Some forty yards away and over to their left, a figure was emerging from the ground.

Christian motioned the others to stay where they were and ran forward at the crouch. 'Over here,' he hissed.

Franz Mohr crawled towards him. They shook hands, both feeling faintly ridiculous.

'Franz Mohr, Oberleutnant.'

'Christian Eicke, same. Where's von Stuerzbecher?'

'Right behind me.'

It was two minutes before von Stuerzbecher's head appeared. Christian was beside him in a flash. There was no danger; the trees took care of that.

The German major-general shook himself like a dog.

'What the hell are you doing here, Christian?'

'Getting senior officers who can't fly aeroplanes out of trouble. Come on, let's get to hell out of here. There are three others in my party, two NCOs and a prisoner. I'll explain it all when we're a million miles away.'

More than a little envious, Mohr watched them disappear into the darkness. It was quite an advantage, having rank. Oberleutnant Eicke would undoubtedly have their escape route well planned.

'Can I come out now?'

Mohr almost laughed out loud in spite of himself. Fritz Uhde sounded like a tired child after a long game of hide and seek.

'Yes. Shake it up.' He waited until Uhde was beside him. 'See you in Germany,' he said, and was gone.

One by one the Rabbit Run escapers emerged from their burrow. After Uhde came Herburg, who felt he'd been walking an hour before the first of the naval officers appeared. But he was a quarter of a mile away, determined to put as much distance as he could between himself and the camp before morning, before Kapitänleutnant Heydt joined his men.

Emke had to widen the hole. Two feet six inches might be adequate for Mohr and the others, but it was at least six inches too narrow for himself. It took him valuable minutes but then he was on his way, heading west.

Blinking, Peter Kaehler came out ahead of Johann Preiss. The filigreeing effect of the trees made the camp lights barely sufficient to read by, but that was for men who hadn't been in almost total darkness for a week.

Once on level ground they each tested their legs, each their balance. The exercises had paid off. Apart from a slight feeling of giddiness they felt ready for anything.

'The hole,' whispered Kaehler.

'Oh Christ, I almost forgot.'

Breithaupt had asked them to fill it in with snow as best they could. It was unlikely the deception would last long, but it was always possible.

'That should do it.'

They took a last look at the camp, sleeping peacefully now.

'Good bloody bye,' said Preiss.

Major Breithaupt lay awake in his bunk, fearfully listening for any sound that would tell him the escape had failed. He heard nothing. An hour passed. Then two. They'd made it.

A few minutes after midnight, more due to nerves than anything else, he found it necessary to go across to the heads. In one of the shower sections he came across Oberleutnant Kapp. The artillery officer had been hanged and his executioners had made a messy job of it.

Breithaupt now realised the significance of Weiss's presence in the compound, and he had to admit that his security officer had been clever about the whole affair. No one would suspect murder, certainly not Thorogood. To all intents and purposes an informer had taken his own life for failing to tell the *Tommis* about an escape before it happened.

16

The blizzard hit them with the vengeful suddenness of an assassin's dagger. One minute they could see the dark outline of Bassenthwaite Lake over to their left; the next they were blinded by a million icy flakes, racing before a nor'-easter.

In the van of the tiny column Christian cursed out loud and glanced over his shoulder. Next in line, von Stuerzbecher was struggling; a month of POW regimen had left him far from fit. Behind him Alan Miles, his hands unbound now, was also feeling the pace. Bringing up the rear Schelling and Schultz were going easily, but the entire quintet could only travel as fast as the slowest.

Christian beckoned von Stuerzbecher to join him.

'It's going to be tougher from now on, but we've got to keep going.' He shouted to make himself heard. 'We have to be within striking distance of the coast by morning, before they start setting up road blocks and covering the countryside with troops.'

'How far d'you think we've come?'

Christian knew the answer to that without referring to his map. They were still on the Keswick-Carlisle road. The next objective was Bewaldeth, where they would swing west.

'About a quarter of the way, perhaps a little less. If it wasn't for this bloody snow we'd make it easily.'

'Perhaps it'll go off.'

But it didn't, and their rate of progress dropped to a snail's-pace. Even when they left Bassenthwaite far behind and a bend in the road brought the prevailing wind slightly to their right, they were still averaging less than a couple of kilometres an hour.

At 1 a.m. Christian came to the conclusion that he was tiring von Stuerzbecher needlessly. If they kept going and the blizzard blew itself out at dawn, the major-general would be too tired to go any further.

He raised his arm and called a halt. 'It's no use, we've got to get out of this. If my calculations are correct Bewaldeth's just up ahead.'

Schelling remembered it from coming in, a tiny hamlet, a cluster of twenty houses or so, and a solitary general store. Because there had been lights showing in two or three downstairs windows, they'd given the place a wide berth by cutting across the fields. 'There was a barn or something in one of them.'

They left the road and were immediately knee deep in snow.

'Over that way,' called Schelling, but they had only covered a few yards before Wolf Schultz yelled at them to stop.

'Listen . . .'

They listened; nothing but the howl of the wind.

'I could have sworn I heard . . . There it is again.'

'Cows,' said Christian. 'Well done, Wolf. You're not going to find cows out on a night like this.'

They struck off at a tangent and found the barn after five minutes' searching. It was open on one side and a dozen or so cows were huddled together miserably against the far wall. Close by were twenty or thirty sheep, who eyed the newcomers nervously. The stench was appalling, but at least they were protected from the worst of the blizzard.

'Up there.'

A ladder led up to an open loft. One by one they trooped up it and flung themselves down on the straw.

Schelling slipped the rucksack from his broad shoulders. 'There are still a few cans of that self-heating soup left.'

'Warm them up. Keep an eye on him, Wolf.'

Christian jerked a thumb at Alan, who still had on the same clothes he was wearing when Christian abducted him; flannel trousers, a roll-neck sweater, a navy-blue donkey jacket. None of these items was waterproof, and he was shivering.

'Are you all right?' Christian called over.

Alan was far from all right, but he realised the futility of complaint. In any case, being a devotee of B-movies he knew what happened to those who couldn't make it.

'I'm all right.'

Von Stuerzbecher beckoned Christian to one side. 'I hope we're not taking this break because of me.'

There was no point in making him feel any worse. 'No, we all need one. But I had hoped to get a lot further tonight.'

'The snow will delay the *Tommis* as well.'

'I wouldn't bank on it. The blizzard may well have blown itself out by morning, in which case they'll have a clear run. Don't forget they have transport, we haven't; they can travel by day, we can't.'

'What do you think they'll do?'

Christian had thought of virtually nothing else for the last two days. Like a criminal who has masterminded a bank robbery, he knew that the easiest part was getting into the bank and out with the money. Far more difficult was getting somewhere where the money could be spent.

'Well, we have a little time on our side, at least for the moment. They're unlikely to discover you've all skipped until morning roll-call, and then they'll spend an hour double-checking because I doubt they'll believe it themselves at first. After that, if I was in command I wouldn't waste much time scouring the immediate area; I'd take all my troops directly to the west coast. Sooner or later we'll have to go towards them, and they know it.'

'That stretch of coastline is pretty massive; they can't comb it all.'

'Agreed. But they'll almost certainly concentrate part of their force around Maryport, and just below Maryport is where Korvettenkapitän Stieff is to pick us up.' Christian realised he was painting a pretty gloomy picture and it wasn't really as black as all that. 'However,' he went on, 'we have one advantage I didn't know about yesterday; it's not just you they'll be looking for. With eleven others on the run the *Tommis* are going to be spread pretty thin on the ground. It's my guess they'll descend like flies on Workington and Whitehaven, which are the obvious exit routes and quite a few miles from Maryport. There's another advantage too. Because they'll be searching en masse we should see or hear them coming miles away, especially at night.'

'If we can move at night.'

'We've *got* to move at night.' Christian fisted his palm in emphasis. 'It would be suicidal to try it by day.'

'Literally,' said von Stuerzbecher. 'I was forgetting. If they recapture me and still fall for my false identity, as an official POW it's just twenty-eight days' solitary confinement. If they take you it means a brick wall.'

Christian shrugged his shoulders. 'We'll just have to make sure we're not caught. Regardless of weather conditions, we're moving out of here at 3 a.m. We might not get very far but we will get further. I can't risk hanging around. If we're not at the rendezvous by the 14th, Stieff has his orders. He'll leave without us.'

Christian didn't bother to add that if Reichsfuehrer Himmler's directive was obeyed to the letter, there would be no prison cell for von Stuerzbecher. It wasn't only his own party's necks that made it imperative they get home, though if it didn't work out that way there was no question of shooting his old friend. Himmler could throw a thousand fits, but if they were retaken he and Schelling and Schultz would be somewhere the Reichsfuehrer couldn't reach them.

Von Stuerzbecher shook his head at Christian's offer of an English cigarette. 'It was a hell of a risk to take, Christian, and I haven't thanked you properly for it yet.'

Christian waved him away. 'Forget it.' He smiled mischievously. 'If the truth were known I was virtually blackmailed into it, or at least bribed. Restoration of my former rank and perhaps a little cauliflower to go with my Ritterkreuz. If you want to thank anyone it should be Feldwebel Schelling and Obergefreiter Schultz. They were in a cosy billet in Russia before I pulled them out.'

'I'll see it's done properly when we get back to Germany.'

'Which we will, providing we keep our heads and do nothing foolish. How's the soup coming along?'

'Almost ready,' said Schelling.

Unknown to Christian four hundred yards south of the barn Leutnant Fritz Uhde was about to do something incredibly foolish.

After Franz Mohr said, 'See you in Germany,' Uhde waited only to see Werner Herburg's head emerge from the tunnel before setting off in hot pursuit of Christian's party. At that time he had no idea how many it comprised, but judging by Major Breithaupt's warning, and including the mysterious Karl, there had to be at least three of them.

Away from the camp searchlights it was unbelievably dark, but he guessed correctly that the group would begin their escape by heading north along the main road. Ten minutes hard running and he had the rear man, Wolf Schultz in his sights. His eyes now accustomed to the darkness, he found that by walking along the bank on the opposite side of the road he could make out the silhouettes of the men up front against the snow without getting any nearer than a hundred metres. There was no chance that anyone would see him if they suddenly turned round.

In spite of Breithaupt's caution, he didn't question the morality of his actions. In any case, he didn't intend joining forces with the group, merely follow. And if they had, as they surely did, a ship or a U-boat or even a plane waiting somewhere for them, they could hardly refuse him a ride if he turned up unexpectedly.

It was all very well for Breithaupt to lay down the law like a schoolmaster, but he, Fritz Uhde, had as pressing a need as anyone for getting home. Besides, in officer training they called this sort of thing initiative.

At midnight they were still on the main road, but Uhde deduced they would swing west when an opportunity presented itself. On reflection it had to be a ship or a U-boat. There was no way anyone could land an aircraft in total darkness in this sort of country.

Fifteen minutes later he felt the first of the snowflakes on his face, and quickly he tried to close the gap. But quick as he was he was too late. The storm was upon him.

As he stumbled into Bewaldeth he knew he had lost them. They had either left the road to seek shelter or changed direction. In either event, short of a miracle he wouldn't find them again.

Sick at heart he crouched in the doorway of the general store. Although an officer in Goering's Luftwaffe and in consequence looked upon as something of a superman by his family and friends, he knew he was a perfectly ordinary young man with no more than average amounts of courage and tenacity. He was not cast in the heroic mould of Emil Wielen, for example, and as the minutes ticked by and he found himself unable to make a decision, he would have given a lot for a companion, someone to talk to and share his predicament. For that matter, he would have given a hell of a lot for a square meal.

With a start he realised that he was standing within a few feet of as much food as he would need in a week's march, probably more than he had seen in a year. Behind a pane of glass was the answer to at least the problem of hunger. It was a general store (the English lessons given in Skiddaw by officers who spoke the language told him that much), but it would undoubtedly stock quantities of food in tins, as well as biscuits, bread, butter, and so forth.

He stepped out into the street and looked up. If anyone lived above the store they were asleep. And with the wind howling like a hundred Loreleis they wouldn't hear much even if they were awake.

It was against everything he'd had drummed into him, of course. Breaking into a house or shop was a sure giveaway. He could hear Major Breithaupt giving the lecture now. 'Whatever you do don't start stealing from shops or private houses. If you're hungry, take something from a field. If you're thirsty, drink water or suck snow. The *Tommis* will only have the roughest of rough ideas which way you're heading. But if a householder or a shopkeeper reports a broken window or a forced door to the police, you might as well leave a map of your route.'

But that was all theory. In the comparative warmth of the Mess on a snowy afternoon, it sounded perfectly logical and reasonable. Out here, at God knows what hour in the morning and with a gale blowing, it was a different matter.

Suiting the action to the thought, he withdrew his fist into the sleeve of his jacket and punched the glass in the shop door, just above the lock. The first blow was nowhere near hard enough so he tried again, full force. This time the pane shattered with what seemed enough noise to wake the whole hamlet, and a jagged edge tore through the sleeve and into his arm. But his nerve-ends were partly anaesthetised by the cold and he scarcely realised he was bleeding.

Holding his breath until he thought his lungs would burst, he put his hand through the broken glass, slipped the latch, and went inside.

A few miles further north, disaster struck Leutnants Kaehler and Preiss shortly after they passed through one of the small villages on the road to Carlisle.

Although last away from Skiddaw they had covered a greater mileage than any of the others by the time the blizzard blew itself out at 4 a.m. Unlike Christian's party they had no rendezvous to make, no need to conserve energy for another day. Their only concern was to get as far away as possible as quickly as possible, and their enforced stay in the Rabbit Run had done them no harm at all. Their exercises had toughened them and their peculiar rest hours had found them still asleep at 6 p.m. the previous day. Even though the packed snow dragged at their feet and for four hours they had been marching straight into the storm, at 4 a.m. they were fifteen miles from the camp and less than that distance from their first objective, Carlisle.

'Bastard.' Johann Preiss swore at the wind, which had dropped without warning. The few remaining flakes of snow were of the gentle, Christmas-card variety. 'Now why the hell couldn't it have done that hours ago?'

'It's a *Tommi* plot.' Peter Kaehler was feeling good. Morale was high even though they were both soaked to the skin and cold. For most of the last hour they had been singing, in particular *Wovon kann der Landser denn schon träumen*—What does the soldier really dream of?—inventing obscene choruses that would have shocked the composers, Plücker and Richartz. At that hour in the morning and in those conditions it was unlikely anyone would hear them. 'Time we started looking for a burrow anyway.'

Neither possessed a wrist watch, but even if they'd known that dawn was still four hours off they'd have come to the same conclusion. They didn't want to be caught out in the open, and it was better to be safe than sorry.

The most risky period for any escaper was the first twenty-four hours. The majority were recaptured within that time because the search-parties could assess almost to the last quarter-mile how far a POW would have travelled from roll-call to roll-call. The pursuers' main problem was guessing direction, and Kaehler and Preiss felt they'd foxed them in that respect. All they had to do now was keep out of sight during daylight for a few days; after that, human nature being what it was, the hunt would lose its intensity.

'Backwards or forwards?' queried Preiss.

Kaehler debated it. The village they had just passed through didn't hold out much hope; a few houses, shops, a garage, something that looked like a school. There'd doubtless be a farm across one of the fields, but farms were always dangerous.

'Let's press on.'

They continued walking, keeping well to the side of the road.

Now that the wind had dropped the night was uncannily quiet, and they had only covered a couple of hundred yards before Kaehler, who was in the lead, stopped and held up his hand. 'Listen.'

Preiss did so. Somewhere up front he heard a peculiar clanking noise. He knew he should be able to identify the source, but his memory cells refused to release the information.

But it was getting louder and therefore closer.

'What the hell is it?'

Kaehler shook his head worriedly. 'I don't know, but . . .'

And then it was on top of them, a horse-drawn milk-cart, the horse's hooves deadened by the snow, the empty milk churns rattling in the back. There were no lights on the cart. The driver—they could just make out his muffled shape as they dived through the hedge—evidently trusted the animal to follow a well-worn path.

Preiss felt his ankle go as he jumped. He was off balance as he made the sideways leap, and he experienced a sudden jab of excruciating pain. He bit his lip and clenched his fists to stop himself crying out.

The sound of the milk-cart receded. Kaehler got to his feet and dusted himself down. 'Christ, that was close.' Preiss didn't move. 'Are you all right?'

'My ankle.'

'Oh Jesus. Here, let me feel.'

It wasn't broken but it was already swelling from the sprain. And judging by the muted grunts of agony, Johann wasn't going to be walking any further that night or for several nights to come.

Preiss swore solidly and without repetition for upwards of a minute. 'Of all the wretched bloody things to happen. You'll have to go on without me, Peter.'

'Don't be a bigger bloody fool than you already are. Cold-water compresses and it'll be all right in a day or two. We'll hole up until then.'

'Hole up where?' Preiss tested the ankle and winced.

'Back there in the village. It's less than half a mile. I can carry you that far.'

'And then what? Knock on the first house we come to and ask them to put us up for a couple of nights?'

'No, in the school,' said Kaehler. The idea had only just occurred to him but it made sense. 'It's the middle of December, right? If English schools are anything like German schools the kids will have broken up for the Christmas holidays. Now no arguments, please. We'll manage.'

Hoisting the feebly protesting Preiss across his shoulders in a fireman's lift, Kaehler retraced their steps to the village. The school was just off the main road, but the iron railings which had once surrounded it were long since part of a Lancaster.

Preiss stood one-legged against a wall while Kaehler circled the single-storey building, looking for a way in. A door at the rear seemed to fit the bill, and he wasted no time breaking a pane of glass and slipping the bolt. Unlike Fritz Uhde, Kaehler would not have considered taking such an action, in spite of Preiss's ankle, if the building had been a shop or a private house. But if he was guessing correctly, no one would come near the school until January.

He chipped out the pane completely. From a distance it would be impossible to see that anything was broken.

Once inside one of the classrooms, Preiss removed his boot. The ankle had swelled considerably.

'You're a fool, Peter,' he said from the darkness. 'A nice fool but a fool nonetheless. I won't be walking on this for a week.'

'Then we'll stay a week.'

'And what will we do for food?'

'We'll survive. Christ, we got out, didn't we? That was the hardest part. Who'd have thought yesterday that tonight we'd be free and sleeping in an English school? Sends me back ten years. I suppose schools everywhere have a special smell of their own.'

'Don't change the subject. This time tomorrow you could have been in Carlisle. Ten days from now you could have been home.'

'And what would I have told Hannah? "Yes, of course Johann came out with me, but he injured his foot so I left him. He's probably in the cooler by now." She'd have been very proud of me. I intend to marry your sister, Johann, and I don't see her marrying someone who'd cheerfully leave her brother to rot.'

'I wish to God you would—marry her, I mean. Then we'd all get a bit of peace.'

'It shall be done, my clumsy friend. It's the first item on the agenda when we get home.'

'If we get home.'

'Christ, what a Jeremiah you're becoming in your old age. Of course we'll get home. It might take a little longer now, but we'll make it nevertheless. Providing we keep out of sight for the next couple of days, the *Tommis* will assume we're out of the area and call off the hounds. After that, we proceed as planned.'

'You make it sound like an afternoon stroll through the Black Forest.'

'Much less dangerous; no wolves. At least, I don't *think* there are wolves in England.'

'You're a good friend, Peter.'

Kaehler was embarrassed. 'I'm only doing it to impress Hannah. Now shut up and get some sleep. We'll see to your ankle in the morning.'

Towards 7 a.m. it became apparent to Christian that they would still be four or five miles short of the coast at daybreak. They had just passed through, or rather round, Bridekirk, and Dovenby, where the man and wife in the car had almost run them down, was a mile or so further on. An empty house wasn't the safest place in the world to shelter for a whole day, but as it was nearing the time when the first of the tradesmen would be starting his rounds, his options were limited.

'Let's step it up,' he called over his shoulder.

All in all they hadn't done too badly, in spite of two wasted hours in the barn, and he was confident that the night would see them safely aboard the U-boat. With luck. Any enterprise such as this needed luck and so far they'd had it. But so far, of course, the *Tommis* in Skiddaw had been fast asleep. In a little over an hour they would be very wide awake and hopping mad.

Christian was wrong in that assessment. The Skiddaw balloon began to ascend several hours before morning roll-call, when the CSM was given the news that Oberleutnant Kapp was dead, found hanged by the neck in the bath-house. Purser immediately called the Adjutant, who experienced a stab of unease. Any other German found dangling from a rope would have pleased him hugely, but this was Kapp, his own man. If Kapp had committed suicide, assuming it was suicide, something must be seriously amiss.

'See that he's cut down, S'arnt-Major, and tell the MO I want the fullest report. Never mind, I'll call him myself. Let's hope to God it's not going to be one of those days.'

Apart from Kapp, the 8.30 head-count, accurate for once, revealed a discrepancy of ten. CSM Purser knew that that was ridiculous, that his NCOs, still sleep-sodden, had miscounted. But when a second check, inaccurate this time, showed Skiddaw to be eleven POWs short, he began to get alarmed.

'Absurd,' snapped Thorogood. 'Out of the question. Take a proper roll-call and teach your NCOs the principles of simple arithmetic.'

Nevertheless, Thorogood knew in his steadily sinking heart that there was nothing wrong with their addition. He didn't believe in coincidences; there had to be a connection between Kapp's death and the shortfall.

By 9.25 he knew the truth. CSM Purser had checked and double-checked. There was no mistake. He was ten POWs missing. Including Kaehler and Preiss, he had lost a dozen in a week. It just wasn't possible, but figures couldn't lie.

'What the bloody hell is going on around here?' he screamed. 'Am I surrounded by incompetents? Doesn't anybody keep guard, keep watch? Every man on sentry duty last night is on a charge! How the hell can ten bloody Jerries disappear overnight?'

CSM Purser stood his ground. 'Perhaps it's some sort of trick, sir—to get us in a flap for no reason.'

'Trick, S'arnt-Major! Are you out of your mind?' Thorogood snatched up the list of missing men. 'Look at the names. Heydt and Mohr, two of the senior officers and up to their necks in any dirty work that goes on around here. That sort don't play tricks. Oberleutnant Stuerzbecher. Good Christ, the bloody man's only been here a couple of weeks. Emke, Herburg, Uhde . . . Are you seriously suggesting that these officers are playing some lunatic game of hide and seek?'

'Perhaps not, sir.'

'Perhaps not, sir! I'll tell you bloody certainly not! They're over the bloody hills and far away. Ten of them, S'arnt-Major. While you and that idiotic bunch of men you call NCOs were sleeping in your pits, ten Germans calmly walk out of this camp as though it were an hotel.'

'That's unfair, sir . . .'

'Unfair, is it . . .'

Thorogood slammed down the list and took a grip of himself. It was a long chalk from being unfair but screaming at Purser would get him nowhere. He was going to need the CSM now, need him as he'd never needed anyone before.

'Perhaps you're right.' It took a supreme effort, but he managed to calm down and apologise. 'I'm sorry I addressed you in that fashion. We're all to blame, every last one of us. They've got away but they won't get far. You're to turn this whole camp upside down. I want last week's hunt for Kaehler and Preiss to be nothing by comparison. Every available man. I don't care if they're off duty or about to go on leave. I want to know how those people got out and I want to know it fast.'

The CSM snapped to attention. 'Yessir.' He hesitated. 'Have you . . . er . . . told Major Mitchell yet, sir?'

Thorogood shuddered at the prospect. 'No. That's next on the agenda, after I've phoned the police and the Home Guard.'

Major Mitchell didn't believe it either. He had already received a brief report from the MO on the death of Oberleutnant Kapp, but that matter paled into insignificance compared to this.

'Ten of them, Adrian?' He was having trouble with his vocal chords. 'Ten of them? Are you sure?'

'As sure as we can be.'

'But how? When?'

'I've got the CSM on that now, sir. I know it might seem like wasting time, using every available man, but I think it's important that we ascertain how they got out before some other bright bastard decides to use the same route.'

'Important? Of course it's important. It's the only thing that matters. What d'you mean, it might be a waste of time?'

'It delays getting after them, sir. While we're looking for the escape hatch we can't concentrate on getting them back.'

'You won't be doing that anyway, Adrian. The escapees are now the responsibility of the civilian police, the Home Guard, the Military Police, and any other units in the area who can be spared. Our job is keeping the prisoners inside Skiddaw, a task at which we are becoming increasingly inefficient.'

Thorogood stared at the CO with disbelief. 'You can't be serious, sir. They've escaped from our jurisdiction. It's up to us to get them back.'

'Wrong, Adrian. The areas of responsibility are clearly defined.'

But not for Adrian Thorogood. This was a personal matter now, nothing to do with the war. Heydt and the rest had stuck out their tongues and he was determined to see they were lopped off.

men, twelve if we include Leutnants Kaehler and Preiss, is bad

'I don't think you've considered the implications, sir. Losing ten enough, but if we allow the civilian police or the Home Guard to bring them back we'll be a laughing stock. What's more, someone may start to think we can't do our job.'

'Which could well be the case.'

'Sir . . .' Thorogood was desperate now. 'You and I both know that's not true. We've foiled any number of escapes. This was just bad luck. But it won't read that way on paper.'

'Nevertheless, I can't have half the garrison chasing their tails throughout Cumberland.'

'I wasn't thinking of half the garrison. Let me take CSM Purser and half a dozen men in a one-tonner. I won't ask for any more than that.'

Mitchell considered it. It could do no harm; in the report it would at least show willing. But he doubted if it would do much good either.

'You won't get very far with a handful of men and a one-tonner, Adrian. Ten prisoners are on the loose and they've probably gone in ten different directions. It'll be like looking for a needle in a haystack.'

'Not entirely, sir. There was a hell of a storm last night. That will have slowed them up. In any case, they'll be heading for the coast—Workington, Whitehaven, Maryport. They always do. And to get there they've got to pass through or near Cockermouth. If I leave within the hour I stand a chance.'

Mitchell sucked at the stem of his pipe. 'Very well; the CSM and half a dozen men. But before you go I think we'd better have Major Breithaupt in.'

Thorogood heaved a sigh of relief.

Otto Breithaupt found it difficult not to look smug; the ill-tempered interview with Major Mitchell was the first solid confirmation he had received that the twelve had actually made it. Missing names at roll-call were one thing; a dressing-down from the Commandant was quite another. There would be jubilation in the German lines this day.

There was only one note of disappointment. Towards the end of the session CSM Purser came in to announce that the tunnel had been found. A sharp-eyed sentry on patrol outside the wire had spotted the exit hole. The snow Kaehler and Preiss had packed in to disguise it had simply fallen down into the tunnel proper.

Adrian Thorogood went across to see for himself. He cursed vilely when he realised that the excavations obviously began somewhere under the chapel. Those bloody choir practices!

'All right, S'arnt-Major—house of God or no house of God, strip the blasted thing.'

It took less than five minutes to find the entrance. Moving around in the dark the previous evening, the POWs had left muddy footprints near the altar. When it was moved and the broken floorboards revealed, Thorogood had no doubts that down there was where Kaehler and Preiss had been concealed for a week. He would have somebody's head for overlooking such an obvious hide-out, but not now.

'Organise a one-tonner, will you, S'arnt-Major, and round up half a dozen men, a Bren team amongst them. I want to get going as soon as possible.'

Lance-corporal Cade saw the CSM coming and suspected something unpleasant in the offing. He disappeared at top speed. Harpo Cook wasn't so lucky and found himself included in the CSM's half-dozen.

Minutes before Thorogood was due to leave, Major Mitchell received a call from the police.

'They say a general store in a little place called Bewaldeth was broken into overnight. The only thing missing is food. Sounds like one of ours.'

Thorogood checked his map. Bewaldeth was too far north for that POW to be making for Workington or Whitehaven. Most likely his destination was Maryport. Bewaldeth, Blindcrake, Bridekirk, Dovenby, Maryport. That was the probable route.

17

Taking a leaf out of Franz von Werra's book, Oberleutnant Mohr had left Skiddaw dressed as a Dutch airman. Dutch papers were among the easiest to forge, and those in his breast pocket proclaimed him to be Captain van Nuy of the Royal Netherlands Air Force. He fervently hoped he would not be asked to produce them. They were adequate, but they wouldn't stand up to more than casual scrutiny. Neither would his command of the English language. He had enough, heavily accented, to ask for directions or the time of day, but far too little to engage in a long conversation. Which was one of the reasons he had chosen to travel as a foreign officer rather than a British civilian.

Mohr's uniform was the Skiddaw version of what a Dutch captain wore: a pair of navy-blue trousers and a cast-off naval jacket, tailored to fit at the waist. To each sleeve were sewn three strips of white tape. On his head he wore a German naval officer's white peaked summer cap. The emblem on this, woven with painstaking care in red and white cotton, was a cross between a shield and a rectangle. The whole ensemble bore no resemblance to a Dutch officer's walking-out dress, but Mohr knew there were so many different uniforms in England nowadays that one more would attract little attention. At least he hoped not.

A final touch was the addition of a small cardboard suitcase. There was nothing inside it save shaving gear and a change of underwear and socks, but he felt it added legitimacy to his appearance.

As a veteran of several escape bids Mohr was determined not to make the mistakes of his last break. Then, like so many others in his position, he had headed for the west coast and hoped for the best. This time he had a plan, one which seemed to be going well as he approached the outskirts of Penrith soon after 10 a.m.

Unlike Christian Eicke's party, once away from the camp Mohr had swung south, along the main road to Keswick. On the other side of Keswick he found the Penrith road without difficulty and got as far as the hamlet of Scales before the blizzard broke. Not wishing to look as if he had slept rough all night, a sure giveaway for a supposed officer, he took shelter until the storm subsided.

6 a.m found him just west of Penruddock, where he rested up and shaved in the beck before tackling the last five miles to Penrith.

As he neared the town he was feeling well pleased with himself. Half a dozen vehicles had passed him, going in the opposite direction, but evidently no one thought it strange to see a uniformed officer trudging along the main road, suitcase in hand. Going for a train, probably. Which was precisely Mohr's intention.

In the months since the Rabbit Run became a viable proposition, Mohr had given a lot of thought to his route. Remaining anywhere in the Lake District for too long was obviously suicidal, inviting recapture. So too, in his opinion, was travelling south down the west coast. The only thing to do was to get to hell out of the area as quickly as possible, and that meant some form of transport. Stealing a vehicle was too risky, which left trains. Trains were speedy, fairly regular when the Luftwaffe wasn't creating havoc on the lines, and anonymous. The nearest mainline station, as far as he could judge from Breithaupt's map, was Penrith; and from Penrith to London was a mere three hundred miles. In London he would be safe until he could reach one of the Channel ports, from where Occupied France beckoned.

He had money, more than enough for a ticket, but he did not intend buying one at the station. That might involve producing an authority to travel, which he didn't have. None of the Skiddaw forgers had ever seen one. Instead, when tickets were inspected on the train, he would pay then, pleading in broken English that he had been in too much of a hurry to purchase one earlier. If that didn't work . . . But he refused to consider that eventuality. Whatever happened, he was not going to be retaken, with twenty-eight days in solitary the automatic punishment.

Theo Emke felt much the same way. This was his second time on the run and he had no intention of there ever being a third.

Twenty miles south-west of Penrith in the village of Grasmere, he was leaning against a wall opposite the church, watching a young man fiddle with his motorcycle. Like Mohr, Emke had come to the conclusion that transport was essential. Unlike Mohr, he was not opposed to stealing a vehicle. He had little choice. His English was virtually non-existent. For him there could be no question of taking a train or any other form of public transport. He would only have to open his mouth for the police to descend like dogs on a bitch. If he was to make it down the west coast to Liverpool or North Wales, he had to be mobile.

Because of his bulk Emke was an imposing figure, even after a night in the open. He had shaved and washed, and the dyed great-coat, now a sodden wreck in the bag at his feet, had absorbed the worst of the storm. The good people of Grasmere were accustomed to seeing burly men, up from the filth of the cities for a week's hiking or climbing, and paid him scant attention.

He drew in several deep breaths. Christ, but it was beautiful country. Under different circumstances he could have spent many happy hours here, just wandering aimlessly from fell to fell, lake to lake. The trek down from Keswick hadn't tired him in the least. With the blizzard at his back and his head tucked deep inside the greatcoat collar, he had felt about sixteen.

The young man opposite was having trouble with the fuel feed. Emke watched him carefully. There was little profit in stealing a motorcycle which broke down on him a mile further on.

People passed him, going about their business. One or two smiled; he smiled back. He had an easy manner with him, he knew that, and people generally liked him for it. He wondered if they would feel the same if they knew he had dropped hundreds of tons of bombs on their towns.

He sighed to himself. He was no philosopher, but people were pretty much the same wherever you found them, whatever their nationality. Some good, some bad. Whatever Goebbels and his idiotic *Voelkischer Beobachter* might say, there wasn't much differ-ence between the average German and the average Briton. It was a great pity it took a war to find that out.

A little later two teenage girls threw him a glance of more than casual interest. He did what all young men do in the circumstances; he tipped them a big wink. They giggled at one another and hurried on.

The youngster was still fumbling inexpertly with the fuel tap and Emke wished to God he would hurry up. Sooner or later the BBC would be carrying news of the escaped POWs and from then on any stranger would be suspect.

Another five minutes elapsed before the problem was licked. The youngster climbed aboard and kicked the starter. The engine fired first time. Emke strolled over.

Two bright-blue innocent eyes looked up enquiringly. Emke smiled and pointed at the front wheel. The youngster's head went down and Emke chopped him across the back of the neck—enough to stun, no more.

One or two passers-by shouted in protest, but by this time Emke had opened the throttle and was heading out of the village. In passing, he wondered how the others were getting on.

Werner Herburg was doing nicely, thank you very much. Although neither of them knew it, and in fact would never know it, he had passed within a hundred yards of Theo Emke not half an hour earlier.

After getting no further than a mile outside Keswick when the blizzard broke, he had sheltered as best he could for the rest of the night. Dawn found him cold, wet and hungry, and he was half prepared to walk straight into the nearest police station and give himself up. But that same spark of character which had got his bomber into the air and over the target when logic told him to report sick would have none of it. So he continued walking, without a concrete plan, without much idea where he was going or what he would do when he got there.

To pass the time he thought of new and original ways to curse his mother and the hundred and fifty pounds in British notes she had smuggled in. Christ, she'd be delighted when she heard her efforts had paid off, that he'd made a break for it (though he wasn't quite sure of the procedure for that). She would no doubt throw a Werner Has Escaped Party and tell all her society friends that while her dear son had not, as yet, been awarded the Knight's Cross (which was of course the result of some bureaucratic mix-up, soon to be rectified by *dear* Reichsmarschall Goering), he had at least done something that few others had achieved and escaped from a British POW camp. There would be champagne for all and the conversation would be nauseating in its effusiveness.

Dear old Mutti. It wasn't really her fault, Herburg supposed. She was a Prussian through and through; patrician might be a better word. She had been brought up in a certain way, and that way was so inbred that it would never change, though the Reich crumble and the world explode. She had rigid concepts of what was done and what was not done. In her code there was no such thing as right and wrong; there was only what was socially acceptable and what was not. In the beginning she had disliked Hitler intensely. 'That shrivelled parvenu.' But Hitler had brought victory and prestige, and her attitude softened. Herburg supposed there were many like her, and God help Germany if that were the case.

He was jolted from his reverie by the sound of an engine behind him. Oh Christ, he thought, here we go.

But it was a lorry, not a military vehicle or police car. Its open back was piled high with second-hand furniture and suchlike, and the driver pulled up beside him.

'You want a lift, mate? I'm going to Preston.'

Herburg had no idea what the words meant, but it seemed pretty obvious that he was being offered a ride. Which was out of the question.

And then the luck which had smiled upon him as a pilot smiled again. The lorry driver pointed over his shoulder and then down into the cab. Wedged between the passenger seat and the floor-boards were half a dozen panes of glass. The meaning was obvious; there was no way a hitch-hiker could squeeze in there.

'You'll have to climb up back.' Herburg would not have understood the thick Lancashire accent even if he spoke English. 'It'll be draughty, but it's better than walking.'

Herburg gave the thumbs-up sign and scrambled over the tail-board. Within seconds he was ensconced in an armchair. The fact that it was minus its stuffing was of no consequence.

At 9.30 they were passing through Grasmere, where Theo Emke had just spotted the motorcyclist. But Werner Herburg was bliss-fully unaware of this. He neither knew where he was going, neither did he care. His head thrust up towards the clouds, he fell fast asleep.

Kapitänleutnant Heydt and his naval officers were the first casualties of the escape, a couple of miles east of High Lorton in the Vale of Lorton. Though had it not been for an adulterous wife returning home early after a drunken row with her lover they might have made it to the coast, and who knows after that? On such tenuous happenings do fates hang.

The affair that Molly Hankin, married woman of Braithwaite, was having with Jack Angus, bachelor of High Lorton, was a year old. She was not a bad woman, she frequently reassured herself, simply a young one with normal physical desires which needed satisfying. And with her husband serving overseas, Jack Angus was the man to satisfy them. Sometimes. Other times he drank too much, and then they quarrelled as they had earlier. Still, quarrels between them were nothing new and it had come as quite a shock to be picked up bodily and tossed out of the house.

There was no chance of a lift at that hour, 6 a.m., and it was a long haul from High Lorton to Braithwaite, up one side of the Whinlatter Pass and down the other. The overnight blizzard had made the going difficult, too, but she'd see herself damned before she asked Jack Angus to run her home. They were finished, however contrite he might feel when he'd slept it off.

At the top of the Pass she paused for breath and was astonished to hear, in the incredible silence of early morning, the sound of voices coming the other way. Quickly she ducked out of sight, and she remained out of sight when five figures, trudging one behind the other, loomed up out of the mist. The words they spoke were unfamiliar, foreign, but she thought no more about it until later.

She did not arrive home until 7.30, much in need of a long hot soak in the bath. In consequence it was not until nearly 10 a.m., with a cup of tea and a slice of toast in front of her, that she switched on the wireless for the morning music programme. Ten minutes into this the announcer interrupted with a news flash. Some German prisoners of war—he didn't give the number—had escaped from Skiddaw Camp overnight and were believed to be still in the area. All civilians were warned to be on the look-out and to report anything suspicious to the police.

But by the time he got that far, with nary a thought that the police might wonder what she'd been doing out so early in the morning, Molly Hankin was through the door, making for the nearest phone box.

A couple of hundred yards off the main road, at the periphery of Thornthwaite Forest, Kapitänleutnant Heydt was feeling more than satisfied with their progress so far. Getting well away from the vicinity of the camp before daybreak had always been considered their prime objective the first night out, and this they had succeeded in doing. He was still patting himself on the back when he heard the cry of alarm from the young Leutnant he had posted as look-out. He was on his feet in a flash.

'What is it?'

'*Polizei*. Police cars. Five, six . . . A whole bloody convoy of them.'

'What are they doing?' The Leutnant was on a mound and had a better view.

'They're going past . . . No, they're not. Christ, they're stopping.'

Heydt swore under his breath. It wasn't possible. Logic told him there was no way the police could know where they were, but his instinct counselled otherwise. This wasn't a routine patrol. Someone knew exactly where to look.

They were on the wrong side of the road to make a run for it south or west. It had to be north and east, deeper into the forest; back towards Bassenthwaite Lake and bloody Skiddaw.

'What are we going to do, Herr Kapitänleutnant?'

Heydt looked steadily into the eyes of the officer who had asked the question. Jesus, had this clown really been in the war?

'I don't know about you,' he said, 'but I intend running like bloody hell.'

Chief Inspector Bartlett had done his homework well and swiftly. The emergency call from Molly Hankin was recorded in the log as being received at 10.14, precisely thirty-two minutes after word had reached him about the break-out from Skiddaw. By 10.18 he had spoken to Molly personally and obtained detailed information of what she had seen and when.

On the wall of his office in Cockermouth police station was a large-scale map of the area, into which he had stuck several coloured pins. A red pin denoted that at approximately 6.45 that morning a group of men—Mrs Hankin thought five—with foreign accents had been seen near the summit of Whinlatter Pass. Three blue pins designated possible routes.

The first he placed on the road between High Lorton and

Cockermouth, and shook his head doubtfully. If they'd wanted to go through Cockermouth on the way to the coast, they would have swung north around Bassenthwaite Lake and come via Embleton. They wouldn't have used the Whinlatter Pass.

The second pin was at the head of the road running between High Lorton and Buttermere, but he rejected that also. It would take them too far south.

The third alternative was the minor road which led from High Lorton to Low Rogerscale and on to Pardshaw. Whether they were using a map or compass or plain blind luck, that had to be the direction they were taking. From Pardshaw they could strike either south-west to Whitehaven or almost due west to Workington.

Satisfied with his prognosis, Chief Inspector Bartlett did a couple of rapid mental calculations.

From Molly Hankin's sighting to High Lorton was around three miles, and in this sort of weather that was about the distance a man could cover in an hour. Which would put them in High Lorton at 7.45. But sunrise was a few minutes before eight at this time of year and he doubted if they would risk travelling in broad daylight. They would hole up until dark. And where better than Thornthwaite Forest?

It was a fair-sized old place, of course, but if he deployed a dozen men to beat down from the north and east while he and the remainder moved from the south, the Jerries should be in handcuffs by lunch.

From the time he put down the phone on Molly Hankin to the time he yelled for his immediate subordinate to round up every available man, dogs as well, only three minutes had elapsed. And it was barely 10.23 when the first of the cars left the station.

Heydt thought his lungs were going to burst. All those months wasting in Skiddaw hadn't prepared him for this, not after a sleepless night in the open. To his right and left he could sense rather than see his companions crashing through the undergrowth. Someone fell, but he had neither the time nor the inclination to find out who or what happened afterwards. This wasn't a ship and he wasn't the captain; it was every man for himself now and the devil take the hindmost.

Four hundred yards to the south, his officers deployed in line abreast, Bartlett heard the commotion up front. 'Nice of them to make it easy for us. Get the dogs to make a bit of a noise, Sergeant. Keep them on the leash but let the Jerries know we're not playing games.'

The youngest of the naval officers paled at the sudden barking. Christ, he hated dogs, always had.

Abruptly Heydt charged to his right. The other played follow-my-leader, as though attached to him by wire. 'Spread out, for Christ's sake!'

But if his officers didn't hear him or were no longer interested in obeying his orders, the inspector in command of the force moving in from the north did, and changed direction.

Heydt's anger at being within an ace of recapture so soon after the break was directed, paradoxically, against his fellow Germans, still tracking him like faithful hounds. Stupid bastards . . . He should have made the run alone. Next time . . . But in his heart he knew that next time was a long way off.

His breath now coming in short, painful gasps, Heydt broke into a clearing at exactly the same moment as the leading two police-men from the northern force reached the other side of it. For a second the three men glared at one another across fifty yards of open space, then Heydt did a quick about-turn and plunged back the way he had come. He collided with two of his own people and savagely pushed them to the ground. Before either could regain his feet the policemen were upon them. In any case, both were too exhausted to run any further.

Heydt veered off to his left, spotted a constable from Bartlett's squad, and immediately wheeled right. His forehead was bleeding from where it had come into contact with a branch, and in spite of the temperature, sweat was pouring down his face.

Weaving as he ran his foot caught a concealed root, but he managed to stay upright.

It was only a matter of time now, however; a few seconds, a minute. Out of the corner of his eye he could see policemen con-verging from all directions. His two remaining companions, realis-ing the futility of further resistance, threw up their arms in surrender.

Heydt kept going. He wasn't beaten yet, though up ahead a solitary middle-aged individual seemed to have other ideas on the subject. He stood four-square, hands on hips, barring the way.

Heydt put his head down and charged. One man wasn't going to stop him, not while there was breath still left in his body.

Chief Inspector Bartlett saw him coming and dropped into the sort of attacking crouch which had made him a feared loose-forward, with something of a reputation for dirty tactics, in his rugger-playing days. He feinted to move to his left and the Jerry went the other way—straight into a right-hander which travelled no more than a foot. It caught Heydt flush on the jaw and he went down like a pricked balloon.

'Nice punch, sir.'

Bartlett rubbed his fist.

In the manner of these things news quickly filtered through to the POWs that Heydt and his fellow officers had been retaken. Few were surprised, but the Obersteuermann who attempted to make book that the others wouldn't last the day was severely beaten up.

Major Breithaupt was informed officially by the Commandant ten minutes after he had been informed unofficially by Hans Geith. He accepted the news with good grace and silence. Seven out of twelve were still free; it wasn't over yet.

In the endless game that was played between the POWs and their captors, the position at the moment was generally considered to be a tie. Only the next twenty-four hours would decide the overall winner.

Corporal Napley was particularly pleased that five of the bastards were back in the can. Escapes were a bloody nuisance. They meant more work, a tightening of discipline, more bloody aggravation for everyone. And James Napley had as much aggravation as he could handle. His bigamous Carlisle wife was now demanding that he take her to London on his next leave 'or she would think he had something to hide.' Bloody right he had something to hide.

In a foul and filthy mood, exacerbated by the fact that it was too bloody cold to be NCO i/c compound guard, he went looking for trouble. He knew exactly where to find it. Getting Lance-corporal Cade stripped of his chevron and a couple of Jerries tossed in the cooler would make him feel a lot better.

Drinking tea in the boiler-room with Harry Cade, Willi

Braune and Hans Geith were in high spirits. By some freak in the postal system they had both received earlier that morning a letter from Lotti Kreipe, the blonde barmaid from Berlin. The information in each letter was identical: Lotti was getting married.

'Good bloody riddance,' said Hans Geith in German, raising his mug of tea.

Willi clinked cups in a toast. 'You can say that again. Christ, I pity her husband. The minute he turns his back she'll be having it off with someone else.'

Hans didn't like the sound of that. 'Did you ever get her into bed?'

'No.' Willi opted to tell the truth. It was all over now, anyway. 'I didn't even get my hand inside her dress. You?'

'A kiss and a cuddle, that's all. She kept promising but never delivered.'

'Bitch.'

'Prick-teaser.'

'Can we play some cards now,' asked Harry Cade, 'or do you two want to carry on this private conversation?'

Willi winked at Hans. 'He'll never learn, will he? Deal,' he said in English.

The game was five-card draw poker and Cade got no further than dealing a single card to each of them before the boiler-room door shuddered under the impact of a kick.

'Open up, you bastards. Open up before I break it down.'

The two Germans got to their feet in a hurry at the sound of Napley's voice, but Cade motioned them to stay where they were.

'Take it easy. If Napley wants to start something I'll beat the shit out of him.'

He removed the iron bar which served as a lock.

Corporal Napley stood in the doorway, grinning with malicious delight. To judge by the way he was holding his rifle, he meant business.

'Well, well, what a cosy little scene. Caught in the act, Cade, fraternising with the Jerries. You won't be seeing daylight for a few months. Let's go.'

Cade stood his ground. 'Don't be so bloody wet. We're not doing any harm.'

'The CO can be the judge of that.'

'You mean you're arresting us?' Cade couldn't believe his ears.

'Damn right. Now let's move it. You know where the guardroom is.'

'Bollocks.' Cade sat down on a box. 'I'm not moving one bloody inch, Napley, and you'd do well to remember that the Jerries might have something to say to the CO if you're stupid enough to go on with this. It's no secret on their side who let Wielen through the wire. You're digging your own grave.'

Napley hesitated, but he had gone too far to back down now. Besides, it was only their word against his on the Wielen business. 'We'll see about that. Now get bloody moving. I won't tell you again.'

To emphasise that he was serious he slipped off the safety-catch and jabbed at Cade with the muzzle of his rifle.

'You mad berk!' shouted Cade. His face white with anger, he leapt at Napley.

Braune and Geith looked on with fascinated horror as the two NCOs struggled to gain possession of the rifle. Napley had much the better grip on the weapon but Harry Cade was stronger, and it seemed, by twisting the rifle through a vertical plane, that he must quickly disarm the corporal. Which made the shot, when it happened, all the more surprising.

Within the narrow confines of the boiler-room the sound was deafening. But it had been heard on the outside too, and soon guards and POWs alike were running in the direction of the noise.

Clutching his chest, his useless fingers covered with blood, Corporal Napley staggered and fell on a mound of coke. 'You . . . silly . . . bloody . . .'

Which was all he managed. Along with his marital troubles, James Napley's life was over. And although they didn't know it yet, so were the lives of Willi Braune and Hans Geith.

18

Police forces and army units as far north as Gretna Green and as far south as Lancaster, west to the coast and east to the Pennines, had been alerted to be on the look-out for the fugitives, and at various major junctions road blocks were in the process of being set up. But Theo Emke was blissfully unaware of these facts as he dropped down a gear to cross Troutbeck Bridge. To his right lay Lake Windermere and the town of Windermere was just ahead. He would have avoided both like a plague of rats had it been possible, but unfortunately they straddled his route south.

It could have been imagination, but as he passed through the town itself he thought he saw one or two people staring at him with more than normal interest. That was the trouble with being so bloody big. He looked like a circus bear on a child's scooter. On the other hand, in the time it had taken him to get from Grasmere, no doubt the theft of the motorcycle and a description of the thief had been circulated by the police. It wouldn't take them long to deduce that he was a POW on the run and in which direction he was heading. At Ambleside he'd had a choice of two routes and only two.

Still, all he could do was keep going until the fuel ran out and hope to get as far as he could. He had money for petrol but no stamps or coupons or whatever the British called them. On the plus side, however, these little machines were very economical. On the minus side they weren't very fast.

Once through Windermere he opened the throttle. The engine spluttered but didn't die. Emke muttered a silent prayer that the rightful owner had managed to correct the feed problem.

If the information he had gleaned from the school map back in Skiddaw was accurate, in English terms of measurement it was around a hundred miles from the camp to Liverpool; call it eighty from Grasmere. Two hours, given luck and fuel. After that, Ireland and home. And Frau Baum first on his visiting list.

He had made up his mind about that. In spite of earlier misgivings, he had made a tacit promise to himself overnight that he would see Baum's mother if he got back to Germany. It wouldn't be so difficult, telling her about her son. She would want to know anyway, and she had that right. One day the war would be over and Hans would be going home too. It would be a terrible shock for his mother if she hadn't been prepared in advance. Perhaps she could make arrangements to book him into a clinic or put pressure on the Red Cross to have him repatriated. It was better than doing nothing.

No one had challenged Franz Mohr walking on to the platform of Penrith Station without a ticket, and nobody challenged him now. But he nevertheless felt conspicuous and as naked as a newborn babe as he waited for the London train. Which was late of course. He had learned that as much by studying the faces of his fellow travellers as by listening to their conversations, only one word in three of which did he understand. Due in at 10.40 it was now 11.15 and there was still no sign of it.

It was the first time he had seen so many Englishmen (and a sprinkling of English women) close up, and in spite of the precariousness of his position he found himself staring. Most of the would-be passengers were soldiers, sailors and airmen, and the majority of these were NCOs and other ranks. The handful of officers were gathered, as if by predetermined arrangement, at the far end of the platform. No doubt, as in Germany, some sort of rank segregation system operated on the railways, but Mohr couldn't risk getting too close to men who held commissions. He wouldn't stand an earthly of fooling them with his ersatz uniform.

They were a healthy-looking lot, the *Tommis*, he thought, pretending to be interested in a timetable. Their physical condition was obviously first rate; no shortage of food here. It was a point worth remembering, as the High Command would undoubtedly quiz him on such matters when he got back. Their morale, too, was unquestionably high. Sitting on kitbags reading newspapers and magazines or playing a quick hand of cards, not a man among them looked as though he considered the war lost. Well, maybe they were right. Only time would be the arbiter of that.

'Did you hear about those Jerry prisoners getting away from Skiddaw?'

Mohr pricked up his ears at the word 'prisoners'. The speaker was a hard-looking sergeant wearing the flashes of a Scottish Regiment.

'Heard it on the wireless just before I came out. They just strolled through the gates or something.'

'How many?'

'Didn't say. But one of the blokes in the billet said it was fifty.'

'Don't be bloody daft. If there were fifty of them on the loose they'd have hauled us in.'

' That's what I heard.'

'Where the hell's Skiddaw, anyway?'

'Carlisle way, I think.'

'Probably why the train's late. Bloody Jerries have hijacked it.'

The Scottish sergeant roared with laughter at his own wit. As he did so he looked straight at Mohr. His eyes narrowed, puzzled, as they took in the strange uniform. At a complete loss but knowing it would be fatal to turn away at this juncture, Mohr smiled broadly, as though he too were enjoying the joke.

The sergeant nodded curtly in acknowledgement but did not smile back. Mohr moved a few yards further down the platform.

Christ, this was worse than waiting to go on a mission, a thousand times worse than sitting in the Rabbit Run. Where the hell was that bloody train?

'Excuse me?' Mohr turned with as much aplomb as he could muster. The Scottish sergeant was holding an unlit cigarette. From their kitbags his friends watched him curiously. 'Have you got a light . . . sir?'

The 'sir' was definitely an afterthought, but the question was well within the compass of Mohr's knowledge of English.

'I do not smoke.' He had matches in his pocket but they were the Skiddaw variety, each match split into three for reasons of economy. He could hardly produce those.

'Oh, foreign, are you?'

'Captain van Nuy, Royal Netherlands Air Force.' Mohr thanked God he'd got out of the habit of automatically clicking his heels.

The sergeant toyed with the unlit cigarette, his eyes never leaving Mohr's face. But eventually he seemed satisfied.

'Thought that was it. I was telling my mates that the uniform was either Dutch or Polish. But you should be at the other end of the platform, sir. They usually put on a special coach for officers.'

Mohr missed most of this, but he caught 'special coach' and 'officers'. Taking a deep breath he summoned up his reserves of English.

'In Netherlands officers and men travel together. What is good enough for men is good enough for officers.'

'Bloody good,' said the sergeant. 'I mean, that's the way it should be, sir. But if you're going all the way to London with that accent, I'd advise you to keep your papers handy. Some Jerries have escaped from a POW camp.'

'They have been captured, sergeant. I hear someone say they have been taken.'

'Oh well, that's all right then. See you on the train maybe.'

Mohr's legs were quivering like harp strings by the time the sergeant rejoined his friends.

Arriving in the one-tonner just as a uniformed police sergeant was in the act of leaving the general store, Captain Thorogood lost no time in making his authority felt. Strictly speaking, this was now a matter for the civilian police, but Thorogood was having none of that and fortunately the sergeant was the cooperative type. If the army was willing to do his job, that was all right with him. The police were short-handed as it was.

'He won't have got far, sir. From what I can make out he must have lost quite a lot of blood.'

'Blood?' This was the first Thorogood had heard that one of them was wounded.

'Blood, sir.'

He showed Thorogood the broken pane in the door and the trail of blood leading to the shelves. A flour sack had been torn apart, the sacking evidently to be used as bandages. An elderly man whom Thorogood took to be the owner was making notes in a cash book and muttering something about 'bloody soldiers who couldn't do the job they were paid for.'

'Of course, it doesn't necessarily have to be one of your chaps,' said the sergeant. 'It could be an ordinary burglar.'

'What was missing?'

The sergeant consulted his notebook. 'Cigarettes, biscuits, butter, cooked meat, a few tins.'

'Then it's a Jerry, sergeant. What else have we got?'

'There were one or two drops of blood leading away from the shop, which means he certainly didn't leave until the small hours, probably later.' The sergeant preened himself, pleased with his detective work. 'The storm didn't blow out until 4 a.m. and we had another shower around 6.30. Even if he left straight after that, he'd look for somewhere to hide out before it got light. It's my guess he's not more than two or three miles away.'

'Direction?'

'I'd say towards the coast, sir. That's the way the buggers always go.'

Thorogood wasn't too happy with the 'always', but he let it pass. 'So would I. Well done, sergeant. We'll keep you posted.'

CSM Purser was acknowledging a signal from Skiddaw on the one-tonner's wireless when Thorogood returned. He told the Adjutant that the police had already picked up five of the runaways in Thornthwaite Forest. Thorogood hoped they would leave something for him.

'All right, S'arnt-Major, let's move out—west towards Blindcrake and Bridekirk. I'll explain as we go.'

If prayer was the common denominator among the surviving POWS that morning, Fritz Uhde had done more than his share.

He knew he should be moving from his hiding place in the ruins of the crofter's cottage, but somehow he couldn't find the energy. The gash was deeper than he had at first supposed, and blood was still seeping through the bandage he had fashioned from the flour sack.

He would move out in fifteen minutes, he resolved. He was quite safe for the moment. Across the field, through a gap in the fallen masonry, he had a clear view of the road. He would see any danger long before it saw him. And as he had taken great care to walk in the tracks made by early morning cattle, he had left no telltale footprints.

His arm throbbed painfully and he pressed a handful of snow against the bandage. Characteristically, Uhde didn't blame himself

for his misfortunes. It was the fault of rotten bloody luck, something intangible over which he had no control.

Seven miles to the west, on the outskirts of Dovenby, Christian
Eicke was also feeling, but without self-pity, that he had temporarily lost control of events.

He had posted a guard at the front and rear first-floor windows
of the empty house, and from his own position he could see the
coast and the sea beyond, a frustrating three or four miles away.
Somewhere out there Stieff was playing a dangerous game of tag
and waiting for dusk, which was five hours off. Christian felt
privately that they were likely to be five of the longest hours he
had ever spent.

Werner Herburg's luck continued to hold. Ten minutes after the
furniture lorry passed through the town of Kendal, the police
threw road blocks across all roads leading south and east.

Heading in roughly the same direction as Herburg but fifteen
minutes behind and by a different route, Theo Emke wasn't so
lucky.

Entering the hamlet of Winster on the Cumberland-Westmor-
land border, he saw, sitting at the kerbside, a red-headed little boy
of seven or eight playing with a mongrel puppy. Instinctively he
touched the brakes, but seconds before he drew level with the child
and the dog, he knew that the dog was going to run at him and
that he was going to hit it.

There was a sickening crunch and a strangled yelp, and Emke
came off the motorcycle. The boy, tears already forming, hadn't
moved, but the puppy's back was broken. It was still alive, but
only just.

Emke let out a cry of angry despair as he picked himself up. He
was unharmed and the motorcycle, its engine still running, appeared
no worse for wear. But other ears had heard the crash and from the
house opposite a young woman in her late twenties, also with red
hair, came running, her face as white as the surrounding snow.

'I'm sorry,' said Emke in German, and pulled the motorcycle
upright.

The woman shouted for him to stop, but he paid no attention.
Glancing over his shoulder as he slipped into gear, he saw her

bend over the body of the dog and knew it would only be minutes before she telephoned the police.

There was no doubt about it, they were checking papers. Mohr stiffened with horror and edged his way further down the platform.

He hadn't seen the two redcaps at first. Because he had moved far away from the barrier and, since his brush with the Scottish sergeant, was keeping close to the wall, he hadn't spotted the two military policemen until they were less than thirty yards away. Whether they were looking for escaped POWs or simply making a routine check for deserters was immaterial. Unless he could get off the platform or the train arrived within the next few minutes, he was in serious trouble. MPs would not be fooled by his phoney Dutch papers. At the very least they would haul him in for further questioning, and that would be that.

Leutnants Kaehler and Preiss knew all about trouble. By mid-morning Preiss's ankle had swollen to twice its normal size and it was patently obvious he wouldn't be walking anywhere for a long time. It would have been impossible to move, anyway. Since 10 a.m. a gang of children had been playing a scratch game of football in the schoolyard, and from time to time the ball thudded against the outside of the classroom wall. Kaehler's assessment that school had broken up for the Christmas holidays had proved correct, but that didn't mean that the yard was not to be used. In spite of the snow, it was the obvious place to play.

'Maybe we could offer our services as goalkeepers,' whispered Kaehler, and grinned reassuringly. He could see that his friend felt guilty and depressed and was determined to keep his spirits up.

'They'd stone us as soon as look at us,' muttered Preiss. 'I don't know, Peter, but the kids seem worse than the adults. If it's like this in Germany, God help the next generation of both countries. They'll never recover from this war.'

Kaehler nodded his understanding and looked at the reasons for Preiss's disenchantment, which were hung up on all four walls of the classroom. As well as childish paintings of Christmas scenes, many of the artists had depicted scenes of war. The most common were rough drawings of German planes, either in flames or in the act of crashing, having been shot down by British aircraft, always shown at a superior height. Neither Willi Messerschmitt nor R. J.

Mitchell would have recognised one of his own designs, but the swastikas and red, white and blue roundels painted on the fuselages left no doubt which side the losers were on. As Preiss said, it was depressing. Judging by the size of the desks and the standard of the artwork, most of the children couldn't be more than eight or nine.

'A thousand years ago they were probably painting Viking ships being burnt,' offered Kaehler cheerfully.

'Which is precisely what I mean. The Vikings, the Bayeux Tapestry, the Hundred Years War, the Elizabethans, the Napoleonic Wars, the First War. It never seems to end.'

'No,' said Kaehler, 'I suppose it doesn't.'

'You should get some rest, Christian.'

Christian turned away from the window. Kurt von Stuerzbecher was holding out a cup of coffee. One thing to be said about their present billet, there was no shortage of hot drinks.

'I'll sleep for a week when we're aboard that U-boat. Thanks.' Christian sipped the scalding coffee gratefully. 'Who's looking after the Englishman?'

'I put him in with Schelling. They could use some sleep too. Schultz and Schelling, I mean.'

'They're used to it. I've seen both of them travel across some of the worst country in the world for forty-eight hours non-stop. And with nothing more to eat than a bar of chocolate.'

'They're first-class men. Strange, isn't it, that we should be losing the war with men like that.'

'The *Tommis* have their own fair share. So do the Ivans.'

'Yes, it was a mistake to take on both at the same time.'

Christian smiled. 'Treason, Herr Generalmajor?'

'If it is, half the Luftwaffe are guilty of the same thing. The Army and Navy too, I shouldn't wonder. If it eventually goes against us, I suppose only the SS will fight to the last man. Sorry, Christian.'

Christian shrugged it off. 'That's all right. I'm no longer SS.'

'But you will be when this is over. Restoration of your former rank and with a crack Division is the least they can do.'

'Perhaps.'

'You'll be needed, Christian,' said von Stuerzbecher seriously. 'Not everyone holds the opinion that all SS are thugs and bullies.

You'll be needed in the east if not elsewhere. If it ever becomes a question of losing it will be better to be overrun by the British and the Americans than the Ivans. Every SS man will be needed to hold them back.'

'To save the Reich for others who couldn't do their jobs properly?' sneered Christian. 'No offence intended.'

'And none taken. You're right. The Luftwaffe didn't command the skies the way Goering promised and the Navy didn't sink enough ships. But that's not the reason we're on the defensive.'

'What is?'

'As always, leadership. The wrong men in the wrong jobs for the wrong reasons. Once in power, the Fuehrer should have sacked all the old gang and started from scratch. Mark my words, Christian, when historians come to write about this time they'll say exactly that; that the fighting was left to politicians instead of soldiers, that good men were killed or removed from office because they held the wrong political views, while lackeys were promoted to the highest positions.'

Christian thought of the sealed orders signed personally by Himmler.

'I can't argue with that,' he said.

The redcaps were only feet away, examining the travel documents of the Scottish sergeant and his companions, when Mohr heard the whistle of the train. The passengers surged forward en masse, all anxious to be first to board.

Mohr sidled to his right, towards the barrier, to put himself beyond the MPs, among those whose authority to travel had been passed as legitimate.

'All right, you, not so fast.'

Mohr kept going. The speaker made a move towards him, but the Scottish sergeant was having none of that. He snatched his paybook and warrant and thrust them into his breast pocket as the train shuddered to a halt.

'Haven't you buggers got anything better to do?' he demanded belligerently, and barged his way to the front of the scrum, using his kitbag as a battering ram.

Mohr had one hand on the door handle when he felt a shove in the back.

'Come on, sir,' pleaded the sergeant. 'You won't get back to Holland that way.'

Seconds later, Mohr was aboard.

Thorogood had been of half a mind to head straight for the coast and beat back from there, but two factors militated against that. The first was the obvious one; that whoever had broken into the store couldn't be far away, certainly nowhere near the coast. The second was that the area around Whitehaven and Workington was already crawling with troops and police. Two companies of Paras had been diverted from an exercise on Scafell Pike and the police covered the ports as a matter of routine. As far as he could see, no one except his small group was following the obvious route via Bewaldeth to Maryport, which was the way he wanted it. With five prisoners already in the bag, the next success had better be his or he would want to know the reason why.

'Pull in here, driver.'

The one-tonner skidded to a halt. Thorogood scanned the surrounding countryside with his field-glasses.

'What do you make of that, S'arnt-Major?'

CSM Purser took the glasses. Two fields away was what appeared to be a derelict cottage or lean-to. The CSM wasn't impressed. Since leaving Bewaldeth they had searched a variety of farm outbuildings, including, although he didn't know this, the barn where Christian and his party had holed up during the night. They had found nothing, no trace of illicit occupancy.

'Not a lot, sir. It's got no roof and not much in the way of walls. He'd freeze to death before the day's out.'

'Maybe, but take one man and have a look anyway.'

Through a gap in the masonry Fritz Uhde gave vent to an oath of despair when he saw what was happening. From this distance he couldn't make out whether the two men now climbing through the hedge were troops or civilians, but he'd have laid long odds that they weren't hikers on a ramble.

He had to get out. Behind him was a dip which led down to a stream. Beyond the stream were trees. If he could hide there until they completed their search . . .

Swiftly he gathered up his belongings.

By common consent among his teachers, Michael Wills was the biggest troublemaker in the school. Not yet ten years of age, whether it was lifting the girls' skirts to see what colour bloomers they were wearing or setting a booby trap of a bucket of water above a classroom door, Michael Wills was usually at the bottom of it. And now, as he trapped the football expertly and prepared to shoot, he knew exactly what he was going to do; he was going to put the ball straight through the window. He would make it look like an accident, of course, and no doubt there'd be hell to pay when the holidays were over. But that didn't worry him.

He evaded a clumsy tackle and put the full force of his boot behind the shot. The other children watched awestruck as the ball sailed up into the air. They could see full well what was going to happen long before it did, and it came as no surprise when the window pane shattered and the ball disappeared into the classroom beyond.

'You idiot, Wills! What did you want to do a thing like that for?'

'It was an accident.'

'Accident my arse. You did it deliberately.'

'I did not.'

'He'd better get it back anyway.' This from a bigger boy. 'It's the only ball we've got.'

'Give us a bunk up then. Let's see where it is.'

Standing on the shoulders of the bigger boy, Michael Wills peered into the classroom—straight into the shocked eyes of Peter Kaehler.

Unkempt as they were, seeing Kaehler and Preiss gave Michael as much of a fright as it gave them, and he jumped down quickly.

'There are two tramps in there,' he said.

19

13 December: 1215—1330 hours.

Fritz Uhde was next of the German dominoes to topple.

Following the progress of CSM Purser and Harpo Cook via the field-glasses, Thorogood spotted the movement in the derelict cottage before Uhde had taken three steps. His pulse racing with sudden excitement, he quickly adjusted the focus screw. There was no doubt about it. He couldn't make out the man's features, but there was someone over there who didn't want to be seen.

He cupped his hands to his mouth to shout a warning, but the CSM's old soldier's eyes didn't miss a thing, and he and Harpo were already proceeding at the double.

Uhde might still have got away with it, or at least remained at liberty a little longer, if he had not concluded that the angle of the bank leading down to the stream was too steep immediately behind the cottage. Rather than add a broken leg to his other problems, he looked for an easier descent. But to find one he had to leave the shelter of the ruins and run across open ground.

CSM Purser was not a man to waste time on subtleties. His own personal weapon was a Sten, useless at this distance, but Cook had a Lee-Enfield .303, standard issue.

'All right, son, put a couple of rounds over his head.'

'Me, Sergeant-Major?' Never in his life had Harpo expected to be ordered to shoot at someone.

'No, Greta Garbo, you damn fool. Shake it up, he's getting away.'

Harpo didn't move. He had shot on the range, at cardboard dummies, and barely obtained a pass grade. He knew only too well

233

that if he aimed over someone's head, the likelihood was that he'd hit him between the shoulders.

In the fraction of a second it had taken him to work this out, Uhde was almost out of sight.

'You bloody halfwit!' screamed Purser, and let fly with the Sten.

Uhde heard the shots and instinctively flinched. But experience told him he was being fired upon by an automatic weapon, of low calibre at that, which was unlikely to do any damage at this range.

Slipping and sliding he stumbled down the bank. His injured arm caught a jutting rock and he cried out with pain.

The stream was wider than he had at first supposed, but if he could make it to the trees . . .

Behind him he heard a couple of rifle shots. If they'd done that in the first place . . .

The water came up to his thighs and was cold, bitterly so. The weight of the pilfered provisions threatened to throw him off balance. But he had to hang on to those. Literally, they meant life or death.

Only a few more metres now. The bare branches opposite beckoned like sirens.

His arm was bleeding again, but he ignored it, did not even feel it.

He had to get away. If they caught him now there would never be another chance. He had to get home. His wife needed him. No, wrong—he needed his wife. He would willingly fly a hundred more missions, a thousand, if once in a while he could share her bed. The war, the bloody war ruined everything. It wasn't just being killed or maimed that was so dreadful about war. It was the other losses, the unseen ones; those no one remarked upon because they were hidden inside.

I hear your wife's been to bed with half the Luftwaffe, Uhde. You're well rid of her, Fritz. Never trust a woman who, sober, is too interested in sex. Have your fun, certainly, but don't spend the rest of your life paying the bills for her hats and dresses. Find yourself a nice dumpling who's content to make the meals and bring up the kids.

What Uhde intended doing when he reached the other side of the stream, whether he thought a few sparse trees would hide him, became academic. As he was about to take the last couple of steps, the CSM and Harpo appeared on the slope behind him. But this time the CSM had the Lee-Enfield and Harpo was carrying the Sten.

For good measure Purser put a shot into the trees, though only fifty feet separated him from the German. Uhde turned slowly, dreams over, hands raised, pale and shaking from his night in the open. He was, thought Purser, not much older than David.

The driver of the furniture lorry ferrying Werner Herburg south was a burly individual named Tom Walsh, who had a special reason for taking the long way round, via Kirkby Lonsdale, to Preston. But Herburg was unaware of this and awoke with a start as the lorry pulled off the A65 and on to the forecourt of a transport café.

As far as he could see they were approaching a town, but which town? Judging by the distance of the Cumbrian Mountains, way off in the north-west, they had covered quite a few miles in the last two hours.

He heard the driver jump down from his cab and the door slam. He shut his eyes, feigning sleep.

Walsh poked his head over the tailboard. 'Pit stop. Time for something to eat.'

Herburg grunted and tried to indicate that he was all right where he was.

'Please yourself.'

Walsh went into the café. His 'special reason' was standing behind the counter, every voluptuous inch of her making some sort of impression in the thin white overall. There were some who said that Janet Higgins, a widow, was over the top at thirty-eight, but he knew different. Feed her a couple of gins and she was hell on wheels. Her nineteen-year-old daughter Jean, who now tipped him a big wink, was going the same way too. It had crossed his mind to take up with her when he tired of the mother.

He fought his way to the counter. Food rationing never seemed to worry Janet, which was one reason the place was always jammed to the gills with drivers. The other reason was the woman herself. Many a man would have given a month's pay to be in Walsh's trousers. Or out of them.

'Hello, Tom. Are you stopping or should I put bromide in the tea?'

'I've got an hour. But food first.'

Janet Higgins felt a tingling in her loins. An hour with Tom Walsh was what she needed. Although big and strong, outwardly he was a mild-mannered man—until he was aroused. Then he was vicious, and lately she'd become very fond of viciousness.

'I'll get Jean to bring it over. I've saved you something special so it'll be a few minutes.'

Walsh helped himself to cutlery and found a vacant place at a table near the window. The other three occupants were all men he knew well and they didn't interrupt their conversation to greet him. The talk was inevitably of the war.

'Of course we're bloody winning.' This from a wiry individual hovering over a forkful of beans. 'Rommel's had the shit beaten out of him in North Africa and the Russians are doing the same in Stalingrad.'

'I didn't say we weren't winning, you daft bugger. All I said was there's no point in taking prisoners if we can't hang on to them. We might as well shoot them on the spot.'

'Can't hang on to who?' asked Walsh.

'The Jerries that got out of Skiddaw last night. The wireless didn't give the exact number but you can bet your life there are hundreds of the bleeders on the run. My argument is that we might as well put a bullet through them if they're going to cause trouble later.'

Tom Walsh hadn't heard the newsflash and his knowledge of geography was minimal, but as a medium-distance lorry driver plying the route between Carlisle and Preston three times a week, he knew he had seen the name Skiddaw somewhere.

'Where exactly is the camp?'

The man with the beans told him, adding that the police had issued a bulletin warning motorists to be on the look-out for anything suspicious—such as strangers hitching lifts.

Walsh's knees turned to jelly. Jesus Christ, no wonder the bloke in the back hadn't said anything. Half the police forces in the north of England looking for Jerries and he'd be coolly ferrying one out of the danger area. If that ever got out he'd be a laughing-stock. Tom Walsh, the driver who runs a travel service for POWs. Neither Janet Higgins nor her daughter would look at him twice after that—unless, of course, he could turn the situation to his own advantage.

'I wonder if they give rewards for capturing one,' he said casually.

'Shouldn't think so. Why d'you want to know?'

'Because I picked one up a few miles up the road.'

The other three stared at him. 'You must be bloody joking!'

'I'm not. Take a gander.'

They looked out of the window. Werner Herburg's head was just visible in the back of Walsh's lorry.

'That's a *Jerry*?'

'Sure. I knew it as soon as I picked him up. I was just waiting for a chance to deliver him to the local coppers.'

'But Christ, he might have made a run for it as soon as your back was turned!'

'He's got nowhere to run to, mate. Besides, I can see him from here. That's why I sat by the window.'

'You're a cool bastard, Tom.'

Walsh shrugged modestly. 'You want to take a closer look?'

The man with the beans fished a heavy bunch of keys from his pocket. 'I want more than that,' he said grimly. 'They're all Luftwaffe at Skiddaw, and those buggers have been bombing the shit out of us for three years.'

Werner Herburg saw them coming. News had quickly spread throughout the café that Tom Walsh had 'captured' one of the escaped POWs and everyone wanted to get in on the act. Some twenty or thirty hard, heavy men, as well as Janet Higgins and her daughter, were now marching towards the lorry. At their head Walsh was angry at his own stupidity, and irrationally his anger was directed at Herburg. The bloody Jerry had almost made him look a complete fool.

Herburg knew the game was up. It was a pity; in the last five minutes he'd started to take his bid for freedom a little more seriously. But if it wasn't to be, it wasn't to be.

He stood up in the back of the lorry and raised his hands.

'Come down from there, you bastard!'

There was no mistaking the command, but Herburg wasn't sure he wanted to obey it. Some of the men were carrying iron bars. He backed away, but half a dozen hands reached for him and pulled him over the side of the lorry. Within seconds, feet and fists were flying, and what should have been a mild roughing up turned into a brutal beating.

Herburg was pulled upright and pushed from one man to another. Those who couldn't reach him shouted encouragement at the others and begged for a turn. The two women—like mother, like daughter—experienced almost identical excitement in the face of so much violence and both were among the most vocal in their exhortations to 'kill the bastard.'

Somebody, somewhere saw what was going on and, not knowing the reason, telephoned the police. By the time they arrived Herburg was almost unrecognisable. His face was a mask of blood, his jaw was broken; both arms and four ribs were fractured. Later, in hospital, it was diagnosed that he had suffered multiple internal injuries. His bruises and minor lacerations were too numerous to count, and it was three weeks before he could even talk.

The police arrested no one. There was no doubt a law somewhere that covered such affrays, but nobody could be bothered to dig it out.

Later on in the day, under the pounding weight of Tom Walsh, Janet Higgins experienced the most intense orgasms she could ever recall, and at approximately the same time as Herburg was having wire inserted in his jaw, her daughter Jean joined the couple in the big double bed.

'Do we take him back, sir?' asked CSM Purser.

Thorogood looked Uhde up and down. 'No, we damn well don't. I'm not wasting valuable daylight getting him to a doctor. If he bleeds to death, that's his hard luck. Do what you can with a field dressing, but we're pressing on.'

Theo Emke was also pressing on, just as fast as the pre-war BSA would carry him. The speedometer was laid out in m.p.h. and the needle was pointing at sixty.

Several miles away the red-headed child's mother had already called the police, who flashed a signal to divert cars from the Kendal roadblock.

With the cold wind bringing tears to his eyes, Emke pushed the motorcycle to its limit. The needle edged towards seventy. There were side roads, minor roads, but God knows where they led to. His recall of the map of England was sketchy, but he knew that somewhere around here the north-west coast jutted out into the Irish Sea. If he took one of the right-handers he could well find himself trapped in Cumberland.

Curiously, only part of Emke's mind was on his immediate plight; the rest was on the boy and the dog.

Like many German pilots, on first being captured he had been astonished by the hostility which confronted him. In the early days of the war it was British Government policy not to conceal captives, especially pilots, from the prying gaze of the public as they were transferred from camp to camp. In Emke's case, after interrogation in the London Cage he had been sent north by rail, and the attitude of British civilians at Euston Station had both bewildered and frightened him. Fists clenched, voices raised in anger. He thought at first he was going to be lynched from the nearest lamppost.

On the drive across London he had seen some of the devastation Luftwaffe bombs had caused, but didn't the British realise that the same thing was happening to German cities? Night after night the RAF dropped thousands of tons of high explosive, though it was doubtful if more than a handful of *Tommi* pilots consciously wanted to kill innocent German civilians. Their deaths were an inevitable consequence of war. The British might call the Luftwaffe Nazi murderers, but surely they knew that the German expression for the RAF was terror fliers.

It saddened Emke to think that somewhere in England a young boy would grow up believing that all Germans were heartless puppy killers. In the way of these things, time would distort the incident out of all proportion to the facts. The boy would become a man without ever realising that his dog's death had not been an act of malice, had only been the result of a single German pilot seeking his liberty.

In the trickle of seconds it had taken to think these thoughts, Emke had travelled a mile. The faster police cars coming from Kendal had covered slightly more ground and were already pulling across the T-junction when Emke was still five hundred yards away.

He cursed when he saw what was happening, but there were no slip roads to escape down. He had to go on. The two cars did not block the entire road, although the gaps were being filled by uniformed constables. They would move, however; they would move when they realised he had no intention of stopping.

Four hundred yards, three hundred, two hundred . . .

He gave the throttle a final twist, and it was then that fate took a hand. The engine spluttered, roared to life momentarily, and died as the last of the fuel was exhausted.

The policemen linked arms. Three of them were on his side of the road. He was close enough to see that panic was their common expression. But they stood their ground.

Fifty yards, forty, thirty . . .

Brave bastards, he thought, and wrenched the handlebars to the left. Even without power he was still travelling at almost seventy miles an hour when he hit the front wing of the nearest car.

There was an ear-piercing crunch of metal, and Emke was flung over the handlebars and over the bonnet of the police car. His neck snapped the instant his head touched the ground. Almost his last thoughts were of the boy and his dog. His very last were of Hans Baum.

20

Young Michael Wills' father hated Germans with an intensity that exceeded anything felt by Adrian Thorogood, though in his case there was a more tangible reason.

One of the last to be taken off the beach at Dunkirk, Frank Wills had suffered for five days under the ferocious dive-bombing of the Stukas. Some said he was lucky to be invalided out with nothing more than total deafness in one ear; others had lost their lives or at least a limb. Wills disagreed. Long after he was safely home he knew he would live for ever with the memory of the Ju 87's sirens, the screams of the wounded, the feeling that death was but minutes away.

His hostility towards Germans in general was surpassed only by his loathing of the Luftwaffe in particular. So when his son ran in with the news that he had seen two tramps hiding in the school, Frank Wills didn't treat it as a practical joke or wild imagination. He knew precisely who they were and what he was going to do about it.

He should, of course, contact the police immediately; that was what the wireless had said. But the police would merely re-arrest them and return them to Skiddaw. That wasn't good enough. Luftwaffe personnel lived like lords in the camps, or so he had heard; they wanted for nothing. The two in the school would be punished mildly, rapped across the knuckles, and in a few weeks would be trying the same thing again.

No, sir.

'Have you told anyone else?' he asked his son.

'Well, the others were there.'

241

'What others?'

'Billy Barnes, Andy Craig, quite a lot.'

'Then run and tell Mr Barnes not to do anything until he's seen me.'

He would see Andy Craig's father himself. Bert Craig had lost a sister in the Coventry bombings.

But before leaving the house he took his 12-bore, a gun he normally used for poaching, from its rack and filled his pockets with cartridges.

'We've got to get out,' said Preiss for the umpteenth time.

He was on his feet, staring unseeingly at the shattered window pane and the football, lying like a severed head between the desks. It was quiet outside now and had been for half an hour, but that wasn't to say that things would remain that way.

'Don't be a bloody fool. How far d'you think you'd get with that ankle?'

'All right, *you've* got to get out.'

'Not by myself,' said Kaehler calmly. 'We've been over this a dozen times, Johann. Either we both go or we both stay. That's all there is to it. Besides, we don't know that the child will tell his parents or that his parents will believe him or add two and two together. We're as safe here as we would be anywhere.'

Preiss lost his temper. 'Of course he'll tell his damned parents, you idiot. He'll want his ball back if nothing else. You've got to go, Peter. Please,' he pleaded. 'You've got a few minutes. How the hell do you think I'm going to feel if we're recaptured because I was clumsy?'

'Would you go if the situation were reversed?'

'Of course I would. It'd be my duty.'

Kaehler smiled. 'You're a damned liar, Johann, and a bad one. We'll sit it out.'

The train was bursting at the seams with troops returning from leave or in transit. As it had started its journey in Scotland and had stopped at Carlisle en route, obtaining a seat was impossible. Mohr found himself standing in the corridor, sharing the same few cubic metres of what passed for oxygen with the Scottish sergeant and his friends. The sergeant's breath reeked of stale beer and tobacco, but Mohr wasn't complaining. The way they were packed, with kitbags, suitcases and rifles taking up any spare space, a ticket collector was going to have one hell of a job getting through.

'Told you you should have gone up to the officers' end,' grinned the sergeant. 'I'll bet it's not like this in Holland.'

'Not now,' said Mohr, catching the drift.

'Never mind, we'll kick the Nazis out one day and you can have it back, windmills and all.'

There was another side to the coin, of course, thought Mohr. Spending hours on a train as close as this meant that his home-made uniform was under constant scrutiny, especially the cap. It might be a good idea to take it off. The weakest part of his disguise was the wretched hand-sewn badge, and at this range the sergeant or one of his companions could well notice that it didn't represent anything.

He removed it and tucked it under one arm.

'You want to watch that, sir. If it drops on the floor it'll come up the colour of a coal miner's neck.'

Mohr smiled uncomprehendingly.

In the back of the one-tonner Harpo Cook knew he was in big trouble for disobeying the CSM's order to shoot at Uhde. Fourteen days' CB was the least he could expect and maybe it would mean a lot more. But even fourteen days was bad enough because it would include the Christmas period. If he was put on CO's orders first thing in the morning, the punishment would take him up to the 28th.

Christ.

Up front, sandwiched between Captain Thorogood and the driver, CSM Purser said: 'Bridekirk coming up, sir.'

Thorogood nodded sourly in acknowledgement. He was feeling thoroughly disgruntled. After recapturing Fritz Uhde he had thought that this was going to be his day, but since then they had found nothing, not even a trace. They had searched every conceivable hideout between Bewaldeth and Blindcrake, Blindcrake and Bridekirk. Barns, byres, farm buildings, even hedgerows. Zero. After Bridekirk there was, on the main road, only Dovenby before Maryport. Perhaps he was on a wild-goose chase. Perhaps only that idiot Uhde had been coming this way. Perhaps . . . Perhaps there was only one real way to find out, and

243

that was to interrogate Uhde without being too fussy about the methods used. But he couldn't do that with the CSM and the men around.

'Stop the truck,' he said suddenly.

The driver applied the brakes. The one-tonner skidded to a halt.

Thorogood pointed through the windscreen with his cane. 'You see those fields over there, S'arnt-Major?' The CSM said he did. 'I want you to beat across them.'

'Across the fields, sir?' Purser looked bewildered. There was nothing across the fields except more fields and nowhere a man could hide.

'That's what I said. Look for tracks. According to the map there's some sort of bridle path leading towards Gilcrux. See if it's been used recently.'

The CSM had seen the map too and knew that if anyone was making for Maryport they wouldn't be going by way of Gilcrux. But it was a direct order and he wasn't going to argue on that score.

'Very good, sir.'

'And take all the men, the driver as well. You'll be able to cover a greater area of ground that way.'

Thorogood waited until they were a couple of hundred yards away before climbing into the back of the one-tonner.

'And now, Herr Leutnant, you and I are going to have a little talk,' he said in German.

Christian switched off the radio and went to relieve Schelling. The weather news was better than he had any right to expect. Gales were forecast for the Irish Sea and further heavy snowfalls for Cumbria, but neither was due before midnight.

'Has he eaten?' Christian indicated Alan Miles.

'Like a pig,' answered Schelling. 'I thought fear took away a man's appetite.'

'Maybe he isn't frightened.'

'Then he's the only one in the house who's not. Can I bring you anything?'

'No, thanks. Leave the Luger.'.

Schelling placed it on the dressing-table and left the room.

Christian shook a cigarette from the Players packet and offered one to Alan. The Englishman declined nervously. Because he couldn't be expected to watch the road and the prisoner simultaneously, Schelling had lashed Alan's hands to the bed-post.

'I'll untie you for a couple of minutes.'

'No, I really don't want one.'

Christian saw that his eyes were on the dressing-table. Maybe he was frightened after all. He certainly looked a wreck, but so, probably, would any man who had a two-day growth of beard on his face and who hadn't slept properly in almost sixty hours.

'Don't worry, I'm not going to shoot you. That's just to remind you what can happen if you do anything stupid.'

'I'm not likely to do that, but is it all right if I ask you something?'

'Go ahead.'

While Alan hunted for the words, Christian turned to the window. The house was at the eastern extremity of Dovenby—a quarter of a mile outside the village, to be accurate—and from his vantage point he had a more or less clear view of the road as far as Bridekirk. Wolf Schultz was watching the west, but Christian knew that trouble, if it came, would come from the east or north-east.

'Why haven't you shot me?'

Christian swung round, astonished. '*Shot* you?'

'Yes, shot me, got rid of me.' Alan's sentences tumbled over one another. 'I mean,' he stammered, 'I don't want to be shot, but why haven't you? I'm in your way, someone's always got to be awake to make sure I don't escape . . . Well, England and Germany are at war.'

'I'm a soldier,' Christian said. 'English soldiers are fighting German soldiers. We don't kill civilians.' At least most of us don't, he added silently.

'That's not what you hear,' Alan hurried on. He was talking as much to reassure himself that Christian was not a monster as for any other reason. 'You hear . . . I mean, *we* hear on the wireless and read in the newspapers that the Germans are murderers, that you kill women and children.'

Christian looked him straight in the eyes. 'We're told the same stories about the English,' he said. 'So now we both know somebody's lying.'

'And you're really going to let me go?'

'Later tonight if all goes well. You can't do us any harm then.'

245

'I wouldn't anyway.' The words came out in a rush before Alan could stop them. He shook his head, embarrassed.

'Thank you.'

'I mean it,' said Alan. 'I don't know why I mean it, but I do.' He paused, looking for the right expression and failing to find it. 'I don't know what the hell this war's all about.'

'I wish I could tell you,' said Christian, 'but I'm afraid I can't.'

At the other end of the house, carrying two mugs of coffee, Schelling kicked open a bedroom door. Kurt von Stuerzbecher turned at the sudden noise.

'I'm sorry, Herr Generalmajor,' apologised Schelling, spilling some of the coffee as he tried to come to attention. 'I thought Wolf . . . Obergefreiter Schultz was in here.'

Von Stuerzbecher pointed to the bed. 'So he is.'

Schelling looked across. Schultz was lying on his back, mouth wide open, dead to the world.

'But if that's coffee you've got there, I could use some. I'm sure Obergefreiter Schultz won't be needing it for a couple of hours.'

'Of course.' Schelling passed over a mug. 'If the General would like to get some sleep also I can keep watch here.'

'No, thanks. It's your turn. I've done precious little to earn my keep up to now and it's high time I started. There are three or four other bedrooms. Take your pick.' He smiled. 'Pretend it's a first-class hotel, the war is over, and you've just inherited several billion Reichsmarks.'

'If the General will forgive me,' said Schelling, 'I'd like to add just one item to that list.'

'A woman?'

'No—that the waiters speak German, not English.'

'Amen to that,' said von Stuerzbecher.

Thorogood brought the cane down sharply for a third time on Fritz Uhde's injured arm. The German cried out with pain.

'I'm trying to help you, Herr Leutnant. You know very well what will happen if Major Breithaupt finds out you broke into that store. It's against everything you've been taught, isn't it? Whatever you do don't leave a trail. I'm sure the good Major must have spent hours drumming that into your thick skull.'

'Go to hell,' muttered Uhde. His arm was bleeding freely now.

Thorogood ignored the remark and the blood. 'But Major Breithaupt need never know how you were captured. You can say it was bad luck and I won't tell him anything different. However, one favour deserves another. Are you listening to me, Uhde?'

The question was punctuated with another blow.

'You bastard. You sadistic bastard.'

'Wrong, Uhde. I'm not like your lot. Bastard I may be but sadistic, never. I'm not enjoying this if that's what you're thinking. You have information, I need that information. Beating it out of you is just an expediency. If I had more time I'd use other methods.'

'It'd be a wasted effort either way. I don't know anything.'

'Wrong again. You might be lying or you might just think you know nothing. But I'll be the judge of that. Just tell me everything that happened from the moment you got out. Which way you went, who you saw. Don't leave anything out. I'll give you five seconds to make up your mind and then I'll really start on you.'

Only two-thirds conscious because of pain and loss of blood, Uhde nevertheless knew that Thorogood wasn't joking. It was useless quoting the Geneva Convention or pleading the laws of common humanity to a man such as this. He would get what he wanted, one way or another.

Fritz Uhde was a realist. Theo Emke or Franz Mohr would have spat in Thorogood's eye, but he wasn't Emke or Mohr. It was a matter of balancing immediate pain against what he knew, and really he knew very little.

Thorogood raised his arm to strike again, but Uhde had had enough. 'All right,' he said quickly, 'I'll tell you.'

Thorogood relaxed. 'That's better. Now you're using your head. Begin at the beginning, from the moment you were on the outside.'

'A cigarette first.'

Thorogood gave him one and took one for himself. He lit both. Uhde inhaled deeply. The events of last night seemed a long time ago and it took him a while to recall the sequence.

'Major Breithaupt had decided the order of escape,' he said finally, 'and I was number three.'

'Who were the first two?'

'Oberleutnants Mohr and Stuerzbecher. Behind me came Oberleutnant Herburg and then Heydt and his naval people, I think.'

'Go on.'

'Well, it was around ten when I got out. I guessed the others

247

would be going north, so I ran and caught them up. At least, I kept them in sight.'

'Mohr and Stuerzbecher?'

'No, Stuerzbecher and the others.'

'Wait a minute, wait a minute. Stuerzbecher and *what* others? You said he and Mohr were the only two out.'

Uhde hesitated. To hell with it. He was committed now and it couldn't do any harm. 'Stuerzbecher had some people waiting for him on the outside.'

'*People*? You mean *Germans*?'

'Yes. Only Breithaupt and Mohr and perhaps a couple of others knew who Stuerzbecher really was, but he wasn't an Oberleutnant in the Luftwaffe.'

Thorogood experienced a surge of adrenalin. Jesus Christ, he'd stumbled on more than he knew. But it made sense. It had puzzled him from the beginning why Stuerzbecher had been included in the break. The man had only just arrived in Skiddaw and in the normal course of events would have been way down the escape list. Now it was becoming clearer. Not only was Stuerzbecher important enough to have been given a major place in the tunnel, the Germans had sent someone in to fetch him, take him home.

'If Stuerzbecher wasn't an officer in the Luftwaffe,' he asked Uhde, 'who was he? A civilian?'

'I don't know.'

Thorogood decided not to labour the point. 'All right, what happened next?'

'I followed them until the storm broke, then I lost them.'

'You keep saying them. How many of them were there?'

'I couldn't see exactly, I didn't want to get too close. Four or five.'

'And when the snow came you lost sight of them?'

'Yes. I tried to close the gap, but I think they must have taken shelter somewhere. I never saw them again.'

'And that was in Bewaldeth?'

'I don't understand.'

'That was in the village where you burgled the store.'

'Just outside it, yes.'

Thorogood lit a second cigarette from the stub of his first and added up what he had learned.

Three, possibly four, German commandos had been sent in to rescue this mysterious man Stuerzbecher. By a coincidence they had arrived on or near the day an escape attempt was to be made. Somehow Stuerzbecher had got a message to them and they'd been waiting for him outside the wire.

They would undoubtedly try to get out the same way they came in, and that meant a ship or a U-boat. An aeroplane was out of the question. The terrain was too rugged for an illicit landing and the weather was too unreliable. So either a ship or a U-boat, with the odds heavily in favour of the latter.

Judging by the route they were following before Uhde lost them, they were making for Maryport or somewhere in that region. But as they had evidently taken shelter when the blizzard broke, it stood to reason they would have remained in hiding near Bewaldeth until it blew itself out, which was at 4 a.m. They wouldn't risk travelling in daylight and from 4 a.m. to dawn was insufficient time for them to reach the rendezvous. Therefore they had holed up somewhere until dark, when they would make their way to the coast. And somewhere off that coast, when darkness fell, a U-boat would be waiting to ferry them home to Germany.

But not if he could bloody well help it.

He should, he was well aware, radio Skiddaw, tell Mitchell what he had deduced and ask for assistance. Had he been working entirely in the dark he would possibly have done just that. But Stuerzbecher and his rescuers were under cover somewhere between Bridekirk, where the one-tonner now was, and the coast around Maryport. It was simply a question of searching every possible bolt-hole, by no means a daunting task in such a rural area, before nightfall. If he failed to find them he would make for Maryport and patrol the coast road. Sooner or later there would have to be a signal flashed between the shore party and the U-boat, and then he would have them.

In the meantime, there was Uhde to be considered. Thorogood doubted if anyone would examine his methods too closely if he were successful, but failure had to be anticipated also. Uhde would complain to Breithaupt about ill-treatment and there could be an enquiry. He couldn't risk that. In any case, Uhde had now outlived his usefulness. A little accident, a recaptured POW making a run for it; that was the answer.

Thorogood's side-arm was a Browning 9mm automatic, and he

249

was in the act of unfastening the holster, watched by the suddenly frightened German, when the CSM's face appeared over the tailboard of the one-tonner.

'No one could get far across those fields, sir. The snow's three feet deep.' He became aware that all was not as he had left it and looked quickly from the Adjutant to Uhde, who was nursing his bleeding arm. 'What's going on here?'

'Prisoner decided he didn't like my company.' The lie slipped easily from Thorogood's lips. 'I had to rap him across the knuckles. Patch him up, will you, then get the men aboard and join me up front. I've had a couple of ideas about what we should do next.'

Thorogood jumped down and vanished round the side of the truck. He would deal with Uhde later.

The CSM examined the young German's arm. Uhde could speak no English, but it wasn't hard to guess what had happened.

'Bastard,' muttered Purser, and fished in his tunic for a fresh field dressing.

Someone had produced a few bottles of beer and the troops around Mohr were busily drinking and singing.

'Come on, sir,' said the Scottish sergeant, 'give us a song in Dutch.'

But Mohr smiled politely and shook his head.

Johann Preiss heard them first. 'Listen.'

Kaehler cocked an ear and heard the sound of footsteps crossing the schoolyard, heels crunching in the snow, and the buzz of excited voices, adult and child.

He scrambled on to one of the desks and peered through the window. 'Christ,' he said, and ducked down.

'What is it?'

'Looks like a lynching party. About a dozen men and the same number of kids.'

'Armed?'

'One of them has a shotgun, the rest sticks and spades.' Kaehler grinned. 'We're a bloody dangerous bunch, you know. I don't think they quite realise how well you can fight with that foot of yours.'

In spite of himself Preiss grinned too. But after a moment his eyes clouded over. 'Looks like we've had it.'

'So it would seem. Maybe next time.'

'She'll wait, Peter.'

'I never doubted it. It'll be something to tell the children anyway; how daddy and Uncle Johann spent the war.'

'*Come on out, you bastards. We know you're in there.*'

The words were meaningless to the two Germans, but there was no mistaking the sentiment.

'We'll do it in style this time,' said Kaehler, 'through the front door.'

'It's out of here and to the left, I think. Help me up.'

Leaning heavily against his friend, Preiss hobbled from the classroom.

If the people in the schoolyard were expecting two proud young eagles to emerge, newsreel Germans resplendent in Luftwaffe blue and jackboots, they were doomed to disappointment. The pair now coming through the main doorway looked scarcely old enough to be out of school themselves. Their clothes were tattered, their eyes tired, their faces unshaven. A good meal would not have gone amiss with either of them.

The one who was limping tried to smile, but as he was descending the steps he missed his footing and pitched forwards. The other made a quick movement to save him, but it seemed to one or two of the bystanders as if he was going to make a run for it, run through the crowd. It was at that moment that the shotgun went off.

After shouting for the Germans to show themselves, Frank Mills broke the 12-bore and made sure that both barrels were loaded. Satisfied, he snapped the gun shut and flicked off the safety.

'They won't come out by themselves, you know,' he told Bert Craig. 'We'll have to go in and fetch them.'

'Don't be bloody silly, of course they'll come out. And watch what you're doing with that gun. You're not Annie bloody Oakley.'

Wills realised he couldn't rely upon Bert Craig to back him up. Only to be expected, of course; Craig hadn't been in the Forces. But you'd have thought you could have counted on a bit of support from a man who'd lost a sister in the bombing.

Wills was disappointed when the school door was unbolted and the two young Germans appeared at the top of the steps.

251

They might have at least put up a fight. He moved a few paces forward.

'They're only kids,' someone said—which was when Preiss slipped.

Years later Wills still wasn't sure whether he had pulled the trigger deliberately or whether it was a reflex action. But in either event the right-hand barrel went off with a devastating roar.

Only a dozen yards separated Wills from the Germans at this point, and in trying to break his friend's fall, Peter Kaehler took the full blast in the face. Bits of gristle and lumps of flesh flew everywhere, but he made no noise as he landed at the foot of the steps.

In the sudden shocked silence of afterwards, only Wills could be heard, bleating feebly. 'I thought he was going to run for it.' No one believed him.

Because it was likely to be a unique event in the annals of the village, someone had brought along a camera. The photograph, when later developed, showed Johann Preiss cradling Peter Kaehler in his arms. It was hard to tell because the exposure wasn't right, but it definitely looked as if the surviving German was crying.

The train had been rattling along at a fair old pace for a couple of hours and the scene in the corridor was becoming rowdier by the minute. In addition to the beer, someone had dived into a kitbag and produced a bottle of whisky. The abandon with which it was being passed from man to man in the Scottish sergeant's group seemed to indicate that no one had paid good British currency for it. Mohr was forced to take a turn. He tried to decline, but the sergeant would have none of it.

'Come on, sir,' he roared, 'it's free.'

Mohr took a mouthful and almost threw up. With one or two very minor exceptions, it was the first hard liquor that had passed his lips in almost two years.

'That's the way. Here, don't drink the bloody lot.'

Mohr wiped his mouth. Not for nothing, he thought wryly, do they segregate the officers from the men in the army.

The songs were seemingly endless. The soldiers had been through *Bless 'Em All, Roll Out the Barrel, The Good Ship Venus,* and were now into *Four-and-Twenty Virgins*. The sergeant had a nice line in original verses for this one, and the train rocked with merriment.

> The vicar's daughter, she was there
> She had us all in fits
> Jumping off the mantelpiece
> And landing on her tits . . .
> Singing balls to your father . . .

'Come on, sir—you're not singing.'

Mohr wondered what they would do if he broke into a couple of choruses of the Horst Wessel song.

There was skylarking, too. One of the soldiers had stolen the sergeant's glengarry and was wearing it back to front, the ribbons over his face. The sergeant was trying to get it back. It was all good-natured lunacy and might have remained that way if, after unsuccessfully snatching the headgear, the sergeant hadn't collided with Mohr, knocking the Oberleutnant's own cap to the floor.

The Scot apologised and picked it up. Mohr reached for it quickly, but the sergeant had drunk enough not to care. He put it on and faced his friends.

'Look, lads, I'm an officer.' The men hooted. 'Now fall in three ranks and say sir when you address me.'

Mohr began to panic. 'My cap, please,' he said stiffly.

Realising that he had gone too far and that Dutch officers doubtless had the same power of life or death over other ranks as British officers did, the sergeant prepared to hand it back. But as he took it off his eyes fell upon the cap badge. He knew he was drunk, but he wasn't that drunk. As he'd thought on the station platform, there was something very fishy about that badge.

'Bloody peculiar, this,' he muttered, and picked at the emblem with a dirty finger-nail. The cotton started to come away.

'My cap, sergeant!' Too late, Mohr realised his voice had gone up an octave. The men shuffled their feet uneasily.

'Give him his cap back, for Christ's sake, Jock,' someone urged. 'You'll land us all in it.'

'In a minute . . .'

The sergeant was a regular soldier, not 'hostilities only', and he'd seen and handled enough cap badges, both officers' and other ranks', to know that they didn't unravel if you picked at them with a finger.

'Look at this.' The cotton was coming away in handfuls. 'Look at this bugger.' One or two heads peered over his shoulder. 'This isn't a cap badge at all. It's been sewn on.'

Mohr edged towards the compartment door, a few feet away. The train was travelling at sixty miles per hour, but it was an unconscious reaction, a flustered brain seeking a way out. It was all over now, thanks to these drunken fools.

The sergeant focussed his bloodshot eyes. 'You know what I think we've got here, lads? I think we've got one of those bloody Jerries. Say something in Dutch . . . sir.'

Mohr didn't get a chance to say anything. At the mention of the word 'Jerries', one of the soldiers reached up and pulled the emergency handle. The train decelerated instantly, throwing everyone to the floor.

It seemed an age, but it was literally only seconds before Mohr was among the first to regain his feet as the train shuddered and screeched to a halt. His hand gripped the door handle until his knuckles were white. The *Tommis* all had rifles, but did they have live ammo? It was unlikely, in transit, but one never knew. In any case, what did it matter? Running and taking a bullet in the back —wasn't that preferable to twenty-eight more days in solitary, going slowly out of his mind staring at the walls? He'd told Otto Breithaupt weeks ago that he'd rather be shot than spend another month in the cooler, but Otto hadn't believed him. In his book, a man stayed alive and carried on fighting as long as he had breath in his body, even if fighting meant nothing more laudable than surviving. The alternative was the act of a coward.

The *Tommis* were getting up now, the Scottish sergeant to the fore. They didn't rush him, however. Curiously, they stood stock still, waiting.

Slowly, Mohr felt his whole body relaxing. He loosened his grip on the door handle. Perhaps it was the thought of the bullet or perhaps it was wondering what Breithaupt would say, but he knew he couldn't run away. It wasn't in his nature. So what the hell was twenty-eight days anyway? He'd done it before, he could do it again.

He shrugged his shoulders philosophically and drew himself up to his full height. In English he said: 'Oberleutnant Franz Mohr, Luftwaffe, at your service.'

He expected to be floored then. They were *Tommis* and he was, to them, a Nazi. He expected them to beat him, land a few kicks and punches before the MPs were summoned. What he wasn't prepared for was the Scottish sergeant's half-smile to become a grin which quickly turned into laughter. Nor was he prepared for the others to join in, and it was with something close to amazement that he watched the tears roll down their cheeks.

The Scot put his arm around Mohr's shoulders. 'You cheeky bastard,' he spluttered. 'You almost had us fooled. Where's that bloody whisky?'

Someone thrust the bottle forward. Like all good soldiers, in any crisis they protected the booze first and foremost.

'Here, take a swallow before the redcaps come along to see what's happened.'

Thoroughly bewildered, Mohr accepted the bottle gratefully. He wasn't quite sure what lesson he had just learned, but he knew that, whatever it was, it had nothing to do with the colour uniform a man wore.

Dusk wasn't far off. It was time to be getting ready.

Christian called them all to the bedroom on the east side of the house. The map was unfolded on the dressing-table.

'We're here,' he said, 'and we want to get here.' He jabbed a finger at a spot on the coast equidistant between Flimby and Maryport. 'We'll be using the back roads so I estimate it will take us a couple of hours. However, we don't know what sort of a reception committee they'll have waiting for us on the coast or whether we'll meet roadblocks or other obstacles. So let's add an hour to that for safety.'

He checked the time on his wrist watch.

'It's now coming up to 1600 and it will be dark enough to move in another half hour, which should put us on the coast at 1930. Stieff will be waiting for our first signal at 2000. If he doesn't see it he'll go away and come back tomorrow. Except I don't think much of our chances of remaining free, outside this house, for another twenty-four hours. It has to be tonight.'

'You're cutting it very fine, Christian,' said von Stuerzbecher.

'I admit it, but we're restricted by sunset.'

'That's not the only thing we're restricted by.' Feldwebel Schelling was doing a stint at the window. 'Come and see this.'

Christian crossed the room in three strides and peered through the curtains. Coming slowly down the road, looking as if it had every intention of stopping, was a British Army one-tonner.

21

13 December: 1615—1730 hours.

It was almost dark now.

'They're not moving.' Wolf Schultz had taken over by the window. 'They're set for the bloody night.'

The one-tonner was parked in the road at the end of the driveway and had been for ten minutes. Christian recognised the CSM immediately and asked von Stuerzbecher to confirm that the troops were from the camp. Von Stuerzbecher borrowed Christian's fieldglasses to get a better look.

'Yes, they're from Skiddaw. The one on the radio is the Adjutant, Captain Thorogood. I remember some of the other faces too.' He handed the glasses back. 'Do you think he suspects something and is calling for reinforcements?'

'I don't know.'

'Maybe they'll go away,' said Schelling hopefully, but they didn't. And as the ten minutes became fifteen and then twenty, Christian began to get worried.

'We're going to have to find out what they're up to,' he said finally.

'How?'

'By going out and talking to them. Me going out, that is.'

'That's madness, Christian,' protested von Stuerzbecher.

'No, it's the only way. Look at it like this. If they are summoning up reinforcements, the one Luger we have between us isn't going to be very effective. We're all dead. But if they're hanging around out there for some other reason, it's up to us to move them.' He tapped his wrist watch significantly. 'It's 4.25. Unless we're out of here and on our way in the next quarter of an hour, Stieff will think we're not coming.'

Von Stuerzbecher accepted the logic of the argument. 'What do you intend doing?'

Christian picked up the rucksack. 'I'll slip out the back door, come up the road behind them, and pretend I'm a hiker. If I get the opportunity, I'll tell them I saw something fishy earlier in the day. That should get them moving.'

'The Company Sergeant-Major knows you,' von Stuerzbecher reminded him. 'Won't he think it somewhat odd to see you once as a van driver and once as a hiker?'

'I'll take the Englishman with me. They know him of old. If there are any queries, I'll say that as a result of the bread business the other day old man Foster fired us both.'

Von Stuerzbecher shook his head. 'It's flimsy, Christian.'

'And staying here is suicide. Have you got any better ideas?'

Von Stuerzbecher hadn't. Christian walked across to Alan Miles and untied his hands.

'There's a squad of British soldiers at the end of the driveway,' he said, 'and you're going to help me get rid of them. We'll be alone, so you might think it an ideal opportunity to raise the alarm. That would be exceptionally foolish. I'll be taking the Luger and I'll have nothing to lose by killing you. Is that understood?'

'Yes.'

'Good. Wolf, you're about his size; give him your boots and waterproof.'

Schultz did so. Alan put them on.

'Right,' said Christian, 'let's go.'

Thorogood had pulled up outside the house because it was the first in the village and the obvious place to park. And he had been stationary for the best part of half an hour because the CO had ordered him to return to camp. At least, the Duty Officer, 2nd Lt. Tom Hastings, had passed on Major Mitchell's message. But Thorogood wanted none of it. He refused to move unless ordered to do so by Mitchell in person, and he had despatched Hastings to find the CO and bring him to the radio room. Until that happened, he was staying put.

'Someone coming, sir,' said CSM Purser.

Christian and Alan Miles hove into view, Christian wearing the rucksack. One or two of the soldiers had their rifles at the ready, but they relaxed when they saw that the newcomers were hikers.

'What's going on?' asked Christian.

'Never mind that.' Thorogood scrutinised Christian with all the suspicion of a butcher buying a bargain calf. 'Who are you two and where are you going?'

Christian explained that they had hiked up from Keswick that day and were on their way to Dearham, a mile or two up the road, where they would spend the night with friends. He was all the time conscious that the CSM was studying him closely, trying to place his face.

'Hello again,' he said.

The CSM got it then. 'You're the van driver.'

'Not any more.' Christian smiled feebly. 'Neither of us. Thanks to that business the other day we both got the sack. Alan for not turning up at all and me for allowing half a load to be stolen.'

'I said I'd speak to your boss about that.'

'Doesn't make any difference. Forty or fifty customers didn't get their orders, thanks to those Jerries.'

This was all going too fast for Thorogood.

'Wait a minute. You know these people, S'arnt-Major?'

'They work for Foster's Bakery, sir.' He jerked a thumb at Christian. 'This one was the driver of the van that was involved in that rumpus the other day. I put the report on your desk.'

Thorogood lost interest. The matter had been dead and buried by the time he got back to Skiddaw.

'Which way have you come today?' he asked.

'Across Whinlatter Pass.'

'Spot anything unusual?'

'If you mean did we see any sign of those escaped POWs, the answer's no, nothing like a dozen anyway. But we did see a couple of suspicious-looking characters.'

'That's near where the police copped Heydt and his cronies, sir,' said the CSM.

Thorogood nodded. 'Did you report it?'

Christian took his cue from the CSM's last sentence. 'Called the police at Cockermouth.'

Thorogood was less than interested. Whinlatter Pass was a long way from Dovenby.

'CO's on the radio, sir.' The soldier who had been given the job of listening watch on the wireless poked his head out of the one-tonner.

'I'll be right there. If you see anything suspicious on the way to Dearham,' he said to Christian and Alan, 'don't ring the police, ring Skiddaw Camp. Tell whoever you talk to to get the message to Captain Thorogood.'

'Okay,' said Christian, 'we'll do just that.'

Thorogood left them to have it out with Major Mitchell. Christian decided it was safe to stick around for a little while longer. He made a move towards the one-tonner, but the CSM barred his way.

'That's far enough, lad.'

'I'm not going to steal it.'

'You're not going to do anything with it.'

'You've got someone in there?' It was impossible to see into the depths of the truck, but the CSM's attitude made it apparent that they'd recaptured at least one of the POWs. Poor bastard, thought Christian. 'Is he dangerous?'

Christ, thought Purser. 'He's a man, just like you. Maybe better than you. Now clear off.'

Christian hesitated. 'Because if he's not dangerous, you couldn't give us a lift, could you, as far as Dearham? The last couple of miles are always the worst.'

'No, we couldn't. We're not going that way, in any case. Now beat it before I have to do something I'll regret.'

That was as far as he had any right to push his luck, Christian thought, and was about to move off when Thorogood called out. There was no mistaking the white-hot rage in his voice.

'We're going back, S'arnt-Major. Get the men aboard.'

Christian waited until the truck had completed its turn and was out of sight before running for the house, urging Alan along in front of him. Von Stuerzbecher opened the back door.

'They say they're going back,' panted Christian, 'but I wouldn't bank on it. I made a big mistake when I was talking to that captain and I'm wondering how long it'll take him to realise it.'

As the one-tonner rounded Bassenthwaite Lake and headed down the Keswick road, Adrian Thorogood tried to work out what had been bothering him for the last hour. It wasn't the peremptory summons from Mitchell to return to Skiddaw or the fact that he would have to explain Leutnant Uhde's condition when he got there. Regarding the former, there was still plenty of time to have it out face to face with the CO, explain his deductions, and be on the coast by 7 p.m. As for the latter, it was only Uhde's word against his. No, there was something else.

For the fourth or fifth time he went over everything he had learned from Fritz Uhde. A squad of German commandos had landed with the object of rescuing this man Stuerzbecher; Stuerzbecher was not who he purported to be; the commandos had arrived on or around a day when an escape was already planned and Stuerzbecher had got a message to them; they had waited for him outside the wire and were now on their way to rendezvous with a U-boat.

What the hell was wrong with that?

He sat bolt upright, almost hitting his head on the roof of the cab. One thing was very seriously wrong and he'd ignored it before because he couldn't find the answer. In order for Stuerzbecher to get word to the commandos about the date and time of the escape, there would have to be some contact between them, a message passed physically from someone on the inside to someone on the outside. Yet physical contact between the POWs and anyone except the guards was impossible. Except, except . . . Except that during the bread riot the day before yesterday dozens of POWs had been within inches of the van driver, the man they had seen at Dovenby . . .

And . . .

And the commandos would obviously include a man who spoke fluent English . . .

And . . .

In an instant he had it, the thing that was troubling him. The so-called van driver had said he had seen no sign of Jerries. 'Nothing like a dozen, anyway.'

The news bulletins had made no mention of the number of escapers. Mitchell had insisted on that from the start. Even if they had, the figure would have been ten, not twelve. Only someone who knew about Kaehler and Preiss hiding in the tunnel would call it a round dozen.

The driver nearly went through the windscreen as, in response to Thorogood's sudden shout, he slammed on the anchors.

'But Major Mitchell, sir,' protested the CSM when he realised Thorogood intended going back.

'Damn Major Mitchell. From this moment this call-sign is off the air.'

22

13 December: 1945—2030 hours.

The U-boat had surfaced fifteen minutes earlier, at 1930, and was riding the choppy sea half a mile off shore, as close as Stieff dared approach. The forward machine gun and the conning-tower searchlight were manned as a matter of routine. The dinghy party, under the command of an Obersteuermann, was ready to push off at a moment's notice.

Stieff huddled deeper inside his duffle-coat. Apart from the danger of coastal radar, he knew he was taking a hell of a risk. Although the sky was overcast, it was far from pitch dark. Behind the clouds, scudding before a nor'-easter, a sliver of moon was doing its best to shine through.

Beside Stieff, Obersturmbannfuehrer Kirdorff scanned the coast with night glasses. 'Tell your men to keep their eyes peeled. It won't be much of a signal, if and when it comes.'

'They're watching. They're well trained.'

'Do as I ask, please, Herr Korvettenkapitän. We want no mistakes.'

Stieff resented being told what to do on his own boat, but he relayed the order via a runner. Kirdorff had made it quite clear that he was in command—until the U-boat was under way or in peril.

Five minutes passed.

'Maybe it won't be tonight.'

'It'll be tonight,' said Kirdorff. 'I have that feeling.'

A quarter of a mile inland Christian was far from certain that it would be this night or any other night. To get to the path, any path, which led down to the beach, it was necessary to cross the road and the railway line which ran parallel with the coast, and the two *Tommis* who were patrolling this sector were there to make sure no one did. Christian would have walked straight into them if he hadn't spotted their silhouettes as a match was struck and heard the crackle of a wireless.

Schelling tapped him on the shoulder. The Feldwebel drew the blade of his hand across his throat in an unmistakable gesture. Christian shook his head and thumbed over his shoulder. Move back. They retreated to the edge of the field they had just crossed. After reaching the outskirts of Flimby they had abandoned the road as being too risky.

The others were waiting in the shadows.

'What's the matter?' whispered Schultz.

Christian told him. 'Though the fact that one of them's carrying a portable wireless means that they're probably spread pretty thin on the ground.'

'You're thinking of going round them?' asked von Stuerzbecher.

'I'm thinking we might have to. What worries me is what the hell they're doing here in the first place. POWs wouldn't head for a remote part of the coast such as this, so why the patrol?'

'Perhaps Thorogood's already rung the tocsin.'

'I don't think so. If he had the road would be littered with troops and we'd have seen the lights of their vehicles for miles. No, I think it's more than likely a day patrol waiting to be picked up.'

'If you'll forgive me, Christian,' said Schelling, 'we haven't got time to debate the point. It's six minutes to eight.'

Christian nodded decisively. 'You're right. Let me have your knife, Wolf.'

Schultz handed it over reluctantly. 'Schelling and I could do it.'

'No, we know exactly where they are.'

'Take care, Christian,' said von Stuerzbecher.

'It's my middle name.'

It was seventy-five yards from the edge of the field to the road. Schelling and Christian moved forward at the crouch, keeping several feet apart. Years of training ensured that their approach was noiseless.

When they were fifty yards away they could hear the *Tommis* talking. A few seconds later they saw them clearly. Both were looking out to sea.

264

Christian put the knife between his teeth and waved Schelling down. The Feldwebel needed no telling. The last few yards were to be covered on their bellies and the executions carried out silently, just in case Christian had made a mistake about the *Tommis* being thin on the ground.

Twenty-five yards . . . twenty . . . fifteen . . .

Christian could hear the conversation now.

'She doesn't look much, but there's nothing she won't do for a bloke.'

'Yeah, any bloke.'

'Come off it, she hadn't been with anyone else since she started going with me.'

They sounded very young.

Because their faces were only inches from the snow, neither Schelling nor Christian saw the headlights in the distance. Schultz did. 'Oh Christ,' he whispered—but there was nothing he could do.

They were at the edge of the road, only feet separating them from the exposed backs of the *Tommis*. Out of the corner of his eye Christian saw Schelling push himself to his feet for the final rush. He began to do the same and simultaneously caught sight of the headlights as the truck rounded a bend. Like a rabbit hypnotised by a torch beam, for a fraction of a second he froze, as Schelling froze, lost in that no-man's-land between decision and indecision. Then they hit the ground together and lay absolutely motionless, two dark shadows among other shadows.

They heard the truck grind to a halt. A voice called out: 'Come on, you pair, we haven't got all night.'

Neither German moved for a full half minute, until long after the truck had moved off with a clash of gears and the sound of its engines was a diminishing hum in the distance. When they did, each was surprised to discover that he was shaking from head to foot.

'There they are.'

In the conning-tower of the U-boat Stieff grunted with satisfaction. Three minutes earlier, after seeing the headlights going down the coast road, he had been prepared to accept that his cargo wasn't coming. But there was the signal. Two long, two short— over to the right. A pause of exactly sixty seconds and the same again.

'Get going, Obersteuermann,' he called out.
But the dinghy was already over the side.

On the coast road, less than a mile away from where Christian's party were waiting on the beach, Adrian Thorogood had parked the one-tonner with its lights off just south of Flimby. Remembering that the so-called van driver had said that he and his companion were making for Dearham, north-west of Dovenby, Thorogood had headed due west, assuming correctly that Dearham was a red herring. He had wasted no time searching side roads. The game was too far advanced for that. His only hope now was to watch for the signal the Germans would inevitably make or catch sight of the U-boat. To this end he had two men on the beach, looking inland to the cliffs for lights. CSM Purser and the remainder were spread out at intervals of two hundred yards along the road. It was the best he could do. If it didn't work and it became known, as it surely would, that he had failed to pass on vital information, the brass would pillory him.

'Truck coming, sir.'

Thorogood stepped into the middle of the road and flagged it down. A Para sergeant stuck his head out of the window.

'Need any help, sir?'

'No, thanks. Where are you people going?'

'Back to Workington. It's as quiet as a grave up coast.'

Thorogood waved them on.

He glanced anxiously towards the sky. Snow had been forecast for later on and snow was the last thing he needed now. What he did want was for that bloody moon to try a bit harder, if only for a few seconds.

A quarter of a mile north of the one-tonner, at the extreme right of a line of look-outs, Harpo Cook stamped his feet to keep warm and stared miserably out to sea. Unaware that at this moment Harry Cade was in the guardroom cells under close arrest, he had made up his mind to see his friend as soon as he got back to the camp. Harry would know what to do about the CSM's charge of disobedience.

Harpo Cook was a shy, humble individual, very uncertain of himself and his role in society; a young man who had achieved nothing of note in his life and never expected to. So when the sudden, momentary break in the clouds occurred and the thin crescent of moon briefly illuminated the sea, he wasn't sure whether or not he had seen the upper superstructure of a U-boat. It all happened so fast. One minute he was screwing up his eyes in an endeavour to see beyond the immediate blackness, and next he was staring at a German submarine, half a mile out and roughly twice that distance north-west of his position. A second after that there was only blackness again.

Harpo had never seen even a photograph of a U-boat, but he knew what a submarine looked like and the CSM had told them to watch out for submarines. But had he seen one? What if he hadn't? What if it was his imagination playing tricks? If he sent the whole patrol off on a wild-goose chase the CSM would have his hide. No one else had apparently seen it. It was probably better to say nothing.

But Harpo's mind didn't work to the rules of self-preservation, and a moment later he was racing down the road, shouting as he went.

Crouched near the water's edge, Christian willed the second-hand of his wrist watch to move faster. He could hardly believe it was only twelve minutes since Schultz had flashed the first signal. It felt more like twelve years. Come on, you bastard. Faster.

A few yards behind Christian, in the shelter of the rocks, Alan Miles was experiencing his first feeling of panic for almost two days. They weren't going to let him go. They were either going to kill him or take him to Germany. He'd been a fool to believe the English-speaking officer. All that talk about soldiers only fighting soldiers had been a ruse to keep him quiet.

He shuffled his feet nervously. Feldwebel Schelling placed a restraining hand on his arm and said something to him in German.

The minute hand of Christian's watch moved on to the quarter-hour.

'Flash them again, Wolf. Now.'

'You're absolutely sure?' demanded Thorogood.

'Yessir.' Harpo was more sure than ever. 'About a mile up coast and half a mile out.'

Thorogood had no option but to believe him and issued his orders calmly and precisely. However lacking were some of his other qualities, he knew how to direct a section attack.

The driver of the one-tonner was told to motor for exactly one mile on his odometer. 'Not a few yards more nor a few yards less unless I tell you otherwise. After the rest of us de-bus, turn your vehicle so that it's facing the sea and switch on every light you've got. Bren team, I'm not sure how these people are armed, but if they start shooting back with anything I want them silenced. I'd prefer them alive, but I'm not fussy.'

'What about Leutnant Uhde?' asked the CSM.

'Damn, I'd forgotten about him. All right—driver, as soon as you've done your business with the lights, get round the back and stand guard over the prisoner. If he tries anything ambitious, shoot him. Okay, S'arnt-Major, get the men aboard.'

In the conning-tower of the U-boat, Stieff was first to see the headlights of the one-tonner as it began moving.

'It may not be relevant,' commented Obersturmbannfuehrer Kirdorff. 'There's nothing we can do about it, anyway. But tell the machine gun crew to be ready, just in case.'

They could see the outline of the dinghy now, the three men straining at the oars. It was still a hundred yards off shore and about twice that distance down coast. At the same time, above the roar of the waves, they heard the sound of the approaching one-tonner and saw its lights.

'Shake it up,' shouted Christian.

'What about the Englishman?'

'Bring him with us.'

This conversation was conducted entirely in German, and all Alan knew was that he was being hurried along in the direction of the dinghy.

In the one-tonner the driver counted off the tenths on the odometer and braked when precisely one mile showed. Being an intelligent man, he didn't wait for Thorogood and the squad to de-bus but swung the vehicle in a wide arc and pulled up facing the sea. There was still the railway line between the road and the cliff top, and had Christian's party been sheltering within the lee of the cliff, the lights would have been ineffective. But they weren't; they were at the water's edge, waiting for the dinghy. And to make matters worse, Alan Miles chose that moment to let loose a shout of fear.

In the U-boat Stieff and Kirdorff knew instantly that this was no passing truck, that it was a pursuit vehicle with a damn good idea where the fugitives were. Even as they watched they saw Thorogood's squad pile out of the back.

'Christ, they've only got a pistol.'

Kirdorff evidently knew that. 'Then we'll have to give them some help, won't we. Give the order to switch on the searchlight and tell the machine gunner to fire at will.'

Stieff hesitated. 'We'll have every *Tommi* plane and ship in the area down on us.'

Kirdorff turned to face him. 'Herr Korvettenkapitän, let me remind you once more that I am in complete command of this operation until the U-boat is in danger. At the moment there is no danger. In ten minutes that situation may have altered, at which time you will be in command and may do as you think necessary. But until then kindly do as I say.'

Suddenly a whole area of beach was flooded with light. Blinded until he turned his head away and half closed his eyes, Christian looked desperately for cover. There was none save a few small rocks. The dinghy was still fifty yards from shallow water, the oarsmen momentarily shocked into immobility. It was either a question of wading out to meet it or not getting there at all. A quick glance over his shoulder revealed a squad of men scrambling down the cliff path. It was a million to one they weren't armed with pea shooters.

All this took under a second to register. The next five seconds were filled with devastating noise as the world went mad and the U-boat's machine gun opened up.

The machine gunner was no newcomer to this business and did not have to be told what his primary targets were. His first sighting burst was way off, but then he got the range. The next twenty rounds shattered the lights on the one-tonner and decapitated the driver, who was in the act of climbing from the cab to stand guard over Uhde. Traversing right, the gunner selected the lead men on the path for his next burst. He hosed the path from bottom to top. Really, it was like swatting flies on a wall.

The CSM was the first to die. No longer a young man, he nevertheless knew that it was both his right and his duty to be in the vanguard of the assault on the beach. Once down there it would be his job to keep the enemy occupied with his Sten while the Bren team got into position and tried to do something about that bloody U-boat. But he was still fifty feet from the bottom when two of the machine gun's shells tore his chest open and flung him against the cliff wall like a discarded rag doll.

Immediately behind the CSM the Bren team were caught in the same upward hosing action. Hampered in their movements by the gun and the spare magazines, their chances had been almost zero from the moment the machine gunner squeezed the trigger. And what little they had was lost when neither man attempted to take cover. Instead they kept running, slipping and sliding in their anxiety to get to the beach. It was not so much that the machine gunner shot them; it was more a question of them running into the bullets. As the number one died he let go of the carrying handle. The Bren fell twenty feet before becoming wedged in the rocks.

The duration of the skirmish was still being measured in seconds when Thorogood realised that it was a complete balls-up. Not only had he lost the CSM and the Bren team, he was about to lose the Germans, who were now wading out towards the dinghy. At least, three of them were. Two were still at the water's-edge. One was on his knees, firing back with a pistol; the other was standing bolt upright, as though paralysed.

'Aim for the bloody dinghy!' he screamed.

Safely behind cover, three of the riflemen opened up in unison, and one of the oarsmen collapsed over his blade. A moment later, it seemed as though another was hit. But Thorogood knew he needed the LMG to become even marginally effective.

'You . . . come with me . . . we're going to get that Bren.'

'Me, sir?' Harpo shuddered at the thought. He hadn't fired a shot yet. He had found himself a big rock and was determined to keep his head down. The ear-splitting noise being made by the U-boat's machine gun was terrifying, and spent shells were ricochetting off the cliff face in all directions.

'*You! At the double before I have you shot!*'

Harpo almost laughed in Thorogood's face at the absurdity of the statement, but like so many youngsters who never quite knew why, he got to his feet.

Knee-deep in water, Christian winced and ducked involuntarily as bullets from the *Tommi* rifles thudded into the bodies of the two oarsmen. The dinghy was only feet away now. They'd make it, providing the machine gunner kept playing his music.

Where the hell was everybody? He glanced around quickly. Kurt was there, just behind him, his eyes bulging with effort. So was Wolf Schultz, the water almost up to the little man's waist. But where the hell was Schelling? Christ, not still on the bloody beach!

Feldwebel Schelling heard Christian's shout but chose to ignore it. Only fifty yards separated the water's-edge from the base of the cliffs and he could see the *Tommi* officer scrambling for the Bren gun. If he reached it and managed to set it up behind cover, Christian and the others would be sitting ducks.

Slipping a fresh clip into the Luger he ran forward, weaving as he went. Behind him Alan Miles, tears streaming down his face, was bellowing. '*I'm English, I'm English!*' But above the roar of the Lee-Enfields and the machine gun, no one could hear him.

Stieff was first to see the headlights of vehicles coming down the main road from Maryport.

'How long have we got?' asked Kirdorff.

Stieff did not like to think about it. 'Five minutes, ten. Fifteen at the outside.'

Kirdorff nodded his understanding. When Stieff turned to speak to him again, the Obersturmbannfuehrer had clambered out of the conning-tower and was standing next to the machine gun, directing operations.

Thorogood reached the Bren while Schelling was still climbing up through the rocks. Sweat dripping from his forehead, he wrenched it free and ducked as the Feldwebel loosed off a couple of snap shots. Frantically he pulled at the cocking-piece. But it was jammed, damaged in the fall.

'*For the love of God shoot him, man, shoot him!*' he raved at Harpo.

As Schelling saw it, he had two choices. Either to kill the officer first, or kill the rifleman. If he disposed of the officer, the rifleman would undoubtedly kill him afterwards. If he dealt with the greater danger of the rifleman first, there was a possibility that he could despatch the officer before the man succeeded in unjamming the Bren. One decision meant certain death, the other gave him a chance.

Schelling was an ordinary mortal who just happened to be in an extraordinary situation, a man who wanted to live if he had the option. He made the wrong choice. He was not to know that Harpo Cook had never shot anything more lethal than a rabbit in his life, and never would. So he killed him first. Steadying himself against a boulder, he took aim with both hands. The single shot from the 9 mm pistol took Harpo in the throat, severing the jugular. He died with the safety-catch still on.

But by this time, with an effort that made his hands bleed, Thorogood had freed the cocking-piece. Schelling saw the barrel of the Bren swing towards him and knew he had no chance. The *Tommi* officer was smiling. His last thought before Thorogood fired the shots which tore him in half was that the man was undoubtedly insane.

Thorogood was on the beach, racing for the sea, before Schelling stopped moving. On the way, firing from the hip, he put a burst into the stomach of the man who was screaming at him. It sounded like '. . . English . . .'—but it could have been anything.

Christian saw him coming, bullets from the U-boat's machine gun kicking up sand and spray at his feet. At that moment he would have given five years of his life for a loaded rifle. Of the two sailors who had been hit, one was only wounded but the Obersteuermann was dead. Christian heaved him over the side before yanking von Stuerzbecher into the dinghy.

'Grab an oar!'

'What happened to Schelling?'

Christian was already rowing. 'Hit,' he said curtly. 'I saw him fall.'

'Bloody fool,' muttered Wolf. 'He never could look after himself.'

As Thorogood reached the sea, the Bren stopped firing. A magazine contained only twenty-eight rounds and he'd had his twenty-eight.

Throwing the now useless weapon to the sand, he pulled out his Browning. With hardly a break in his stride he began wading after the dinghy.

Standing next to the U-boat's machine gun, Obersturmbann-fuehrer Kirdorff totted up the odds. The action had lasted under five minutes, but that was five minutes too long. The headlights of the vehicles from Maryport were growing brighter by the second, and it could surely not be long before the Royal Navy and the RAF decided to take a hand. At a rough guess it would take at least a quarter of an hour, rowing against the tide, for the dinghy to reach the U-boat. Long before then, Korvettenkapitän Stieff would have reassumed command and given the order to dive.

'Why have you stopped firing?' he demanded of the machine gunner.

'The *Tommi* is too near the dinghy, Herr Obersturmbann-fuehrer.'

'Never mind, continue.'

The gunner was a veteran of a thousand surface and sub-surface battles and was not afraid of the SS. He stepped a few paces back from his weapon. 'I regret, Herr Obersturmbannfuehrer, that I must disobey that order.'

Kirdorff pushed him to one side. 'You'll be dealt with later.'

It was not the first time Kirdorff had handled this sort of weapon under these circumstances. He drew a bead on the dinghy and held it in the machine gun's sights. He too had his orders.

While the gun crew looked on with horror, he raked the dinghy from end to end. One in six of the machine gun's bullets were of the tracer variety, and there was no chance he could miss such a simple target. He saw the *Tommi* fall, cut down in mid-stride. Two of the dinghy's occupants stood up, waving their arms, facing the U-boat. Then they too fell.

He held the burst for thirty seconds, until he was certain that no one was left alive. Then he went to find Stieff.

The three remaining riflemen saw the U-boat's searchlight go out and heard the wail of the emergency klaxon. The night was suddenly dark again. 'Jesus Christ,' said one. 'Jesus Christ.'

In the back of the one-tonner, only half-conscious, Leutnant Uhde listened to the wind and the waves and the sound of engines in the distance. And he wondered how long it would be before someone came to collect him.

EPILOGUE

Operation Hammer, Generalmajor Kurt von Stuerzbecher's plan for the mass escape of German POWs, never did take place, though an updated version of it was tried from Devizes Camp in December 1944. Details of the plot were revealed to the British before the attempt could be made, however, and the ringleaders were transferred to Comrie Camp, in Scotland. There, a Council of Honour was instituted in an endeavour to ascertain the name of the traitor, and suspicion fell upon two men. One was quickly exonerated of all blame, but the second, Wolfgang Rosterg, was executed by his fellow POWs for his apparent part in the betrayal and his anti-German sentiments.

Five men were eventually tried for the death of Rosterg: Pallme Koenig and Jupp Mertens; Kurt Zuelsdorf, Heinz Brueling and Joachim Golitz. All were found guilty of murder under British law, and hanged.

It may be argued that they were executed not so much for the murder of Rosterg, guilty of treason in German eyes, but because they had proved themselves to be thoroughly intransigent. What, for example, would have been the attitude of British officers in, say, Colditz, if one of their own kind had ratted to the Germans on the eve of an escape? What the Devizes POWs had tried once they might well try again, with greater success. When examining the crimes, and they were many, perpetrated by the Nazi regime, it is as well to sit back and reflect that not all the men in the black hats were on one side.

Of those who survived the events of 13 December, Leutnant Fritz Uhde made no further attempts to escape. Nor did he complain of the ill-treatment he had received at the hands of Captain Thorogood. With Thorogood dead he thought it best to keep his mouth shut. Doing otherwise would have meant an enquiry in the course of which his burglary of the Bewaldeth shop, the first link in the chain which led Thorogood to the coast, might have been revealed.

When the war was over, Uhde was among the first to be repatriated and was quite surprised to find his wife waiting for him, loving as ever. Try as he might, he could find no evidence of infidelity.

Oberleutnant Franz Mohr survived his twenty-eight days in the cooler and indeed made one more (unsuccessful) attempt to escape before the war's end. This time he got as far as Liverpool before being recaptured, but he decided that was his last throw of the dice. Completely bald before his thirtieth birthday, a fact he attributes to the camp diet, he now lives in Düsseldorf, where he is the proud and somewhat corpulent grandfather of three girls.

Johann Preiss became an inveterate troublemaker during the rest of his time in Skiddaw and an incurable alcoholic soon afterwards. When he can think clearly, which is rare these days, he blames his drinking partly on a feeling of guilt for Peter Kaehler's death and partly on the death of his family, who were all killed in the Dresden bombings. In a way, he is glad Hannah Preiss did not survive long after Kaehler.

Otto Breithaupt was promoted to Oberstleutnant, in his absence, in 1943, and continued to head the Escape Committee until that body was no longer needed. But security, under a new Commandant, tightened up after the night of December 12/13, and an escape attempt on such a scale was never again feasible.

When he returned home in 1946, it was to a son, now aged eleven, who didn't know him, and a wife who had lost five stone and aged twenty years. Whatever they had had together, both in bed and out, had been eroded by the war, and they were divorced in 1950. Frau Breithaupt died soon afterwards.

Otto Breithaupt remarried and was fortunate in the fact that his new wife got on famously with her step-son. But talents acquired in the Luftwaffe and in Skiddaw were not much use in the new Germany, and Breithaupt found it difficult to earn a living. In 1952 he emigrated to Australia, where he still lives, the owner of a small restaurant, the old days forgotten.

Heinrich Weiss could not forget the old days and could not become accustomed to living in a Germany where the Third Reich was but a distant, unpleasant memory. Because of his scars he divorced his wife without ever seeing her again and set sail for Argentina. There, until he died of a heart attack in 1968, he lived among Germans who still thought as they had done during the great days of the Thirties, who believed that only a battle was lost, not a war. It wasn't the perfect end to a career, but it was better than democracy.

Kapitänleutnant Heydt went into politics. A born opportunist, he began his career as a right-winger but quickly realised that extreme conservatism was a thing of the past. With an adroit sidestep that left opponents and allies alike gasping with admiration, he joined the Christian Democrats and now wields considerable influence in Bonn. Walking the corridors of power he occasionally comes across a face he recognises, a face that once peered at him from beneath a peaked cap, but both men studiously ignore their recent history. It was as if yesterday had never happened.

Werner Herburg recovered completely from his beating and, as he had expected and dreaded, was feted by his mother when he arrived home. She knew nothing, of course, of his escape attempt, but to hear her talk her son would have won the war single-handed if only that fat oaf (no longer the dear Reichsmarschall) Goering had seen fit to promote him to the General Staff.

Herburg stood it as long as he could, which was nine months, then wangled himself into America. From New York he went to Los Angeles and Hollywood, where he started writing screenplays. His first few efforts were rejected as hopeless, but showing that quiet determination which had always been a characteristic, he persevered. Nowadays, on either the big screen or television, his name is frequently among the credits.

Oberleutnant Hans Baum never recovered from the effects of seeing his crew fry in their own fat. The newest techniques, the most brilliant specialists, even a handful of quacks—they all tried their luck and failed. Hans Baum hasn't spoken to this day, and lives in a State-run home on the outskirts of Munich. His mother, now in her eighties, never forgave Theo Emke for deluding her. It is her private opinion that Emke lacked guts.

Major David Mitchell, MC, was removed, quietly, from the post of Commandant of Skiddaw after the debacle of 13 December. The escape record of the camp was not good and it was decided by the brass that tougher measures were needed. Mitchell was given an unimportant desk job in Whitehall, which bothered him not a whit. As soon as he was out of uniform he returned to his civilian occupation of accountancy, and quickly prospered. With masses of new fiscal legislation coming in right after the war, anyone with half a mind for figures was at a premium.

He now lives in a large detached house in Surrey and once in a while some event, a book or a film, will bring back memories of Skiddaw. To this day he doesn't know what possessed Adrian Thorogood to do what he did with a mere handful of men.

Lance-corporal Harry Cade, Unteroffizier Geith and Obergefreiter Willi Braune were tried for the murder of Corporal James Napley. In vain did Cade protest that not only was Napley's death a grisly accident, Braune and Geith had been no more than innocent bystanders.

The Court was unsympathetic. Too much had happened in Skiddaw that day, and the result had been the death of a British soldier. There was circumstantial proof that Geith and Braune had had a hand in the escape, and it seemed possible that Corporal Napley had discovered their complicity and was going to challenge them when he met his end.

All three were sentenced to be executed, though Cade was later reprieved and imprisoned for life. Not so Willi Braune and Hans Geith. On the morning of 24 March 1943, bewildered and frightened, they paid the ultimate penalty.

It's hard to believe that the young men who tunnelled their way out of Skiddaw and who suffered the hardships of being on the run in a hostile country are now in or approaching their sixties. War may take its toll, but the fee is small compared to that demanded by time. But that applies to all of us.